Cahill tried to scrabble upright by putting his arms behind him, but I kicked a wrist out from under him and he fell onto his right side.

He howled and shifted his weight from his side onto his stomach so that he could push off the ground. His mouth was open, his fangs still bared, and I brought both my hands and all of my weight onto the back of his head and slammed down hard.

Cahill's fangs anchored in the floor. He tried to pull his face loose with just his neck muscles and couldn't, then braced his right hand against the floor. That's when the tiny part of Cahill's brain that was still a detective heard a sound that it had heard many times before... the sound of the fire selector switch on Cahill's own Glock 18.

The Glock I had just lifted from his side holster.

The Glock I was holding pointed at the side of his head.

Praise for the Pax Arcana series:

"The Pax Arcana books are seriously good reads. Action, humor, and heart with unexpected twists and turns. If you are (like me) waiting for the next Butcher or Hearne—pick up Elliott James. Then you can bite your nails waiting for the next James, too."

—*New York Times* bestselling author Patricia Briggs

"Loved it! *Charming* is a giant gift basket of mythology and lore delivered by a brilliant new voice in urban fantasy. Elliott James tells stories that are action-packed, often amusing, and always entertaining."

—*New York Times* bestselling author Kevin Hearne

"I loved this book from start to finish. Exciting and innovative, *Charming* is a great introduction to a world I look forward to spending a lot more time in."

—*New York Times* bestselling author
Seanan McGuire

"Grab some snacks and settle back as splendid debut author James serves up a Prince Charming tale yanked sideways. John Charming comes from a prominent line of dragonslayers, witchfinders and killers trained by the Knights Templar, but now he has a problem: He has become what they hunt. James's reluctant hero faces threats and danger with a smartass attitude that keeps the narrative fast-paced, edgy, and amusing. Mark this name down—you will undoubtedly be seeing more from James!"

—*RT Book Reviews*

"In a saturated literary realm, James's tale stands out for the gritty, believable world he builds...This is masculine urban fantasy in the vein of Jim Butcher and Mark del Franco."

—*Booklist*

"James's world is rich and complex and well worth diving into."

—Richard Kadrey

"Supernatural chills and thrills with a hefty dose of humor... James should be on your must-read list!"

—*RT Book Reviews* (Top Pick!)

"This debut introduces a self-deprecating, wisecracking, and honorable-to-a-fault hero who can stand up to such established protagonists as Jim Butcher's Harry Dresden and Seanan McGuire's October Daye. Combining action and romance— with an emphasis on action—this is a top-notch new series opener for lovers of urban fantasy."

—*Library Journal* (Starred review)

By Elliott James

Pax Arcana

Charming

Daring

Fearless

Pax Arcana Short Fiction

Charmed, I'm Sure

Don't Go Chasing Waterfalls

Pushing Luck

Surreal Estate

Dog-Gone

Bulls Rush In

Talking Dirty

Fearless

PAX ARCANA: BOOK 3

ELLIOTT JAMES

www.orbitbooks.net

Copyright © 2015 by Elliott James LLC
Excerpt from *Pax Arcana: Book 4* copyright © 2015 by Elliott James LLC
Excerpt from *Jinn and Juice* copyright © 2014 by Nicole Peeler

Orbit
Hachette Book Group
1290 Avenue of the Americas, New York, NY 10104
www.orbitbooks.net

Printed in the United States of America

RRD-C

First Edition: August 2015

10 9 8 7 6 5 4 3 2 1

Orbit is an imprint of Hachette Book Group, Inc. The Orbit name and logo are trademarks of Little, Brown Book Group Limited.

The Hachette Speakers Bureau provides a wide range of authors for speaking events. To find out more, go to www.hachettespeakersbureau.com or call (866) 376-6591.

The publisher is not responsible for websites (or their content) that are not owned by the publisher.

Library of Congress Cataloging-in-Publication Data

James, Elliott.
    Fearless / Elliott James.—First Edition.
        pages ; cm.—(Pax Arcana ; Book 3)
    ISBN 978-0-316-25344-4 (paperback)—ISBN 978-0-316-25343-7 (ebook)
I. Title.
PS3610.A4334F43 2015
813'.6—dc23
                                                              2015001508

*To my father—the most decent and
honorable man that I know*

I am well satisfied that being awake, I know I dream not; though when I dream, I think myself awake.
                                        —Thomas Hobbes, *Leviathan*

A man cannot be too careful in the choice of his enemies.
                                        —Oscar Wilde

PART THE FIRST

A Small Price to Pay

A BRIEF RECAP OF WHAT HAS GONE BEFORE, SCREENPLAY STYLE

The clip begins with John Charming's voice doing a voice-over.

JOHN (VO): Previously on *Tales of the Pax Arcana:*

[CU of John Charming standing in a river up to his waist. It is night, and he is stripped down to his boxer shorts. He is leanly muscled and scarred, holding a crude staff in his hands while a longbow is slung over his shoulder. He is facing a patch of shifting darkness where a wila hides in the woods at the edge of the water.]

WILA: What are you?

JOHN: Would you believe room service?

WILA: There are no rooms here. And you didn't bring me anything. In fact, you took something away from me and tried to kill me.

JOHN: I didn't say I was very good at it.

WILA: What is this really about?

JOHN: Perhaps this is about the fact that my name is John Charming. Perhaps my family has protected humanity from things like you for more than a thousand years. Perhaps, sometimes, on nights like this, I remember who I really am.

[The wila's voice begins to thicken, to deepen. There is a sense of shadows growing larger.]

WILA: Are you telling me that a Charming still lives, and he's a werewolf?
JOHN: I did say perhaps.

Cut to a scene where John is naked in a forest, surrounded by growling wolves, on his hands and knees. He is changing into a wolf.
Cut to a scene where a six-foot-tall athletic-looking blond female, Sig Norresdotter, stands in the doorway of a bar while the narrator has another voice-over:

JOHN (VO): She smelled wrong. Well, no, that's not exactly true. She smelled clean, like fresh snow and air after a lightning storm and something hard to identify, something like sex and butter pecan ice cream. Honestly, I think she was the best thing I'd ever smelled. I was inferring "wrongness" from the fact that she wasn't entirely human. I later found out that her name was Sig.

Cut to a scene in a dark alley where John is unarmed and facing a vampire coming at him with a machete. The vampire's fangs are bared. A spear flies over John's shoulder and impales the vampire so that the metal point is emerging from his back and the wooden haft is lodged directly in his heart. Sig's voice reverberates from some point above and behind John.

SIG: I'm a valkyrie.

Cut to a scene where John, Sig, and a vampire hunter named Stanislav Dvornik are talking to Ted Cahill, a homicide detective, over breakfast:

JOHN [reaching for a cup of coffee]: Has Sig told you about the Pax Arcana?

CAHILL: That's the big "don't ask, don't tell" magic, right? She told me that before the elves went back to where they came from, they made the spell to protect all the little half-elf bastards they were leaving behind. The knights are like magical bouncers or something.

JOHN: It's a little more complicated than that. Knights are immune to magical compulsions because they're already under a spell called a geas, a magically binding oath. The knights swore to not harm any supernatural beings who aren't threatening the Pax Arcana, and to eliminate any who are as quietly as possible.

A montage of scenes where monsters are being eliminated follows. Cut to a scene by a riverbank where a watery humanoid soaked in Greek fire is screaming and thrashing as it catches fire.

Cut to a scene where a pug-nosed humanoid with purple blotches on its skin has been impaled by a copper pipe from behind.

Cut to a scene where John and Sig are sitting on the ground with their backs against a suburban house in a lower-class residential neighborhood, staying low so that they cannot be seen through the window they are poised beneath.

JOHN: I'm not going to be able to stay in Clayburg after we deal with this hive, Sig. You know that, right? It would be too dangerous for both of us.

Cut to a scene where John and Sig are making out in a parked car on a dark street in front of a health food store.

Cut to a scene where John is in a forest reading a letter. Sig's voice is recounting the words.

SIG (VO): I have feelings for you, very strong feelings, but that's why you're not good for me right now. I'm sorry, but that's the way it is.

Cut to a scene where John is standing on the doorstep of Sig's new apartment on a wintry night. John is holding a red rose.

SIG: You realize that if you pursue this, you're going to get punched a lot.
JOHN: I'll heal.
SIG [leaning forward to kiss him]: Yes, you will.

Opening credits begin to roll to the sound of Eminem's "The Monster" featuring Rihanna.

❦ 1 ❦

IT TAKES A VILLAGE IDIOT

Once Upon a Time, Ted Cahill had changed. The only real question was whether Cahill had changed too much or not enough.

For example, when I first met Cahill, he had been a mouthy homicide detective in Clayburg, Virginia. Now he was the sheriff of Tatum, New York, which basically meant that he was better paid, had more administrative responsibilities, and was forced to be a lot more polite to a lot more people. But when someone in Cahill's jurisdiction died in a suspicious manner, he was still a homicide detective at heart. And Tatum and Clayburg had a lot in common: Both towns are nestled in mountains, both towns are hosts to small private universities, and both towns call themselves cities, as if saying the word could make it true. So, how much of the change in Cahill's status and environment was really all that significant?

Another thing about Cahill that was different—but not unrecognizably so—was his physical appearance. Cahill's skin was a little paler than when I'd first met him, and I was willing to swear that his freckles were disappearing. His excess body fat had melted off like wax from a lit candle, and his cheek-bones were still pronounced, but in an angular way rather than chubby. His brown eyes were still small but now burned with an intensity that might be compelling or disturbing depending on how you looked at them... or how those eyes looked at you. This quality is actually fairly common among supernatural beings struggling with predatory instincts.

And that, of course, was the biggest change, the catalyst for all of the cosmetic alterations in Cahill's life. Ted Cahill had become a dhampir, a vampire who still retained some of his humanity. It was when trying to figure out *how much* humanity Cahill still retained (or what humanity meant exactly) that things got confusing.

"So, what about it, wolf boy? Do you smell it?" Cahill had been pushy and snappish ever since we arrived. He seemed to feel like he was doing us a huge favor by letting us help him, because asking for help had been so difficult.

"I smell it," I confirmed. Sig Norredotter, Cahill, and I were standing in the middle of a frosty and fenced in horseback riding ring next to Kincaid University's stables. It was that kind of private school. Tatum in January was a lot colder than Virginia, and I was wearing a grey hoodie under a brown Flying Tiger fighter pilot jacket. I was also wearing black leather gloves, thermals under my dark blue jeans, two pairs of socks beneath my running shoes, and a slight frown.

The scent in question had been dissipating for twenty-four hours and was now too faint for normal human senses, but I could discern a weird, flat tang in the air. It was the slightly off, kind of wrong, almost burnt smell that writers of the old tales used to describe as brimstone. When someone or something from another plane suddenly materializes on this one, molecules from the visitor's dimension get shoehorned into ours, and molecules from our plane get sucked into the visitor's home to fill up the empty spaces left behind. It's like the alternate-universe version of swapping spit. And the surrounding air has a neutral but not quite natural feel to it afterward.

Cahill gave me an impatient look. "And?"

"And why don't you shove an orange cone up your ass and go direct traffic, you doorknob?" I said. "I'm trying to concentrate so I can do your job for you."

Well, okay, I didn't really say that. I might have a year earlier, but I've been working on my social skills. Instead, I confirmed Cahill's suspicions. "Something supernatural manifested in this corral."

"Was this thing summoned?" Sig spoke up, wearing some kind of cream-colored, soft-shelled female outdoor jacket unzipped. She wasn't bothered by the cold any more than she was by the heat of the huge steaming cup of drive-through coffee that she was gulping instead of sipping.

By way of answering, I fished out my wallet and flashed the driver's license I was currently using. "Does it say *Gandalf* on here or something?"

I really did say that one.

Sig gave me a look, and her glare is a formidable thing: icy-eyed, intense, full-lipped, and framed by long golden hair flowing over Scandinavian cheekbones. I stared back and saw how smart and strong and beautiful she was, and smiled.

Seeing that smile, her eyes softened, and the corners of her lips curved upward slightly. Being around Cahill again had us both a little on edge, so I relented. "Yeah, it was probably summoned deliberately. Things that break into our universe without an invitation are rare, and they usually kick up a shitstorm right away. They don't go bump in the night; they go boom."

Sig nodded and addressed Cahill without looking at him or

using his name. "This missing college student... What was her name again?"

"Lindsey Williams," Cahill supplied. "I was thinking maybe you'd see her ghost around here."

"I don't," Sig said shortly. She doesn't particularly like the I-see-dead-people part of being descended from Valkyries, but she doesn't deny it either. "So, a security camera caught this Lindsey Williams heading this way at three thirty in the morning, right? What was she doing here that early?"

"Normally, I'd say she was meeting someone she shouldn't," Cahill said. "Some married professor, maybe, or her BFF's boyfriend, or her drug dealer. But after a little nudging, her roommate admitted that Lindsey used to sneak out here at night pretty regularly. She said that Lindsey was horse crazy and that the upperclassmen in the equestrian studies program get to choose all the best horses for themselves. So Lindsey liked to come out and take some of her favorites for a night ride."

"You say it took a little nudging?" Sig's voice was tight as she repeated the words. Cahill had carried a major torch for Sig back in Clayburg. I couldn't really blame him for that, but vampires are low-grade telepaths, and as a dhampir, Cahill had some of those abilities. When he'd partially turned, he'd started broadcasting his feelings for Sig and made her experience them too. From what I understand, they flirted around for a few days before going out on a date. Then they had dinner, and at some point while talking about how strange it was that they'd known each other so long and now this new thing was happening, Sig had a distant idea in the back of her mind. Sig is nothing if not strong willed, and the suspicion kept drifting back to the surface of her thoughts despite the tide of hormones trying to bear it away. After dinner, while Sig and Cahill were kissing in the parking lot behind the restaurant, Sig wrapped her arms over

Cahill's shoulders and pulled him close…and broke his neck. Lo and behold, the sudden rush of new feelings that had come into Sig's life completely disappeared.

Cahill's neck improved. Relations between him and Sig did not.

Cahill claimed the whole thing had been an accident, a result of having new powers that he didn't fully understand and was still learning to control, and that was entirely possible. On the other hand, Cahill had used Sig's unavailability as justification for using other women like Kleenex to wipe off excess sperm while his marriage fell apart. So it was kind of hard to say whether Cahill's feelings for Sig were real or whether they were just his excuse for being a player, and that was a difficult uncertainty to deal with. If Cahill's telepathic seduction of a woman he truly cared about had been unintentional, it was tragic, and he was kind of a victim. If it weren't an accident, Cahill had mentally raped Sig as a means toward physically raping her. People are complex, so there was the whole question of what Cahill had done consciously or subconsciously too, or how much of the event he had reinvented or lied to himself about.

Which was why Sig had compromised. She left Cahill breathing but told him to get his dick out of Dodge if he wanted to stay that way. And Cahill, whatever his other faults, knew Sig well enough to take her seriously. Hence Cahill's new job running a small police force in a town in upstate New York. I don't know if Cahill had called Sig reluctantly or if he'd been looking for an excuse, but when he came across something he didn't know how to handle, he'd called her just the same.

And she had answered. Sig is like that. She tends to have an "it takes a village" attitude toward monster hunting. I have mostly hunted supernatural predators alone, partly because I had no choice and partly because I'm an idiot. But Sig is worth going outside my comfort zone for.

"I gave the roommate a mental push," Cahill's voice resonated with a complex mixture of defiance and anger and shame. "If I don't practice using my powers, I'll never get better control of them. And this was for a good cause."

Sig considered that while taking a big slurp of her coffee coco mucho mocco whatever (I'm a coffee purist), then turned her focus on me again. "So, what are we dealing with here, John? I saw your lips do that I-smelled-a-fart twitch they do when you connect some nasty dots. Spill it."

Being attracted to a smart woman has a lot of rewards. It also comes with a few challenges.

"Yeah, I've put some pieces together," I grumbled. I would have liked another minute to think about them, but I went ahead and squatted down closer to the ground so that I could outline a wide area with a sweeping index finger. "Did you notice how this part of the corral has the outline of hoofprints frozen in the mud much clearer and deeper than the rest of the riding ring?"

They had not.

"This patch of ground got moister than the rest and then froze. I figure the creature that manifested a physical body here used water as its elemental base."

Cahill made a "time-out" sign and gave Sig an exasperated look. "Whoa! Whoa! Whoa! I asked you to bring Professor Peabody here because I don't know a lot about this stuff, remember? What do you mean, element base?"

Professor Peabody was a cartoon character on the old *Rocky and Bullwinkle* show who had a lot of doctoral degrees. He was also a talking dog.

Grrrrrrrrr.

"Elementals are monsters from other planes who create a physical body from scratch and wear it around our universe like a cheap suit," I explained. "They make that body out of whatever primary element is most similar to their own home environment." I began to tick some examples off on my fingers. "A gargoyle might use earth. A sprite might use air. A salamander might use fire. And so on."

It could get more complicated than that—a lot of otherworldly beings can possess human hosts, for example. Some of the rarer and more powerful ones can even incorporate more abstract forces like darkness or imagination, but I wasn't set up for a PowerPoint presentation.

Sig squatted down to get a closer look, and I indicated the ground again. "I think Lindsey Williams snuck over here and found the riding ring empty except for a beautiful, harmless-looking horse that she didn't recognize. I think Lindsey was drawn to the horse. She couldn't help herself. It was like poetry made flesh. She looked into its deep dark eyes and climbed up on it, and the creature began to change. It took off with Lindsey on its back and jumped the fence."

"How the hell do you figure all that, Charming?" Cahill challenged, but his voice was more subdued and curious than before.

"Because there's a water elemental called an Each Uisge," I said. "It assumes the form of a beautiful horse when it first manifests, and anyone who comes across it feels compelled to climb on its back and take a ride."

"And it's more like a highway to hell than *My Little Pony*," Cahill guessed.

"Right. The person is compelled to cling to its back, and the Each Uisge changes into a scarier-looking beast and heads for the nearest large body of water. Once it has its rider submerged, the Each Uisge tears its victim apart with its teeth and eats them whole, clothes and all, everything except the liver. When it's done digesting its victim, the Each Uisge dissolves into the water and goes back to its home plane. Basically, it uses our world like a drive-through window to pick up some fast food."

"Everything except the liver?" Sig's face had a strange I'm-trying-not-to-make-a-joke-about-not-even-supernatural-creatures-liking-liver expression.

"Jesus," Cahill exhaled. It didn't sound like a prayer. On the other hand, the word didn't burn in his mouth like battery acid either, so that was good.

"Summoning an Each Uisge this close to so many bodies of water was definitely murder magic," I said. "But how would anyone who wanted to kill this Lindsey Williams know that she was going to show up at 3:30 in the morning? And what did she do to piss a cunning person off?"

"What's with this cunning person shit? Why can't you just say witch or wizard?" Cahill complained.

"Ted, shut the fuck up," Sig told him. "You wanted an expert. Be glad you got one."

I stood up and offered Sig a hand. She didn't need it any more than I needed her to help me deal with Cahill, but she let me pull her up anyway. "The question still stands. Is there anything to suggest that this Lindsey Williams is mixed up in our world?"

"Not that I can find," Cahill admitted. "But I haven't been on this long. We didn't do any of that wait-forty-eight-hours bullshit here. Lindsey's boyfriend is a local whose parents are big people in this town."

"Maybe this Lindsey is new to our world?" Sig hazarded. "If she was as horse crazy as Ted says, maybe this is a case of some amateur witch using magic she didn't really understand and getting killed by it."

"Then who cleaned up the spell components and ritual items after she was killed?" I nodded at the stables where the sounds of an equestrian studies major getting the horses ready were obvious. "I guess she could be part of a group of witches, but I don't see a whole coven being horse crazy. Or all of them being equally ill informed either. I can think of a more likely scenario."

Cahill got it at once. "You think the spell was meant for whoever was supposed to show up and feed and groom the horses that morning."

"Yeah. I think Lindsey snuck in, doing her little midnight ride routine, and accidentally triggered a trap set for someone else," I agreed. "It would explain some things."

"Maybe," Sig said thoughtfully. "But maybe not. Maybe the spellcaster didn't care who got hurt, because this was some kind of random act of magical terrorism. Maybe somebody has a grudge against the university or horseback riding programs in general."

"That's possible too," I admitted. "But it doesn't feel like it. Terrorism is about causing terror. This event removed a student quietly and discreetly. One of you should find out who was supposed to take the morning shift in the stables and make sure they're safe."

"One of us?" Cahill's voice was suspicious.

"The other one ought to come with me and track whatever made those hoof marks," I explained. "Or do you want to just take my word for it and not really find out what happened here?"

They both considered this.

"We could get Molly and Choo to do it?" Sig offered hesitantly. Molly Newman is our group's holy person, and Chauncey "Choo" Childers is our weapons maker. They had gone to find us some hotel rooms and check out research material on Tatum when the local library opened: survey maps, town history, local legends, Native American tribes that had lived in the area, that kind of thing.

"Even if I'm right about the Each Uisge, we don't know who summoned it or why or if they're done," I reminded her.

Molly and Choo are normal humans and a lot more vulnerable to surprise attacks than Sig or me, which is why Sig likes to keep them in reserve when we don't know what we're dealing with.

"I guess you are the best suited for tracking the horse," Sig granted reluctantly, then turned to address Cahill. "And I should probably go investigate whoever was supposed to prep the stables yesterday morning. Anybody who pissed off a magic type might also have some ghosts that I can talk to following them around. But it's your turf, Ted. Do you want to check on the student who might be the real target or go with John?"

Cahill sighed. His Jedi mind tricks wouldn't work on me, and he probably knew it wasn't a coincidence that neither of the choices we'd given him involved Cahill being alone with Sig. "I owe it to this Williams kid to find out what happened to her. I'll help Charming test out his hypothesis."

Yippee.

"No sense wasting time, then." I pointed northwest. "The nearest lake is that way."

Cahill squinted suspiciously. "How do you know that?"

"John memorized the campus maps on the ride up," Sig said with a trace of…what? Fondness? Pride? "In case we wound up chasing something here."

"I also brought a copy of the *Junior Woodchuck Guide*," I added.

Cahill's expression remained a bit sour, as if he'd bitten into something he didn't like. Well, that was fine. It was what he liked biting into that I was worried about.

∾2∾

A HORSE OF A DIFFERENT CHOLER

"How long do you think we have before more people start waking up and moving around?" I asked. It was a little after seven, the time when the dining hall on the other side of the campus opened.

Kincaid University was large for such a small population, just a few thousand students, and some of those students would be in overseas exchange programs or away on internships. Rolling hills had stone stairways built into them, and bicycle and walking paths threaded through the various halls, dorms, libraries, gymnasiums, common rooms, auditoriums, administrative buildings, and gazebos (it was a no driving campus), but the paths were empty.

"On a weekday, the gophers would already be climbing out of their holes," Cahill mused. It was a Saturday. "But there aren't any eight o'clock classes to worry about, and the cold will keep a lot of the early risers who weren't out partying last night in bed. I'd say we have at least an hour."

"That ought to be enough," I assured him. The stables were

on the fringes of the campus proper anyhow, and we were headed into an increasingly thick-wooded area. I had a dark blue sling bag across my back, a tight cylinder rather than the teardrop-shaped kind. "One way or the other."

Cahill ignored that qualifying remark and put on a pair of dark sunglasses though the sun was just barely starting to make its presence felt. Most dhampirs can function in sunlight, but their eyes are weak during the day, and they get sunburn or sun poisoning easily. "You're dressing a little sharper than you used to there, Charming."

"I got most of my clothes from Goodwill or Salvation Army centers when I was being hunted by knights," I explained.

"Some of the sharpest dressers around wear consignment stuff," Cahill countered. He himself dressed well when he wasn't wearing a sheriff's department jacket.

"That's true," I acknowledged. "But I mostly wanted to pay in cash and travel light and keep changing my appearance. My clothes were disposable."

What I wasn't saying was that Sig had given me the jacket I was wearing for Christmas. I'm not a big fan of men letting their women dress them like Ken dolls, but it was the first Christmas gift I'd gotten in a long, long time.

The trees were leafless and the ground frozen, but Cahill still wore an expression of mild distaste, moving awkwardly despite his inhuman agility as he avoided the occasional curling bramble or fallen branch.

"I take it you weren't a Boy Scout," I observed.

Cahill actually laughed before he remembered that we were being tense around each other. "Not in any sense of the word. I grew up in Queens. The only reason I moved to Clayburg before you met me was that I was still trying to save my marriage back then. My ex-wife wanted me to be a cop someplace where there wasn't a huge gang problem."

And he'd wound up hanging around a bunch of monster hunters instead. Cahill didn't particularly want to talk, but he really didn't want to linger on his ex or Clayburg either, so he tried to switch topics. "So, an Each Uisge huh? Wasn't there some book about taming a sea horse?"

"There's a line from that Browning poem, *My Last Duchess*," I said. "The guy in the poem mentions a bronze statue of a sea horse. He calls having the statue made taming a sea horse."

"You're kind of a fucking know-it-all," Cahill observed. "Did you know that?"

"What I know is that the statue of the sea horse is a dead thing," I answered. "It doesn't have any of the wildness or beauty or magic of the original. But the narrator is a control freak who tried to do the same thing with his wife. He couldn't dominate her, so he had a beautiful painting made of her and then killed her. The poem is about what happens when you try to control the people you love. You wind up killing the things you loved about them in the first place, or the things they loved about you. You become a monster."

Silence.

"I meant the book by Robert B. Parker," Cahill said finally. "*Taming a Sea-horse.* I like mysteries."

"Oh," I said. "I forgot about that one."

I could smell the approaching lake when Cahill said, "You're talking about me and Sig. You think I tried to control her."

Actually, I hadn't had any intention of opening up a big emotional discussion on the brink of a possible monster battle. But sometimes, conversations have a mind of their own.

Sometimes, things need to be said, and if you dam them up, they just find another way of getting around to the subject.

"I don't *think* that," I said. "You *did* try to control her. The only question is whether you meant to or not."

"I didn't," he ground out. His right hand was a little too close to his gun for my taste.

"And you asked for help and we're here," I reminded him. If I ever discovered that Cahill was using his mental whammy to make women have sex with him, I was going to cut his head off and burn his body down to ash. But there was no point making threats. If I decided to do it, I'd do it.

Cahill bared his teeth. His fangs were showing, just slightly. "So, this hunt wasn't just an excuse to get me out here for some he-man ass-kicking contest?"

"We're not rivals, dumb-ass," I informed him bluntly. "I don't need to protect Sig from you. She already did that."

Those words hit him harder than the whole sea horse thing.

"What do you fucking know?" he hissed. "You're a man who got turned into something else, just like me. You had people chasing after you, and you put Sig right in the danger zone! And you've done all kinds of fucked-up things; any cop could tell that just looking at you."

"What do you want me to say, Cahill? That life isn't fair?" I asked quietly. "What was your first clue?"

It didn't take enhanced senses to hear his teeth grinding.

I took my sling bag off of my shoulders. Might as well use the time wisely, since we were stopping anyway. "The question is, are you going to man up and deal with it or not?"

"You're not sleeping with her," Cahill said. "I'd be able to smell it if you were."

It was true. I was courting Sig, and she was setting a slow pace. And it wasn't any of Cahill's business.

"I left Sig alone when she said that's what she needed," I said evenly. "And she came and found me again. I don't know why. To be honest, I thought she was smarter than that. But she did."

Cahill let out a long, harsh breath. It sounded like some of his soul came out with it. "If I leave her alone, I don't think she's going to come looking for me."

I pulled out a sledgehammer that was rolled up in my sling bag. The sledgehammer was already smeared with mud, which was good. I'd gotten it from a room in the stables while Sig was talking to the student in charge of morning cleaning. "So grow a pair, or freak out and attack me, or shut up while you decide. I'm about out of bullshit."

"Fuck you," Cahill said, but his heart wasn't in it. Maybe because he didn't have one.

Next, I pulled a bottle out of the sling bag. I usually carried the bottle and a few other things around in a specially made guitar case, but I was in Tatum as an expert tracker, and that would have looked awkward. Cahill watched me pour a small amount of liquid over the metal head of the sledgehammer. Then he watched some more while I removed a matchbook from my pocket and struck a match, causing the top of the sledgehammer to flame briefly.

Finally, he gave in to curiosity. His voice wasn't apologetic, but it wasn't angry either. "What the hell is that stuff?"

"Absinthe," I said. "Distilled down to the point where it's basically jet fuel. Absinthe is made from wormwood, and wormwood is potent against water elementals."

"Why?"

I sighed. One second, he was griping about me giving explanations; the next, he was asking for them. "My best guess? There's a prophecy in the Bible about a fallen star called Wormwood poisoning large bodies of water at the end of time. It may be that so many people have read and repeated that verse over the centuries, believing it, that it became a kind of crude magical ceremony, and now wormwood has taken on symbolic properties. Magic works that way sometimes."

"Do you even hear yourself talk?" Cahill's voice was flat, all of the emotion drained out of it.

"Here's the other piece," I held up the weapon while the flames burned out and left a scorched patina behind. "I just combined fire with the earth that makes up this sledgehammer. When I swing this thing fast and cause it to whistle through the wind, I'll be combining air too. That's earth, fire, and air. Three natural elements against the truce this thing made with water to move around our home."

"What am I supposed to do?" Cahill's tone was showing some small signs of becoming normal again.

I sealed the bottle of absinthe and handed it over. It was shaped like a World War II Nazi hand grenade, though a little bigger. "Break this over the Each Uisge and light it on fire. Then grab the biggest branch or rock you can find and go at it."

I removed my jacket and rolled it up in the sling bag, careful not to knock the katana inside to an odd angle.

"I don't like you very much," Cahill pointed out, as if that were directly relevant.

"So ignore my friend request on Facebook." I stood and shifted the sling bag back over my chest and shoulders. "Are we going to do this or what?"

He didn't answer, which meant that he sort of did. I started walking again and he followed. We were almost at the lake when Cahill spoke again. "Do you even have a Facebook page?"

"No," I answered tersely, and we emerged from the woods at the edge of a large lake. The Kincaid University material I'd printed off said that the name of the lake was Contemplation, but that sounded like something the university founders had come up with. As opposed to Lake Intoxication or Lake Procreation or whatever the students actually got up to around those waters. If I'd known we would be dealing with a water elemental, I would have looked up the lake's original name. True names are important.

Hell, I would have brought some rotisserie chickens from the local grocery store too. Back in ye olde days, knights used to lure Each Uisge out of their watery bolt-holes with roasted meat while the creatures still had the taste of flesh in their mouth. But you can never prepare for everything.

"Here's what I don't quite get," Cahill ventured. "This thing just wants to leave? Why don't we let it?"

"Because it broke the rules and killed someone from our home." I didn't take my eyes off the lake. I didn't know much about this Lindsey Williams. I knew she had a passion for horses. I knew she had people who cared about her. And I knew she'd deserved a chance to fuck her life up and learn and love and try to figure out what she wanted to leave behind. And some thing had taken that from her. It wasn't right.

Cahill grunted, so I gave him an answer he could be happier with.

"Besides, it's easier for cunning folk to summon creatures that they are already familiar with," I said. "Letting this thing live so that the person we're really after can summon it again would be like leaving a loaded gun lying around."

He nodded but still didn't look convinced. Fuck him.

I yelled out over the water: "SCIO ENIM QUIA HOC! VENITE CERTAMEN! ET FERTE PRESIDIUM! VENENUM EFFUNDAM EN LECTO! ET MATREM TUAM TERPIS!"

Nothing happened.

"What was that?" Cahill wanted to know.

"Latin."

He snorted. "No shit. What did you say?"

"I challenged and insulted it." The sledgehammer was balanced casually on my shoulder, my feet comfortably apart and my left hip angled toward the lake. The terms of the Pax Arcana actually keep me from attacking supernatural creatures unless they have done something to make their presence known to the world at large, but if I let a creature smell werewolf and give them a little attitude, they usually attack me.

We waited a while longer. Cahill started to say something but I interrupted. "All right, we're going to have to pull out some juju. Take your badge out and hold it toward the lake. You're the closest thing we have to a symbol of local authority."

He did so, cautiously, as if the badge might catch fire.

"Now stand on one leg—that symbolizes meeting someone halfway between worlds—and hop widdershins... That means in the same direction as the sun travels because it's our earth. Hop in a circle to symbolize the rotation of the earth, and yell *Ego sum stultus* three times."

He started to argue and I cut him off again. "Magic rituals are meant to look stupid. It's one of the ways cunning folk keep random people from messing around with them. Just do it."

Gritting his teeth, Cahill held out his badge, stood on one leg, and hopped in a circle yelling "EGO SUM STULTUS! EGO SUM STULTUS! EGO SUM STULTUS!¹"

Still nothing.

"Your ritual didn't work," Cahill's jaw was clenched. It sounded like every bodily opening he had was clenched.

---

1. I to be foolish, I to be foolish, I to be foolish

"That's because I made all that up," I admitted. "I just wanted to see if I could get you to do it."

"You ass—" Cahill started, and the Each Uisge erupted out of the water. It was an enormous horse, as big as a draft animal but shaped like a war steed. At some point in the last forty-eight hours, it had begun to turn a dark and virulent green. Its eyes would have been bloodshot if the threads lining its black irises hadn't been violet.

And it was headed directly at Cahill while he was off guard, moving faster than any normal horse. Fortunately, I move faster than any normal human, and I stepped between the damnable thing and my sort-of partner, sliding my topmost hand down the sledgehammer's haft and twisting my hips for maximum impact as I swung.

The Each Uisge halted as if momentum were just a wild figment of some physicist's imagination and went up on its hind legs. The swing I'd begun would have missed if I'd followed through on its natural extension, and the Each Uisge could have brought a front hoof down on my skull, but instead, I whirled into a side step that brought the sledgehammer upward into the side of the Each Uisge's jaw. The elemental came down awkwardly on its front hooves, and I was already stepping back into another whirl that would bring the sledgehammer around when I was ready to move forward again.

Not my first rodeo.

Unfortunately, Cahill didn't anticipate my back whirl, and shoulder checked me slightly off-balance while he was surging forward to smash his bottle over the nightmare horse. Cahill succeeded in soaking the thing in absinthe, but when I tried to stop my swing, the end of the hammer still grazed Cahill's forearm, and I lurched closer to the Each Uisge than I'd intended.

A strike from a foreleg dislocated my left shoulder and sent me hurling into a tree trunk some four or five feet behind me. I am ashamed to admit that I lost hold of the sledgehammer.

Vampire-strong or not, Cahill still got slammed off his feet by the Each Uisge's charge and dropped the lighter he was pulling out of his pocket. The monster came at me while I was hauling myself to my feet by using my right hand to grab a small overhead broken branch. The problem with regeneration is that it doesn't heal a dislocated shoulder because nothing is broken, and jamming my left arm back into its socket wasn't going to be as easy as they make it look in the movies.

So, I didn't try. I snapped the top off the branch stub I was holding and kicked off the tree, snarling and lunging to meet the damned thing head-on. Again, my speed and decision took it off guard. I don't think the Each Uisge had ever fought something that was human-shaped but not entirely human before. It brought its right foreleg up and sent me spinning off again, but not before I anchored that jagged section of wooden branch in its right eye.

It screamed.

The Each Uisge was careening and stamping wildly, and I was scrabbling on the ground with one bad arm and a few newly cracked ribs, trying to stay in its blind spot. I was close to getting a knee broken or a breastbone smashed or a skull crushed when Cahill finally set the horse on fire.

Which would have been awesome, but apparently, some of the absinthe had spilled on the left front of my hoodie. When the Each Uisge went up in flames, so did I. Ever yanked a burning jacket over a dislocated arm? Personally, I don't recommend it.

The Each Uisge homed in on my yell and swerved its head around to see me, but I retained enough presence of mind to swing my burning hoodie at its good eye. The Each Uisge screamed again and went up on its hind legs so that its forelegs could drive me back, but when it came back down on all fours, a sledgehammer came down on its skull.

A sledgehammer that had been picked up by a hundred and ninety pounds of pissed-off dhampir. The Each Uisge's skull shattered. Then its entire body shimmered and slipped and dripped down into a smoking mound of black jelly chunks. A piece of partially digested riding boot was sticking out of the mess.

Cahill sank down onto one knee and leaned on the sledge-hammer like it was a walking stick. Apparently, he had caught a back-kick at some point. I could hear a grinding click as part of his jaw popped back into alignment. Speaking of which…

I grabbed my left bicep in vise-tight fingers and lined my shoulder up with a tree trunk. It was the slight lifting motion that I had to use to position the arm that sucked. For some reason, it made me arch my chin violently to the right as if some unseen puppeteer were pulling my strings.

"What are you—" Cahill began, and my angry grunt cut him off as I slammed my arm back into its socket.

"Shit," Cahill observed when I was done. "You're lucky I was along to save your ass."

If stares could physically impale people, the look I gave him would have been a fourteen-foot-long jousting lance. With spikes on it. And a power cord. But if getting into an emotional discussion with someone right *before* a life-threatening situation is a bad idea, getting into it with someone right *after* a fight is an even worse one. So, I didn't speak until I trusted myself not to comment on Cahill's looks, intelligence, sexual preferences, competence, or probable parentage.

"Thanks," I finally said.

ᮣ3ᮣ

INSANITY IS ALL IN YOUR HEAD

You know you're in a college town when there's a restaurant called "Pancakea." The establishment was a pancake/coffee house, and Choo, Molly, Sig, and I were sitting in a booth arguing about the place and its name and their relative merits. I thought the name was a take on *panacea*, implying that pancakes are a cure for everything. Sig thought the owner wanted the place to become the IKEA of pancakes. Molly thought that given how large the pancakes were, the title might be a riff on Pangea, the first continental landmass. We all agreed that the owner was probably an ex-college student who couldn't get a job with his or her major, but we couldn't agree on whether that major was philosophy, marketing, anthropology, or just heavy drinking. All of us except Choo, that is. Choo was feeling a bit surly and wasn't saying much.

Whatever the reason behind its name, the establishment was clean and brightly lit by large windows on three sides, and there were wood floors and red tablecloths and lots of pictures by local artists all over the place. The kitchen was separated from the dining area by a half wall that functioned as a counter, and the layout helped distribute heat so that the kitchen was cooler and the large common room warmer.

More importantly, Sig had found the student who was maybe supposed to die instead of Lindsey Williams, and she'd followed him here. His name was Kevin Kichida.

The place was packed—it was a cold Saturday in that limbo between late morning and early afternoon—but this actually made it easier for us to talk privately in our corner booth. The customers were mostly families with little kids or single people engrossed in their electronic devices whether they were being single by themselves or not.

Choo's silence was becoming louder and louder, and I followed his eyes and realized that he was glaring at my breakfast. I had ordered something called the junk plate that had Italian sausage and eggs and cheese and bacon and broccoli and red peppers and potatoes all cooked together in an omelet, plus a steak. Choo, on the other hand, was currently trying to win back an ex-wife whom I'd never met, and part of that entailed giving up weed and trying to slim down a little. Hungry, horny, and unsoothed, he had ordered a poached egg and toast, and the toast was already crumbs.

"I feel for you," I told him. "But I just went head-to-head with Mr. Ed. If you think I'm going to order a salad out of solidarity, you're dreaming."

"Don't start with me." Choo leveled a dull butter knife in my direction. "I'm not even playin'." He was, though. Choo's hands give him away when he's really upset. They are big calloused hands, dark brown with long, thick fingers that are surprisingly deft; I have seen those hands play a piano with some skill and weave around wiring and machine parts that should have been too small to be accessible. And Choo's hands were gripping the knife lightly, not tightly.

I was about to make some response—I honestly can't remember what it was, but there's at least a seventy percent chance that it involved Choo's knife, Choo's ass, and some kind of action verb—when Molly chimed in from her own more modest plate of waffles. "Don't look at me either. It takes heavy food to hit my B spot."

We all stared at her. Molly looks a little bit like a hobbit—short, robust-cheeked, thick-spectacled, and with brown hair that tends to go a little crazy when it grows out—but she is an oddly formidable presence. I finally ventured, "B spot?"

"It's a sensitive ridge of tissue about one third of the way up my belly lining," Molly explained. "Repeatedly dropping carbs and chocolate against it gives me intense pleasure."

"That might fall under the Too Much Information category, Molly," Sig remonstrated gently. Then Sig took a bite out of her plate-sized chocolate pancakes covered with whipped cream and hot fudge sauce. She released her next words on a sigh of pleasure. "Although you might be on to something."

"I don't really blame y'all for not wantin' to diet with me." Choo's expression was caught between grumpy and amused. "But the food porn is a little much."

I changed the subject. "So, where's Cahill?" I kind of wanted to see if Cahill could sit close to Molly or not. Molly had recently left the Episcopalian priesthood after being on some kind of mental or emotional leave for over two years, but her ability to affect unholy beings hadn't been hampered by her decision to defrock or her newfound freedom to make pseudo-sex jokes. If anything, her holy mojo seemed to be getting stronger lately.

Sig finished another bite before answering. "Ted's trying to make it look like Lindsey Williams had an accident while taking a night ride in the woods, and got torn apart by wild animals. He's hypnotizing another riding student into believing that she went back to the stables early to look for her cafeteria card and found a horse fully saddled walking back to the corral."

We had found plenty of Lindsey's splatters and tatters on the edge of the lake shore where her liver had washed up, but I frowned anyway. "I don't like it. Someone's missing and can't be found? That's simple. Staging a death? That's complicated."

Molly reached across the table and patted my forearm. "It's one of the things Ted did for us before you came along. He's good at it."

"He wants Lindsey's mother to have closure," Sig added a little tersely. "He doesn't want the FBI or tons of media converging on his town, either."

I put my hand between Sig's shoulder blades and rubbed lightly.

It was Molly's turn to switch subjects. "So, what's the deal with this Kevin Kichida?"

Sig got caught with another mouthful and swallowed politely before looking down at her magic lamp—I mean, smartphone. She made a wish and rubbed it until some info Parth had sent her came up and started scrolling down the screen. Parth is a naga, one of the snakelike immortal beings who spend eternity chasing forbidden knowledge, and as such, he has evolved into a hacker of some skill.

"Kevin's a sophomore at Kincaid," Sig recited. "No declared major but seems interested in history. Father is an ex-Ranger lieutenant named Jerry Kichida, a third-generation Japanese-American. Jerry was a sniper but left the military four years ago. Kevin's mother, deceased, was named Yuna Satou, a Japanese immigrant. She died of cancer three years ago. Maybe that's why the husband left the military? Kevin was homeschooled.

He played soccer in some kind of traveling community league, took cello lessons, belonged to some cult that sacrifices people to Yoth Hoggoth, had a membership at the rec center—"

"Wait," Molly sputtered. "Go back. What!?!"

Sig grinned, a hint of mischief flaring in her bright eyes. "Just wanted to see if you were still paying attention."

Choo indicated me with a head yank. "You've been hanging around him too much, Sig."

I put on my most intent, serious face. "So Kevin doesn't really play the cello?"

Sig bumped her shoulder against mine playfully before continuing. "He's a fourth dan in aikido. No criminal record. He's apparently heterosexual, though Parth says his porn history is pretty tame and infrequent. He plays video games, mostly sim and puzzle-solving, not role-playing or shoot-em ups. He has no online profile to speak of. No Facebook, no Twitter, no Instagram, no Snapchat, or any of the other sites teens visit to be sneaky, as far as Parth can tell. No obvious girlfriend. No red flags in his permanent record. No medical history to speak of. No pictures of him on the Internet that Parth can find."

"That's pretty strange for a millennial," Molly commented.

"That's freakish for a millennial," Sig corrected. "It looks to me like Kevin's parents had him on a pretty tight leash, social-media-wise."

"What about his college transcripts?" I asked.

"No mention of a third nipple or strange protuberances in his college medical records." Sig almost sounded regretful. "He's one of two males in the equestrian program. He's into fencing too."

I looked over at where Kevin Kichida was sitting alone at a table by the front window, drinking copious amounts of hot chocolate and doing something on whatever the hell the latest electronic notebook was called. He wasn't a bad-looking kid; he was clear-complexioned and slender and wiry, around five feet ten and wearing it with good posture. He had a retainer that you could see when he smiled at the waitress, which he did every time he talked to her. His hair cut was a little edgy, spiky on top and shaved down to stubble on the back of his head, and he was dressed all in black and charcoal grey, casually so in clothes that looked loose and soft and comfortable. I didn't see anything remarkable.

Nothing remarkable...why did that hit a chord? Oh. "That mother's name sounds kind of generic," I said reflectively.

"What do you mean?" Choo demanded. "It sounds Japanese."

"That is what I mean," I explained. "It almost sounds too Japanese. Kind of like a female Japanese version of John Smith. I'll bet you it's a fake."

"How do you know about Japanese names?" Molly asked curiously.

"The only way I stayed alive when the Knights were after me was by traveling through Eastern countries where the Templars didn't have as many resources," I informed her. "I spent the better part of the '60s and '70s that way."

"Even if you're right"—Sig recommenced her assault on her pancakes—"we need to figure out how we're going to investigate and protect young Mr. Kichida at the same time."

"I could follow him and see if any more nasties jump out," I offered.

Sig chewed that suggestion over. Apparently, it didn't taste as good as her pancakes. "You mean, use him as bait."

"I like it," Choo said firmly. "The best way to figure out if anyone is after the boy is to smoke them out. We can't watch this kid forever."

"The problem with that is, Kevin might know something that would help us protect him and figure out what's going on." Sig's use of Kevin's first name made me groan internally. She'd already personalized the kid. Valkyries were bred to judge warriors, and sometimes, Sig does a weird meta-focus thing where she goes into a trance and perceives all kinds of clues and keys and phenomena when she first meets a person. I tease her about judging people she just met, but generally, it's easier to just go along. Speaking of which...

"Maybe you should just tell us what you're thinking, Sig." I leaned over and planted a kiss on her cheek.

She stuck her tongue out at me but obliged. "We could just tell Kevin that I'm a psychic and that we were asked here to investigate Lindsey Williams's disappearance. It's the truth as far as it goes."

"Bad idea," Choo responded without hesitation. "Right now, the boy's acting clueless. You tell him his ass is in danger, he might get all twitchy. It might warn whoever's after him that something's up."

Sig was acting just a little off, and Choo was being a bit confrontational, and I didn't know what was up with that, exactly. It might just have been that our team had variations of this argument a lot. Or maybe seeing Cahill again was causing tension because Choo blamed Sig for Cahill's transformation and/ or departure. Or maybe Cahill seemed like a ghost of Choo's Christmas future to Choo, a tense reminder that he was swimming in dangerous waters. Whatever was going on, the group had a lot of strong personalities, and the planning stage rarely went without some friction anyhow, so I wasn't too worried. But I took note.

"Here's something else to consider," I suggested. "If someone is after Kevin, they might have a good reason. Even if this kid is a good person, it doesn't mean he's not involved in something bad. People can make mistakes."

"Right." Choo jumped on that. "They can get blackmailed or fooled too."

"All the more reason to start communicating clearly," Sig said a little more grimly.

"We're not even sure this boy really does have a magical target painted on his back. We could scare him for no reason," Choo argued. I could tell Choo didn't really believe that. His pessimistic streak might be worse than mine. "We tell the boy to watch out for magic monsters, he might think we're crazy and call the cops."

"You want the truth?" Molly shook her fist and made an outraged face. "You can't handle the truth!"

Molly watches a lot of movies.

"Let him. We know the police in this town," Sig countered. "And John's not being hunted by knights anymore. We can handle a little scrutiny."

"Seriously," Molly told Choo. "If you're worried that Kevin will think we're crazy, I could do it. Most people think I'm a little crazy, anyhow."

"You're the sanest person here, Molly," Sig scolded her.

"Well, sure," Molly agreed. "But that's not saying much."

Choo laughed softly and held out his fist. Molly obligingly reached across the table and bumped knuckles.

"John?" Sig said.

I was distracted because I was watching a guy who had a vagrant vibe—he could have been anywhere from early thirties to early fifties but they were hard years either way—standing in front of the window where Kevin Kichida had stopped typing. The guy was just staring. At Kevin. The man—if that's what he was—was big and gaunt, his head and face covered with stubble and his body covered with fresh sores and old clothes. His skin had a slightly bluish tinge around his mouth and the hollows of his cheeks, though I suppose that might have been the cold. A white T-shirt had been pulled on over a green flannel shirt instead of worn beneath it, and painter's overalls completed the ensemble. There were dark circles around brown eyes that were a strange combination of wide open and burnt out and dead, as if someone had stubbed out a giant cigarette in his face. His forehead was pressed against the windowpane.

The windowpane that wasn't fogging. In the cold. Where the guy's breath should have been.

Kevin frowned and made one quick sideways glance. His body posture shifted uncomfortably, but Kevin quickly returned his attention to the monitor screen, which didn't seem to be working properly.

I started to move, but Molly was already up and motioned me to stay put. "I've got this."

I didn't protest.

The thing—I won't call it a man any longer—drew back a large hand and clenched it into a fist, and there was something about the certainty and power and purpose of that gesture that let me know the fist was about to smash through Pancakea's plate glass window and yank Kevin through the storefront like a small fish on a big line. But when the fist finished drawing all the way back, it stayed back.

Molly was approaching now, and the thing took the terrible intensity of those insane eyes off of Kevin for the first time. It looked up... and then it leaned forward as if straining against something and then stumbled back violently when Molly continued to move toward the window. She was wearing a cross prominently on a silver necklace—she always did—and there was no hesitation in her stride.

Maybe that was why Molly was drawn to hunt things in the dark. Some people are wired to shut down fear when they are actively in danger, and Molly never seems to be afraid or spacey or distracted when she is intent on exorcism or survival. It is only in relative safety that she needs medication and calming rituals like her movies or her dog or her daily meditations. Perhaps Molly needs those paradoxical moments of inner stillness that the presence of danger gives her.

Or maybe she is answering a call.

The thing continued to stumble back, reluctantly, straining and giving way as Molly's approach inevitably pushed it away from the store, from Kevin. It turned its head as if it couldn't even stand to look at her while she gazed at it through the fragile glass barrier between them.

"It's some kind of walk-in spirit," Sig whispered. "It's got that blurred-focus look."

I had no idea what kind of blurred-focus look she was talking about, but I didn't need to. I stood up and grabbed the much smaller sling bag I was now toting about. This one was originally the cover for a portable unfolding canvas chair, and I had adopted it as a temporary means of discreetly carrying my katana around. "Let's go."

I started making toward the door to the side of where all the action was going on, and Sig stood up to follow me. Choo's voice came dryly behind us. "I guess I'm picking up the check."

"Whoever summoned this thing might be watching," Sig reminded him. "He or she might even be in this restaurant. Stay alert."

Choo's response must have been nonverbal, because I didn't hear it.

Molly is one of the most powerful and unorthodox warders I've ever seen. All priests have their rituals, but those rituals are generally steeped in thousands of years of tradition, drawing on whatever energy comes from that cosmic soup of prayer and archetype and dream floating around in a place that is not bound by Time or Space. If physicists are right, and thought is electricity, and the molecules that make up our reality are bound by electricity, and no energy is ever destroyed, it may be that the prayers and dreams of people long dead or never dead are still embedded in the very atoms that make up our world. It may be that we are literally living in the thoughts and dreams of all the people who have ever been and ever will be.

That, as I understand it, is the essential foundation of magic.

But Molly's faith is a vibrant, living thing, and she often makes up her own rituals on the fly. History has been full of people who are able to do this. Sometimes, they are called wizards or witches. Sometimes, they are called saints or madmen. Whatever you call them, they rarely have happy lives. Molly blew a kiss at the thing on the street, not a mocking kiss, and it flew back and smashed into a car behind it, then reeled sideways and began urgently striding away. Molly moved closer to the window until her nose was an inch away from the pane, her hands clasped behind her back as if she was merely stretching and enjoying the view.

By this time I was out the front door, and I could see the thing moving rapidly down Tatum's main street. The figure definitely had a physical human form—I could smell it, a pungent mix of unwashed body and the beginning stages of decomposition—but that didn't make any sense. The sidewalk was covered with a light dusting of frost and snow...and the thing wasn't leaving any footprints. It was walking into the morning sunlight and cast no shadow.

ᔕ4ᔐ

KICKING BHUT

I stared after the shambling figure, and I think my mind must work more like a slot machine than a Magic 8-ball; options and choices and clues whirred behind my eyes: walk-in spirit—animating a corpse—not touching the ground—dressed mostly in white—not casting a shadow—bluish tint to the skin... and ding ding ding! Jackpot! Only instead of dumping a pile of coins in my lap, the slots behind my eyes usually drop a big steaming pile of crap into my life.

The thing was a bhut.

I passed Sig coming out of the restaurant as I stuck my head back in. Dropping the canvas chair tote bag, I quickly pulled my fighter pilot jacket off. It was freezing outside, but I was probably going to have to smear earth all over myself at some point, and I didn't want to mess the jacket up even if keeping it intact was becoming a major pain in the ass.

I tossed the jacket to Molly and indicated Kevin Kichida with my eyes. "Watch my jacket, okay?" She saluted me with a casual swipe of her hand. Pursuing things rapidly down city streets isn't really her thing.

Shouldering my tote bag again and still wearing a replacement hoodie, I pulled on my stocking cap and gloves while I caught up with Sig. She was trailing the bhut from about ninety feet, walking briskly but not quite jogging in her cream-colored winter coat, no hat, no gloves, no sign of discomfort or weapons though I knew she had a SIG Sauer holstered under her jacket. When I caught up with her, she stopped and addressed me. "Do you think this thing is going to disappear or start attacking people if we fall back a little?"

"Probably not," I said.

Sticking her hands in her pockets, Sig nodded. "Then let's follow it from further back and see where it takes us."

"Okay," I agreed. My nose could follow the bhut's trail if we lost visual contact, anyway. "But if we wind up fighting it, smear yourself with mud and find something iron or steel to hit it with."

Sig grimaced, probably at the mud part. "Anything else I should know?"

I slapped my hands together energetically and blew out a big puff of steam while we lingered. "Well, let's see. Donkeys kill more people every year than plane crashes. If you get lost in the woods, you can figure out which way is north by—"

Sig gave me a small punch on the shoulder and started walking again, but not before I saw the faint smile flickering at the corner of her mouth. "About this thing we're chasing."

I followed her. "It can make that body it's using strong. Lift-a-burning-car-off-a-child strong. It has some telekinetic powers too, but they're mostly maxed out keeping it floating a fraction of an inch off the ground."

Sig nodded. "So it's one of those has-a-dysfunctional-relationship-to-the-earth types."

"It is," I agreed. "Holy things will work against it. And burnt turmeric root."

"That would be great if that health food store we passed wasn't half a mile in the other direction." Sig sounded a little impatient.

I shrugged. "We don't really want to drive it off, anyway, do we?"

"No." Sig began picking up her speed slightly. Our prey was roughly a quarter mile ahead of us now. "So, what is this thing?"

"It's called a bhut." I matched her pace. "It's a kind of evil Hindu spirit. What makes it different from other ghosts is that it doesn't have to form an obsessive attachment to anyone or anything to hang around."

Sig eyed me peripherally. She knows a lot more about ghosts than I do, and what she knows, she knows more intimately, but I could tell that this was a new one on her. All she said though, was: "Maybe that's why it can't touch the ground."

I nodded. Almost all ghosts are defined by the anchor that keeps them on this earth. Ghosts that obsess on a place can possess anyone in their territory, but they can't leave it. Ghosts who fixate on a person can follow that person anywhere, but they can only possess others who are connected to that person. Ghosts who fixate on an object can only focus on people who come into contact with that object. Bhuts just don't give a shit.

Sig's eyes stayed focused on the bhut in the distance like an eagle staring down at a field mouse. "So, this thing doesn't have any limits? It can go anywhere? Possess anyone?"

"Yeah, but not for very long. As soon as a bhut moves into a person or object, its new body starts breaking down," I expounded. "That's what the bluish tinge in that guy's face is all about. Whoever was there before the bhut moved in? That's a dead body up ahead of us now. A bhut is like ghost poison."

Sig absorbed that. "These bhuts must have been some seriously toxic assholes when they were alive."

I agreed. "They were all extremely violent people."

"Well, so are we." Sig said that as if she was grimly determined, not as if she was struggling with self-doubt. Along the way, Sig plucked a snow shovel out of a display rack in front of a privately owned hardware store and kept walking, casually ripping the plastic top and the handle off of the wooden haft as if she were plucking leaves off fruit. A small nail went flying past me and bounced off the side of a Volkswagen Jetta. Sig dropped the plastic accoutrements in a public trash can a moment later and used the haft that was left like a thick cane.

"I don't know if that turns me on or if I'm worried about your hands being on my tender places now," I commented.

She smiled a little wider this time even though her mouth was still tight. "Did you have a particular tender place in mind?"

"Would you believe me if I said my heart?" I asked.

She laughed, just for a second. "No, but you get points for trying."

Hold on. We were on a points system?

Before I could ask for clarification, the bhut ducked down a side alley. When we reached the opening, we found it filled with a light fog that got denser as the alley got deeper.

"I thought you said this thing didn't have much mojo left." Sig's tone was mild as she twirled her makeshift weapon—its length somewhere between a baton and a Bo staff—in one hand.

"It doesn't take much to move a few air molecules around." I listened and took a whiff before adding quietly, "About thirty feet away and bearing left. I think it's trying to cover its scent by hiding behind a Dumpster."

In answer, Sig darted into the fog cloud at a run, wielding her new weapon the way a blind man uses his cane, probing, smacking it before her, the feedback of sound and impact helping her chart her way down the alley fast.

I cursed and followed. There was no way I was swinging my katana around in a confined space with limited visibility and Sig, but I still had my silver-steel knife, and I unsheathed it fast. Maybe too fast. My right foot slipped on cold, wet mud, and after a moment's hesitation, I slid and rolled into it, coating myself from shoulder to shoes in the slush. Somewhere ahead of me, the sounds of wood on bone cracked loudly in the air, and the unnatural mist filling the alley began to dissipate. I rolled onto my feet and saw Sig by a Dumpster, holding the snow shovel haft in one hand and tugging on it. She had crushed the bhut's throat, and he had ignored the damage and trapped the haft by tucking his chin down over it. Why not? He didn't have to breathe.

Sig yanked on the stick at the same moment that the bhut broke the haft with the palm of his hand. The sudden lack of resistance caused Sig to stumble and turn slightly, and the bhut kicked her across the alley and into the opposite brick wall, where she lost her footing and fell down.

That's the problem with taking on the ghosts of lifelong violent souls. The bastards know how to fight.

I came in hard and fast and hammered the hilt of my knife against the bhut's jaw in a sharp crack of broken bone, and when its head turned, I snapped off a low kick that should have smashed or splintered its knee. Unfortunately, in the heat of things, I'd forgotten the bhut was actually floating just off the ground and not putting weight on that knee. It made it almost impossible to knock the thing off-balance. I had to bring both my forearms up and lean into a block to keep the bhut's return backhand from lifting me off my feet.

Then the bastard put one hand on the Dumpster beside it and lifted its entire body parallel to the ground in a way that would have been impossible if the bhut'd had more than a passing familiarity with gravity—I threw myself backward to keep those pile driver feet from hammering into me and breaking bone.

It was a desperate move, but I managed to hold on to my knife without stabbing myself and rolled into a crouch just in time to see a heavy manhole lid fly through the air like a Frisbee and half cave the side of the bhut's skull in. Well, I'd told Sig to find something steel to hit it with.

"Ha!" Sig's voice was triumphant, and the bhut decided she had a point. I was crouched, and the bhut charged and got past me by running sideways up the alley wall above me, its body at a 45 degree angle to the ground.

I cursed and took an extra second to adjust the katana that was still slung on my shoulders before pivoting and following. The bhut jumped back down to the not-quite-ground and made it out of the alley...where it ran past the sidewalk and headlong into the path of an oncoming box truck—one of the large kind used for hauling furniture. The massive vehicle tried to hit its brakes, but it ran over the bhut with a sound that was half like a thump and half like a thunder burst with some wet thrown in.

Shit.

A slender woman with short curly brown hair and glasses, dressed in jeans and a red all-weather coat, was standing at the entrance of the alley where the bhut had emerged. Her mouth was wide open and her body was stiff with shock. Possibly, the fact that I was covered from head to toe in mud and holding a fourteen-inch knife also had something to do with that.

I pretended to be more winded than I was and put my palms on my knees as I looked at her. "That guy was seriously messed up on something," I gasped. "Meth, maybe, or heroin. He tried to rob my girlfriend."

The woman was inching backward carefully when Sig appeared behind me.

"Hey, sweetie," I greeted. "Are you all right?"

Sig brushed a few strands of hair out of her face. "I'm fine, but that poor man! You should have just let him have my purse!"

"He had this knife!" I exclaimed defensively, gesturing with my blade. "What was I going to do, let him wander off and hurt the next person who came along?"

The woman visibly relaxed a notch or two. I turned slightly to keep the knife's sheath on my hip hidden.

"What if he'd killed you?!" Sig said angrily. "I can cancel a few credit cards!"

By this point, the truck had ground to a halt and its driver— a large, somewhat beefy man with bad skin and short grey hair and big glasses—jumped out of the cab and left the door open as he dropped to his knees and looked under his vehicle.

I pulled this week's cell phone out of my pocket with my free hand and checked it. There was no signal, which meant the bhut was still active in the area. The woman was still watching as Sig and I began to walk toward the "accident," and I called over my shoulder: "The police are going to want to talk to eyewitnesses! You'd better call anyone who's expecting you and tell them that you're going to be in a police station for most of the day."

I had judged her right. The next time I looked over my shoulder, the woman was gone.

"What are we looking for?" Sig murmured.

"A flickering light," I said grimly, finally sheathing my knife and unzipping the top of my tote bag. Another car appeared, and then another, but both simply went around the halted truck without bothering to see why he'd stopped. The truck driver himself wasn't paying any attention to us, weeping and cursing while he looked at the thing that was hanging from his truck's chassis. "My katana is blessed. It should destroy the thing if we can find its true body."

Or lack thereof.

"Let me handle that part," Sig told me. "I've picked up a few tricks for dealing with disembodied ghosts that don't involve waving a sword around."

I didn't have time to agree. The flickering light we were looking for appeared from beneath the truck. I stepped aside and Sig lunged forward, but the light disappeared into the truck's exhaust pipe as if sucked up a vacuum nozzle.

What the hell?

The truck started. By itself. I ran forward and yanked the truck driver back off the ground before he was run over by his own wheels, and the truck continued to roll forward, gathering speed. For a second, I thought the bhut was just trying to use its new body to get away, but then I remembered what the bhut had been intent on in the first place.

The pancake house. Kevin Kichida. Molly. Choo. Even if the bhut couldn't get near Molly, it could aim the truck at Pancakea's front window like a runaway missile and then depart, letting momentum do the rest.

I tossed my tote bag back toward Sig and kept running. Maybe the bhut had enough control over its truck-body to close the front door that was swinging open, but if it did, it was concentrating on swerving to smash me aside instead. I darted between two parking meters, and the side of the truck swiped into them and sent the short metal poles flying up into the air like launched missiles. I had to jump over the rolling hood of a Fiat that the truck sent tumbling toward me, maybe jumping a little higher than a normal human being technically could. Fortunately, by the time the truck was ready to crush me against the side of a local art museum, I was parallel to the cab. I leaped into the doorway, shouldering the door further open, and when the bhut tried to slam the door shut on my hands, it wound up knocking me into the cab.

It took about four frantic seconds to hook my shoulder under the seat belt strap and click the horizontal part of the belt over my waist, and as soon as I did, the mechanism unlocked again. The door reopened and the truck swerved violently, trying to throw me out the side; only the fact that the truck's long body wasn't made for sudden turns saved me. Fucking bhut.

Then the seat belt strap started to pull me back against the seat, the strap slithering over my throat to choke me, but the harness recoiled when it pressed firmly against my mud-covered body. Thank God.

I grabbed the steering wheel with both hands, and I'm not sure how to account for what happened next. It may be that the bhut hadn't gotten full control of its new body yet. It might be that I'm stronger than a normal human and that made the difference. It might have been that the mud my chest and arms were caked in saved me again, or that the bhut only had control over the truck body and gears, not the tires that were touching the ground. Whatever the reason, I managed to wrench the steering wheel into a sudden turn despite its resistance. The truck lurched back into the street and slowly tipped over on to its right side in a skid.

The whole thing was incredibly loud, and I clung to the

wheel with one hand and the shoulder strap of the safety belt with the other as my body was yanked violently sideways and down, smacking against the dash. Still, the action kept me from being ground like so much hamburger against pavement and shattering glass and crumpling metal. Shrapnel flew around me in a hailstorm of small notebooks and flashlights and wrappers and cups.

When the truck finally came to a stop several smashed cars and a broken utility pole later, I was fairly certain that the bhut didn't have enough Jedi juice to lift that massive metal body back on to its side. The bhut apparently didn't think so, either. The truck's engine shuddered and gave up its life, and the truck lay there like a big metal beached whale.

I didn't see what happened next. I was slightly rattled and battered and disoriented—it felt like I'd been trapped inside a giant kettle drum—trying to work my way out of an upturned truck cab quickly and failing. So I didn't see Sig run up to the truck and wait beside the exhaust. I didn't see her jab her hand into the center of the flickering lights that emerged and use her index finger to trace some Norse sigil into the bhut's very core. I didn't see that disembodied being evaporate into a thousand smaller points of fading light like some kind of cosmic dandelion burst by a sudden wind.

But I hear it was oddly beautiful.

The first thing I did see when I climbed out of the truck cab, ears ringing, bruised and bleeding from multiple cuts and contusions and scrapes, was the front window of Pancakea. Molly was still standing there, though she had been joined by a dozen other customers, Choo and Kevin Kichida among them.

Molly gave me a small wave.

❧ 5 ❧

TRUCK ACCIDENT ESCALATES, WRECKS MAIN STREET

Sunday, February 8, 2015—9:57 a.m. by WhatsNews WithU

Tatum, NY.—A homeless man is dead after an accident involving a moving truck on the main street of Tatum, New York. Several eyewitnesses saw the man walk into the path of the oncoming truck while seemingly disoriented.

The truck's driver, Lamont Patrick, stopped and got out of the vehicle immediately, but in a twist that added to the tragic turn of events, Patrick may have failed to park the truck properly in his haste or possible shock. The vehicle continued to roll down Main Street causing tens of thousands of dollars' worth of property damage before a passerby ran alongside the moving vehicle and climbed onto the driver's side. Tatum's sheriff, Ted Cahill, believes that the passerby grabbed onto the steering wheel while trying to climb into the cab and caused the truck to overturn. However, Sherriff Cahill is also quick to point out that the runaway vehicle was headed for a crowded restaurant and is not pursuing charges at this time.

The unidentified Good Samaritan left the scene and has yet to come forward.

The police have declined to identify the homeless man until his family can be found and notified, but they have issued a statement that the subject was a local with a known history of arrests and convictions involving the abuse of illegal substances.

~6~

CAUGHT BETWEEN A COP AND A HARD CASE

You know, when I was Kevin Kichida's age, interrogation rooms didn't mess around," I commented. "There were drains in the concrete so that cops could hose the blood away, sweat lamps the size of miniature football field lights, and steel benches bolted to the floor."

Molly's voice did something weird while she talked out of the side of her mouth. "It was a hard time, with hard men and hard drinking."

"Yeah, easy there, 1937," Sig said, dropping my birth year.

I smiled but still indicated the Tatum Police Department interrogation room that Kevin Kichida was sitting in. "I'm not saying it was better. I'm just saying, this place is a spa."

It was sort of true. The walls of the climate-controlled room were warm-colored, probably because some social psychologist from Berkeley had theorized that people would be more willing to open up in a nurturing environment. Kevin's chair looked reasonably comfortable, plastic but curved to accommodate a spine, and there was even an empty chair on Kevin's side of the table to remind interviewees that they had the right to request a lawyer. Not that Kevin was being charged with anything.

Instead, Kevin had waited in the community room while Cahill interviewed other witnesses of the truck "accident." People were being asked to look at a composite sketch to see if it resembled the man who had climbed out of the truck. Me. It had been a pain in the ass sneaking into the station around the witnesses too, but Cahill was being crafty. Molly had been sitting right next to Kevin, and Cahill had apologized to her for the inconvenience and explained that they normally would have just interviewed people on the scene, but that they were trying to track the movements of the man who had climbed out of the truck because he might be involved in another investigation. Cahill asked if Molly would mind being interviewed in an interrogation room, half laughing and explaining that she wasn't a suspect or anything, that it was the only clean and quiet place in the police station right then. She had agreed. Then Cahill had apologized again and said that she would have to leave any electronic devices with a clerk because there were security regulations about allowing recording devices into the area, and again, Molly had agreed.

Ten minutes later, Cahill and Molly had returned, laughing and being polite, and then Cahill had let her go and repeated the process with Choo. When Cahill and Choo came back after a short interval, Cahill had done the same with a waitress and three other customers. When Cahill finally came to Kevin Kichida with the same proposition, what was the kid going to do? Scream that he wanted a lawyer?

But as soon as Kevin and Cahill sat down, a deputy had come in as arranged and called Cahill away on some administrative matter. Cahill had apologized to Kevin saying he would be right back. Now Kevin was just sitting there, stewing in his own juice.

For our part, we—that is, Sig, Choo, Molly, and I—were with Cahill in the observation area adjacent to the interrogation room, watching Kevin Kichida through the one-way glass. Cahill's being the sheriff really did have some advantages.

"We still have places and ways for making things uncomfortable for a perp," Cahill said, but he didn't take his eyes off Kevin and he didn't get specific. "But we have to be more creative now."

"I'll bet," I shifted in my chair. Ironically, our room was actually less comfortable than Kevin's. We weren't in New England, but we were damn close, and the furniture was that strange combination of utilitarian and ornate: polished walnut chairs with elaborate scrollwork carved into them. I would have preferred some cushions. The only decorations on the plain white walls were an intercom phone and a fire extinguisher.

Sig patted my knee. "You just don't like being near interrogation rooms, period."

"Got yourself a bit of an authority complex there, Charming?" Cahill asked mildly.

"I don't know why they call it a complex," I grumbled. "It's more like an authority simplification. I don't like authorities."

"Unless you're being one," Cahill sniped.

"Oh kiss my ass," I shot back. "I was trained by professional monster hunters, and I've been doing this kind of thing for more than half a century. How long have you known about the supernatural again?"

Cahill gave me just a bit of a warning glare. "Before I started living it? Four years."

"Holy shit! Four years? Four whole years of not knowing what you were doing and picking shit up as you went along?" I put my coffee cup on the floor so that I could drop down on my knees and clasp my hands in front of Cahill imploringly.

"Oh Great Master! Forgive this blind fool's impertinence in even presuming that his humble self might have some paltry crumbs of knowledge worthy of passing on to one so wise and learned. Teach me! Teach me! Teach me!"

"Fuck off!" Cahill was pissed but he was also laughing. "Why do you got to be such a smartass all the time?"

Choo jumped in with his own contribution. "What I want to know is, why are you actin' so antsy? I'm the black man in a police station. Hell, that boy in there looks more comfortable than you do."

It was true. I was having some bad memories and couldn't get comfortable. I had been on the other side of an interrogation the year before, and the Knights Templar don't much care about Miranda rights. Sig was the only one in the room who knew the details. She reached over and rubbed my arm as I got back in my seat, but before I could deflect Choo's question, Cahill decided to take control of the situation again. "Choo's right. This Kevin Kichida isn't acting like a normal kid."

We all looked at Kevin. He seemed composed and self-contained.

"I've seen professional killers who weren't this patient," Cahill added. "I don't think the waiting is getting under this kid's skin at all."

"He was acting kind of squirrelly after the truck crash," Molly offered. "He got a little impatient when he couldn't get his waitress to bring him his check quickly."

"He didn't volunteer anything when you showed up so fast and asked if anyone had seen John leave the truck either," Choo told Cahill. "If I hadn't pointed him out, I don't think he would have said nothing."

"He didn't look too happy at showing me his identification before I asked him to come to the station now that I think about it," Cahill recalled. "Has Parth broken into the kid's cell phone yet?"

"No," Sig said slowly. "He says it's registered to a Terry Woods, but he hasn't gotten any further than that. Parth also says Kevin's normal phone is back on campus."

"So Kevin was hanging out in a public place with an emergency phone that's not under his own name," I commented. "And he's not carrying the normal phone that could be tracked easily. You know what that sounds like, right?"

"Fuck this." Cahill stood up. "I'm just going to trance this kid. We'll find out what we need to know, and we won't have to wonder if he's telling the truth either."

And that was my real issue with Ted Cahill in a nutshell.

I mean, yeah, there was the Sig thing, but honestly, that was more Cahill's issue with me. Sig was coming out of a seriously messed-up relationship that was all tangled up with a history of substance abuse and codependence, and one of the reasons she and I were taking things slow was that she wanted to make sure whatever we had was real and strong enough to build on. She could never be into a man who had made her feel things that weren't true, however briefly or unintentionally. That's just the way it was. If Cahill thought he was in a love triangle...well, that was his problem.

My problem was that Cahill didn't seem to think what had happened between him and Sig was that big of a deal. He wanted to flex and explore his new powers, and maybe that's understandable. Being able to get inside someone's head must be every homicide cop's dream. I mean, let's be honest, what if *you* suddenly had the ability to make people answer any question you wanted, or forget anything you wanted, or behave any way you wanted within reason? Would you immediately say to yourself, "This power of mine to play with someone's innermost psyche is a form of molestation or rape, and I won't do it"?

Or would you maybe ask a few people what they really thought about you? Or ask the person you're seeing to open up about what's been bothering them? Would you make your best friend stop singing that annoying song that they don't even know the right lyrics to? Just to be naughty and daring, would you ask a really hot stranger to strip and then make them forget it ever happened? Would you tell your boss to give you that promotion you deserve, or make someone quiet down in a theater, or tell your sibling's husband or wife to treat them better? Is there anyone you would like to "help" give up cigarettes or stop drinking or lose weight? It all sounds pretty good, doesn't it? Like the premise of a romantic comedy.

Now imagine someone else—and I don't know which would be worse, a complete stranger or someone you love—having that kind of power over you.

Does it still sound great? Or did the movie in your head just turn into a psychological thriller with a bloody ending?

"We should try to talk to this kid first," I objected. "Trancing him ought to be a last resort."

Sig looked over at me curiously. "Didn't I say we should talk to him back in the coffeehouse?"

"We know Kevin really is in danger now," I said. "That changes things. If Kevin doesn't know anything about it, he needs to. And if he does know something, we should give him a chance to come clean."

"Or we could just stop dicking around and I could just ask him my way right now," Cahill repeated. "And we'd know he was telling the truth, the whole truth, and nothing but the truth. It's not like I'd hurt the kid."

Molly intervened before Cahill and I could get into it again.

"This is your town, your rules, Ted. But speaking just for me, I'd rather focus on how we're going to protect Kevin than how we're going to violate his rights."

"Who even says we should protect him?" Cahill demanded, feeling defensive now. "So far, two innocent people have gotten killed because they got between Kevin and the person who's after him—and we still don't know anything about whoever that is or why they have a beef with the kid."

"We know some," Choo corrected. "We know whoever it is likes to send monsters to do their dirty work."

We were interrupted by a hesitant knock on the door.

"Come on in, Eric," Cahill's spine straightened. His chin tilted downward slightly and his face assumed a professional and polite neutrality.

A thirty-some-year-old man dressed in a deputy's uniform stuck his head in the door. He had the thinness and slightly cured skin of a longtime smoker. "Pam Williams wants to talk to you about the search we've organized for her daughter. I wouldn't bother you, but she's spiraling out of control again. She's sent me twenty texts in the last hour."

Cahill rubbed his forehead with the palm of his hand. "Tell Mrs. Williams that I put you in charge of it because I'm dealing with a truck accident on Main Street."

"I did. I just…well…Her daughter is dating Ryan Arnold's kid," the deputy reminded him.

Cahill digested this information silently. His predecessor had left the Tatum Police Department suddenly after a mild stroke, and I found myself wondering if Cahill had used his new mental powers on the board or council that had interviewed him for his interim position. Either way, sooner or later, Cahill was going to have to run for election if he wanted to stick around, and he couldn't hypnotize an entire town.

Cahill sighed. "Tell her I'll update her myself as soon as I'm done interviewing witnesses."

The man nodded, hesitated, and then indicated Kevin. "Is everything okay with that kid?"

"Witnesses saw Nate Johnson hanging around this boy right before he wandered into that truck, and Nate was on drugs," Cahill said shortly. "The kid is also in Lindsey Williams's horseback riding class, and she's disappeared. It might be a coincidence, or maybe bad things are happening around this kid because he's dealing drugs. I'm going to lean on him a tiny little bit."

The cop still lingered and looked at us. Sig was supposed to be some kind of psychic that Cahill had discreetly contacted about Lindsey Williams's disappearance, and I was supposed to be an expert tracker. Molly and Choo had both been witnesses at the accident. You could see him trying to make those puzzle pieces fit.

Cahill didn't take the hint and explain. "Is there anything else, deputy?"

It was a curt dismissal hiding behind a question mark. The man mumbled a "No, sir" and closed the door.

After a moment, Sig picked up where we'd left off. "We know something else about whoever's doing all this. If that Eek Usage spell had worked, Kevin would have just disappeared without a trace. And if the bhut had killed Kevin and then abandoned that homeless man's body, you'd just have a case of some vagrant going crazy and killing a college student before dropping dead. Whoever we're after doesn't want to violate the Pax Arcana or leave any fingerprints."

"For now." Cahill's expression was sour. "Another thing we *don't* know is how far this unknown son of a bitch—no offense, John—is willing to escalate if we keep making things difficult."

"We at least need to protect this kid until we know what the stakes are," I argued. "And that includes not giving his head an enema. Kevin might know something that an evil person doesn't want getting out. Or the kid could be part of a prophecy. Or maybe his death is the sacrifice that's going to summon some butt-ugly fuckmunch—no offense, Ted."

"Or maybe the kid isn't some innocent victim at all," Cahill shot back. "Maybe he's in this up to his eyeballs."

"Kevin Kichida is an essentially good person," Sig said firmly.

"You said that about me once," Cahill reminded her shortly, his face flint. "And that didn't turn out so well."

Sig didn't blink. "I knew you had the potential to be a selfish prick. But there's no way that you've become someone who will let an unknown person come into your territory and kill whoever they feel like, so stop posturing."

"Who's posturing?" Cahill didn't blink, either. "You broke my main street."

"If you want us to go home, say so," Sig challenged.

He just stood there. It struck me as ironic that Kevin Kichida was keeping his cool, and our group was falling apart. If this was what working with Sig's team was like, I wasn't sure I wanted to do it. Monster hunts get messy enough without a bunch of personal drama.

Cahill stalked toward the door. "Fine. I'll question the kid the old-fashioned way. For now."

We sat there for a few moments after the door closed, no one saying anything until Choo said: "Huh."

He packed a lot of meaning into that grunt.

"That got a little too intense for my tastes," Molly confessed. I'm not sure if that was connected to her next comment or not, but she added: "I have to pee."

"So go pee," Sig told her.

"As soon as I leave, something bad will happen," Molly explained.

"Something bad is going to happen sooner or later anyway." It was an odd way to reassure her, but Sig and Molly understood each other. "You don't want to have a urinary tract infection when it does."

"Fine. But it's on your head." Molly left.

Cahill entered the interrogation room with a clipboard that had a sketch that vaguely looked like me on it. Kevin got up from his seat and stepped up to offer Cahill his hand. Cahill gave the hand a short pump. "Thanks for waiting, Mr. Kichida. Hey, do you mind if I record this? It would save someone else from having to read my handwriting."

"Sure." Kevin's face and voice were affable, but he stiffened when he touched Cahill's hand. What had he sensed, and how had he sensed it?

"Thanks." Cahill sounded sincere. "Sorry I kept you so long. I had to talk with a mother whose daughter is missing. A college girl."

When Kevin stepped back to the table, he sat down on the police side with his back to the observation window. Maybe he didn't know better, but I kind of thought he did. "Is she all right?"

Cahill sat down across from him with no sign of disgruntlement. "No. No, she's not. Her daughter's missing. Maybe you know the girl. Lindsey Williams?"

The muscles between Kevin's shoulders began to stiffen again, but it stopped there, as if his brain were reaching down and squeezing the neurons before they could travel any farther down his spine. "She's in my equestrian studies program."

Cahill blinked. "What, you're in that program too? Huh."

He packed a bit of *I'm sorry; I thought you were a man* attitude into that *huh*, but Kevin didn't rise to the bait. "Hey, since you're here, maybe you could tell me. Did Lindsey have a wild streak? Did she seem like the kind of kid who would run off without telling anyone?"

Kevin shook his head emphatically. "If Lindsey's missing, it's because something happened to change her reality."

"Philosophy classes," Sig murmured next to me under her breath.

Cahill just stared at him blankly. "What do you mean?"

"Lindsey stayed hunched inside her bubble like a fetus." Kevin ticked off points on his hand. "Horses. Grades. Boyfriend. If it didn't have something to do with one of those three things, she wasn't interested."

Cahill gave a friendly chuckle. "You asked her out and she shot you down, huh?"

Kevin looked surprised. "I don't even know her."

"So, how do you know all this bubble stuff?" Cahill seemed puzzled. "It sounds like you knew her pretty well."

"I pay attention." There was a slight hint of *That's why I know you're full of shit* in Kevin's tone. His intelligence and focus were palpable things, and if he'd grown up a military brat and studied aikido, he'd had practice being around authority too. But he was still young and male.

"She did keep to herself, mostly," Cahill muttered distractedly as he put his clipboard on the table. "It's making my job a lot harder." He made a production out of looking for a pen.

"Did?" Kevin raised an eyebrow. "She doesn't anymore?"

For a second, something pissed-off and menacing flickered across Cahill's face, but he covered it by continuing to pat himself down. "I mean, before she disappeared."

Kevin offered him a pen. "Keep it."

Cahill took the pen with a small laugh. "Thanks. It's probably good you don't know Lindsey well. I have to tell you it's not looking good."

"Is that why I'm really here?" Kevin asked softly. "Because if it is, I would like to call my father."

Cahill acted surprised. "Is that why you *should* be here?"

Kevin's voice shook for the first time, just a bare hint of a quaver. "Do you know what it feels like when someone is staring at you?"

"No," Cahill lied.

"I do," Kevin said. "You've been watching me through that mirror. Several other people still are. I would like to call my father."

I found myself standing up.

Cahill didn't answer directly. "Did you feel Nate Johnson looking at you too? One of our witnesses says Nate was staring at you through the restaurant window as if he knew you. Nate's the man who went down the street and stepped in front of a truck."

Kevin didn't raise his voice. "I want to call my father. Or I want a lawyer who will call him for me."

Cahill leaned forward across the table and stared directly into Kevin's eyes. Cahill's body language clearly said *Enough of this shit.* "Hey Kevin, look at me."

Kevin did. And maybe Molly should have held her water after all, because everything went to hell.

ᵔ7ᵔ

IT'S SO HARD TO MAKE A
CONNECTION THESE DAYS

Cahill and Kevin both froze, dramatically so. Cahill's body was leaning forward at an angle that should have been uncomfortable. Kevin was caught in a position that had been moving to back away slightly. It wasn't as if time stopped—it was more as if their muscles were locked and contracted in some painfully unnatural fashion, their bodies straining but going nowhere.

Then . . . have you ever stood next to an active power line? There's this invisible pressure against your skin, a vibration. Whatever began emanating from Cahill and Kevin was like that, except it wasn't moving on air currents. The wave went straight past the one-way glass and through my nervous system; it sent me running out the door.

There was no one in the short hallway between the observation area and the interrogation room, and the latter wasn't locked. I flung the door open and saw the forms attached to Cahill's clipboard tearing loose and shooting up into the air as if sucked into some kind of vacuum. The power in the building went out, then came on again as emergency generators kicked in, hesitated, went out, and sputtered back on, so that there was a kind of retarded strobe light effect. I caught scatter-shot glimpses of a dozen sheets of paper floating above Kevin and Cahill, contorting and folding in on themselves until they looked like origami bats. As soon as their metamorphosis was complete, the paper bats began flapping their wings and flying around Kevin and Cahill hurricane-style, rustling frantically.

"What the hell?" Choo was frozen in the doorway behind me. As I moved closer, the paper bats began circling me, not gliding like paper airplanes but flapping like panicked animals while light and darkness struggled for control of the room. The paper edges of the artificial bats' wings began making cuts in my skin as they brushed against my face and hands, trying to drive me back. Sig's skin was harder than mine...Where was she? The clipboard came hurtling toward my face and I smacked it away with a forearm only to have it come back painfully against the side of my head. I caught a flash of the pen Kevin had given Cahill darting toward my left eye while the room was light, and I grabbed it out of the air as the room turned dark again.

Screw this. Cahill and Kevin still hadn't moved, and I launched a round kick that cleared the edge of the table. It wasn't textbook perfect, but I caught Cahill in the forehead and threw him backward violently. His chair tipped and he landed on the floor, hard. Pure instinct or not, the move severed the connection between Cahill and Kevin. The lights came back on with an audible *clunk*, and the clipboard dropped to the ground with a loud crack. The paper bats fluttered down after it.

Kevin slid down against his chair, boneless, and I caught him before he fell. He was unconscious, but his eyes were wide open and only showing the whites. Thin trails of saliva were visibly glistening below the corners of his mouth.

Cahill groaned.

"What happened?" Choo was reluctant to enter the room; he had only become a monster hunter after being briefly possessed by a geist, and he was in no hurry to repeat the experience.

I didn't answer because I didn't know. Kevin's pulse was too fast, but I could also tell that it was slowing down. Then I set him down on the floor because Cahill was awake and coming to his feet. His fangs were bared and his eyes were wild and he was snarling. Ted's not home right now. Leave a message and maybe he'll call back later.

Cahill sprang forward, completely focused on Kevin. His jaw was pulled back so that his upper fangs were poised to tear flesh. His fingernails weren't clawed, but his hands were extended as if they were. Cahill was stronger than me, so I stepped inside his reach and turned my block into a grab for Cahill's lead wrist, moving in a waterwheel motion that was pulling the top part of his body instead of pushing against it, shifting my body weight into my hips, my hips into Cahill's lower half, bending so that I was pulling him over the curve of my descending shoulder in a natural progression as his body pushed forward. At his speed, with his power, he went feet over head and landed flat on his back, hard.

Cahill tried to scrabble upright by putting his arms behind him, but I kicked a wrist out from under him and he fell onto his right side. Cahill went with it, turned all the way onto his right shoulder and swiveled so that he could grab my ankle with his left hand, but I yanked my ankle out of the way by knee-dropping onto his extended wrist. There were cracking sounds. He howled and shifted his weight from his side onto his stomach so that he could push off the ground. His mouth was open, his fangs still bared, and I brought both my hands and all of my weight onto the back of his head and slammed down hard.

Cahill's fangs anchored in the floor. He tried to pull his face loose with just his neck muscles and couldn't, then braced his right hand against the floor. That's when the tiny part of Cahill's brain that was still a detective heard a sound that it had heard many times before... the sound of the fire selector switch on Cahill's own Glock 18.

The Glock I had just lifted from his side holster.

The Glock I was holding pointed at the side of his head.

If I'd been in a movie, I would have screwed the gun into the side of Cahill's ear for dramatic emphasis, but personally, I prefer not to make it easy for opponents to disarm me.

Training and conditioning warred with vampire instinct until Cahill calmed down. "Mu'er fu'er!" he drooled before pulling his fangs loose with a pop.

"Kevin Kichida is under my protection," I informed him.

Cahill spit whatever the floor tasted like out of his mouth while he pushed himself to his knees very, very slowly. An ordinary bullet in the side of his head wouldn't kill him, but it would briefly immobilize him and give him the mother of all migraines. "That little bastard got inside my head!"

I'd figured that out, actually. The paper bats had been some kind of psychic projection of Cahill being a vampire.

"You tried to rape his head first," I pointed out grimly.

"Hey!" Choo yelled. In his right hand was a retractable baton made out of some kind of highly durable plastic; it was fully extended and down by his side. The end of the baton had been sharpened to a point, and it glistened with a coating of God knows what. Choo's left hand held a glass vial that he wouldn't have had any problems getting through a metal detector. The odds were pretty high that it was filled with something that would make a small explosion if exposed to oxygen or impact. "I said, *What the hell is going on?*"

"He got inside my head," Cahill repeated. He ground the words out of his mouth like they were broken glass.

"We just got another clue about whatever the hell is going on," I informed Choo. "Kevin Kichida is an untrained psychic. A powerful one."

"How do you know he's untrained?" Choo asked doubtfully.

I indicated Cahill with my chin. "Because if Kevin was trained, Mr. Mindfuck over here would be the one drooling on the floor right now."

The hallway outside was freezing, and not just because the building's furnace had been hiccupping. Grey tendrils of mist were gathering in sudden pockets of cold. It made it hard to see who was standing by Sig in front of the door to the detectives' work area, and I couldn't smell anyone.

Which meant ghost. As I got closer, I could see that the spirit was a slightly tubby young guy with blond hair and small squarish glasses, dressed in nothing but shorts and a pale blue tank top. There were purpled strangulation marks on his throat left by strong fingers.

"This is Taylor," Sig said solemnly. "I think he wants someone to solve his murder."

Sig said this before demanding to know why I was carrying Kevin Kichida in my arms, so it was important to acknowledge Taylor fast and first. I nodded at that empty-eyed, expressionless face and said, "Hello." I sure as hell wasn't going to say, *Pleased to meet you.*

Sig must have sensed or seen Taylor the moment she entered the police station, and by encouraging Taylor to manifest fully in a visible form, Sig had invoked the Pax Arcana, the mass enchantment that prevents mortals from paying any heed to the supernatural. Anyone who approached the door to the interrogation area would see Taylor without seeing Taylor. The Pax would make them stop blankly in front of the door and forget why they had been about to try to go through it. Eventually, something else to do would occur to them and they would wander off.

The security cameras had stopped working as soon as Taylor began to manifest too.

The truth is, Sig is better at working in a team than I am. I had reacted to the immediate threat, but she took a moment, looked at the big picture, and moved to cover our group's collective ass.

"What happened to Kevin?" Sig demanded.

I stuck to the short version. "He's in some kind of psychic coma. We need to get him out of here."

Sig looked at me. Then she looked at Cahill behind me, who had torn clothing and visible injuries. The bruises would fade soon, but at the moment, they stood out dramatically from the combination of pale skin and blood that was a little darker and thicker than it should be. But Sig didn't waste the time we didn't have. "Follow me and Taylor."

And Sig walked out the door. Taylor followed her without giving me a backward glance.

"Get Kevin's personal effects and bring them to us," I said to Cahill as I shifted Kevin's weight in my arms.

"How was I supposed to know—" Cahill began.

"Not now." I walked after Sig. "But if you can still say a prayer, you might want to offer one up that this kid doesn't die."

Sig, Taylor, and I walked through the police department, and the only person who gave us a glance was Molly, who had been making her way back from the bathroom through the dark. In fact, people actively avoided looking at us and moved out of our way, though they didn't realize they were doing so, and no one saw us exit the building. They were too busy checking the computers and cell phones that had just gone out of commission again.

When we got outside the police station, Sig turned and looked at the ghost she had gotten to fully manifest, then looked at Kevin in my arms. Seeing that look, I wondered what I would do if Sig ever decided that she had a greater obligation to the dead than the living.

On that day at least, I didn't find out. "I'll come back soon, I promise," Sig whispered to the echo of a boy named Taylor, and then she led the way to Choo's van.

∾8∾

MINDFIELDS

Bonaparte Bakery." Sarah White's voice had a certain power to it. She was a confident woman, half earth-goddess type and half no-bullshit independent business owner. More importantly, Sarah was a cunning woman with a good reputation who lived in Bonaparte, New York, only forty-five minutes away. I'd met her once before when I needed help breaking a curse.

"Hi, Sarah." I had my burner phone on speaker so that everyone else could hear. "This is Tom Morris."

"You're still alive." She didn't seem disappointed, but she didn't sound overjoyed, either. "And you're tense."

"Yes, I am."

"And you're still using that fake name." Sarah was one of the sharpest women I'd ever met. Not just intelligent—if cunning folk weren't abstract thinkers with a lot of questions, they wouldn't become druids or shamans or witches or houngans in the first place. But unlike a lot of cunning folk, Sarah had common sense too. Somehow, we'd met and parted on reasonably good terms anyhow. "You never have told me your real one."

"You know who I am," I said.

"That's true," she admitted. "Should I hang up and start running now?"

Beside me, Sig snorted. We were in a backseat that Choo had bolted down in his van, with Kevin Kichida's unconscious form propped between us.

"Probably," I said. "But I would count it as a personal favor if you didn't."

There was a moment of silence. I was telling Sarah that I was willing to formally place myself in her debt, and neither of us took that lightly. Favors are one of the primary currencies that cunning folk trade in, and the price they exact is always more than you bargained for. The last time I owed Sarah White a favor, I was almost drowned by a pissed-off Scandinavian water spirit.

"Who's that with you?" Sarah finally asked.

"I'm with some friends. You'll meet them if you say yes."

"Knights?" Her voice took on a slight edge.

"Come on, Sarah," I chided her. "I said friends."

"Then you've changed," she said. "That's good. Will your friends owe me a favor too?"

"No," I denied flatly.

"Yes," Sig insisted.

Sarah heard her and laughed, a quick, quiet, almost reluctant laugh. "So, it's that kind of friend."

I didn't ask what kind she meant.

Sarah sighed. "What kind of trouble are you in this time, Mr. Not-Tom-Morris?"

"I have an untrained psychic in a coma," I said. "He's one of your people."

"Yes, because everyone with the sight is the same." Her voice was sardonic. "Just like all knights."

Okay, she had me there. "His name is Kevin Kichida."

"I don't care what his name is or how gifted he is. I choose who my people are," she re-emphasized, just in case I hadn't gotten the point the first time.

I tried a different tack. "What about me, Sarah? Am I one of your people?"

Another silence. Instead of answering the question, she said: "You really have changed."

"I've changed some," I admitted. "But my word is still good."

"Yes it is." She sighed again. "And you're one of the few people I know who would put himself in my debt for a complete stranger, even if you are a killer."

I didn't know what to say to that. Next to me, Sig grunted and stirred restlessly.

Sarah briskly got down to business. "Is this Kevin person breathing fast and shallow, like he's going to vomit in an aspirator? Or does he seem dead?"

"It's like somebody pulled a drain inside him and his soul went down it," I said. "He's barely breathing at all, and his body is cold. We're keeping him bundled up."

Silence again.

"Is that worse?" I wondered.

"It means he'll probably still be alive by the time you get here," Sarah told me. "But I'm going to have to go looking for him in the Dreamtime. And when you're looking for a frightened person lost or hiding in the Dreamtime, it can be a minefield."

Speaking of danger...Shit. I had to tell her. "Hey, Sarah? Another cunning person is trying to kill this kid, and I'm still trying to figure out why. So if you take us into your place of power, you might be putting yourself in danger. You should know that."

"You're right. You have only changed in some ways."

The phone hung up.

"Women," Molly commented.

"Does that mean *come on over* or *stay the hell away from me*?" Choo wondered.

Sig didn't have any trouble translating. "It means *come here but I'm pissed about it*. How well do you know this woman, John?"

Something in Sig's tone made me obscurely defensive. We had spent the previous night driving from Clayburg and had been through three supernatural incidents in the space of twelve hours before maybe killing a kid. We were all stressed out and tired and cranky. "I barely know her at all. We spent two days together total."

"You only knew me for one day before you decided you liked me." Sig had a strange tone in her voice. It was supposed to sound lighthearted and cute, but it was a bit like encountering a six-foot-seven, three-hundred-pound mugger dressed in a pink tutu and a tiara.

I didn't know what to say, so I just looked at her.

"And you weren't exactly tripping over your feet in your rush to tell her you were involved with someone just now," Sig went on.

"I was focusing on the essentials," I said. "But that reminds me—would you mind pretending to be my sister?"

Sig turned her blue eyes on me with that full intensity that makes me feel like I'm standing on a subway rail and liking it. "I would."

"That was a joke. She's not an ex," I told her.

"But you wanted her," Sig said with complete certainty.

"She's a cunning woman," I protested, and that didn't even sound like a direct answer to *my* own ears. "I'd rather have sex with a power outlet."

"Because dangerous women are such a turnoff for you." Molly wasn't being helpful.

Choo put his ten cents in. "She sounds hot." Choo was actually sitting in the shotgun seat while Molly drove because he was examining Kevin Kichida's smartphone. Molly is the only person who Choo will let drive his van without an argument, by the way. He has a bit of a bias against demi-humans. I think Choo pictures fire-breathing dragons and twelve-foot-tall scaled dogs with horns and such attacking the van the moment Sig or I get behind the wheel.

Sig lowered her voice and spoke in a throaty way. *"You know who I am."*

"Since when do I sound like Antonio Banderas?" I demanded. "Not that there's anything wrong with that."

"I would count it as a personal favor if you didn't," Sig continued on in the same voice, waggling her eyebrows up and down suggestively for emphasis. *"Am I one of your people?"*

Look, I have a lot of experience with a lot of things, but real relationships aren't one of them. I once fell in love when I had no business doing so, and that selfishness got a woman killed. If there was a way of escaping that fact, I would have found it by now. I lived a kind of half-life under that weight for a long time, and then I met Sig, and she saw right through my smokescreens and aliases, saw me through the eyes of the dead woman I'd loved, as a matter-of-fact. I could sense Alison behind Sig too, or in Sig even though I didn't know that's what I was sensing, and suddenly it seemed like I had a real intimate connection with someone again whether I wanted one or not. Sig had been stuck in her own bad patterns, and we had come into each other's lives like runaway trains crashing through a living room from opposite sides.

So, I seriously didn't know when I asked, "Are you really jealous?"

"Maybe a little," Sig admitted. "You never mentioned this woman before today. And I can tell she's attractive from the way you talk to her."

For some reason, I had a mental flashback of Molly in the pancake house, shaking her fist and going, "You want the truth? You can't handle the truth!"

I shifted Kevin's body so that I could give Sig a stare of my own. "I've lived a long time, Sig. There are a lot of things I haven't mentioned."

"This seems like a pretty important one," she said.

I might not know much, but I knew better than to ask why. "Come on, Sig. You're the woman I'm trying to build something with. You have to know that."

"You still need to say it sometimes." Her voice was both affectionate and exasperated. "Especially when we're in messed-up situations."

"I'd tell you two to take it to the back of the van, but this ain't that kind of a van," Choo interrupted, holding up Kevin's smartphone. "Besides, Parth finally broke into this phone's account. We found something."

Thank God.

∿9∿

A CLUE, A CODE,
AND A CLOSE CALL

Kevin did know something was going on," Choo informed us. "He's been deleting all of his texts, but Parth managed to retrieve them."

"You should still take the battery out of that thing," Sig said.

Choo gave her a *Who do you think you're talking to?* look over his shoulder. "I already did. But we might want to pop it back in soon."

Okay, I definitely wasn't imagining the tension between those two. I interrupted their Dance of the Tense Glances by asking the obvious question. "Why?"

"Because Kevin's been sending messages to a Jkichida every eight hours since yesterday," Choo said.

"J. Kichida. Kevin's father is named Jerry." It was a pretty useless observation, but I felt like somebody ought to make it. "It sounds like Kevin's father is having Kevin check in with him because he's afraid there might be trouble."

"The messages are kind of weird too," Choo noted. "In the first one, Kevin just texted *Anne is fine,* and this Jkichida wrote

Bridgett is doing okay too. Being around other people is good for her. Then Kevin texted *I'm hanging out with Catherine at the coffee shop tomorrow,* and his dad sent back *Good, Dorothy has been worried about her.* The next one is a little different. Jkichida wrote first, and he did it a couple hours early too. The message says, *Something's wrong with Aunt Emily. You should go wait for her at that vacation spot we talked about.* And Kevin responded. *I'll tell Aunt Frances. Be careful."*

Choo looked up from the screen. "That one came in while Kevin was at the coffee shop. Looks to me like it would have been right around the time the bhut thing was going down."

"So that's why Kevin was acting like he wanted to get out of there fast," Molly said pensively.

I waved that off. "The real question is, why did Jkichida send that last text, and what's up with the female names?"

Sig regarded me curiously. "It's obviously a code."

"That's their code?" I demanded incredulously. "Including female names in the texts in ascending alphabetical order?"

"Looks like it," Choo said cautiously. "I could just type in *Gail is alright* on this thing and Jerry wouldn't know it was me."

"It can't be that easy," I protested. "The man was a sniper. The code is a dummy wire."

"What does that mean?" Molly asked.

"You know…the obvious trip wire that's supposed to make you overconfident so you don't see the real trap. I guarantee, if we just text *Gwen is having a good solid bowel movement* or whatever, Jerry will know something is up."

Choo grunted agreement. "I know what you're sayin'. I plugged the names into a search engine, but so far, I'm just gettin' ten thousand hits for baby names and dating sites."

"Maybe they're only using the names of women they know

personally," Sig speculated. "That would make it hard to anticipate or duplicate."

"They're using the names of female saints," Molly informed us.

Shit. I should have known that. I was the one raised by an order of Catholic knights.

"So what female saint starts with G?" Choo asked.

"There's Gertrude," Molly suggested. "I love that one."

"Genevieve might be better," I pointed out. "I think using the most ordinary female saint names they can find is part of it, Molly. Even a couple of chumps like us could have figured it out if they'd been using names like Agnes or Dymphna or Fortunata."

"I guess that's true," Molly admitted. "It was Dorothy and Frances that tipped me off."

"Hold on a moment," Sig protested. "Am I missing something here? Why are we even talking about sending a message to trick Kevin's father in the first place? Kevin has been letting Jerry know that everything is okay, and everything isn't okay. We should contact Jerry and tell him that."

"We're just talking options," I said. "We've got some time to decide how to handle this."

"Besides, how do we know that's what the messages are about?" Choo objected.

"I told you Kevin is a good person," Sig said curtly. I think she was blaming herself for what had happened to Kevin, which was at least partly why the discussion about Sarah White had gotten a little tense. Sig is the hardest to be around when she's being hard on herself. She gets defensive, and she knows the best defense is a good offense. The other part of it is that we were dealing with the most fundamental difference between me and Sig. Neither of us grew up in what you'd call nurturing environments, but we responded in very different ways. Giving people the benefit of the doubt is important to Sig because she always felt unfairly judged growing up. Me, I'm willing to take things on faith, but only after I've exhausted every other option.

Sig narrowed her gaze. "I thought you wanted to be upfront with the Kichidas, John."

"That was with Kevin when we were all in the same place," I said levelly. "All we know about Jerry is that he was a sniper in the Rangers and he's not taking any chances. I'm not sure I'm ready to call him and say *Hey, you don't know us, but we're magical beings who have your son, and he's in a coma and can't talk to you. Tell us what you know and please don't call any authorities!*"

"We don't have to give him our names or location," Sig pointed out.

"Yeah, cause that'll make him trust us," Choo griped.

"Maybe we will have to try to set up a meeting," I said. "But I'd like to try to wake up Kevin first. Right now, there's no way Jerry's not going to investigate us, and unless we tell him everything, what he finds will be weird or incomplete. I don't want this guy trying to stake us out, or get leverage on us."

"Because that's what you'd do." The tension in Sig's voice was cranking up a notch.

My own voice was getting more intense. "Yes. If I were him I'd be looking for a trap."

"That's what Ted did," Sig pointed out. "Instead of just talking to Kevin, he went in with his dick swinging and tried to take control of the situation. And look where that got us."

"I told you that Cahill was messing with people's heads too much," I pointed out tightly. "Now you're saying I'm the same as him?"

"I'm saying if we had just talked to Kevin back at Pancakea like I wanted to, none of this would have happened," Sig growled like she was the werewolf. "And I'm not going to sit back and watch you play the same kind of stupid male dominance games with Kevin's father."

"I'm new to this whole working with a group thing, so let me get this straight." My voice was taut. "You're saying the only way to *not* play dominance games is to just do things your way?"

Sig's temper finally snapped. "Oh, go get spayed!"

"Fuck you and the flying horse you rode in on!" I shot back.

"All right, ZPPPT!" Molly interrupted. "INTERDICTION!"

I was momentarily taken off guard. "What?"

"This conversation is now under sanction," Molly informed us.

"Stay out of this, Molly." Sig's voice was stark.

Molly ignored this. "Sig, you're not listening to any of us right now. Am I playing male dominance games too?"

"You're being pretty damn bossy," Sig gritted out.

Molly nodded. "You almost got me killed the last time you got like this. I still have nightmares about those vampire tunnels."

It was an oblique reference to Sig's dysfunctional relationship with Stanislav Dvornik and the spectacular way it had blown up—literally. Sig turned a bright red. It was probably her most vulnerable area. "You think I don't?"

"And John," Molly continued. "Sig was right when she got you to reach out to some of the other werewolves in your pack when things went bad with that Bernard guy, right?"

"Okay," I grunted.

Molly held her hands out as if she were displaying a marquee, ignoring the grab Choo made for the steering wheel as she proclaimed: "Headline: SCIENTISTS DISCOVER NO ONE IS RIGHT ALL THE TIME!"

Sig started to say something, and it's probably for the best that she stopped herself, took a deep breath, and reconsidered.

When she released the breath, she wouldn't look at me. "Why do you all think Jerry Kichida is a threat?"

"Not necessarily a threat," I amended. "A delicate situation."

"It's the e-mail address," Choo said at the same time.

Sig tried to consider those words, realized that she was still too stirred up to focus, and just said, "What about the e-mail address?"

"Why have his kid send texts to an e-mail address?" Choo asked. "Why not send 'em straight to Jerry's phone? And why codes? Why not real conversations?"

"We already talked about this. Someone is after him," Sig said. "Cell phone numbers can be tracked by anybody with an Internet connection these days, and he's afraid someone might capture or hack into his cell phone. Or Kevin's. And he was right. We did."

"He was damn right," Choo said. "So what if whoever Jerry is scared of did catch him? That last text message didn't sound too good from Jerry's end. We might wind up sending a message to whoever's trying to kill us."

"We don't know what kind of person this Jerry is, either," Molly reminded Sig. "Just because you get a good vibe off Kevin, it doesn't mean his father isn't a bad guy. What if Kevin's in trouble because of something his father did? Like a kid getting shot at because his father is a gangster or a drug lord or something? We should find out as much as we can before we do anything definite."

"I'm not against contacting him," I added. "I just want to take a little time and size things up first."

"Those are good points," Sig admitted grudgingly, and we all gave her some time to percolate a bit. When she spoke again, it was so quietly that no one but me could hear her. "You were right about Ted. An innocent boy got hurt because of me."

"Maybe I wasn't right," I admitted reluctantly. That self-righteous rage in the police station had felt good at the time, but it wasn't the whole story. "Cahill didn't mean to hurt Kevin."

Sig sighed and rubbed her hands over her eyes. "I didn't expect being around Ted again to be this hard. It's not because I like him. It's because I don't. I feel bad about that."

I just nodded. Whatever else Cahill was, he had been Sig's friend. Or she'd thought he was.

"Not knowing if Ted tried to take advantage of me or not is messing with me," Sig admitted. "I feel like I should either kill him or forgive him, and I can't make myself do either one."

"For what it's worth, I'm starting to get the feeling that Cahill is fucking up and pushing his mind mojo so much because he's trying too hard to apologize," I told her.

That surprised Sig. Hell, the words surprised me. But I've spent most of my life assessing people trying to figure out if they're threats or not, and I guess I'd been going over what had happened in the police station in the back of my head. Sig focused on me a little more intently. "You really think so?"

I held out my palms helplessly. "I think Cahill's screwing up because he made a mess of things and doesn't know how to fix it. He's trying to treat it like a math problem. He did something bad with his mental powers, so now he has to do good with them to prove that they're not all bad."

Sig laughed then, if a little raggedly. "That might be. Ted's not all that emotionally developed. And people will do really stupid things to say *I'm sorry* without actually saying it."

"That's true," I admitted.

Reaching over a comatose body to take someone's hand is a little strange, but I did. After a moment, Sig squeezed my hand back.

∿10∿

BAKEN, NOT STIRRED

It was past the bakery's closing hours when we got to Bonaparte, and Sarah met us at the back door. There were no vagrants or lurkers hanging around the Dumpster behind the bakery, and it should have been a prime scavenging site. I glanced at the rear wall of the building; it was covered in a lot of graffiti that didn't quite go with how clean the rest of the alley was. The spray-painted tags and messages and pictures probably hid all kinds of protective wards and sigils that would make it hard for anyone who didn't have direct business at the bakery to hang around. Come to think of it, Sarah had fed me from leftover goods she set aside for homeless shelters when I first met her.

Sarah herself was still fit, curvy but lithe, and if her long black hair had a few more wisps of grey in it, the contrast looked good on her. She was dressed simply in a taupe sweater and a green cotton skirt, wearing more jewelry than when I'd first met her. But then, she'd been baking at the time, and wearing jewelry and kneading dough don't go well together.

If the outside of the bakery was magically protected, there were bound to be layer upon layer of guards and charms on the inside. One advantage to operating a bakery was that Sarah could perform all kinds of spells without having the resulting odors seem out of place. I could smell rosemary, lavender, cinnamon, and ginger among the rich blend of spices in the air. There was a faint lingering hint of smudge sticks too.

Of course, none of that could affect me. I'm a knight. Well, an ex-knight. Or since I've sort of been pardoned, maybe an ex-ex-knight. I'm definitely *knight-ish* anyhow, and knights of my order can blow past detection spells and curses and compulsions like they're not even there. This is one of the reasons witches generally hate knights. Well, that and centuries of religious persecution, slander, and torture.

People can be so petty.

"You look better, Not-Tom," Sarah told me. I was carrying Kevin Kichida in my arms, and she reached out and touched my right bicep. It wasn't a flirtatious gesture, maybe not even a conscious one—psychics often touch people when they are evaluating them—but there was empathy there, and I was suddenly conscious of Sig's eyes on us. "You seem more solid somehow. Less haunted."

"Less hunted maybe," I offered. "I've come to a truce with the Knights Templar. And my name is John. John Charming."

Sarah wasn't exactly delighted with my news, but she didn't comment directly. "Charming? Are you serious?"

"Occasionally." I proceeded to make introductions, and Sarah offered her hand to Choo and Molly. Sarah was grave with Choo, smiled at Molly, who smiled back. When I introduced Sig, though, Sarah hesitated.

Sarah addressed me without taking her eyes off of Sig. "And Sig is…"

Normally, this was the point where I would have made a smartass comment, but Sig was having a bad day, and something about the tautness of Sig's body language and facial expression warned me that this would be a bad idea...would, in fact, be an idea that other bad ideas would cross the brain to stay away from when they saw it come lumbering down their side of the frontal lobe.

"She's the woman I'm courting," I said.

Something in Sig relaxed, though she was watching Sarah as intently as Sarah was watching Sig.

Sarah spoke quietly. "A death-walker. That's perfect. And terrifying."

"I prefer the term *Valkyrie*," Sig said, still a bit stiffly.

"I can see that," Sarah was agreeable without actually agreeing. "I'm sorry if I gave offense. You are all welcome to my home."

As soon as Sarah said those words, Sig and Choo relaxed. It was subtle but noticeable, as if a giant invisible hand that had been gently squeezing their chests had just released. I didn't feel any different, and interestingly enough, Molly didn't seem to be affected, either. "Is there a place I can set Kevin?"

"Follow me." Sarah led us down to a dark cellar with nothing but a candle to light our way. It occurred to me that if we were in a folk tale, Sarah would be leading us down to Hell. I wasn't worried, though. I've traveled a lot, and I'm pretty sure that if there is a Hell, you have to ride a Greyhound bus to get there.

"Electricity doesn't work down here," Sarah explained. She lit another candle with the one she was holding, and immediately, the wicks of fourteen other candles placed around the room caught fire. Cute trick. We were basically in a root cellar that had storage bins built into the walls, and none of them seemed to hold anything scary: There were no bat wings, no dried eyeballs, no beating hearts, no cobwebs, no musical CDs made by former Disney child stars. "Go ahead and put him on the table."

The table in question was one of those brown padded jobs that masseuses use, with a hole at the top where clients can stick their face so that they can lie flat on their stomachs and still breathe. I set Kevin down face up anyway.

"Would anyone like some tea?" Sarah actually had a teapot brewing on the lid of a cast iron wood stove, and several mugs were set out on a shelf above it.

I asked for a cup just to emphasize to the others that I really did trust Sarah, but then I couldn't resist telling Sig, "Don't forget: If I turn into a frog, kiss me."

Sig didn't blink. "What if you turn into a handsome prince?"

A really graphic suggestion as to exactly what Sig could do then shot through my mind, but she was still a bit tense, so I toned it down. "The kissing still goes, but you can use tongue."

Sarah finally showed a hint of impatience. "I need to know everything." So my team found seats, and between the four of us, we managed to get the story out without contradicting or correcting each other too much. Sarah mostly listened without interruption, though she did have a few questions about the bhut and more than a few about what had happened in the interrogation room. Her expression was disgruntled at first, but by the time we were done, she had downgraded to pensive.

"Whatever or whoever you're dealing with," she said, "it's powerful."

I was about to say *Well duh* but Molly got there first. "Relative to what?"

"I've never even heard of someone summoning a bhut deliberately before," Sarah said "They're hard to contain or control by their very nature. But it's more than that. The rituals for summoning an Each Uisge mostly come from Celtic and Scandinavian cultures. Bhuts are a largely Hindu phenomenon."

Sig got it at once. "This would-be killer is cross-referencing magic systems."

Choo looked at them both. "So?"

"The really powerful magic spells take a long time to master," Sarah explained. "It's possible for a gifted idiot to dabble just enough to learn one spell, but that tends to end in disaster. Real practitioners of magic prefer people to take their time and learn the entire system and philosophy that created the spell from the ground up. And no one managed to summon an Each Uisge and then summon a bhut the next day by being a lucky dabbler twice. Whoever you're after has been studying magic for a very long time. It's not just that, though."

"It never is," I griped.

"Kevin's aura has been..." Sarah faltered. "I'm not sure how to describe it. He looks like he's two people at once."

"You mean like multiple personalities?" Molly asked cautiously.

"I mean, it's as if I can almost see someone else when I look at him with the sight." Sarah squinched her eyebrows. "Like a photograph where someone has superimposed two different peoples' photos on top of each other."

"Just cut to the chase, Sarah," I said a little brusquely. It had been a very long day. "What's been done to him?"

"Someone is using Kevin's body like an old ham radio," Sarah said. "They've keyed in to his psychic frequency to make it match their own. And if they're trying to kill Kevin, I'm fairly certain that means they're connected biologically."

"Because..." Sig encouraged.

"There are certain kinds of dark magic where someone can prolong their life by sacrificing their own flesh and blood,"

Sarah said somberly. "It's why there are so many old stories about children being isolated and raised by evil witches or sorcerers who don't love them. The children those stories were based on were probably being raised like cattle to be sacrificed when they became young men and women."

This was a new one on me.

Was Sarah talking Rapunzel in the witch's tower? Was the witch who wanted to kill Snow White because she was obsessed with youth and beauty really Snow White's stepmother? There were a lot of stories where evil wizards had young servants whose parents were unknown, come to think of it.

"Is there anything else involved?" I asked.

Sarah didn't like talking about it, but she understood the question's relevance. "The person being sacrificed has to be old enough to bear children. But the person also has to be a virgin."

That also explained a lot of the emphasis old stories put on abducting virgins and keeping them isolated, come to think of it.

"It's got something to do with the sacrifice being part of the cycle of life and death and outside of it at the same time," Sarah added when we all just sat there processing what she'd said. "I don't know much about that kind of magic."

"And some cunning person has begun this process with Kevin?" I asked. "All that's left is that he needs to die?"

Sarah shifted her shoulders as if a heavy weight had settled on them. "It would fit the facts that you've given me."

"Well, there's another reason not to trust Kevin's father," Sig sighed.

"No, he's been acting like someone who's trying to keep Kevin alive," Molly disagreed. "This might be the mother that supposedly died. John said he thinks she has a fake name."

"It could be a grandpa or grandma too," Choo agreed. "Maybe even a great-great-great grandma or grandpa if this dude has been doing this kind of thing for a long time."

That was a comforting thought. I addressed Sarah directly. "Magic trades are quid pro quo. Does sacrificing a descendant only prolong someone's life for a span of fifty or seventy years? About a normal mortal lifetime?"

She looked approving then. "Yes."

Sig cut to the chase. "Can you help Kevin?"

Sarah sighed. "I think so. But I'm going to have to look for him in the Dreamtime. And if your enemy is as powerful as I think, I'm going to need help."

"What kind of help?" I tried not to sound suspicious.

Sarah smiled crookedly. "I've been thinking about this ever since you called. I want you to go into the Dreamtime with me, John."

"It won't work," I protested. "You can't link up mentally with me because of my geas."

"I know that," Sarah said gravely. "But knights know enough about meditation that I can help you get into the Dreamtime on your own and meet you there. You know how to achieve a lucid dream state, right?"

I seriously thought about lying. "Yes?"

"And I can give you some herbs that will help you retain a more alert level of consciousness while still dreaming," Sarah said. "Your protections don't extend to chemical influences."

"Didn't you just say something about how people shouldn't dabble to learn one spell?" Sig demanded.

Sarah shook her head. "You don't understand. Clairvoyants can't see knights. If a powerful mage is looking for Kevin and can't find him on this plane, the next logical place to look for Kevin would be in the Dreamtime."

I got it then. "You want the protection of my geas. A cunning woman."

"That's right," Sarah agreed. "I think it will work."

"Okay, what are you two talking about?!?" Choo sounded exasperated. He hates the metaphysical stuff and doesn't want to think about it, but then he gets frustrated when he has to play catch-up.

I tried to put it in military terms. "Sarah wants to mount a stealth operation into the Dreamtime, not a full scale assault. She thinks someone else is going to be looking for Kevin there, and she wants to hide behind my shields while we complete a search-and-retrieval mission."

Sig exhaled disgustedly.

"What?" I said. "I didn't say I was going to do it."

"John," Molly said gently. "It's one of the worst ideas I've ever heard. Of course you're going to do it."

That was totally unfair. I want that on record.

Sig and I had a little bit of time alone. Sarah's tea had steeped—she made it as thick and potent as the Brits do, so it was almost like coffee—and we were sitting in the empty bakery with the lights out, eating some kind of light croissants with cheese baked into them. "Don't eat any of the pastry puffs called Bonaparte Bites," I warned. "Some of them have real fortunes in them."

Sig didn't care about pastry puffs. "Listen, I know I've been a little erratic lately."

"You have been a little off ever since Cahill called," I agreed cautiously.

"My father committed suicide," Sig told me.

The suddenness and the seriousness of that total non sequitur shut me right the hell up. Sig had never talked about her father before.

"When my mom overdosed, I left home." Sig kept the shifts terse and abrupt, saying everything robotically just to get it over with. "I was seventeen, and my father was just so...empty. All he did was watch TV and eat peanuts and sleep. If I tried to communicate with him or snap him out of it, he just got angry. I didn't have what it took to deal with it."

"You were grieving too," I ventured.

"My dad and I were never close," Sig said. "He was a cop, this big tough guy with everybody but my mom, but with her, he was this weak asshole. Our relationship basically amounted to him telling me all the horrible things that would happen to me if the world found out what I was, and then him threatening to reveal what I was if I didn't stop making things so hard for my mother. The fact that I became stronger than him when I got older threatened the hell out of him."

"Nurturing." I left it at that.

Sig wasn't listening to me anyhow. "And the thing was, I'd always planned to leave. That was how my aunt Amy always kept me going. She used to say, *Don't think of your home as a crazy house; think of it as a crazy hotel.* She was always telling me to become someone who could take care of herself, to not become addicted to anything or hook up with some asshole."

Sig released a sigh then. It sounded like she was decompressing. "Of course, I went and did both of those things later."

"You never talk about her," I noted.

"Aunt Amy?" Sig smiled sadly and pushed her pastry around on its plate. "She was an ex-Army captain. She practically raised me. Practically raised all of us, really. My family didn't come off the rails until Amy died."

That was a lot of death for one family. "How did she die?"

Sig got a little impatient. That wasn't the point of the story.

"She dozed off while she was using a kerosene heater. It was fumes that got her, not a fire. I was thirteen."

I shut up again.

Sig finished a croissant but didn't seem to take any pleasure from it. "Anyway, when I graduated, I couldn't wait anymore. I was dating this rich boy who was going to take a year off and backpack across Europe with some friends, and he bought me a ticket. I don't know why—he cheated on me two weeks after we got over there—but he wasn't the main reason I went, anyhow."

She stopped. Not for dramatic emphasis. More like she was emotionally worn out. I encouraged her to go on, still saying as little as possible. "So what was the reason?"

Sig sighed. "I didn't know what I was back then. All I knew was that my mom was a liar and came from Sweden or Switzerland or Iceland or someplace like that. Trying to find out something about where I came from or what I was . . . That was something that I could actually do something about. Can you understand that?"

"Yes." My tea was getting cold, but I drank some anyhow. "I can understand that."

She smiled sadly then. "I know you can. I think it's one of the reasons we seem to get each other most of the time."

I just kept looking at her.

Sig rubbed her left collarbone with the palm of her hand absent-mindedly. "And I felt like I was just one more burden my dad didn't want to deal with anyway. He seemed relieved to get me out of the house."

I reached out and took her other hand. She didn't notice.

"But then he changed his mind. When I was home, he was just mad at me for not letting him watch TV or sleep, but as soon as I was gone, he decided I was just like my mother."

She looked to me for some sign that I was listening, so I said, "He decided you had abandoned him too."

Sig yanked her chin in a violent motion that might have been agreement. "And he was right. We didn't talk much. I was bumming around Europe and phone calls from overseas were expensive."

Sig stopped talking again. Tears had begun welling up, and she laid her hands along the side of her head as if she were making a face sandwich, rubbing her cheeks. "But I ignored some stuff I shouldn't have ignored. I won't pretend that I didn't. And then one day, I called and I couldn't get in touch with him, so I just put it off for another week. And then I couldn't get in touch and I put if off for another few days. And then I couldn't get in touch so I started calling every day, and then..."

Sig trailed off.

"What?" I nudged.

"He contacted me." The words had this quiet desolation about them.

Why did she say it like that? What was I miss...oh. Oh, shit. "His ghost?" I said quietly.

She just nodded. I sort of had a sense that her father hadn't come to Sig to bring her closure or make his passing easier on her emotionally. A shudder traveled up from the base of her spine and convulsed her shoulders. "It wasn't good."

"You had to...exorcise him?" I asked slowly.

"Eventually." Sig didn't mention her father again. I wasn't sure that she was ever going to mention her father again. "I lost track of what I was doing then. I hooked up with some people who were hobnobbing around Europe in Iceland, and somehow, I wound up doing the club scene in Paris with them for a while. It was easy to have no money and party if you were young and pretty and in Paris. And I was different enough from all of the slender, dark-haired women there that I was a bit of a novelty."

She said this matter-of-factly, without pride or shame, like she was talking about being color-blind or left-handed. "There had always been people offering me free drinks and free drugs and free food, but I had my mother's example keeping me...I don't know...not careful, exactly, but...tethered maybe? But after my father died, something in me just broke. I just wanted to run away, but the thing I wanted to run away from was me. I can't even tell you how long my life went on like that. At some point my passport was revoked and I can't even remember why. I woke up on a plane with a couple of days missing."

I cleared my throat. "I've never done drink or drugs." It was true. I grew up fearing a loss of control that would take my soul with it. It's one of the reasons I work so hard to study things, to hone my skills, to stay vigilant. I was an anxious kid in my own way, if not a stereotypical one, and those rituals calm me. "But I can see how getting obliterated would be a great way to feel better and punish yourself at the same time."

Sig was starting to come out of soliloquy mode, but she still wasn't really talking to me yet. "And now, I still wake up sometimes and realize that I'm being loyal to men I shouldn't. Or I'm taking my anger out on men who are trying to be good to me, because I feel bad for not deserving it." Sig's voice was dead. "My compass for that kind of thing is damaged and I don't know how to fix it."

"You're talking about Cahill now?" I just wanted to make sure.

Sig nodded and went back to her pastry. I didn't say anything, and eventually she started talking again. "Ted is a dhampir because I got him involved in our world. It was to save someone a lot more innocent than Ted ever was, but it still messes with me. I knew Ted wanted me, but he was married and a shit about women, so I didn't take it too seriously."

I got it, or I think I did. Guilt. Resentment about feeling guilt. Guilt about feeling resentment about feeling guilt. All of it mixed in with genuine concern and anger and a sense of social obligation and confusion. It was probably the kind of emotional cocktail that she associated with the worst time of her life.

"I'm working on my shit," she told me. "But it's hard. Are you still going to be all Lover Boyish when the fantasy wears off and you start to get how messed-up I really am?"

"Well," I said contemplatively. "It is a little unfair considering how baggage-free I am." She snorted and I pretended not to notice that she blew a little snot, kept going with it so that she could locate a napkin. "I mean, here I've gone to all this trouble to build a sane, normal, orderly, predictable life…"

"Shut up." Her laugh was a little ragged, but it was a laugh.

"I'm tired of fairy tales, Sig." I leaned across the table and took her bottom lip between my lips, pulled it slightly into my mouth and kissed her.

∾11∾

DREAM ME UP, I'M WAKING

I have been to the Dreamtime before. Everyone has been to the Dreamtime before. But I'd never been so...well...awake...or had such clear memories as when Sarah and I went looking for Kevin Kichida.

What is the Dreamtime?

Imagine Aboriginal creation myth wearing tight shorts and delivering a pizza to a place where Carl Jung's theory of a collective unconscious is making out with the Hindu belief about reality being a kind of communal illusion. "Hey, there," says Aboriginal creation myth with a cheesy moustache and blank facial expression. "Are you the ones who ordered the sausage extra large?" And then the porn music starts and they have a threesome while Plato's hypothesis about layers of reality pounds on the walls and yells, "Hey! Keep it down over there! I'm trying to read Neil Gaiman's *The Sandman!*"

That's what the Dreamtime Sarah White described to me sounds like. I don't know if it's an ocean that our minds take a swim in while we sleep...an ocean where powerful and mysterious things live in the depths—or a power strip with infinite sockets that all of our minds are plugged into. It is the very stuff of metaphor and defies metaphor.

But I know the Dreamtime is real. I just don't know if it's sort of real or more real than real or neither or both.

It took a long time for me to sync my body rhythms up to Kevin Kichida. I was holding his hand in my left and Sarah's in my right, and she managed to slow her pulse rate until it throbbed in the same steady beat as Kevin's much sooner than mine did. I breathed in when they breathed in and breathed out when they breathed out. I had drunk something...Sarah wouldn't tell me what it was, but it had contained mugwort and wormwood and dream herb and something else I'd never tasted or smelled...It could have been moley, for all I knew, but it was taking me somewhere. The scent of lemongrass candles filled my nose while the sound of Molly beating a Mongolian shaman drum thrummed in my blood.

"Are we there yet?" I asked.

I surprised muffled sounds from Sig and Molly. Sarah wasn't amused. "Do you want my help or not?"

"Sorry." I resumed my efforts to relax and not make it an effort, and finally, my body temperature began to drop to match Kevin's. I could feel the aches and pains and pulses in his body as naturally as I could feel my own, and it was only then that I did what Sarah had told me to do, did what I had done a thousand times before, and imagined myself as a white pulse of light traveling through my body, traveling in time with the tidal flows of my breathing. But when I reached the hand that was a part of Kevin's hand, I imagined moving myself though his palms, up his arms, until...

I found myself walking in a massive and crowded subway junction. Placing two fingers on my carotid artery, I concentrated on my pulse until I could hear/feel Kevin's heart beating in the background.

"You *are* a natural."

I turned around and Sarah was standing behind me. She was dressed the same way she had been in the real world, but I was wearing a Kevlar vest and carrying my katana. When it was clear that I wasn't going to respond to her words, Sarah just walked past me. "Come on."

I did. Just out of curiosity, I looked upward while we were walking. The "ceiling" of the subway tunnel was several hundred feet high, and I saw the floor of a vast museum where upside-down people strolled about. A Masai tribesman standing in front of some kind of ice sculpture waved down at me. I didn't wave back.

I stopped when Sarah looked down and found a golden tomcat brushing against her leg. She bent down and rubbed the fuzz beneath his chin with her thumb while her index finger stroked behind his left ear. "Hello, Stevens."

I suddenly remembered that I could speak. It felt like talking underwater. "You have a cat here?"

"I had Stevens when I was a child." Sarah and I were the only people in the whole subway station who were talking or noticing anyone else, as far as I could tell. Everybody else seemed to be in their own private universe, even if their eyes were open. "I don't know if this is his soul or a projection of my imagination. Cats have no regard for rules, you know, even metaphysical ones."

Other dreamers in various states of dress and undress were around us. A young woman in a professional blazer and skirt with high heels and an attaché case walked briskly past us while the blurry outline of what might have been someone in a bathrobe fell behind. When I turned to look at the fuzzy distortion, it was gone. A boy on a skateboard zipped over the tiled floor effortlessly, weaving in and out between the crowd as openings miraculously appeared and disappeared. Ahead of us a bear was standing on its hind legs and looking about over the throng. An old woman half jumped and half floated past us in thirty-foot leaps.

Suddenly, the cat took off with a startled and angry yawp. I looked ahead and saw something or someone scrabbling about the platform, moving among the tranquil procession and staring intently at the faces of passersby, most of whom went about their business without paying any particular heed to the bony hag with mossy teeth and pupilless eyes. The slightly elongated arms sticking out from under her ragged shawl had long jagged nails.

"Something's not right," Sarah muttered. "Maeres don't come here."

That thing was a maere? Shit. Maeres are soul vultures who steal slices of life from the terrified breaths of sleepers caught in horrifying dreams. They are one of the few beings who can move freely between the land of dreams and that place we optimistically call reality. The very word nightmare comes from *nacht maere*. "What do you mean? They usually haunt dreams, right?"

Sarah shook her head irritably. "They're scavengers. They prowl among the shadows of the Dreamtime: the back alleys and caves and basements and dark woods. Not here in the Junctions."

As we watched, it slowly became clear that the maere was only interested in males. Young males. Asian males. The maere stopped in front of a boy wearing pilot goggles and a bomber jacket.

"I know him," Sarah breathed softly. "That's Mark Duong. His mother, Tiet, owns a nail salon one block down from the bakery."

"Coincidence?" Sarah had told me not to be surprised if I saw people that I knew in the Dreamtime, but a maere concentrating on young Asian males in and around Sarah's physical proximity?

"There are no coincidences here," Sarah said tensely.

Mark stood stock-still as the maere got up into his face. Within a moment, Mark was flat on the tiled floor, the hag crouched over him, her bottom resting on his chest as she peered intently into his eyes. He made little convulsive jerks, but his body seemed paralyzed.

Sarah's hands clenched into a fist, and suddenly, she was holding her holly staff—or at least a representation of it. Sarah had always made it clear that she avoided physical confrontations when she could. Metaphysical confrontations too, for that matter. She viewed violence as a chain reaction more than a solution, a breeding contagion that caused three more problems for each one it pretended to deal with, and the whole process seemed infantile and pointless to her. But if that crone started inhaling deeply with her mouth right next to the nostrils of a boy Sarah knew...

I drew my sword and snarled.

The maere released Mark from her clutches and he disappeared. Somewhere, Mark's physical body was bolting upward as he awoke from a dream of lying down and being unable to move while some strange presence that he couldn't see loomed over him.

Troubled, Sarah watched the maere stalk off.

"You think she's looking on behalf of our mystery enemy?" I asked.

"Maeres are no one's servants," Sarah muttered.

"Neither are bhuts," I reminded her. It occurred to me then that a maere fit the MO of the other creatures that had been sent after Kevin. Supposedly, people who die in dreams die in real life, and a maere would be ideally suited for killing a boy in his sleep without causing any undue suspicion in the real world.

We made it to a subway platform where a crowd was waiting with unquestioning patience, and we pushed our way through them until someone called out Sarah's name. She turned and didn't seem particularly surprised to see a sixtyish woman dressed as a flower child with long grey hair braided and beaded into locks. "Jackie!"

The woman waved distractedly and started shambling toward us.

"Jaqueline Laughlin, an old philosophy teacher of mine," Sarah murmured out of the side of her mouth. "This is the only place I ever see her dressed unprofessionally."

The woman stopped in front of us and then didn't say anything. Sarah didn't say anything either, and I was content to stay silent myself. We just waited until a gigantic snake the size of a train came undulating down the subway tunnel and halted with its head in front of the commuters. The snake opened its massive jaws and a forked tongue flickered out at a slight angle and anchored at the edge of the platform. People began to walk across the tongue and down the snake's maw.

"Come on," Sarah said, and motioned for Jaqueline and me to follow.

Jaqueline's face contracted in slight distaste. "It's ... a snake?"

Sarah laughed. "It's Wagyl. You taught us about Aboriginal Dreamtime archetypes, Jackie. Remember?"

Jacqueline stared at her blankly.

"Anything beings like Wagyl do in the Dreamtime has repercussions in the waking world," Sarah said gently. "Wagyl's going to take us through the dreams of architects and city planners and miners and engineers. Subway tunnels and dam conduits and sewers and mine shafts will be made because of it."

Either Jaqueline Laughlin was a better teacher than student, or she just didn't like snakes. At some point while Sarah was speaking, the woman disappeared. Me, I followed Sarah across the snake's tongue and down its gullet, and it didn't occur to me until later that this was strange.

Wagyl's insides were shaped like a subway car, although there were no windows. Its tongue kept extending backward through its gullet like a red carpet of sorts, threading between benches on either side of its interior walls. Sarah sat down next to an animated stick figure. The stick figure was drawing on a sketch pad, and when I peeked over, the picture it was drawing looked like a real-life photograph of a pleasant-looking woman with red hair.

"She's beautiful," Sarah commented, but the stick figure did not respond.

I sat next to Sarah, and a stout middle-aged man with a towel wrapped around his waist and a mining helmet on his head sat next to me.

"Are you going down the central shaft?" he asked me dreamily. What? That's how he asked me.

"I hope not," I said.

The man fell quiet. Eventually, he reached down between the folds of his towel and absent-mindedly began fondling himself.

"Yo, Wee Willie Winkie," I said, and Sarah dug her elbow into my ribs.

I turned around to talk to her and realized that I was sitting alone on a park bench. The city I was in looked like Tokyo, but that probably didn't mean anything. Unless it meant everything. A red car of some kind careened past, veering wildly over the street. I could see that the driver was screaming and turning the steering wheel frantically, making the steering wheel revolve in complete revolutions, but the car did not seem to be responding.

I hate that dream.

It didn't feel particularly cool, but I concentrated until a few flakes began to fall from the sky and my skin goose-pimpled with a memory of cold. I exhaled, still keeping my breath in time with Kevin's breath on some level, and a plume of mist came out of my mouth. The tendril of condensed breath twisted and turned until it drifted in a specific direction and dissipated. Kevin was that way.

Wait a minute. How the hell did I know how to do that?

For the first time, I panicked. Where was Sarah? How was she going to find me? She couldn't track me here... that was the whole point. Was she in danger now? I could feel my consciousness beginning to expand as if I were about to float up out of the world, or shatter it, and I suddenly knew without knowing or caring how I knew, that if I didn't get my fear under control, I was going to wake up. I forced myself to breathe slowly, then remembered that I was supposed to be matching my breath to Kevin's. The wind was coming in at patterned and regular intervals that were distinctly unwind-like, and it occurred to me that maybe the breeze was in sync with Kevin's breath here, so I slowed my inhales and exhales to match. It calmed me.

Soon, I found myself walking down the street alongside a long wall made of panelboard. No plan as of yet, but at least I was moving. I paused and stared at the wall beside me. Bands with improbable names, some cheesy and some clichéd and some bizarre, were featured on fliers that announced their performances at coffeehouses and bars. I wondered if these were groups that existed only in people's dreams, if the businesses were ventures that other dreamers planned on owning some-day. Were the movie posters of films yet to be made? Listing the credits of people who knew they could act or write or direct if someone would just give them a chance? Were the articles announcing the victories of fantasy league teams cut out of imaginary newspapers, taped on the wall next to announcements of weddings that were only in people's fantasies?

Or were there people who lived here in the Dreamtime? Coma patients and madmen and artists and cunning folk and curse victims who decided they liked it better on this side? Had they put these posters up? Did they have careers? Go to shows?

There...the picture of the cabaret performer named Maxine something or other...The photograph's eyes were moving. I pretended not to notice as the eyes slid over me, and it was clear that their gaze wasn't registering me at all. The eyes were disconcertingly brown in a black-and-white picture, and I saw them again a moment later, peering out through the eyes of a poster about a missing dog, but again, the eyes did not seem able to focus on me.

I thought about that while I stared at a poster about a circus I'd never heard of coming to a town whose name I didn't recognize. I'd heard of a clairvoyance spell of eastern origin—what was its name again? Whatever it was called, the spell made eyes manifest in the openings of walls. I vaguely recalled that it was first created to make eyes appear in rips and tears in the paper walls of Japanese houses. And the dream had brought me to a place that looked like Tokyo too...

"There you are."

I looked to the side and saw Sarah standing a ways down the sidewalk. I strolled over to her and found her standing in front of a picture of a door drawn on the wall in what looked like green chalk. Like the piece of green chalk in Sarah's hand actually.

"I told you to stay focused on me," Sarah reprimanded. "I was about to go in without you."

"Go in?" I should have told her about the eyes, but my mind wasn't quite firing on all cylinders.

Sarah reached out to the picture of a door and opened it. I never entered but suddenly found myself in a hospital operating room, as if I were moving in snapshots. Men and women in green surgeon gowns and masks were standing still, just staring at us. I walked over to the operating table and saw that it had sheets and a pillow just like a normal bed instead of those thin, paper-like blue covers. The blankets were thrown open where someone had gotten up.

"This is where Kevin came into the Dreamtime," Sarah said.

"How do you know?" I didn't doubt her. I was just curious.

She pointed at a heart monitor next to the operating table, and it was still beating although it wasn't hooked up to any patient that I could see. Listening to its beep and following its spiking digital lines with my eyes, I realized that the machine was monitoring Kevin's pulse. "On some level, Kevin knows he's in a coma, and we're in his mind now. Let me lead, John. Kevin will be more powerful here, but he'll be more vulnerable too."

Sarah continued on to where two swinging wooden saloon doors with nothing but darkness behind them were standing still. She pushed the saloon doors open and I saw what looked like a set of peeling grey wooden cellar stairs. There was a soft glow coming from somewhere down at their base, and Sarah walked down. The stairs creaked alarmingly. "I'm coming down," she called out. "It's all right. I'm not here to hurt anyone."

No one answered.

I followed Sarah to what looked like a hurricane cellar. The walls were whitewashed concrete and lined with jugs of water and canned vegetables. Kevin Kichida was sitting on a folding cot, clutching a baseball bat and listening to an old-fashioned radio by the light of a kerosene lamp. The radio was playing the rhythmic beat of a Mongolian shaman drum.

"Hello." Sarah didn't say Kevin's name, and I wondered if that was dangerous here. "I'm here to take you back home."

"This is home," Kevin replied, then looked around as if seeing the cellar for the first time. "My old one."

Sarah slowly stepped forward and gestured at the far end of the cot. "May I sit down?" He made a chin jerk that might have been an affirmation, though he did not release the baseball bat, and she carefully positioned herself on the edge of the cot. "Your father was a Ranger, wasn't he? I suppose you lived in a lot of places growing up."

"Yeah, we did," Kevin agreed. He seemed to be coming out of the unquestioning acceptance that was the default state of most dreamers, but it still hadn't occurred to him to ask who we were. "This is the house we lived in when Dad was stationed at Fort Sill. Our first civilian house off base."

"You liked it." Sarah didn't sound like she was guessing. I guess it made sense that Kevin would have come to a happy place. And the storm cellar was probably where his family came during violent storms, a place young Kevin had always associated with safety during scary times.

"It was great." Kevin didn't elaborate.

"So, why are you hiding?" Sarah asked.

Kevin seemed to fully see us for the first time. "Who are you?"

"A friend. Do you remember the man in the police station?"

He shuddered. "He was a vampire."

A dhampir, actually, but Sarah didn't disagree. "He put you in a coma. I'm here to help you out of it."

Kevin didn't pursue the matter of her name. "Why?"

Sarah shrugged. "You need help. I can help you."

"You can't help me," he disagreed. "He's coming for me."

"Who?" Sarah asked. "The vampire? We've dealt with him."

"No." When Kevin shook his head, it was almost violent. "My grandfather."

Sarah might have pursued that point, but even half aware, I was more attuned to environmental danger than she was. One of the shadows stretching out from the far end of the basement moved in a way that I did not like. I didn't bother to feint or cut or jab or thrust. I unsheathed my katana without thinking and flowed into a quick strike, one hand at the base of the hilt to guide and anchor and one hand higher up to flick the sword forward.

The blade didn't hit anything, but the shadow of my katana stretched out and disappeared into the shade created by a water heater. A muffled scream emerged from the dark patch.

Sarah rose to her feet then, and her staff burst into flame. She held the staff out before her as if it were a torch and advanced on the shaded patch. Darkness receded like a black wave returning to some ocean of night, revealing the stooped form of the maere. One of its hands was clutching a bleeding wrist stump and the crone was squinting intently forward. A hand with long gnarled talons was scuttling around her on the floor, its fingers moving like crab legs.

"You've stuck your nose in it now, little witch." The maere's voice was raw rage, scraped clean of any pretense of civility. "Run fast, you stupid fool. Run as far as you can."

"I'll leave at my own pace, and I'll take the boy with me when I do." Sarah's voice trembled, but that didn't mean anything. Trying to hide a negative emotion from a maere would have been like trying to hide a bleeding wound from a shark, anyhow. Sarah wasn't going anywhere.

"The boy is a lost cause, witch bitch." The maere straightened and the dark brown shawl covering her rippled in places where a shawl should not. "Save yourself."

"He's my apprentice." I didn't know where that had come from, but I heard the truth in the words as soon as Sarah spoke them. Fucking Dreamtime! But I didn't have time to get freaked out again. Sarah added, "And you're nothing but echoes and shadows, you old hag."

The maere made a mocking sound that was supposed to be a laugh. "This is the land of echoes and shadows. You're the tourist, you dumb slut!" The maere began to grow then, to narrow, and suddenly, the brown shawl emptied and vomited forth a stream of vermin, black rats and black snakes and black spiders with glowing yellow eyes. I snatched the kerosene lamp out of Kevin's hand and threw it into the horde before us. I don't know if it was just the fluid nature of that place, but more kerosene poured out than a lamp that size should have held. The snakes and rats and arachnids hesitated, began to shift into bats and hornets, but the kerosene coated their wings and impeded their flight, and Sarah brought her flaming staff down onto the approaching edges of the spreading puddle and set the cellar on fire.

The verminous creatures screamed, all of them in unison and forming one long shriek of anger and agony. Bats fluttered upward already aflame and spiraled into the nearest surface, and when they died, their bodies dissipated into oily smoke.

The screams didn't last for long.

I could actually feel the heat from those flames, and I turned to motion Kevin up the stairs and saw that he was no longer holding a baseball bat. He was staring at the flames and holding a long wooden match the size of a club.

In retrospect, I don't think Sarah or I were the ones who had made that kerosene flow or flame up so dramatically.

Sarah stepped in front of Kevin, forcing him to look at her. "Let me take you to a safe place in the Dreamtime. Once I show it to you, I think I can teach you to go there when you sleep from now on."

"Then let's hurry," I urged.

Sarah shook her head solemnly. "This is a refuge I made with some help from a few others. I can't take someone with a connection to the knights there without talking it over with some friends first. I'm sorry, John."

I actually didn't have a problem with that. I did have one problem, though, and I waved at Kevin to redirect his attention my way. He still seemed a little out of it. "Who was this grandfather you mentioned?"

"Not now," Sarah said impatiently.

And at the same time, Kevin said, "Mom would never tell me his name, but he's like me."

That was annoying, but it actually made sense if the mom was hiding Kevin from divination spells. Names resonate. "So what *can* you tell me about him?" I pressed.

"John, not now," Sarah repeated.

I heard her, but I didn't listen. My friends' lives were in danger because they'd gotten involved with this boy and his problems.

"Dad said it might finally be happening," Kevin's calm, semi-befuddled state of acceptance seemed to be wearing off as he became visibly more upset. A crack appeared in one of the basement walls around us with a loud ripping sound.

"John," Sarah interrupted.

I faced her. "What?"

"Wake up," she said.

And I did.

~12~

WELL, GLAD WE GOT THAT UNSETTLED

The first thing I saw was Sig standing over me, her hand going to the hilt of the sword sheathed behind her back when I gasped. It was oddly comforting. Sarah and Kevin didn't open their eyes. I carefully lowered Kevin's hand to the futon cushions he was propped up on, then released Sarah's too.

"Is everything okay?" Sig asked.

I unfolded myself out of my sitting position gingerly. "No, but Kevin is good for now."

Molly spoke as softly as she could over her drumming. "He doesn't look any different."

"Sarah is taking him to some place in the Dreamtime where he can sleep safely." I gestured at the drum. "I think you can stop that. It helped though. Thanks."

"Sarah can keep Kevin safe without you now?" Sig asked.

"She seems to think so." I hunched my shoulders and my neck made crunching sounds. "She tossed me out of that place like a four-hundred-pound bouncer."

"Why?" Sig pressed.

I rotated my neck some more. "Because the universe is in a conspiracy to keep us from finding out what the hell is going on."

It wasn't much of an answer, and they both just stared at me.

"I guess I was kind of being a pain in the ass," I admitted. Strangely, Sig and Molly didn't both jump in and start protesting about how unlikely that was. They were probably preoccupied with concern for Kevin.

Molly played it off, anyhow. "How big an ass pain were you being? Sarah seems like a compassionate person."

"She is," I granted. "But we were under a lot of stress, and her priorities aren't the same as ours. Or mine, anyway. Kevin just became her apprentice."

"What?!?" Sig said. "How? You were only out of it for a minute."

I stared at her blankly. She was serious. "It was a hell of a minute."

"Maybe you should tell us the whole thing," Molly nudged.

I stood up and stretched. "All right. Just let me make some coffee and get my thoughts together. Whatever Sarah gave me is making it a little hard to wake all the way up."

"Hold on! You're not going anywhere until you answer a few questions!" Sig declared. It made me smile. "Did you find out anything about who's sending us monster-grams or not?"

"Spoiler alert," I said. "It's Kevin's maternal grandfather."

I remembered where the coffee was and dragged myself upstairs. My mind and movements felt sluggish, but at least my memories of what had happened in the Dreamtime weren't slipping away the way dreams do sometimes. Choo wandered in from his self-imposed sentry duty on the first floor while I waited for the coffee to brew. I didn't know if Choo needed some time alone, or if he couldn't relax closed in by basement walls while things were out there looking for us, or if he just wanted to stay in the area where he could use his smartphone. I didn't ask either. We were both terse, Choo because he still had something up his ass that he wasn't ready to talk about, and me because I was preoccupied and groggy.

"Cahill will be here soon," Choo said when I'd filled him in on the basics. "Kevin's dad isn't answering his phone, but Cahill tracked the cell phone's location. Not the one Jerry's using to check his e-mails. The one listed under his name."

"That's good," I said though I wasn't really sure it was.

Choo wasn't sure it was all that great either. "Cahill says it's about an hour and a half away from here."

"I'll pass that on," I promised.

Sarah was awake and making herself some tea when I went back down to the basement. She was also responding to something Sig had said about waking Kevin up. "Do you think bringing someone out of a coma is like popping a cork on a champagne bottle? You're as bad as your boyfriend!"

That seemed a little snippy for Sarah, but she had made a peaceful life for herself because she really didn't like this kind of thing. Sig kept her temper, but I didn't have to see her face to know that a warning was flashing in her eyes like heat lightning. "John is risking his life for that boy because I dragged him into this mess. *Bad* isn't a word I would use to describe him."

For a second I felt a tingling warmth start to build in my chest.

"Idiot, maybe," Sig added. "I use that word a lot. Mule headed adrenaline junkie with a hero complex..."

"You can stop there," I called out from the stairs. "I don't want to tear up."

"If you thought I could just snap my fingers and wake Kevin up from a coma, and he'd be ready to go, that's on you, not me," Sarah informed us. "His mind is healing."

Molly stepped in. "But Kevin's not in danger anymore, right? His mind anyway?"

"He shouldn't be," Sarah admitted. "But the Dreamtime is an odd place. Sometimes, releasing bad stuff there is therapeutic, and sometimes, nightmares can scar us in ways that traumatize us for the rest of our waking life."

"Fine. We won't wake him up." I could smell Sig's frustration. It did seem a little unfair that she was being cast in the role of someone who wanted to endanger Kevin when Sig had been his most steadfast advocate from the very beginning.

Sarah probably sensed that. "Thank you. Now, if you'll excuse me, I need to use the little witches' room."

Sarah passed me wordlessly. Molly was watching Sarah disappear up the stairs when I rejoined them, and she commented softly. "I like her."

"I do too." Sig made the admission as if it was something she was blaming Sarah for. Then she turned her focus on me. "Now tell us everything."

So I did.

Sig sighed when I was done. "How many monsters does this grandpa from hell have on a string anyway?"

"It's like we pulled this kid out of the way of a falling rock," I agreed. "But it was just the first stone in an avalanche. We need to get behind this thing and find the guy responsible, not just keep reacting to what he throws at us."

"Witchie-Poo says we need to let Kevin sleep," Sig reminded me. "Not that it sounds like he knows too much anyway."

"We can follow up on Jerry Kichida's phone," I said cautiously.

Sig smiled wryly to let me know that we weren't going to fight about Kevin's father this time. "You said Cahill has tracked it down?"

"Yeah. And that bothers me," I said. "Jerry Kichida took all those precautions with the way he and Kevin were communicating, and then he leaves his regular cell phone on so that anybody can trace it? Does that sound likely to you?"

"Jerry wants someone to find the phone." Sig didn't have any doubt about that.

"Maybe it's a decoy," Molly said. "Kevin left his ordinary phone behind."

"Maybe. But Jerry's a sniper," I replied. "He's used to being a hunter, and he's being hunted. I'll bet you anything he's set up a rat trap, and that cell phone is the cheese."

Molly winced. "You want to walk into the trap anyway, don't you?"

"Why does everybody think I look for trouble?" I protested. "I am reason and calm."

"You have the survival instincts of a lemming," Sig retorted. "The only reason you're not dead is that you heal fast and get so much practice at almost getting killed."

I ignored that. "Cahill's going to be here any minute. He says the phone is an hour and a half away, and we've got about two and a half hours before Jerry is expecting Kevin to check in again. Let's get close to those GPS coordinates while we wait for Kevin's check-in time to roll around."

"How close?" Sig asked thoughtfully.

"Depends on the terrain," I said. "Say half a mile to a mile. I'll look for good sniper positions and listen and sniff around a little. If I hear any screams or pick up any monster scents, we can follow them. If I don't, and Kevin hasn't woken up by the time he's supposed to text his father, we'll contact Jerry ourselves and hope for the best. No tricks."

Sig smiled crookedly at this compromise. "I see what you're saying. That way, no matter what kind of response we get, we'll be in a better position to deal with it."

"Right," I agreed, and meant it. If Jerry wanted to meet up, we'd be close by. If nobody answered, we could check the cell phone out faster. If we alerted somebody and made them run, we'd have a lot better chance of spotting and tracking them. If somebody answered and said Jerry was dead and we'd better hand over the boy, we'd be in a better position to attack.

"That's assuming Jerry really did stake out his cell phone," Molly said.

"Yeah. Assuming that," I conceded. "I like those odds."

I didn't get the response I expected.

"There's a small problem," Sig said reluctantly.

Sarah had rejoined us at some point, and now she chimed in too. "I have one as well."

I stared at them. I had lived on my own for decades, and I got used to doing things my own way and taking my own chances and not having to be responsible for anybody else. Having to consider all of these group dynamics was a pretty big adjustment, and I wasn't sure it was any way to run a monster hunt. If it hadn't been for my recent experiences working with a werewolf pack, I'm not sure I could have handled it.

Sig and Sarah began to explain, and at some point Choo came downstairs and informed us that Cahill had arrived and couldn't get past Sarah's wards, and then Sarah had to go bring him in and all kinds of mediating and debating ensued. The fact that the maere had found us so quickly had rattled Sarah, and it didn't exactly settle her down when I remembered to tell her about the eyes I had seen in the Dreamtime. She wanted to keep Kevin safe behind her wards until she figured out a way to get him out of there safely, and she wanted at least one of us to stay while she tended him in case some God-knows-what showed up. Sig, on the other hand, had encouraged that young ghost in Tatum to manifest by promising that she would follow him and find his mortal body. She had brought the ghost to an active state where it was more likely to cause trouble, and now that Kevin was out of his coma, that obligation was pressing on her. So Sig wanted to go back to Tatum and take care of that while we handled Jerry Kichida. This made Cahill change his mind and want to go back with Sig as it was his town and the matter smacked of official police business, but Sig wanted Cahill to stick with the cell phone angle because Jerry Kichida was less likely to fire on a police officer and dhampirs were hard to kill, anyhow. Molly wasn't convinced that the cell phone wasn't just a decoy, and she thought it was foolish to send the whole team haring after something that might be designed to lead us further away from Jerry. Choo had missed all of the initial interplay with Sarah and wanted to go ahead and wake Kevin up and have him call his dad. He asked Sarah if the mental or emotional damage she was hinting at was more like pulling off a Band-Aid or amputating a limb, and Sarah refused to speculate.

After all of the back-and-forth and questioning and alternate ideas that we proposed and shot down, we eventually decided to spread the muscle and the mojo out evenly. Molly would go with Sig since they worked well together. Cahill would stay with Sarah and her bakery. I would take Cahill's police jacket and go with Choo to track down those cell phone coordinates; if some unknown thing was hunting Jerry Kichida or had found him already, I had the most experience tracking and identifying and dealing with random supernatural menaces.

Cahill, perhaps not surprisingly, was the least cooperative. "You guys are the ones who promised to pay back Glinda the Good here. No offense, lady, but I don't know you or owe you anything."

Choo'd had even less sleep than me. I'd at least managed to

grab some naps in the van, but he'd driven all night the night before. So Choo was a little close to the bone when he indicated Kevin's inert form. "Did you want that boy to die?"

Cahill's jaw worked tightly. "No."

"Then you owe the woman," Choo said. "Quit bein' an asshole."

And Cahill tried. At least Choo and Molly's opinions still seemed to matter to him.

A little later Sig and I said good-bye in the kitchen. We held each other for a long moment, and when we kissed this time, we weren't kidding around. We finally separated, and Sig gave a strange little laugh and put her forehead against mine. "I am so fucked."

"Good," I told her. "I think."

When it was time to leave, I met Cahill outside the bakery. He held his police jacket out while I put on a Kevlar vest. I'd had to remove the silver steel knife sheathed between my shoulder blades and transfer it to my left hip again. Finally, I pulled my green shirt on over the vest and took the jacket from him.

"Congratulations," Cahill said a bit sourly. "You are now officially impersonating a police officer. That's called a felony."

"What's it called when you do it?" I asked.

"Life," he said, and I kind of knew what he meant. How many of us actually know what the hell we're doing? Cahill had heard everything Sig and I had said—his hearing was almost as good as mine—and he tried to sound casual when he noted, "Looks like you and Sig are all in."

"I don't think you really want to have this conversation any more than I do," I observed. "So how about we just don't?"

For another minute or so, we didn't say anything. Then, as if he couldn't stop himself, Cahill said bitterly, "Sig made me see the monsters in this world. And now I am one, and she's left me alone in it."

Oh, boo fucking hoo.

"You called. We're here," I pointed out. "And that world you're talking about? I was born in it. Sig's helping me *not* see monsters everywhere."

Maybe Cahill and I were staring at Sig from opposite sides of the same tunnel. He was coming from a lighter place, and pursuing her would lead him farther into the dark. And I was coming from a darker place, and maybe the direction I was going in would take me someplace lighter. It was a nice hope to hold on to, anyhow.

∼13∼

SICK TRANSIT GLORIA

Kevin's mother may have been a prostitute." Parth's voice came through radio channel 88.5 via Choo's iPod, which was plugged into his dash like an IV.

"Why just *may have been*?" I probed. I was driving Choo's van while Choo rode in the passenger's seat. Choo had been reluctant to let me drive—had, in fact, pointed out that the last time he'd seen me drive had been while I was wrecking a truck. But he was exhausted and it was dark, and I was nocturnally inclined, so there.

"A Yuna Satou worked at a hospitality house in Okinawa while Jerry Kichida was stationed there," Parth reported. "But that same Yuna Satou was born in Nagoya in 1960. The Yuna Satou who married Jerry Kichida had all of the same information except that she listed her birth date as 1975. It seems likely the original Yuna Satou was a prostitute who died or got sent somewhere else when she got old. The question this raises is, did Kevin's mother just take the first Yuna's papers, or did she take over her position in the brothel too? And who was she before?"

"I went to one of those Okinawan hospitality houses when I was stationed there," Choo recalled. "It was all bright and out in the open. Kevin's mom mighta gone to a place like that for some fake papers because it was easy to find and full of women. She mighta felt more comfortable there than walkin' into a place like Whisper Alley."

Parth contemplated this possibility. "If so, that might suggest Kevin's mother was a desperate woman who came from wealth."

"Or Jerry Kichida might have been the one who bought the papers from a hospitality house to help a woman he loved," I pointed out.

"I know someone who has been involved in prostitution one way or another in many different places all over the world," Parth revealed. "She may be willing to investigate further on my behalf."

I pursued that comment a little. "Is this someone a naga like you?"

"Does that matter?" Parth wondered blandly.

"There's a homicidal spellcaster tied up in this somewhere," I explained. "If your acquaintance is a naga, it means she can protect herself."

"Ah." Parth chuckled. "Yes, Chavi has been taking care of herself for a long time."

Which didn't precisely answer my question.

The conversation petered out after that. Parth and I have both spent most of our lives trying to pry out other people's secrets while keeping our own, and our conversations tend to have this weird, guarded, circular, probing quality when we're not focused on something specific. Choo alternates between being chatty and taciturn at the best of times, and he wasn't having the best of times.

It wasn't until Parth signed off that I asked, "So, you went to some hospitality houses, huh?"

Choo made a rueful sound. "I did some things over there that I wouldn't want to talk about in church. Stupid stuff. It wasn't as much fun as it sounded. What about you?"

He knew I'd been alone for a long time. Four to five decades moving around and avoiding any deep connections because I didn't want to endanger anybody else. It doesn't even seem like a real number anymore. And then when I finally . . . oh fuck it. "Yeah," I said quietly. "I've done some things just trying to get enough human contact to stay sane or fake it."

"Me too." Choo leaned back in his seat and closed his eyes.

We rode in silence for a time, and then I asked him something that had been on my mind. "So, what's up with you and Sig? You've been giving her a hard time, and she's already having one."

Choo kept his eyes shut. "I know it. It's all this stuff with Cahill. I look at him and I'm like, well, this is what happens when you mess around with this shit. I guess I'm next."

That was kind of vague, but I was following. "Sig didn't pull you into this world. You and Molly got jacked up by a ghost all on your own. She's not keeping you in it, either."

Choo sort of answered that sideways. "You remember tellin' me I should get out of this business?"

"Yeah."

"I thought about it," he confessed. "But I can't. It's like . . . I see all these people who don't call me until it's too late. I mean, as an exterminator."

"Sure," I said.

"There's a kind of person . . . thinking about things like bugs or mold freaks 'em out so much, they just don't think about it." Choo laughed. "Then they call me when the termites and carpenter ants are about the only thing holding their house together."

"Sure," I repeated.

"Ever since I found out ghosts and shit are real, I just have this feeling things are eating away at the foundation of my house." Choo shivered slightly. "And I don't want to be one of the fools who look the other way. Who just sit back and pretend everything is cool while things get more and more out of hand."

I took a shot in the dark. "You keep mentioning trying to work things out with your ex, but you don't really talk about her. Is that what happened in your marriage? Did you ignore some problems that kept getting bigger and bigger?"

Choo laughed but he wasn't really laughing. "Sometimes you're pretty smart, and sometimes you're a dumb-ass. I don't know which one you're being right now."

"Okay."

He sighed and went on. "Sex with an ex, baby. It's like looking at the front of a train. It's powerful and movin' so fast, it makes you forget what's behind it. Car after car after car of baggage. Me and Chantelle, we love each other, but there's a whole lot of pain in that train, man."

I would have asked him more about Chantelle, but Choo closed his mouth as well as his eyes after that, pretending to be asleep. A few minutes later, he really was.

I like driving at night. I like the feeling of going somewhere, and I like the feeling of going nowhere in particular. I grew up in a hostile environment, and quiet and solitude and darkness were my safe places. If they weren't, I would have cracked up a long time ago. Of course, I'm a werewolf knight who spent a long time running from a secret society before falling for a Norse battle goddess. And I was trying to keep some kid I didn't know from being killed by a Japanese wizard, and my allies were an ex-priest writing blank reality checks, a semi-vampire cop who wanted my girlfriend, a witch who couldn't decide if I was working for her or with her or against her, an immortal naga who wanted to peel away the secrets of my psyche and my DNA, and an exterminator who was kind of ambivalent about my existence. So, maybe I went crazy a long time ago. Maybe I'm really an accountant who cracked during tax season, sitting off to the side of some craft class where other patients are making dollhouses out of macaroni while an orderly checks my med chart or something.

Nah.

I was almost half a mile from the GPS coordinates when Cahill called. "The kid's awake and made contact with his father. Jerry knows you're on the way."

"Kevin seem okay?" I said.

"The kid doesn't really want to talk to me," Cahill observed.

I didn't comment on that.

"Do you think it was really Jerry?" I asked.

"Kevin only talked to him via texting and e-mails, but he says it was really him," Cahill said. "He asked him some questions only his father would know just to be safe. Jerry said he'd meet you at a specific address and then went into radio silence mode."

"I don't have a way to talk to him directly right now?" I asked.

"Nope," Cahill said. "He's not answering his cell phone, surprise surprise. And his e-mail doesn't exist anymore."

"He knows his son is with you, and he cancelled his e-mail address?" I verified.

"Yep," Cahill said. "As soon as he sent his last response."

Damn. I'd been prepared for all sorts of scenarios, but I

hadn't expected that. "This address he gave you," I said. "Is it the same as the cell phone's GPS coordinates?"

"Yep," Cahill said.

"Awesome," I commented. Jerry was making sure I couldn't negotiate a different venue by threatening his son. With no way to contact Jerry, if I wanted him, I would have to come to him, period. And if I was hostile and wanted to use Kevin as leverage, I would have to keep Kevin alive and take him to Jerry's designated meeting point as a hostage. From Jerry's point of view, that was a lot better than having to turn himself in to someone who might just kill him and Kevin anyhow. But cancelling his e-mail address had still been pretty hard-core.

"You know he's going to be checking you out through a sniper scope when you get there, right?" Cahill probed.

"Yeah, but that doesn't mean he's outright hostile," I said. "I'd do the same."

"As I recall, you're pretty good at sniffing out snipers," Cahill ventured.

"In every sense of those words," I agreed. "But Kevin vouched for Jerry, and he's on full alert. Right now, the worst case scenario is that Jerry wants to take me alive so that he can ask me questions or trade me for his son. If I go in hot, there's too much chance of me hurting Jerry or him blowing my head off for no good reason."

"I was reading the kid's texts when he sent them," Cahill said. "Kevin doesn't know you're a werewolf."

"Then Jerry probably won't have silver bullets," I speculated. "That's something. Does Kevin know about Choo?"

"He didn't mention him in the e-mail, either." Cahill sounded thoughtful. "You, me, and Sarah are the only people Kevin knows about, and me and Sarah are here. Kevin made it sound like you were coming alone."

"That's something too. Has Sig checked in yet?"

"No," Cahill said shortly, and hung up.

I thought about calling Sig, but if she was hanging around a ghost, her cell phone wouldn't be working anyway, so I nudged Choo awake. "You ready to wake up and be my plan B?"

"I was having nightmares, anyway. I kept dreaming my wife had left me and I was hanging out with freaky-ass people and monsters were real." Choo finished rubbing his eyes and looked around the van as if for the first time. "Oh, hell."

∿14∿

THE PIED SNIPER

The house at Jerry Kichida's cell phone coordinates was built near the Hudson River, a large home painted grey and shaped like a barn, though it had a white porch sticking out of its base. The second level was mostly windows. At a couple of hours until sunrise, the house was the only thing around that had lights on. It looked like a giant bug zapper.

There was a lot of land around the house, and Parth had said that the family who owned it was fairly affluent and just used the place for vacations. The sole connection that any of them seemed to have to Jerry Kichida was geographical. He only lived a half hour away.

I opened the van door and immediately smelled something undead. I wasn't exactly sure what kind of undead, but at least there was only one of whatever it was. And amidst all of the other scents was a faint coppery hint of human blood and some kind of antiseptic chemicals.

Either Jerry Kichida had been hurt while bagging and tagging a monster, or some unholy rectal deposit had gotten Jerry, or they had taken each other out.

I stepped out of the van and closed the door without unholstering my Ruger Blackhawk. The gun was loaded with hollowpoints that had been soaked in the holy herb verbena, with a small dose of silver melted and fused into the notches in their tips. Molly had also etched a small cross into the bullets' casing and blessed them.

And if that didn't work, I'd piss on 'em.

There was a deep wheelbarrow furrow in the grass where something heavy had been carried up to the house. I followed that furrow all the way up to the porch and pounded on the front door. It fell over with a crash.

The hinges had been ripped out.

I drew my gun and went in slowly, calling Jerry's name. The front living room was a mess. A coffee table was pancake-flat with its legs splayed out. Piles of plaster and dust were scattered over the hardwood floor, and I could see mud smears and several places on the stairway where chunks of the wooden edges had been snapped off. More interestingly, the ceiling at the center of the room was sagging dramatically.

Something heavy had been dragged up those stairs. I considered firing my gun into the sagging patch of ceiling just to get the party started, but not too seriously. Instead, I straight-armed my gun in front of me as if I were waterskiing behind it and started to check out the lower floor, just to make sure nothing came up behind me when I went up those stairs. I didn't smell anything living or hear anything moving, but you never know what kind of stealth abilities unknown creatures might have. There are more things in heaven and earth, Horatio. Hell and earth too. At least there was no basement this close to the river.

Satisfied, I made my way back to the living room and took my cell phone out and dialed Jerry Kichida's number. A ring tone came from upstairs, right where the sagging patch of floor was. Okay, then.

The upper floor wasn't hard to search. There were only three rooms in it, and it didn't take long to work my way to the studio where the cell phone was still ringing and cold air was rushing in. The room had hardwood floors, and three large windows made up most of its outer walls. There was hardly any furniture: a desk with a computer and a printer, one of those huge plastic water bottle coolers like you see in the reception areas of business offices, a sofa, some long slender metal rods with floor lamps mounted on them, and a lot of easels with mediocre paintings of rivers and wildlife.

Oh, and there was also a corpse.

The undead thing was dressed in a loose mud-covered cotton blue suit over a black T-shirt. Its body was only five-foot-sevenish and compact, but from the way the floor was bending, the corpse weighed at least three hundred pounds. And the dead being had been an albino with Asian features too. Its pale complexion had been disguised by a pretty good makeup job, but there were big streaks of white skin where something— bullets, probably—had torn holes in the clothes and created tangible smears in the facial makeup without breaking the thing's skin. It was the eye that had been shot out that had finally put the thing down.

The ringing cell phone was on the pale corpse's chest.

The piece of cheese in Jerry Kichida's rat trap.

I saw a small black object on the floor and bent down to examine it closely. It was a flattened bullet, a wisp of blue fabric stuck where the tip had accordioned off the creature before dropping to the floor. It was a shame, really. All that precision shooting wasted on bulletproof skin, marble-hard muscle, and dense bone. No wonder the corpse was so heavy.

I turned off my phone and the ringing from the other cell phone stopped.

I was pretty sure the thing on the floor was a chiang-shih, a kind of Chinese undead. I'd never seen one before, but chiang-shih are dense as hell, and the longer they live, the harder their bones and muscles and skin become. Chiang-shih aren't really vampires, but they are sometimes confused with them, and chiang-shih are where the myth about vampires becoming stronger as they get older comes from.

I carefully walked around the body in a wide radius and made my way to the southeast window kitty-corner to the river and hidden from the driveway. The glass in the window frame was gone. There were a few shards of glass still hanging from the frame, but that was it.

I leaned out the window with my gun held at my side. It was still dark outdoors, but in the radius of the house lights I could see that the majority of glass fragments were on the ground below, not the studio floor, and there was a large depression where something heavy had impacted. Just at the edges of my vision was a second noticeable depression where grass had been torn asunder. Something heavy, probably the chiang-shih, had gone through this window in an outward explosion of glass.

I holstered my pistol and tried to visualize the scene.

Maybe the chiang-shih had knocked on the front door downstairs hoping to draw Jerry out, or maybe it had just ripped the door off the hinges from the start, but it had made its way to this room, tracking the same cell phone coordinates that had brought me here. Perhaps the cell phone was lying in the center of the room, maybe even ringing, and the chiang-shih had knelt down to pick it up in a preselected kill zone.

Had the cell phone been ringing? I thought maybe it had. I imagined the chiang-shih picking the phone up and listening to it.

"Tell me whatever it is I want to know, or you're dead," Jerry's voice had said through the phone, or said something like that anyhow. Maybe there had been a big dramatic red dot over the chiang-shih's heart. Or maybe Jerry hadn't said anything at all, just skipped the talk and made the shot that creased the chiang-shih's forehead, hoping to knock it out.

In any case, things hadn't gone as Jerry planned. Whether Jerry shot the damn thing first and it charged the southeast window where the red dot was coming from, or it charged the window and then Jerry shot it, both of those things happened. The shot didn't have any effect on the chiang-shih, and it jumped through the window and landed on the ground below with a massive, earthshaking thud while glass showered around it. Jerry shot it again, then again, but it was moving fast as it charged the area where the shots were coming from. Chiang-shih are sometimes called "Hopping Corpses" because they travel in ten- to twelve-foot leaps when they're in a hurry. Their skin and muscles are so hard that they actually limit the chiang-shih's flexibility, and it is faster and more efficient for them to travel in stiff-legged leaps that require less repetitive motion.

Jerry got off several more shots, but the chiang-shih made it to Jerry's vantage point. Maybe the damn thing smelled him out, or heard him. Chiang-shih are supposed to have incredible senses to make up for the fact that they are almost completely blind in even faint light. Somehow, Jerry had gotten hurt while being close enough to shoot the thing through its eye socket... I'd have to see the actual site to even speculate about that.

However it happened, the chiang-shih forced Jerry to kill it before he'd gotten the information he wanted when he set this rat trap up in the first place. So, Jerry reset the trap. He had figured out that chiang-shihs could track like bloodhounds at this point, so Jerry fetched a wheelbarrow to help transport that heavy body and wheeled the chiang-shih around in circles to confuse the scent trail, then back here in case others of its kind followed.

Yeah, if Jerry was expecting whoever was after him to keep sending more assassins, his actions made more sense. The chiang-shih's body was meant to draw me into the kill zone to investigate, and also be a warning for me to cooperate. There was probably a red laser dot on my forehead, centered right between my eyes. I waved my open left palm at the tree line in a casual, friendly fashion.

The cell phone on top of the chiang-shih lit up and made that generic service provider ring tone again, but there was no way I was getting near that phone or that corpse. I took a piece of paper out of the printer one-handed, laid it on the desk, found a pen, and scrawled the words "Hi Jerry" while keeping the pistol holstered. Then I wrote my cell phone number under the words and held the paper up to the window.

After a few seconds, the phone on the chiang-shih's chest turned off. Then my phone began ringing. I fished it out and answered it, still using one hand.

"Are you a real policeman?" a voice demanded.

"No," I admitted.

"My son seems to think that you and your friends saved his life." The voice had a very slight accent. Pennsylvanian, maybe. "But it sounds to me like all you've done is wake a boy up from a coma that your friend put him in."

"I'll try to answer any questions I can, but there's one important question I have for you first," I told him.

"What is it?" the voice asked cautiously.

"What kind of ammo did you use on the chiang-shih?"

Which is when the chiang-shih lunged upward.

～15～

KUNG F.U.

I tried to fire some rounds into the chiang-shih, but my finger wouldn't pull the trigger. It was my fucking geas. The chiang-shih hadn't done anything to endanger the Pax Arcana, hadn't directly threatened me or anyone I cared about. I stood there and strained mentally and physically, but my index finger wasn't budging on the trigger. I was going to have to wait for the chiang-shih to attack me.

At least I didn't have to wait for long.

It was one thing to read about the way chiang-shih jump about, another to see the ungainly stiff-legged leap that pushed off with one foot and propelled the chiang-shih toward me. It landed in front of me in a spray of wood chunks, the floor sagging beneath us and throwing me off-balance. The big plastic water bottle on top of the blue stand tipped over and water seeped into the depression around our feet.

The chiang-shih gave a scream that sounded something like a bat, lurching and whirling in jerky, robotic motions that were swift despite their limited range. I tried to discharge my gun into its empty eye socket then, but the tilting floor kept me off kilter, and the chiang-shih knocked the gun out of my hand with a forearm block that only moved from the elbow. The bullet hit the chiang-shih high on its right temple and lodged there, steam hissing around its edges.

I ducked under a jerky backfist and came up fast, slamming my palms over the chiang-shih's ears and forcefully compressing the air inside its ear canals. The chiang-shih screamed as its eardrums ruptured with a muffled but audible pop. You have to understand, the inner tissues of the chiang-shih's ear canal were far softer than its outer skin—maybe even more vulnerable than a normal human's because the ears had to channel vibrations to function, and chiang-shihs have ultra-sensitive hearing.

I hadn't just deafened the chiang-shih...I'd as good as blinded it.

There was no time to celebrate, though. The chiang-shih hit me while the hitting was good with a short, straight-armed blow with the heel of its left hand. The damned thing was using its freakish strength to skip a lot of the movements that build momentum and center the body behind a blow, and its herky-jerky fighting style was hard to anticipate. If I hadn't been wearing a Kevlar vest, I think that blow would have caved my chest in. As it was, I went flying backward and skidded over the floor, cutting the wooden legs out from under an easel with a painting on it while I did so.

What was Jerry Kichida waiting for?

The skidding saved my life. The chiang-shih focused on the direction it had sent me and made another stiff-legged hop to cover the increasing distance between us. Its trajectory was a little short though, and the chiang-shih was coming down towards my ankle when I curled my back, rolled on to my shoulders, and straightened so that I could shoot my feet straight into its midriff. I knew how heavy it was now, knew it in my muscle memory, and I launched its top-heavy form backward. The floor that had risen when the chiang-shih went airborne sagged alarmingly again when the undead thing landed on its shoulders. Water from the overturned cooler flowed back into the new depression. That and the chiang-shih's own density and inflexibility had it struggling like a turtle on its back for a few precious seconds.

I was lighter on my feet than it was, even with a chest that felt like a metal plate. I didn't exactly bounce, but I got up and grabbed a four-foot-long standing floor lamp that was teetering back and forth. I had about ten feet of cord to play with, and I smashed the lamp tip against the floor, shattering glass and brass fittings. The broken fiberglass tip and the exposed wires made contact with the puddle of water the chiang-shih was trying to rise up in. Something sizzled and all the lights in the room went out while the chiang-shih jerked.

Chiang-shihs are vulnerable to electricity. Maybe because electricity travels faster through tightly packed molecules, or the disruption of covalent bonds is more serious in denser organisms. I'm not a physicist. What I do know is that lightning is one of the few things that kill chiang-shih quickly in the old stories.

The chiang-shih swayed back on its heels, and I swung the lamp around again and smashed the base alongside its jaw while it was momentarily stunned. The base flew off, the cord snapped, and I stabbed the exposed jagged rod into the chiang-shih's empty eye socket on the backswing. Whatever neural bypass the chiang-shih's fast-healing body had come up with to get it moving again, the synaptic connections inside its skull were still fragile, and the chiang-shih dropped to the floor.

So did I.

Jerry Kichida had just shot me through my left temple.

~16~

CHOO ON THIS

To be fair, Jerry had a pretty good idea that the shot wouldn't kill me. He wasn't using armor-piercing or explosive rounds, much less silver bullets, and I'd been moving fast enough that he knew I wasn't human. And Jerry was some kind of Christian, having grown up going to military chapels that were roughly Protestant, and his son's life was at stake, maybe his son's soul, and I had just fallen into the hellish-creature category in his estimation. So, yeah, Jerry was going to talk to me, but when he did so, my limbs would be broken or I would have explosives wired up my ass. Something like that. Jerry wasn't taking any unnecessary chances.

So, he took me out.

Then Jerry Kichida waited and scanned the environment before he finally began walking back to the house. It is possible that Jerry rushed it just a little. Jerry hadn't slept in two days and wasn't sure how much time he had when dealing with things that regenerated. He didn't have a spotter, and it would have been natural if the chiang-shih's apparent resurrection had rattled him a bit.

Whatever the case, Choo was watching Jerry from ninety yards away when Jerry walked across the clearing. Choo, my backup, who I had let out of the van a ways back and who had followed behind me on foot in case I ran headfirst into a trap. Choo, who was not a former Ranger sniper—was in fact a former Army supply sergeant—but who'd had a lot of audible and visual cover while I was fighting the chiang-shih. Choo, who had spent the last few years learning to hunt things that saw in the dark and had sensitive hearing.

Choo had done enough long-range shooting to know the area that would give Jerry the maximum field of fire, and he was wearing a black wetsuit that had been iced down so that he wouldn't show up in the dark to anyone using infrared—at least, not until the insulated heat inside the suit built up and spilled over. He had some time. Choo was armed with an old-school tranquilizer rifle powered by .22 blanks, and the rifle was good for at least 170 yards, though Choo wouldn't want to fire at anything smaller than a rhino at that distance. There were a variety of darts in the Velcro bandolier he wore... darts that injected juice from a mandrake root, darts that were poisoned with curare, darts that were tipped in wolfsbane, and a few with narcotics powerful enough to put down a gorilla or bear.

Jerry felt a sting in his neck and reacted instantly. He estimated Choo's location from nothing more than the placement of the sting and an automatic assessment of which areas offered the best cover. Jerry fired several shots, and Choo later told me that one of the bullets smacked into the tree he was kneeling half beside and behind.

But Jerry went down quickly, the way he was supposed to go down if he attacked us.

I wasn't taking unnecessary chances either.

~17~

GETTING AROUND TO GETTING DOWN TO IT

Having your brain shredded is a funny thing, even for those of us who regenerate. Choo had taken in the sight upstairs, figured out that I was either going to come back or not, and experimentally tried to hack the chiang-shih's head off with a machete slung around his back. No way, no how was he going to mess around trying to take something he didn't understand prisoner. When the machete didn't work, Choo went back to the van and got a diamond-toothed chainsaw that he keeps in the back for such emergencies. Then he had wrapped both the chiang-shih's parts and my body in plastic tarps, tossed it all in the van, and set up a machine that would liberally spread industrial cleaner into the atmosphere while he was gone—the kind of professional-grade stuff that you can't use without a license and an EP suit because it unbinds molecules and DNA strands in organic residue.

Jerry Kichida was bound but treated gently. Have I mentioned that Choo has a bit of a bias against those of us who aren't entirely human?

Apparently, I was screaming for a while toward the end there, in the van, I mean. I have vague impressions of darkness and jolting agony and confusion and consciousness without coherent thought and waking up repeatedly but not entirely before passing out again.

And I remember gradually coming to something resembling awareness with the worst headache I'd ever had in my life. I was in a strange bed in my boxer shorts, and I celebrated being alive by leaning over the edge of the sheets and vomiting. Sig was waiting with a large metal bowl—apparently, it wasn't the first time I'd done this—and caught most of it.

She spoke, and I couldn't understand a word. My language centers were fucked up, and it was maybe the weirdest and scariest thing that has ever happened to me, which is saying something. I tried to speak and didn't recognize the sounds that came out of my mouth. Sig put a finger to her lips, and I did understand that, and then she tried to get in bed with me and discovered that I had apparently wet it at some point.

It wasn't the way I'd always imagined getting in bed with her.

Eventually, though, I was lying down next to her, even if Sig was clothed, her head on my shoulder, my hand clasped in her hand, and I spent a good while drooling and making undignified gargles and squawks while a searing and sickening white-hot pain filled my skull. We were somewhere above Sarah White's bakery and the room was full of rising warmth and the smell of fresh bread, in a king-size bed backlit by candlelight, and I didn't put any of that together until Sarah came in and gave me some tea that tasted like unwashed ass with a hint of honey. I fell asleep again.

When I woke up the next time, it wasn't gradually. I came to completely alert with Sig's face inches from mine. She was lying on her side and watching me intently, her face unreadable and maybe the most beautiful thing I had ever seen. A sentence came out of my mouth fully formed before I realized I was going to say it. I gazed into those blue eyes that I still found startling in their brightness and brushed her cheek tenderly with my hand and said, "I'm going to kill Jerry Kichida."

Sig brushed aside a few strands of hair that had fallen over her face. She was wearing a blue top, almost a leotard, over dark slim-cut jeans. "I thought about it myself."

"I'll make it quick," I said. "Almost painless."

Sig leaned over on her side and kissed the tip of my nose. "It would hurt Kevin, too."

I still had a dull headache, but I tried to think about that. "I guess killing both of them and calling this whole thing a wash is out of the question."

Sig smiled crookedly. "Sarah made Kevin her apprentice, remember?"

"Shit." I tried to think that through. "How about I just kill Jerry a little bit?"

Sig started to put her hand on the side of my face, hesitated, probably remembered drawing an emerging bullet out of my ear with needle-nose pliers, and put her palm over my heart instead. It was pounding. "You need to calm down."

Something occurred to me. "What about the chiang-shih?"

"It's dissolving in a big metal tub full of holy water in Sarah's cellar." Sig placed another kiss on my forehead and dug something out of her pants pocket and handed it to me. "And Choo found these on him."

It was a plain plastic sandwich bag, like you can get in any grocery store, but the items in it were anything but ordinary. They were scales of some kind, pearly and iridescent scales about the size of a quarter. Five of them.

"Do you know what they are?" Sig asked.

"Not this time." I gave the bag back to her.

"I've been trying to figure out what that thing was using them for," Sig said. "The best I can figure out is that the scales are either currency or spell ingredients."

"Makes as much sense as anything else," I agreed. "It wouldn't need five of them just for identification. Where is everybody?"

"Choo and Molly went back to the house on the Hudson River to finish cleaning up the place. And Ted went back to Tatum to officially find the body of Taylor Halsey. I gave him an anonymous tip."

Taylor Halsey? I had forgotten all about the ghost Sig had gotten to manifest in the police station. I didn't ask her if it was bad. I just asked: "How bad was it?"

"It was ugly." Sig shivered. "The man who killed him is a backhoe operator. One of the ways he makes money is digging graves. I had to walk through a cemetery. Me."

I took her hand, put the underside of my fingers beneath hers, and curled them together so that our hands were two fists interlocked like train couplings. I pulled the side of her index finger into my mouth and nibbled on it with my teeth, just slightly, then moved my lips down the back of her hand, then turned it slightly and planted a lingering kiss over her pulse.

Sig sighed like she was depressurizing. "I don't like seeing you hurt and helpless. It scared me."

I kissed the inside of her forearm. "I've seen you like that. It scared me too."

"No." She pulled her arm away from my mouth, though she still held my hand. "You don't understand. I knew you were going to heal. I didn't like seeing you hurt. That's what scared me. Not that you were hurt—how much I didn't like it."

"I do understand." Something in my voice seemed to get through to her.

"This is becoming real." Sig squeezed my hand. "And it's freaking me out a bit."

It was a little different for me. The knowledge that Sig would be in danger whether I was around or not was actually one of the things that made her attractive. It took the pressure off me in a strange way, relieved some of the weight I carry with me wherever I go.

"You're the one who told me that death wasn't anything to obsess about," I said. "And you should know, right?"

Sig snorted bitterly. "Sometimes, I talk out of my ass. I see the part of people that can't let go of this world, John. I see white fingers on the edge of a cliff, and sometimes, I coax those fingers into unclenching, and sometimes, I stomp on them. But I never get to peer over the cliff."

There was this pain in the right side of my skull, and I couldn't really get too metaphysical. "Look, Sig. If you're breaking up with me, just do it."

She kissed me on the head, where it hurt. "I said that we're getting in deep and it's a little scary. I didn't say I wanted to end it."

"Good." I released her hand and put my palm under her shirt, the tip of my fingers beneath her navel.

She didn't protest my hand, though she did reach down and lay hers on my forearm. "What are you doing?"

I made a small circle trailing the tip of my middle finger beneath her navel. "Comforting you?"

Sig grinned crookedly. "Do you seriously want to have sex right now? Your head must be killing you."

"It still hurts." I leaned over and kissed the curve of her chin, and when she arched her neck, I kissed the soft spot on the underside of her jaw where a knife would go up between the ligaments and tendons if I wanted to shove the tip upward all the way into her brain. "I'm being unselfish."

She laughed, one of those skeptical little *rigggghhhtt* kind of laughs, and released my forearm. Her hand moved down my stomach, not slowly or playfully but briskly going between my legs as if she were taking a temperature or checking the oil in her car. "Wow. You *do* want to have sex right now."

"I'm very giving," I gasped. I put my hands flat on the small of her back, pressed in firmly with the heels and slid my palms up her until my fingers were between her shoulder blades. The bra unclasped easily. Press each side towards the opposite shoulder, then down and away from the body. I don't know why that's supposed to be so difficult. But the straps were trapped around her shoulders, under her shirt.

Sig's body and brain seemed to be traveling down different tracks. She groaned and flexed her back again and moved her right leg so that it was over my hip, pressing our waists together, but she also grabbed my wrist while I was moving my hand toward the right cup of her loosened bra. "When I thought you had died, do you know the first thing that went through my head?"

"Was it a bullet? If it wasn't a bullet, I don't want to hear any whining," I grumbled against her cheek.

She laughed a little raggedly. "Shut up. I wished we'd made love. A lot. So, I'm not saying that I don't want to do this."

"What are you saying?" I asked.

She patted me on the cheek. "I'm saying the first time we have sex isn't going to be in this woman's bed while some butt-ugly could attack at any moment."

"Oh, hell, are you one of those women who put a lot of pressure on the first time?" I asked without thinking.

Her back muscles got tense under my hand and her voice suddenly had a bit of hurt anger crawling around its edges. "What do you mean?"

I knew I'd made a mistake, but I had to go on. "You know…
arrange everything so that it will make a nice mental snapshot
later. Pick a certain time or place. Play some preselected music.
Light some candles."

"Is something wrong with that?" Her voice definitely held
a dangerous undercurrent.

I took her hand and kissed it again. "No. You just didn't
strike me as the sentimental type. The closest we've come to
making love was in the front seat of a car."

"I have a lot of ugliness in my life," she said softly. "I could
use a few beautiful memories."

"I can get on board with that," I assured her. "Just so long
as you understand, the first time I see you with your clothes
off, I'm not going to be thinking about the color scheme of the
walls or what the potpourri smells like."

She smiled, if a little crookedly. Then she became the woman
who had cleaned up several of my bodily fluids without blinking again, got brisk and businesslike and slapped me on my
ass, though she wasn't fooling me now. Somewhere beneath
the hard shell she'd developed to deflect bad things, there was
a marshmallow center. "Whatever. You smell like vomit and
baby wipes."

I focused on my scent for the first time. Gahhh. "You're
right, I stink!"

"Very much," she agreed.

I coughed feebly and gasped. "Could you maybe help me
take a shower? I'm so weak…"

She laughed a little shakily and kissed my forehead.
"Nice try."

Look, anything worth having takes some combination of
patience and desire and risk. I was willing to wait the year Sig's
sponsor had suggested—hell, a lot longer than that if I had to.

And Sig had a lot of raw, powerful stuff churning around, and most of it probably wasn't a turn-on. I really did get that.

But it was still hard to pull back. I think maybe the near-death thing had a lot to do with that. My subconscious was screaming, "YOU CAN DIE! PROCREATE, DUMB-ASS! PROCREATE BEFORE IT'S TOO LATE! PROCREATE!"

What if I started screaming that at Sig? Would it put her in the mood? Probably not, I decided. So, instead, I said, "I'm not going away, Sig."

She unwrapped her leg from around my hip and kissed me briskly but with real feeling. "Good. Now go brush your teeth."

"Jerry Kichida is ready to talk," Sarah White told me.

I was showered, shaved, wearing a slightly-too-large T-shirt that Sarah had dug up from somewhere, and sitting on the bed while I worked my way through a tray of bruschetta. The grilled bread was still warm and the smell of tomato and garlic and olive oil and salt and pepper had my stomach making earthquake sounds. I hadn't been able to keep anything down while I was getting my head together, so to speak.

"Great," I said. "But I'm going to need more food."

Her answering smile was faint but genuine. "You came to the right place. I'll be back in a moment."

Sig examined Sarah's rear end as she turned and left the room. It was a nice rear end. I saw a lot of women examining other women when I was a bartender in Clayburg, and Sig's gaze wasn't sexually interested. It was the sort of cool, clinical evaluation that a woman gives a potential rival.

And okay, I'll admit it, Sarah White is attractive. There were even times where I used to fantasize about going back and looking Sarah up again and trying to make something happen. But those were just fantasies. Sarah didn't want someone like me in her life. I eat meat. I kill people. I'm sort of a knight. I have all sorts of inappropriate or outmoded assumptions or attitudes from the 1930s buried under my surface like landmines that blow up unexpectedly at odd times, though I try to recognize them and deal with them honestly when they do.

There were just too many deal-breakers.

"And she cooks too," Sig muttered after the door closed. Sig herself does not.

"You know you really don't have to worry about Sarah, right?" I said.

"Oh, I know. I just wonder if she knows." We had worked through the bruschetta and a few other things by the time Sarah came back into the room with three baguettes, some brie, and a small box of chocolate muffins.

Sig reached over and took one of the muffins, and it was all I could do not to nip at her hand. Hell, it was all I could do not to cram a baguette into my mouth like a plank into a wood chipper and start spraying crumbs through the air.

"John . . ." Sarah hesitated. "I understand that you might be upset with Jerry Kichida."

"You're a very understanding person," I said. "Thank you."

The sarcasm wasn't all that subtle, but Sarah went on undeterred. "There has already been some . . . unpleasantness. He's not an evil man. He's just scared about his son and wants to feel in control. And he doesn't."

"Just say what you're trying to say," I mumbled around a mouth full of bread.

Sarah switched to hardball. "All right then. You're in my debt."

I chewed on those words and a baseball-sized lump of bread at the same time. I finished the bread first. "And?"

"I want you to protect Jerry Kichida the same way you've been protecting his son," Sarah finished. "That's my price."

I didn't like it, but if that was her price... well, that was her price. "Then let's go talk to the man."

"I want you to go easy," Sarah reiterated.

"Like a Sunday morning," I agreed.

She still glared at me suspiciously. Have people forgotten Lionel Richie already? It's hard to keep track. "It is Sunday morning, John."

"See?" I said. "It's working already."

There was a cramped narrow box of a stairway in the back of Sarah's bakery that led to a room with a large wooden table and metal racks full of kitchen supplies. Kevin and his father were sitting there alone, which pissed me off for a moment, but after that initial reaction, I realized that Sarah was no fool and that we were in her place of power. If Jerry Kichida even held a butter knife the wrong way, his muscles would probably lock up and he would start getting sleepy, very, very sleepy. Someone named Dylan called out through a door with a question about a delivery, and Sarah bustled out and left Sig and me to sit down and introduce ourselves.

I tried not to imagine doing sudden, violent things to Jerry while I examined him. He was an average-sized man, compact and evenly proportioned, maybe five ten or five eleven. He was wearing cotton camouflage clothing, and the rolled-up sleeves revealed disproportionately large forearms. His black hair was buzz-cut close to his flat skull, and he had managed to shave while maintaining a stakeout for at least two days. His eyes were a dark brown and every bit as focused and intent as his body language. And he looked like shit.

The entire left side of Jerry's face was bruised and his mouth was swollen. He was holding his right shoulder at a slight downward angle, tilting his head in a way that suggested he was trying to take pressure off of a rib, and there were purple marks on his throat left by fingers that had squeezed very hard. A wooden chair had been pulled up close to him so that he could drape his foot over the edge of the seat without putting any weight on the recently bandaged ankle.

I made an attempt at conversation. "The chiang-shih messed you up that much? How did you manage to drag him around?"

Jerry's eyes flickered toward Sig, and Kevin cleared his throat. "It was the blond woman. Mostly."

Huh. Well, Sig had said that she thought about killing Jerry. From the look of things, she'd thought about it pretty hard.

"Choo had you wrapped up in a plastic tarp," Sig explained with a complete lack of expression. "When I first saw you, I thought you were dead."

I tried to be charitable. "Well, I expect I was leaking all over the place."

"Choo and I had a little talk too," Sig said grimly. "He might be leaving us after this is over."

Yeah, well, that was for later. I addressed Jerry again. "So... you're the guy who likes to shoot people who are trying to help him."

"I don't like anything about any of this." Jerry scowled. "When I saw you were like the things that are trying to kill us, I decided to chain you up and ask you some questions with a shotgun pointed at your face." It was a statement of fact, not an apology or a confession. I liked him better for that.

"It's not that simple. You could have killed me. The command signals to regenerate come from up here." I tapped the side of my head. "If you destroy a large enough part of my brain, I die."

"I'll keep that in mind," he assured me, and after a second he added, "No pun intended."

I smiled. It was a brief and tight and kind of cold smile. "You do that."

Sarah came back into the room with a tray full of mugs of hot coffee. "That's enough tension. We're intelligent people, and we have a mutual enemy. Let's act like it."

"How do I know you won't try to kill us as soon as I tell you what you want to know?" Jerry responded. "You say you want to help us. Why?"

"Because it's the right thing to do," Sig said. "We're not monsters. We're just humans with bells and whistles, Mr. Kichida."

That wasn't going to fly, coming from the woman who had kicked his ass. Jerry gave an impatient eye-twitch and straightened the way people do when they instinctively want to make themselves seem taller because they feel threatened. Sig noticed too and decided to shut her mouth for a while.

Sarah pointed a finger at Sig. "She's here because two innocent people in Tatum were killed by traps set for your son. The sheriff in Tatum is a friend of hers."

"My son didn't have anything to do with that," Jerry stated grimly.

"Not by choice. But they followed a trail and here you are." Sarah pointed a finger at me. "He's here because he's in love with her and he owes me a favor. And I'm here because I'm like your son. And I like your son. So, why don't you tell us who's trying to kill Kevin?"

Jerry didn't answer that. Instead, he addressed me. "Where did you get your training?"

"My family hunts monsters," I said. "That's sort of how I became one. I'll hunt the person who's trying to kill you too, if you'll stop acting bashful and point me in the right direction."

Again, Jerry ignored the prompt and indicated Kevin with a jerk of his chin instead. "I don't want any of this for him. Werewolves. Vampires. Witches." He looked at Sig. "Whatevers."

"Then help us find whoever's trying to kill you," I said. "And work it out from there. The person who's forcing you to deal with our world isn't going to stop. We take him out, and all you have to worry about is whether your son wants to become Sarah's apprentice or not. She won't force him."

Sig sighed with exasperation.

"Let's get it all out," I said stubbornly. "This guy's going to be a live grenade if we don't."

Jerry looked at me, and something like understanding passed between us. At least we spoke the same language. But he focused on the part he didn't like. "Apprentice?"

"I want to learn how to control what I do. I can't keep drugging myself," Kevin interjected miserably. "Those pills you have me taking turn me into a zombie."

"Zombies aren't just an expression anymore," Jerry pointed out. "You could become one for real if you keep messing with this world."

"Dad, this world is messing with me!" Kevin argued.

"The things you can see weren't meant to be seen," Jerry said softly.

"The things you don't want me to see are looking for me now!" Kevin replied. "People are dying because of me! Maybe I can see the things I see because I'm supposed to do something about them!"

"So, you want to become like your grandfather?" Jerry's voice had gotten even quieter.

Okay, maybe turning this into a family counseling session before I got a name had been a mistake after all. I carefully didn't look at Sig.

"Mom taught us how to make wards to keep people from finding us with magic." Kevin pulled up his shirt sleeve and revealed a swirl of sigils and glyphs tattooed on his shoulder. "Was she like my grandfather?"

Jerry's voice became steel. "Your mother was a brave person who loved you and learned what she had to learn to protect you. You will honor her memory."

"I want to. I want to be brave and learn what I have to learn to protect the people I love too," Kevin countered. "What could honor her more than that?"

I've never had a parent around or been one, but I think every father or mother must have a moment where his or her child turns the values they were taught around and takes them in a direction the parent never wanted or anticipated. Jerry looked like he'd been punched in the stomach.

"I don't know what I want to do when this is all over." Kevin's expression was scared but stubborn. "But I want it to be over. I can see your aura, Dad. You're not being strong right now. You're scared."

To his credit, Jerry didn't deny it. "You should be scared too. Everybody dies, Kevin. I'm worried about your soul."

"I can see most of these people too. They aren't evil, Dad," Kevin insisted. "They could just have that vampire who tried to get inside my head look inside yours. They could just threaten me to make you talk, or try to torture you. But they're not doing that."

Jerry gave his son a sour don't-give-them-ideas kind of look, but he saw the truth in what his kid was saying. Whatever else Jerry Kichida was, he didn't seem like the kind of person who denied things when the truth was evident. He released a sigh so deep that it sounded like he'd been punctured. When he started talking again, it was to the whole room. "All right. I'll tell you about my wife and her father. Maybe I'll get lucky and you really will all kill each other."

"That's not the only reason." Sarah was regarding Jerry intently.

"My wife got help from...magical beings...when she needed it to deal with her father," he admitted reluctantly. "A fox woman saved her life once."

"That sounds like a hell of a story," I observed.

It was.

~18~

YUNA'S STORY

My wife grew up in a house of magic, but it wasn't like a kid's movie," Jerry said. "Her father was some kind of Japanese sorcerer, and Yuna thought roses grew wherever he walked. He wasn't around much, but he wasn't cruel to begin with, or if he was she didn't know it. He was some kind of priest..."

"What kind of priest?" I interrupted.

He understood why I was asking. "Yuna would never be specific. He wasn't *any* kind of priest by the time she was grown anyhow, and she didn't want me trying to track him down. Whatever you call him, he was into some weird stuff. They lived in a house on the side of Mount Fuji, near a shrine that he was keeping up, and their place didn't look like much. That humble abode exterior was all a sham though. The inside of the house was a lot bigger than the outside, and it was full of all kinds of treasures and servants."

"Did your wife ever use the word *onmyouji*?" Sarah asked.

Jerry didn't blink. I'm not sure he'd blinked the entire

time he was there, though that's supposed to be impossible. "Yes."[2]

Sarah nodded and gestured for him to continue.

"The house was full of those sliding paper doors." Jerry paralleled his hands and made a sliding gesture. "But if you went in them in a different order, they'd open up to different rooms. Like that toy that had different colored squares on it. You could turn the rows around to make different color combinations...."

"A Rubik's Cube, Dad." Kevin sounded a little impatient, and it made me like Jerry more. If Kevin felt free to take that kind of attitude, maybe Jerry wasn't a martinet.

"The house was like a Rubik's Cube, then. Except instead of different colors, you could make different...spaces. It was full of servants too. Faceless servants." Jerry's expression became full of distaste. "I don't mean faceless like no one noticed them, either. They really had no faces."

"Noppera-bō," Sarah said under her breath. Jerry paused and looked at her. She explained. "This man was binding a kind of ghost and making them serve him."

"Was that evil?" Kevin asked.

"Yes," Sig said.

Sarah looked troubled. "Some farmers put baby calves in a confined space so that they can barely move—the farmers don't want them developing tough muscle. These beings spend their

---

2. Editorial note here: Onmyouji are diviners and summoners and are human, which means there have been good ones and bad ones. I just want to make it clear that they are not inherently evil. I don't really think anything or anyone is inherently evil with the possible exception of Auto-Tune, entertainment news, and books that translate Shakespeare into modern English.

entire lives alone in darkness, unable to move. Then they're slaughtered. We call that veal. Is the farmer evil?"

"No," Jerry said.

"People disagree," Sarah said tersely. "Personally, I think the man does an unspeakably cruel thing, but he doesn't think of himself as an evil man, and some people agree with him. He's not breaking any laws."

"Maybe we should avoid talking about political hot topics," I suggested. "At least while there's a powerful cunning man trying to kill us."

Sarah's lips quirked. "It wasn't a very good metaphor anyhow. Noppera-bō aren't helpless calves, Kevin. Wrong or not, what your grandfather was doing was dangerous and arrogant."

Jerry decided the interruption was over. "My wife grew up like a princess. These faceless servants made her meals for her, prepared her baths, brought her clothes. But she felt useless. Her father wanted a son, and when that didn't happen he made it clear that Yuna would give him grandsons."

"So Yuna didn't have any brothers or sisters?" I asked.

Jerry shook his head. "No. Her only friend when she was a child was the being who looked after her."

"What do you mean by *being*?" Sig asked.

Jerry regarded her expressionlessly. "I mean, a woman who could turn into a fox with four tails."

Sig and Sarah and I all exchanged glances. Holy shit. The onmyouji had enslaved a kitsune, a kind of were-fox, except that kitsune aren't humans who turn into foxes...they are magical foxlike beings who can make themselves look human.

"When did things go bad?" I asked.

Jerry almost looked at me approvingly then. "When Yuna's mother couldn't have any more children. Her father got more and more angry and started treating Yuna's mother like there was something wrong with her. Yuna had started going to school by then. They were a real family, you understand? They were a part of the world."

"Why didn't you or Mom ever tell me any of this, Dad?" Kevin looked like he was working up a good case of hurt outrage.

"Just listen," Jerry said gravely. "Yuna's mother began acting strange. She told Yuna that they might take a trip very soon, but that Yuna shouldn't tell anyone. It was a surprise. And then one day, Yuna's mother disappeared. Her father told Yuna that her mother had run off with another man. He was so angry, he barely seemed like the same person. He told Yuna that she couldn't go into any parts of the house where the mother used to spend time. Then he did his magic with sliding doors and somehow made that part of the house disappear."

Son of a bitch. Hocus-pocus, abracadabra, childhood begone!

"Yuna didn't know what to think. Her father was so scary that Yuna was afraid to ask him questions. But a lot of her favorite clothes were missing."

Sig got it immediately. "The mother had packed Yuna's bags. She planned to take Yuna along."

"Yes." Jerry's face was grim. "The father had never been around much, but he began leaving the house more and more and acting like a stranger when he was there. Then one day, when a faceless servant was pouring Yuna her tea, Yuna saw a scar on the faceless servant's index finger. A scar that Yuna recognized."

He hadn't said anything about a scar before, but this wasn't a story to Jerry. This wasn't something to tell artfully or lace with foreshadowing and irony. Jerry's voice became clogged with some deep emotion. "It was her mother's hand. Yuna's mother was dead and had been turned into a faceless servant."

"Goddess," Sarah breathed.

"My wife had a breakdown," Jerry said simply. "She tried to leave, but some of the faceless servants dragged Yuna through rooms that she had never seen before. After they left her, Yuna tried to get out, but the house was like a maze. She tried to rip through the paper in the walls, but something always stopped her."

"It was her father's place of power," Sarah said ruefully.

"Yuna tried to find her way out, but no matter how many different combinations she tried, the sliding doors always led her back to where she started." Jerry paused as if he was hearing what he was saying out loud for the first time and realizing how crazy it sounded.

I gave him a little prod. "And then the father came home?"

Jerry looked down at his hands. "Yes. He didn't deny killing Yuna's mother. He told Yuna that her mother had become involved with another man and that there were things going on that Yuna didn't understand but that someday she would. She yelled and cried, but he just left her there again."

"How did Mom escape?" Kevin's whole body was tense. He looked miserable.

"It was the fox woman." Jerry looked a lot like his son. "One night during one of her father's absences, Yuna woke up and saw the fox sitting on the floor, staring at her. It spoke inside her head somehow and told Yuna to be quiet and follow her. When it walked, doors slid open for it. It didn't lead Yuna back out of the house, though. It led her to a room with nothing but a Japanese sword on a pedestal."

"This sounds like a fairy tale." Kevin wasn't complaining so much as shaken. "Why wouldn't this fox woman just stay in human form?"

"Maybe staying in its true form helped it resist whatever hold the onmyouji had on her," I offered.

Jerry looked at me, but only because his eyes didn't have anywhere in particular to go. "My wife wanted to use the sword to kill herself, but when she drew it, the sword spoke to her. It told my wife that it held the spirits of Yuna's ancestors."

Kevin made a sound that was at least half admiration, and Jerry gave him a warning glance. "It sounds wrong to me, but I was born and raised in Pittsburgh. Native Japanese people have a different attitude about spirits than we do, especially family spirits."

Sig looked at me. "You lived there for a few years. What do you think? Was this sword holding echoes or living souls?"

I shrugged. "Japan has more than one belief system, and I'm a gaijin. Stories about objects holding kami are everywhere, and as far as I can tell, the attitude toward those kinds of spirits generally seems to be that they aren't trapped...that our ancestors are everywhere in everything all the time anyway."

"Like atoms," Kevin said. "Except holy."

"Or unholy," Sig commented darkly.

I shrugged again. "Either way, spirits who had sacrificed themselves for their family would be royally pissed off at someone who wanted to sacrifice his family for himself."

"I don't think the sword was evil. Yuna's father was keeping it hidden because his ancestors had rejected him," Jerry said reluctantly. Then he nodded at me. "Like the werewolf said, they were pissed. The spirits told my wife that they'd cursed her father so that he couldn't have any more children and she was in danger because of it."

I leaned forward. "Wait a minute. This is important. Did his ancestors do this because the guy had killed his children before? Has he been doing this for a while?"

Jerry nodded his head. "Yes. Yuna's father had been having children with different women and killing them so that he could steal their youth, but I don't know for how long. That's why his ancestors made him sterile. The curse caught him completely off guard too. Yuna was his last child. If he killed her, he wouldn't be able to sacrifice another heir."

"That doesn't make sense," I argued. "He wouldn't be trying to kill Kevin if all this was true. He'd be trying to take him prisoner and start a new breeding farm."

"Kevin?" Sarah said abruptly. The blood had completely drained from Kevin's face.

"Kevin?" Jerry's tone was sharper.

"I'm a sperm donor," Kevin whispered.

Nobody said anything. The statement had come out of nowhere, and it was so unlikely and so unexpected that it was hard to take in.

"Kevin?" This time Jerry's tone was a warning.

"My friend Max talked me into it. We started last year," Kevin said miserably. "I've been putting aside money to go to Vegas. I figured I could use my... gift... there, but I needed a stake, and there wasn't any place around that would pay for my blood..."

"Just stop," Jerry commanded. He was breathing rapidly through his nose though I'm not sure anyone else could hear it. He did that for maybe forty seconds before saying, flatly, to his son, "You've disappointed me on so many levels I don't know where to start."

"That's how the onmyouji found out about you!" Sarah exclaimed, then put a hand over her mouth.

"What are you talking about?" Jerry's voice became dangerously tight.

"Some of the onmyouji's divination spells would have been

geared to tracking his own bloodline," Sarah said reluctantly. "Like calls to like. Yuna warded you and Kevin, but if some woman used Kevin's sperm to grow an unwarded baby with the onmyouji's DNA..."

"Can we just stop?!" Kevin's face had gone dark with rushing blood. His father was looking at him as if seeing him through a sniper scope.

I wanted to say that there was nothing morally wrong with sperm donors, or mention that Kevin was nineteen, even if he seemed to be an introspective and decent and smart nineteen. But it was Kichida family business, so what I said instead was: "So, one of the grandfather's divination spells finally gets a hit, and he finds some pregnant American woman with his DNA growing inside her and no father. He would have wanted the father, right?"

"Yes," Sarah said.

"So, the grandfather does a little more digging and he finds out the American woman got her sperm from a clinic," I reasoned. "Kevin being a sperm donor would have been like a dream come true for this guy. A whole bumper crop of future breeding stock that he could keep in a freezer."

"John..." Sarah started, but I kept going.

"Just listen for a minute," I insisted. "This whole kill-Kevin thing only makes sense if those sperm donations have been bought up or stolen. The onmyouji has to wait for his descendants to be young adults before he can sacrifice them, right? And this guy has been getting older for at least twenty years now and it's probably been driving him crazy. Or crazier. He wants to kill Kevin so he'll live long enough to harvest the next crop of his DNA."

"Excuse me!" Sig spoke the polite phrase in a rude way that kind of negated the effect. "Could we please finish the story before one of the Kichidas has a heart attack? Your wife was holding her family sword, Jerry."

It took a little more coaxing, but Jerry eventually agreed that he and his son needed to talk in private later and got back to his narrative, though he was clearly distracted. "My wife didn't know how to use the sword, but when she held it, it...she said it wasn't like it possessed her. She said she was still her, but the sword moved through her like electricity. She said that doors opened for it, and the sword guided her through the halls of that house, cutting down paper lanterns and setting fires behind them. Some of the faceless servants tried to stop her, but the sword cut them down. When my wife finally found herself outside on the mountain, her family home was burning behind her. The sword wanted to track down and kill Yuna's father, but Yuna dropped the sword and ran away."

She dropped the sword? I guess she was a freaked-out and traumatized teenager, but that still made me stifle a groan.

"But how did she get to Okinawa?" Kevin protested, then clearly regretted it when his father returned his attention back to Kevin with a look that made him flinch.

"It doesn't matter," Jerry said curtly. "The Army sent me there because I looked and spoke Japanese and some idiot in Military Intelligence thought I could actually pass for a native. And then I agreed to take some friends to a hospitality house and interpret for them, and I met your mother there. She was using some of the things she'd learned in her father's house to keep accounts and tell fortunes and practice feng shui."

"So, she wasn't a..." Kevin faltered.

"No!" Jerry's face darkened. "I wanted to kill some time there because I wasn't going to..."

Jerry looked at his son and halted. I wondered if he was

telling the truth, but I can't say I really cared one way or the other. "We get it," I said.

Jerry gritted his teeth. "Yuna told my fortune. She said I was going to come back to see her again. And she was right. I knew it the second I met her. And I'd never even dated a Japanese-American girl before, much less a native Japanese one. My parents and I used to fight about that. But I knew."

"There's still something you haven't told us, Mr. Kichida," Sig noted. "What is this onmyouji's name?"

"I don't know," Jerry admitted.

I considered killing him despite my promise to Sarah.

"My wife refused to tell me," he elaborated. "She was afraid that I would do something stupid. She wouldn't even tell me her real name. I loved my wife, and she loved me, but she would have divorced me or killed herself before she told me that. She said that me not knowing his name helped her hide us from him."

Jerry looked down at his hands. They had become fists, very tight fists. "I never knew my own wife's real name."

"There's something else you haven't told us," I said. "How did you know this onmyouji was after you after all this time? Why did he focus on you at all?"

"When I was a sniper, I interacted with men who were in Military Intelligence a lot," Jerry said. "A week ago an old acquaintance told me that someone was making unofficial inquiries about me."

"That's when you set up your trap and told Kevin to go hide or hang out in public places?" Sig asked.

"No," Jerry said. "That's when I asked my friend to find out who was asking questions."

"And what did he find out?" I asked.

"I don't know," Jerry said bitterly. "Two days ago, a man from the NSA contacted me. My friend had gone missing, and they were questioning all of the people that he had recently been in touch with. Even then, I didn't assume it was Yuna's father. I thought he was probably dead by now. I don't know if you know much about how the spy world works, but my friend could have made up that story about someone asking about me because he wanted to manipulate me into killing someone for him off the books. Or he wanted me to think I owed him a favor. And if he was doing something complicated or shady, it could have backfired."

I actually understood that completely. "But you told Kevin to take some precautions, and then you set up a trap anyway."

"There are a lot of people who might want to kill me if they got into secure military files," Jerry explained. "Terrorists. A cartel family. A Bosnian weapons dealer. It was possible that I was a target, but even then, I didn't really think Kevin was. Not until that whatever it was showed up. That's when I knew Yuna's father was still alive."

"And that's when you sent that message telling Kevin to go hide at a prearranged location," I finished.

Jerry wasn't inclined to say anything about the prearranged hiding place. "Yes."

Sig addressed the table at large. "So does anybody have any ideas on how to find this grandfather?"

"We can check out burned-down priest's houses on Mount Fuji," I offered. "Or have Parth do it for us. There can't be that many of them. We can look into who's been acquiring Kevin's sperm too."

"That's fine, but Kevin is staying with me until this is done," Sarah said, then looked at me a little wryly. "And at least a few of you ought to stay with me and help guard him."

"Sounds good, but we can't just play defense, Sarah," I said. "If the onmyouji can't find Kevin, sooner or later he's going to try to make Kevin come to him. It's only a matter of time before he starts kidnapping or killing Kevin's family or friends to draw him out."

"My only other family is a brother who's in the Navy," Jerry said. "He's on a battleship."

Surrounded by iron, miles and miles of salt water, and lots of witnesses. That wasn't too bad, actually.

"I have a few friends." Kevin made this sound like a confession. "I guess I could tell them my grandfather is yakuza and some bad people might come around looking for me. They'd kind of get into that."

"You should do whatever you can do," I said. "But we still need to find this onmyouji and shut him down fast."

Sarah gave a distinctly unhappy sigh. "I have an idea."

∽19∾

SECTS AND THE CITY

Apparently, the most powerful cunning woman in Tatum was a seamstress. The store that Alyssa Ballard ran, Darn Good Clothes, was your basic consignment business, but it specialized in altering and custom-fitting specific garments to specific people on-site. The thought made me a little tense. A cunning woman who was gifted with a needle and thread would be able to stitch all kinds of subtle magical knots, charms, and designs into a garment. But I contented myself with this observation: "This place is pretty huge for a small-town consignment shop."

It was too. The consignment shop looked like it had been a grocery store once, anchoring down a strip mall that was nestled right between the town proper and an interstate exit. The location also contained a pet store, a nail salon, a used-book store, an antique shop, a health food store, and some kind of café. I couldn't really gauge how successful the strip mall was based on customer traffic—we were in that time after Christmas and before spring when most businesses go into a kind of economic coma, and it was a Monday morning to boot, an hour before the stores opened. But the place didn't have that grimy pallor that strip malls acquire after they've been on fiscal life support for too long, and the parking lot was trash-free.

"Alyssa married into money," Sarah informed me tartly. She had just parked her car in the strip mall's lot and we were taking our time getting out of it. "And her husband died soon after." Something about her attitude suggested that the two events weren't unrelated.

"So, it's not just policy or general principle. You really don't like her." Molly was sitting in the shotgun seat. I was in the back. Sarah wanted Molly along because she shone like a small star for people who can see auras, and cunning folk would see her and both trust her and not want to have anything to do with her. People who shine like Molly are holy people, and saints or prophets or other divinely inspired types are nothing but trouble. They are the kind of people who generally live lives of suffering in the middle of god-awful events and don't care anything about social ladders or material wealth or how they're supposed to act in order to make people comfortable, and they walk a thin line between madness and inspiration.

Also, magic has a harder time affecting them.

"If I liked Alyssa, I wouldn't be taking you to her." Sarah's expression was flinty. "She's the reason I don't belong to a coven."

I grimaced, and Sarah spotted it in her rear view mirror. Even if she couldn't see me with her second sight, Sarah's physical eyes didn't miss much. "What is it, John?"

"I can't figure out if I wish we had more people here or if I wish I were doing this alone," I admitted. "Working with other people is a pain in the ass, but it's got advantages too."

"Making relationships work isn't easy, no matter who you are." Sarah's tone became a little wry. "There's a reason I'm in my forties and don't live with anyone."

"Because you turn all of your lovers into small animals and make them pets as soon as they get annoying?" I guessed.

She smiled. "No. I'm just not good at it."

We got out of the car. There seemed to be an unusually high number of employees present for so early in the morning. Such places are usually a mix of small-business owners opening up early because they live in their shops (sometimes literally), and part-time employees dragging their asses in just a little after the last minute because they're not getting paid enough to do otherwise. Here, though, all of the stores showed signs of life.

When I pointed that out, Sarah responded, "Everyone who works in this shopping center belongs to Alyssa's coven."

I blinked. "Everyone?"

"She calls it enlightened socialism," Sarah said dryly.

"What do you call it?" Molly wondered.

"Micromanaging. Bullying. Petty tyranny." Sarah smiled tightly. "Take your pick. She wasn't gentle about getting the nonbelievers to take their businesses elsewhere to make room for her followers."

A young woman was already setting up clothing racks on the walkway outside the store.

She had flat long brown hair, a pale, oval face, wide hips, and a body that somehow gave an impression of solid strength without being noticeably big-boned or toned. Her designer jeans, pale blue sweater, and pink scarf didn't really go with her unstyled hair or lack of makeup, but I guess it was good advertising for the store. She smelled like homemade soap and pomegranate.

"Brazil," Sarah greeted. I wondered what the story behind that name was. The girl didn't look remotely South American.

Brazil didn't say anything. She just stared at me while surprise turned to alarm and then to a slow-building hostility. Her second sight wasn't registering me, and Brazil knew what that meant. She thought I was a knight. If Molly's presence was a carrot, I was Sarah's stick. Molly was the velvet glove. I was the iron fist. Molly was... Well, you get the idea.

"It's all right, Brazil," Molly said gently. "You don't have to know what to do with us. Just take us to someone who will."

The cunning woman's face cleared. "Wait here."

"No," Sarah contradicted. "You can lead us in or you can follow us. I'm letting you decide which as a gesture of respect."

"That's a pretty empty gesture," Brazil said sharply. "You brought a knight here!"

"No." Sarah didn't elaborate.

"I'm not taking you inside," Brazil said defiantly.

"All right." Sarah smiled a little sadly, and Molly and I followed her into the store. If the property was warded against enemies, none of us cared.

Brazil came in after us, yelling, "Alyssa! Someone's coming!" But the store was mostly filled with long rolling clothes racks, and anyone over five feet tall was immediately noticeable, so Alyssa had already seen us by that point. She was about thirty feet from the entrance, a stout woman with broad hips, broad shoulders, and an extremely large head that was somewhat moderated by long blond hair that covered the sides of her face. She wore a long, shapeless mauve dress with elaborate lace trim, and if there weren't runes and sigils woven into that garment, I'd eat it. Alyssa also wore some seriously high heels; she was probably five six in bare feet and at least six feet the rest of the time. At a guess, Alyssa liked to be taller than most of her employees.

There was a young man too, talking to Alyssa. He was dressed in a sort of retro sixties way with a white shirt and a black sleeveless vest over black jeans. He had a mop of brown

hair and a beard that was trimmed to be thin and angular—
it was the only thing about him that was. He was maybe six
foot three, beefy but going soft, with cheeks that were way too
ruddy for someone in his early twenties. He had a big ass, big
hands, and a big head, but I really hoped he wasn't related to
Alyssa in any way. When we got close, I could smell her sex on
his breath and smell his sex on her hands.

Alyssa didn't waste any time. She looked at Sarah with real
outrage. "You brought a *knight* here?"

I sighed and removed a pocketknife from my jacket pocket.
Alyssa gasped and backed away as I unfolded the blade. The guy
beside her assumed some kind of half-crouching stance with
his palms out—at a guess, he had wrestled in high school—but
he didn't step between us. You have to understand, these were
just ordinary people. I mean, yeah, Sarah didn't like them, and
they were cunning folk, and some of them could see things that
most people couldn't see, and they ran a coven, but they also
had a favorite television show and romantic issues and went to
concerts and worried about cholesterol and talked to people on
some kind of online social site and had favorite animals and so
on, and if they didn't have those specific habits or traits, they
had others like them. They were probably more used to seeing things like a man taking out a pocketknife and making a
bloody gash on the back of his hand than most people, but that
didn't mean they liked it. Or liked the way that the gash was
healing in front of their eyes either.

"I'm not a knight." I transferred the knife to my left hand,
then turned it to display the regenerating wound clearly. "See?"

"What are you, then?" Alyssa calmed down somewhat while
I was matter-of-factly getting a handkerchief out of my pocket.

"These are my allies," Sarah told Alyssa. "We have a mutual
enemy."

"You're not talking about me are you?" Alyssa asked archly. She was looking at Molly now.

"I hope not," Sarah said. "But I think you know the man we're after."

"It's a little late to ask for my protection now," Alyssa said coldly. "You had a chance to join us, and you spit in our face."

"Covens weren't meant to be run like fast food franchises." Sarah's lips were tighter than I'd ever seen them. "You have too many rules for the sake of having rules. Too many members and too many managers and too many penalties and too much territory."

Just for the record, I have no idea what they were talking about.

"Too much power, you mean." Alyssa smirked. "You can see the future in sifting flour, Sarah. You know the Pax is weakening. We're going to need power in the times to come."

"Your mouth says *we*," Sarah stated levelly. "But your actions say *I*."

Molly cleared her throat.

Alyssa smiled. "I don't think your *allies* want to listen to your babble any more than *we* do."

Sarah let it go. "The man we're looking for is Japanese. An onmyouji. I don't think he would have come into another's territory without going through the proper channels. He seems to be very careful about observing the rituals and proper forms while perverting everything they are supposed to protect."

Alyssa didn't respond one way or another, but the guy next to her obviously knew something. His poker face was a poker farce.

"The young girl who disappeared right after he came here? The accident on Main Street?" Sarah inquired. "You must have known these things were no accident. I don't know if he bribed you or threatened you or flattered you to stay out of it, but he came here."

"Go away, Sarah," Alyssa said.

"He's trying to kill my apprentice," Sarah informed her. It was the truth, but Sarah made it sound like Kevin had been her apprentice all along, before the onmyouji came to town, and I wasn't going to contradict her.

Something flickered behind Alyssa's face then. Behind us, Brazil gasped. Sarah continued, "He murdered his wife, imprisoned his daughter, and deals with unholy spirits, among other things. That's the man you're protecting, *priestess*."

Alyssa spat, "You made your bed. Go fuck yourself in it."

"If it was just me, I might," Sarah admitted. "But it's not."

Now it was Alyssa who turned red. "You stupid bitch! I've let you have your little bakery and play out your fantasies in Bonaparte, but we'll level curses on you that would bring down a small nation! We'll charm your zoning commissioner and hex your customers and enspell your health inspectors and send plagues and diseases down on your head and in your house! There'll be rats in your walls and maggots in your bread! By the time I'm done with you, you'll be lucky if you can hold down a job behind a fast food counter!"

By way of answer, Sarah held her right hand out as if she were going to squeeze Alyssa's breast, her brow furrowed. Then Sarah moved her hand up, then across, tracing the lace spirals across Alyssa's dress with a frown of intense concentration. "Interesting design work here. But you always get greedy. Some parts are straining to burst free."

Alyssa laughed. "You might as—"

The fingers of Sarah's outstretched palm suddenly tightened, and she pulled her hand back as if yanking something. The end of a white thread came loose from Alyssa's dress and flew toward Sarah's fingers, and Sarah snatched it out of the air. Alyssa shrieked a startled shriek. Sarah continued to draw her hand back, and the white threadwork on Alyssa's dress began to writhe like a mass of slender white snakes. Sigils and symbols etched in white briefly stood out, straining outward from the fabric, only to unravel.

The young beefy guy lunged forward then, but he didn't lunge far. He had palmed something while Sarah and Alyssa were talking, and he was trying to bring his hand up front and center while saying something in Greek, but I stepped forward and shot a stiff, fast left into his face. I snapped my wrist into a straight punch at the end and tilted my body weight into it. He bit off a word and the tip of his tongue at the same time, went down, and stayed down while some kind of black powder trickled out of his relaxed fingers. The spurt of blood left a stain on his lips.

When I looked back, Brazil hadn't moved, staring with her mouth open as Alyssa was slowly encircled by hundreds of parallel lines of white thread rustling across her body, binding her arms to her sides. Sarah held the loose thread in her hand up directly in front of Alyssa's face and said, softly, "Want some fries with that?"

"Brazil," Alyssa croaked. "Get help."

"Don't move," Sarah countered, and Brazil didn't. "We don't have time for this. Molly?"

Molly stepped forward and addressed Alyssa earnestly. "Good things can still come from this, Alyssa. It's not too late for you and Sarah to take a step toward healing this rift between you."

Alyssa didn't call Molly a liar, so Molly's sincerity and good intent really must have been manifest. Instead, she just snarled, "You wouldn't torture me, and you won't let them do it, either. Get out of my store."

Molly sighed and addressed Sarah and me. "She's been putting something in Brazil's tea to keep her from becoming pregnant. Brazil is too useful to lose to some screaming little shitpot right now. Alyssa's thoughts, not mine."

Brazil gasped. Alyssa's eyes were already shocked and uneasy, but they managed to widen further. "That's not true!"

"She's taking several dabblers with no real talent into the fold because they have money," Molly continued.

"Alyssa always does that," Sarah said dismissively. "What else?"

"This is utter garbage!" Alyssa protested. "I'm warded! No one can read me!"

Molly furrowed her brow. "Alyssa's encouraging someone named Mariah to divorce someone named Carlos because she thinks he's a pain in the ass, and hasn't decided whether or not to get rid of him yet."

"This is a trick!" Alyssa looked at Brazil wildly. "Brazil, don't listen to them!"

The expression on Molly's face grew increasingly distasteful as she went on. "She sent someone named Cassidy to join a coven in Manhattan because she wants Cassidy to seduce the leader and convince her to join up with them."

Alyssa's face went from red to bone white and Brazil whispered, "How could she know that?" Brazil still seemed more hurt and scared than angry, but there was something sullen and defiant creeping around the very edge of her voice. She hadn't forgotten Molly's assertion that Alyssa was drugging Brazil's tea to keep her non-fertile.

"I don't want to know all of this," Sarah commented. "Can't you narrow your focus?"

"Alyssa," I commanded. "Try not to think about the onmyouji. Try *not* to put it in the forefront of your mind."

"This is insane!" Alyssa shouted.

"There we go," Molly said. "She's scared of him, but she's greedy too. The onmyouji gave her something from a magical animal. Something golden...a feather...wait...now something she's afraid I'll find out just popped into her head.... Oh, that's dark..."

"STOP IT!" Alyssa shrieked. "STOP IT! He's in New York City!"

"You'll have to tell us more than that," I insisted.

"He's involved in the Crucible," Alyssa hissed.

Somehow, I didn't think she meant a production of an Arthur Miller play.

"The Crucible," Sarah repeated.

"A place where monsters who are tired of repressing their true selves can fight each other," Alyssa gritted out. "There's wagering."

"You're talking about some kind of supernatural cage fights," Sarah ventured.

"Yes," Alyssa muttered. "A place for predators who are tired of hiding what they are."

"How do we find this place?" I asked.

Alyssa looked at me with malice. "If you're not human, go hang out in the warehouse districts. Their recruiters will find you."

"Thank you," I said. "Now Brazil is going to bring us the golden feather the onmyouji gave you."

For a moment, the world froze.

"What?!?" Alyssa demanded.

"John," Sarah warned, but I wasn't her dog, and the look I gave her said as much.

"The onmyouji touched it," I explained. "I can use it to get his scent. More importantly, the moment we walk out the door, Alyssa here is going to start thinking about contacting the onmyouji and warning him about us. She'll think she can cover her ass with the onmyouji and get some risk-free revenge for the way you just embarrassed her."

"And how is a feather going to prevent her?" Sarah's voice was edged and curious at the same time.

"Because Alyssa will never be able to tell him she sent us on our way and didn't say anything, not if we have the feather," I said. "He'll never believe she gave it to us willingly. He'll want to know how we knew about it, why she gave it to us, what else she told us while we had leverage over her. He'll know she told us how to find him. And no matter what she says, he'll kill her because she's proven to be a weak link and a loose end."

"And what if he kills you and finds the feather himself?" Alyssa demanded, forgetting that she hadn't admitted to owning the feather yet.

I smiled, but not as if I was amused. "Now you're getting it."

It took a few more words and a threat that wasn't a bluff, but Brazil finally took me to fetch the feather—a siren's feather, by the way—without Alyssa's permission. Brazil apparently knew a lot of Alyssa's secrets and precautions, and from the look on Brazil's face, that wasn't good news for Alyssa. We left the store and made our way back to Sarah's car, pointedly not hurrying. "You did good, Molly," I told her.

Molly looked troubled. "I don't think I did."

The private information that Molly had been announcing out loud in the store had come from me. As soon as Sarah had told us her intent, I'd asked Parth to see if he could hack into Alyssa's e-mails while I spent the evening locating her private residence. With my enhanced hearing and ability to blow past most wards and charms, crouching in Alyssa's backyard and listening in on her side of several phone conversations had been easy.

"What's wrong?" I asked.

"I made her think that I was getting that information from a higher power," Molly said. "And I wasn't."

"Deception is a part of war," I insisted. "Appear weak when you're strong, strong when you're weak. Act like you know what you don't know and act like you don't know what you do. That's basic Sun Tzu stuff."

Molly's troubled expression didn't ease. If anything, it became more intense. "I don't like pretending I'm something I'm not. I spent most of my life doing that because I didn't want to hurt my parents or the people in my church. I wound up marrying a man I liked, but I couldn't make myself love him the way he needed me to, the way I needed to, and I hurt him and my parents and a woman I did love worse than I ever would have if I'd just been honest."

Molly had once told me that she was a lesbian and never mentioned it since. We reached Sarah's car and Sarah opened the passenger's door, but Molly didn't get in. I was getting a little alarmed. "None of that stuff you said was a lie. Alyssa is lying and manipulating and using people."

"And now we are." Molly sighed heavily. "What if God does want to speak through me now? I've turned the idea of being inspired into a scam."

My throat was suddenly dry. I'd still lie my ass off to an enemy in a heartbeat, but Molly wasn't me, and the idea that I'd somehow gotten Molly to betray her truest self...it hit me hard. "Molly, I'm sorry."

Molly took my arm. "It's alright. It's okay not to be perfect. This has clarified some things for me."

"I don't mean to slight the importance of this conversation, but could we have it in the car?" Sarah asked. She had been deep in her own thoughts since leaving the store.

"No," Molly said, and turned around and began to walk away. "I'll walk back to the bakery."

"Molly, that's fifty miles!" I called after her.

"It's something I have to do." Molly didn't say it like she was happy about it. "It'll give me time to think. It's okay, John. Nothing is going to hurt me."

Somehow, I believed her. But I stood there staring after her anyhow.

"Let her go," Sarah advised.

"Everything I did, I did so we wouldn't have to hurt Alyssa," I protested. "The smart play would have been to kill everyone in that store." I don't know who I was arguing with: Molly, maybe, or God, or myself. Not Sarah, at any rate.

Sarah smiled wanly. "People like your friend have their own path, and it's never a good idea to stand in their way."

I didn't try to argue with that.

"Do you really think that feather will keep Alyssa from betraying us?" Sarah asked. "She's smart and cunning, but she's not wise."

"I think it will give her pause for at least a day. And maybe by that time, Parth will have broken into her system and can contact her and let her know that he's downloaded her e-mail history," I said. "And if that holds her a little longer, Cahill can come by in another day or two to inspect her store for safety violations and show her his fangs. It's the best I can do."

"But not the worst," Sarah reflected, and she patted my arm kind of the way Sig does. "That does count for something."

We passed Molly as we drove out of that place. I don't think she noticed us. She was staring straight ahead but seeing something only she could see.

∽20∽

DECISIONS, DERISION, DIVISIONS

That burnt-down priest's house on Mount Fuji got us some-where. Parth says the onmyouji's name is Akihiko Watanabe. Or at least, that's one of his names," Choo informed us. He was in the bakery's cellar, mixing and thickening homemade dyes that Sarah had made from various herbs and berries into paints—spell ingredients turned into pigments. Sarah had decided that the best way to keep Kevin safe was to stay on the move, and she was helping Choo turn his van into a warded fortress on wheels. "Maybe he pretended to be some kind of Shinto priest for a while, but he got kicked out of the order. Then he did feng shui and fortune-telling for rich people, but the government came after him. They thought he was using information from his sessions to blackmail people. Then he did some stuff for the yakuza, but he pissed somebody off there too. He disappeared about ten years ago, and most people think he's dead."

"That would all fit what we know about him," Sarah mused. "Sociopaths and narcissists tend to leave a trail of burnt bridges behind them wherever they go."

Sarah and Sig and I were all standing around, half leaning against various tables or walls. Jerry had finally fallen asleep after three days standing, and I'm still not sure Sarah didn't find some way to slip him something despite Jerry's refusal to eat anything but food he randomly selected from her counter.

"I checked into that sperm clinic," Sig said. "Last month, it had a serious fire and lost its supply of...um...."

"Frozen pops?" I suggested, and got the same dour glance from three different people.

"Akihiko probably broke in, stole Kevin's donations, and set the place on fire to cover his tracks," Sarah speculated.

"Probably," Sig said glumly. "Do we have a picture of the onmyouji yet?"

"No," Choo said.

"Well, we've got a concrete lead as to his whereabouts." I was munching on a slice from a vegetarian pizza that was bigger than a manhole lid and smaller than a tablecloth. "Akihiko is apparently running some kind of underground fighting tournament for supernatural beings in New York City."

From Sig and Choo's blank expressions, I might as well have said that Akihiko had begun marketing edible fire hydrants.

"Why?" Sig asked.

"It's not as crazy as it sounds," I said. "A lot of supernatural beings stay hidden by repressing seriously predatory instincts. A venue that allows them to let off some steam might draw a lot of them out of hiding."

"I understand that," Sig said a little impatiently. "But what does Akihiko get out of it?"

"We've been wondering how he's been summoning all of these different exotic creatures," I pointed out.

Sig's troubled expression cleared. "You think he's using this tournament to recruit supernatural muscle from a lot of different cultures?"

"Not just that," Sarah interjected. She held up the feather we'd taken from Alyssa. "I think those scales you found on the chiang-shih were given to him by the onmyouji as a form of payment. Akihiko paid Alyssa off too. He got this feather from a siren, and it would be useful for all kinds of powerful love charms."

"So, we...Wait, sirens have feathers?" Sig asked. She was probably thinking of all those weird mermaid tangents that had sprung out and deviated from the original siren stories.

"Just the bottom half," I assured her.

"Think of all the monster bits and pieces Akihiko must be collecting just from cleaning up after the fights," Sarah said. "Blood...scales...feathers...teeth and skin and glands and organs. Exotic, hard-to-get items. You could use that to cast a lot of spells or make a lot of charms and potions."

Choo whistled. "Is there gambling involved too?"

"Sarah's source said there is," I said.

"So, he gets money from that end of it," Choo speculated. "He makes contacts with the kind of monsters who like to kill. And he gets hard-to-find spell ingredients. That's slick."

"Let's cut to the part where you want to fight in this underground tournament," Sig said.

It was my turn to stare at somebody.

"We all know that's where you're going with this," she explained. "You do realize that I'm going to fight too, right?"

"Hold on," I protested. "I can't be mind-read or psychically spied on. I'm the logical person to go undercover."

"Sarah can provide me with wards against mind reading, and we're looking for information." Sig was making a point of speaking reasonably. "I can speak to ghosts."

"I'll need to focus. I'll be distracted if you're there." I knew that was the wrong tactic to take the moment I heard the words coming out of my mouth.

"Then I'll fight, and you can sit around waiting to find out if I'm coming back or not." Now Sig's tone was becoming a little grim. "It can't be that big a deal. That's what you want me to do, right?"

And then we were off.

Guess who won that argument?

Life is full of strange pivots and twists and weird compromises. Two years earlier, I would have stolen a car and made for New York City the moment I found out that the onmyouji was there. Every moment wasted was another moment where Aki-hiko might get fed up and kill or kidnap somebody close to the Kichidas, and I felt that urgency pressing on me. But now that I was part of a group, you know what I was doing eight hours after I got my first real lead?

I was making cupcakes.

Let me just say that again: I was making cupcakes.

Cupcakes.

I understand the individual steps that led to it. If Sig and I were going to both go undercover among creatures with enhanced senses, pretending not to know each other, we couldn't just take off; we had to eradicate all scent trails. We had to go to separate locations and get medieval on our skin and hair, get new clothes, acquire new and separate transportation, and avoid physical contact with each other or anything we'd touched. That was step one.

Step two was that Sarah wasn't ready to leave yet, and she still wanted either Sig or Cahill or me around in case Akihiko somehow located Kevin despite Sarah's attempts to ward him.

Again, I could see the sense in this. So, Sig and I had flipped a coin, and Sig had left to make preparations to leave first.

And Sarah wasn't used to leaving her bakery in the hands of her employees for an unidentified amount of time. She was almost as fretful about that as she was to any threats on her life. That's a factor. And I've had a lot of jobs in diners and bars and construction sites and fishing boats and lumber camps and farms over the decades, the kind of knock-around jobs that a nomad can get without inviting too much scrutiny. And while I've never worked in a bakery, I've made a lot of pizzas and biscuits and pancakes and pies and cakes in my day, and Sarah must have had some weird enhanced senses of her own, because it was as if she could smell it on me. So...

Put all that together and somehow I wound up helping Kevin make cupcakes. Another one of Sarah's employees, Courtney Stewart, was coming in and out of the kitchen to check on some cheesecakes, but she was barely talking to us. I had met Courtney once before, briefly, the first time I came to Sarah, but she had mostly been out of it at the time, and Sarah had woven some spells to help Courtney well, not forget, exactly, but remember those events fuzzily, as if her mind's eye was peering through cheesecloth. Courtney had said hello to me uneasily and then proceeded to pretend that I didn't exist, which was fine.

"Sarah says I should talk to you," Kevin said.

"About what?" My voice was neutral, not because I meant to be unfriendly so much as I was ready to start hunting the man who had been hunting us, and I was used to having more alone time to plan and analyze and turn things over and around in my head.

"She says you know what it's like to..." Kevin visibly struggled for words or the strength to say them. "Grow up being blamed for who you are naturally."

"That's true," I acknowledged. "But so does Molly, I think. And she's a much better person to talk to than I am."

I was breaking eggs into the sifted cake and pastry flour while Kevin measured out tablespoons of sugar and baking powder and salt. I say measured, but he wasn't bothering to check the instructions Sarah had laid out, or carefully leveling out the spoons. When I'd asked him if he knew what he was doing, he'd said no, but the cupcakes did. Seriously. At any rate, he didn't argue my point about Molly. "Molly's not back yet. And you might be dead soon."

I didn't take that personally. "Also true."

"This underground fight tournament thing…Are there really that many supernatural creatures around?" Kevin asked.

"Can't you see that for yourself?" I was genuinely curious, not trying to put him on the defensive. "You have the sight."

"I was homeschooled in a small town." There was a little bitterness in this observation. "I still saw some strange stuff, but Mom kept me away from places with a huge population. And now I'm in a small private school. So, I don't really know. Are there that many?"

"Well, you'd have to define *many*," I said. "There are a lot more of us than there were before the Fae created the Pax Arcana eight centuries ago, but the fertility rate is low for most supernaturals, and the mortality rate is high."

"Because of people like you?" It was an incautious question asked carefully.

"Partly. And a lot of noobs like you get killed by other supernatural beings because they don't understand the rules or the players," I added.

"Is there a handbook or something?" Kevin asked.

"I'm working on that," I said. We paused a while to add in the wet ingredients: the milk and softened butter and teaspoons of sweet-smelling vanilla. "Speaking of supernatural beings who don't know what they're doing, you realize there's a good chance that any kids you have will have the sight, right? And if you're just an anonymous sperm donor from some catalog, you won't be there to help them deal with it."

It was the first time I'd brought up the whole sperm donor thing, and Kevin didn't take it well. Anger spilled out of him like lava. "There might be babies out there right now who came from me, being raised by my own grandfather so that he can kill them! I don't need you to tell me I fucked up, okay?"

"I'm not judging," I said, not entirely truthfully. I was pretty sure they didn't have a BIG HONKING PSYCHIC box to check on one of those sperm donor cards, but it seemed like something prospective parents ought to know. "I'm just trying to figure it out. I don't know you well, but it seems like you would have thought about your kids having the sight."

"I was tired of feeling like a freak!" Kevin shot back, then got a little calmer. "A lot of people experiment with different types of drugs trying to do the kind of stuff I can do naturally."

"That's true," I said. "So what?"

"I..." Kevin struggled internally. "I thought maybe I'd be helping seed the universe with people who could see past the usual walls. Like maybe there wouldn't be so much violence if people could see past the surface stuff. And I figured most of the women who'd go to those clinics would be kind of liberal, wide-open types. Not like..."

Not like his parents? How angry a phase had this stage of Kevin's been? It would have been his freshman year, his first year away from an apparently regimented life, not too long after his mother had died from cancer. People can react to the death of a loved one in all kinds of unpredictable ways that don't seem to make sense on any kind of surface level. But

I didn't go there. Instead, I said, "I imagine lots of different kinds of people go to sperm clinics. And I'm pretty sure they all have a right to know that their kid might be able to see ghosts and alternate futures and stuff."

"That mortality rate you were talking about..." Kevin faltered. "Would my kids be...I mean....Do a lot of people like me get killed? I mean, my situation is weird even for weirdos, right?"

"True psychics have it rough," I said bluntly. "A lot of sensitives get medicated into a coma or locked away somewhere until they shut up and pretend to be normal. A lot of them figure out a way to commit suicide too. Are you telling me that you've never thought about it? You and all those things you can't stop seeing?"

His silence was answer enough.

"You need to tell your father that," I said.

"You never had a father," Kevin muttered. I couldn't tell if he was saying that like I had it easy or if he was telling me to go fuck myself.

"No," I admitted. "But I've had people I was trying to work with do screwed-up, sneaky things that almost got me killed. I don't want your dad to join that club."

"What do you mean?" he asked warily.

"I don't want your dad biding his time until he can hunt my friends because he thinks we're seducing you to the dark side," I elaborated. "If he tries to betray us at a critical moment, I'll kill him."

"Maybe he'll kill you first." Kevin's face became closed off and stubborn. "Or I will."

I didn't respond directly. We had to stop talking while I used an electric mixer to turn the floury mixture into batter.

Maybe Kevin could have gently coaxed the cupcakeness out of the sticky mess, but I just beat it into submission. When I was done, I gave Kevin the batter so that he could pour it into muffin tins.

"Is that what you want?" I inquired mildly. "Do you want your father to hurt my friends or them to hurt him? Do you want to kill me or for me to kill you?"

"What do you want from me?" he blurted out. "My father won't listen to me."

"You'd be surprised at what people can handle if they really love each other," I said. "And I really think he loves you, even if you don't fit into his worldview."

"I need time," he said.

"Then tell Sarah thank you but get lost," I said. "Just leave. I don't think she'll try to stop you."

"I can't." Kevin's voice was wistful. He loved all of this: Sarah and the pseudo-maternal thing she had going on around him, dream worlds, valkyries, bakeries full of wards and charms— he loved it. He was young and male and stupid and at least one of those adjectives was probably redundant.

"Then tell your father you love him, but if he does something messed-up to keep you from making your own decisions, you can't be in his life anymore," I said, still neutral.

"I can't," he said quietly.

Neither of us said anything for a time. "Look, Kevin," I said finally. "I've fucked up a lot. I've gone into denial and fought who I am and run from things longer than most people have been alive. I don't think I'm better than you. I'm asking you to be better than me."

Eventually, Kevin drew in a deep breath, held it in his chest before releasing it again. "All right."

"All right," I agreed.

"Why do you care about any of this?" Kevin asked.

Because someone ought to. Because not many could help him, and I could. Because at the end of the day, the evils that happen to someone else and seem like they can safely be ignored are more insidious than the threats that occur on an apocalyptic scale. But what I said was: "Well, saving virgins is kind of a family tradition."

"Shut up." Kevin's face was a bright red.

"Just talk to your dad," I advised.

And he did talk to Jerry too. Molly told me later that Kevin and his father got into a huge fight, a real one, and that by the end of it, Jerry wasn't agreeing to anything but he wasn't trying to leave and he was treating everyone like real people, not species traitors or monsters who looked human. I didn't see any of that, though. Like I said, a sense of urgency was pressing on me, and by the time Jerry was awake, I was gone.

PART THE SECOND

Bite Club

ᗞ21ᗞ

GETTING TAILED

I don't like being in New York City. It's partly a 'thrope thing; there's too much noise, too many smells, too many people moving around me from all angles, but mostly, too many monsters with attitude. There are two basic ways for supernatural beings to hide, and the ones who want to live a quiet life find some place isolated, and the ones who want to spread their wings— sometimes actual wings, mind you— find somewhere crowded.

Maybe that's why I've never been to the Big City without getting into big trouble, and I'm not talking about getting into it with a cab driver because the GPS on my phone says he's taking me on a roundabout, or dealing with aggressive panhandlers, or holing up in my hotel room during a power outage while looters hold the New York version of a Mardi Gras kind of trouble, either. I'm talking the kind of trouble where you hear a child's voice coming through a sewer grate and spend two hours wading through all kinds of shit—literally and figuratively—only to find out that the child is actually an ahuizotl (and if you don't know what an ahuizotl is, trust me, you're not missing anything). I'll innocently follow the smell of a lamb kebab down a street I'm not familiar with and wind up spending the night running through back alleys and over rooftops, being pursued by were-jackals who think I'm the scout for a wolf pack invading their territory.

Which is why I sighed when the pretty Asian woman who smelled like a fox dropped a folded slip of paper on my table. I'd been waiting for something like this, but it still felt like it was time for my New York rectal exam. But at least I was eating some seriously good spiessbraten on a terrace outside a German restaurant, and I continued to do so.

"What's this about, Foxy?" I murmured softly, carefully watching the buttocks of her high rear end alternate up and down in red slacks as she walked away. Young kitsune have a hard time making their tails disappear when they assume human form, and I was just trying to get a sense of how experienced she was, honest.

Her light voice came running beneath the cacophony of car engines and pedestrian nattering. "This is about self-expression."

"That sounds painful," I observed.

She just laughed a distinctly non-demure and feminine laugh and disappeared into the herd of street cattle as they mooed into their cell phones. She was maybe five foot four and not wearing heels, so she disappeared fast. I thought about trying to follow her, but tracking a fox who knows you're tracking it is difficult under the best of circumstances, and a crowded city sidewalk was far from the best of circumstances. Scent trails would be confused, sounds would be submerged, and it would be easy for her to bob and hide among the taller pedestrians around her. So, I stayed put.

I did wonder if this was the same kitsune who had helped Kevin's mother though, and how much that mattered. I opened the slip of paper. It had the next day's date, an address, and a time on it. The time, of course, was midnight.

*   *   *

The address turned out to be waterfront property, a warehouse in the middle of a bunch of other warehouses and docks and shipyards. The most obvious place to watch the warehouse from was a diner down the street, so I didn't go there. The best place was a neighboring warehouse that appeared to have been under construction when it was abandoned for one reason or another, so I didn't go there, either. No point being predictable when trying to spy on a fox.

Eventually, I settled on a small alcove formed by two improperly stacked storage containers in a neighboring dockyard. The site was downwind and about forty feet above the ground, and the shadows the two immense metal containers formed between them were so thick that I was hidden while lying down. It hadn't been hard to get up there unnoticed. All the younger guys working the yard were bundled against the cold. They dressed the same and moved the same: stocking caps, vest jackets, thermals or hoodies, work gloves, all of it pulled over a kind of sauntering slouch, so it was easy to blend without having to get a specific uniform. The field glasses I'd picked up from an army surplus store weren't anything fancy, but they were compact, collapsible, and had great glare reduction.

It turned out the warehouse address was owned by an Asian man in a white overcoat, an older fellow beginning to wrinkle like cured meat but still spry, with an iron-grey beard and a buzz cut. Probably Akihiko, but I wasn't assuming anything until I got close enough to smell him. He was definitely the owner, though, whether it said so on any piece of paper or not. It was in the way Probably Akihiko moved when he walked into the place.

Probably Akihiko had servants too. A woman walked in front of him like a bodyguard instead of behind him like the traditional idea of a proper Japanese woman, and when she opened the door for him, she went in first. The woman was taller than Probably Akihiko, almost six feet, unusually lithe and muscular in dark clothes that wouldn't impede movement. She was wearing pants too, just like the kitsune I'd met. This new woman had long black hair that went all the way to her waist and had small spiked metal spheres anchored at the end of it like beads. It was too far away and the dockyard made too much noise to tell if she clacked when she moved, but she smelled bad. An attempt had been made to cover that smell with some heavy, flowery perfume, but her stench was so strong that I caught a whiff of it on a breeze almost six hundred meters away. She wasn't undead, exactly, but her meat smelled sour.

I didn't know what she was, but she wasn't a kitsune.

Nothing else of note happened for roughly two hours, and then something did. A very weird something.

The door to the warehouse opened, and nothing visible came out, but the light in front of the door warped, kind of the way air will shimmer above hot concrete, though it had been a couple of months since the city had last seen a hot day. A stray fast food wrapper that was floating in the wind smacked dead against some large object or person that I couldn't see, and if I couldn't see it, that meant the person or thing was physically bending light waves around itself, not using mental magic. I knew it was large because I could hear the boardwalk creaking as if under assault. The scrap of paper came to a dead halt in midair before something invisible plucked it, held it suspended, maybe looked at it, and threw it away.

Sweet Mary, mother of God.

Sorry, sometimes I forget that I'm not a practicing Catholic anymore.

The breeze had died down, and I couldn't smell whatever

had opened that door, but I knew it was large, probably Japanese, and capable of bending light around itself. I also knew that Akihiko had spent a lot of his life among the mountains of Japan. To me, that spelled oni. T-R-O-U-B-L-E. Oni.

Except that didn't make any sense. Oni hate large bodies of water. That's why they live on and beneath the mountains and hills of Japan and hardly ever leave their island nation; their massive muscles aren't quite as dense as a chiang-shih's—oni run from six and half to nine feet tall—but they are just as strong because what they lack in compactness they make up in mass. An oni's skin is as tough as Kevlar too, all of which means that oni sink like rocks. Drowning is one of the few things oni are actually afraid of, and for this one to be here, Akihiko had to have either gotten an oni to fly over an ocean or float over it and then hang out on a waterfront.

Things started to heat up in the dockyard and a crane began redistributing storage containers in my vicinity—a big shipment must be coming in—and I decided to go get a little food and check in with Sig and the others before the sun went down and the yard lights came on. As I was making my way out of there by jumping from one row of shipping containers to another, I leaped on to an unevenly formed ledge that smelled like fox urine. Fresh fox urine. I wondered if the kitsune had been in her true shape when she did it, or if the human she was pretending to be had just dropped trou while hanging out behind me downwind. I have no idea why that mattered. What did matter was that the kitsune hadn't just needed to pee. She had been watching me trying to spy on her in her territory, and she wanted me to know it. Foxes like to mess with you that way.

Did I mention that I don't like being in New York City?

ᗄ22ᔆ

GAME ON

Swords and Wards isn't quite as popular an online fantasy game as *Worlds of Warcrack*—I mean, *Warcraft* (and *Swords and Wards* isn't the game's real name, either). *Swords and Wards* only has five million subscribers, but it has still made Parth a lot of his multimillions. And five million subscribers are almost impossible to monitor in real time, especially when the monsters and magical matters the players are talking about sound like they belong in an online fantasy game anyhow. It also helps that the number of subscribing players is bolstered by another million or so people constantly logging on and logging off as they play the first five levels of the game for free.

So, we'd decided to use Parth's online game as a way of contacting each other.

My character, Yohan Frogpants, woke up in the dorm room of WizardMarch, the academy where young wizards are trained for warfare. There was a virtual knock on my digital door, and then a herald appeared. A scroll unrolled on the right half of my computer screen while his reedy voice read from it. There was a list of events going on in the game that particular day, some of them listed in blazing bright green letters that meant I could click on them and teleport my avatar to the locations instantly; the highlights were a tournament where various wizard academies were competing, a special fair where new goods could be purchased, and the news that my home village was being invaded by mysterious beings. The headmaster wanted to see me at once, but after the herald left, I ignored all of the messages and checked my friends list.

Somebody from Sarah's group was supposed to be online and in the game at all times in case Sig or Cahill or I needed an emergency contact. We were supposed to check in at least once every two days, trying to hit agreed-upon eight-hour intervals. Svava Ravenshield—Sig's avatar—was online, and so was Kevin's alias, Hiro Grande.

I opened the virtual wardrobe in my room and looked in. There were no shelves, just a big, empty cabinet slightly taller than I was with a full-length mirror hanging on the door that didn't actually reflect anything. I walked my avatar straight into the wardrobe like Parth had told me to. Apparently, Parth was a C. S. Lewis fan because a strange thing happened. The screen went dark, and as I kept walking, I passed into another room. My avatar's body shimmered, began to...what, pixelate? Suddenly, my avatar looked more like a virtual version of me, wearing the kind of jean jacket I'd been wearing when I first met Parth. The name Yohan Frogpants and my avatar's basic stats disappeared from the bottom of the screen and were replaced by....nothing.

The virtual room my avatar was in was a digital duplicate of the large common room of Parth's mansion back in Clayburg, designed something like the central chamber of a beehive. I could even see glass walls with digital fish swimming behind them down the entranceway. For a moment, I could almost smell the thick incense Parth uses.

An avatar that looked like Sig, again, no stats, was sitting in a version of one of the papasan chairs that Parth has set aside for people who don't want to sit on meditation mats. The words appeared above my avatar's head in big blue letters: DO YOU WANT TO TEXT OR TALK JOHN? Since one of the points of this exercise was to not be overheard by potential spies with ultra-sensitive hearing, I clicked text, and our real names appeared in a scroll at the bottom of the screen.

SIG: What's up frogpants?
JOHN: Milady. Where's Kevin?
SIG: On his way. He cant IM us here from the regular game.
JOHN: He's playing the game?
SIG: I guess he got bored. He's young.
JOHN: Old enough to know better.
SIG: Relax. Jave a seat.
JOHN: How?
SIG: Have. Just stand in front of 1 and click on it.
JOHN: Okay.

I moved my character over to the papasan chair she was sitting on and started clicking.

SIG: What are you doing?
JOHN: Trying to sit in your lap.
SIG: Sorry player.
JOHN: Serious flaw in the game.

I went ahead and clicked on the adjacent empty papasan chair, and my character swiveled and sank down into it. When

I did so, my view of the room rotated on the computer screen, and I saw a feature that wasn't in Parth's actual home. A digital waterfall was cascading down the far wall, but it wasn't water that was being channeled in round trenches that circled the foundations—it was binary code. Nearly transparent rows of repeating zeroes and ones were flowing as if on a conveyer belt. As I was staring, I saw a figure appear on the other side of the cascading numbers. He was wearing a horned helmet over some kind of face wrap and scale mail, and the name Hiro Grande was floating over his shoulder.

When it walked through the waterfall, the avatar briefly looked like it was being transported in one of those science fiction movies, breaking down into little light bits, and then it became an approximation of Kevin Kichida.

KEVIN: wait a mo molly's coming.

A moment later, a character who looked like a female friar with the name JONA VARC appeared, shimmered, and reappeared in the image of Molly. We exchanged some virtual greetings, and I continued my ongoing campaign of making a bad impression on Kevin by chewing him out for playing the game, while Molly and Sig talked about life shuttling around in a van with five people in it and camping in warded tents in holy places of power. But we didn't waste too much time getting down to business.

JOHN: I met a kitsune. Meeting her again tomorrow at witching hour.
KEVIN: u dont have to talk around times no censor function here like in the game shit fuck fire bastard ass hair horse piss at 221B Baker Street.

Molly: language

Kevin: is all language so u met a kitsune?

Sig: Where did she find you?

John: Between the harbors and the meat packing district.

Sig: I'll try hanging out there later tonight.

Kevin: this is the kitsune who helped mom?

John: I don't know, Kevin.

Sig: I think the onmyouji is having trouble with his neiighbors. There were some other players patrollling the area today.

Molly: are we sure we can't negotiate with this man? are we just planning to kill him?

John: 1 person at a time please.

Sig: They were dressed like gangbangers and could smell that I wasnt human. I let them chase me off. And yes, Molly.

Molly: sorry you have typos i type slow

Sig: fuck typoos I didnt want to star t anything with them in case theyre rivals we can side with against Akihiko later.

Molly: oops I did it again.

Kevin: ha ha u r britney spears

John: How much time have you spent online gaming, Molly? You're doing the no grammar thing just like Kevin.

Kevin: free your mind grampa theres no grammar here

Molly: i refuse to answer on the grounds that I may incriminate myself

Sig: EVERY1 STFU TILL I FINISH!

Sig: Back to the gangbangers please. I coulsdnt tell what they were, John.

John: Daylight. Sensitive noses. Pack. Territorial. Some kind of weres?

Sig: They moversed like werewolves but also not. Stayedclose to each other in a weird way. Qolves wouldhave spread out more. I couldnt spot a leader.

JOHN: Could be a lot of things. I'd need a scent.

MOLLY: lets get back to this assassination business

KEVIN: u should try to get close to the kitsune

SIG: Molly, the man imprisoned his daughter and is trying to sacrifice his grandson.

KEVIN: my mother

JOHN: He also has an army of supernatural beings on his speed dial.

MOLLY: sorry kevin. and as 4 you 2...I don't know what's scarier

SIG: ?

MOLLY: when u r arguing or when u r thinking the same way

SIG: I wanna know more about Akihiko, but not optimistic here Molly.

MOLLY: has anyone gotten any more specific info on Akihiko yet?

JOHN: I might have seen him tonight. Sixtyish looking. Grey-beard. Trim. White robe/coat.

KEVIN: the kitsune helped mom escape she could help us if we figure out y she working for him

JOHN: She might have helped your mom for her own reasons.

SIG: Johns motto. Trust no one.

JOHN: Except you, Cuddlecakes.

SIG: Cudddlecakes?

MOLLY: did you take a picture of akihiko

JOHN: Didn't try.

MOLLY: ?

JOHN: Guy oozed magic. It blurs photos.

SIG: You just didn't think about it cos you arent used to sharing.

JOHN: That too.

SIG: John you should contact Ben Lafontaine. Get him toplant some werewolves in the audiences for these fights.

JOHN: It's not the Round Table's fight. Not even ours, really.

SIG: Your one of them. Itsa time you started acting like it. G2G Sugar-tush.

JOHN: Sugar-tush?

SIG: Cuddlecakes?

MOLLY: barf

JOHN: Hold on. Akihiko has more servants besides the kitsune. An oni for sure, and they can be invisible and are very strong. Stronger than you. Be careful.

SIG: Hello pot? This is kettle. Put a lid on it.

And then Sig's avatar disappeared.

The rest of us exchanged some more info, nothing big, and then I clicked out and left the community college whose computer lab was open to the public.

∽23∽

WELCOME TO THE RUMBLE

I didn't like the cold mist that sprang up out of nowhere around quarter past eleven that night. The cloud was thick enough to obscure visibility and formed a quarter-of-a-mile bubble surrounding the warehouse. The surface breeze died down as if sharply reprimanded, and it was harder to smell things effectively, almost as if odors were falling off of bodies with a thud.

I climbed up onto a nearby roof where there was a heating vent directly beneath it on the ground below. The unit was sucking up scent particles and blowing them up into the atmosphere where what air currents there were picked them up and scattered them out over the ocean. Over the next half hour, I smelled a number of different were-beings—a leopard woman, a bearwalker, and three werewolves who were together and talking in very thick Irish accents. I also smelled a half-elf, at least one other kind of Fae, two vampires, and two things I'd never smelled before.

I had a hard time wrapping my brain around that many predators from different gene pools and similar mind-sets meeting in one enclosed space. I wasn't used to seeing members of the supernatural community actually acting like a community. There are generally no ice cream socials, no neighborhood watches, no block parties, no bowling teams, no million-monster marches, etc. There are barbecues every now and then, but that's only when one of us gets burned alive.

I was still wondering if things were changing in the information age or if I'd been oblivious to a lot of supernatural networking because of my mind-set and circumstances when Sig appeared. She moved through the mist and into the warehouse without more than a brief exchange. Suddenly, I found myself breathing a little more rapidly. I forced myself to take deeper, slower breaths, looked at my five fingers, counted them one by one and folded them into a fist, willing my adrenaline to settle. What we were doing seemed a lot more stupid and risky suddenly, and I had an odd moment of panic. I feel fear all the time—I hardly even notice that background buzz anymore, like people who live next to an airport and stop hearing planes. But when I saw Sig disappear into that unnatural fog, I felt something like emotional vertigo.

She and I weren't going to make it if I couldn't get this kind of thing under control, not on any level. Breathe deep. Sig would be in that warehouse whether I was there or not. I increased her chances of survival, or tried to, and that was all I could do. If anything came after death, it would whether I wanted it to or not, and if nothing came after death, it didn't matter anyway, and we had to make this life count. The only thing I could do for Sig was get my shit together.

I was still trying to find some solid ground when I heard it, a black bird the size of a man flapping down toward the roof I had claimed as John Charming Land. The wolf didn't like being intruded on, but I kept the growl in. The giant winged creature actually changed into a man before it landed, dropping that last yard on bare human feet and running forward a few more steps to burn off its momentum. Its human form was short—perhaps five inches past five feet—male, Asian, long-haired, and wearing a white loincloth that looked like a giant diaper. His fingernails were at least two inches long, sharp, thick, and curling slightly inward.

"Gormless, are we?" Apparently, it was British or had learned English from someone who spoke the real thing, which was a little disconcerting because the British never occupied the Philippine culture its progenitors came from. But supernatural predators are often nomads, and globalization doesn't always color in the lines.

"Absobloodylutely," I said. I could see that his eyes were blood-shot, and I suspected that if I got closer, I would be able to see my reflection upside down in them. I didn't need to do that to verify that it was an aswang, though (I pronounce that Oz-wong, by the way, not Ass-wang). Lots of tales claim that aswang have holes under their armpits, but that's just an exaggeration of a physical truth: the ribs of an aswang in humanoid form are very concave beneath the armpits, probably to make room for the feathers that sprout from its arms when it shape changes.

"No need to faff about. These Nips are bazzin'!" The smile wasn't precisely unfriendly, I decided. It was more that the smile was assuming a kinship that I did not claim, and with a cruel joy that I did not share. Aswang have a reputation for especially enjoying the flesh of unborn fetuses and preying on pregnant women. I wondered if this one bothered to fight those instincts.

"You're not one of them?" I asked, nodding toward the ware-house. Aswang tend to be Filipino.

"It's horses for courses down there, wolfie." In a moment, I was going to tell it to stop smiling and tone down the slang. "I'm still learning to be meself."

"What's this all about, then?" I held up the slip of paper with a time and place on it.

"It's the bleedin' Crucible, innit?" He laughed and ran for the edge of the roof again, spreading his arms. I let him. He jumped off the ledge and was a birdman again before he had dropped five feet. He didn't look all that aerodynamically sound to me, but there was probably some element of magic involved. Hell, for all I knew, he farted gravity. What was certain was that he disappeared into the mist, and a few seconds later, I heard his human feet land on the ground.

That was twice I had been spotted while trying to be stealthy. It wouldn't happen again.

Well, okay, so it happened again. This time I was spotted by a pack of were-hyenas, although to be fair, I wasn't particularly trying to be slick. It was about five minutes to midnight when I vaulted down into the mist and made my way toward the warehouse. Atmospheric conditions being what they were, I smelled and saw the were-hyenas coming from the opposite direction at the same time they smelled and saw me. There were at least twelve of them, and we halted in front of a large Japanese man at the door of the warehouse. He looked like a sumo wrestler and smelled like ogre. The oni I had seen earlier, or more to the point, hadn't seen.

Now the oni appeared seven feet tall and slightly more than three feet wide. He was wearing sunglasses at night just like that '80s song, probably to cover eyes with vertical slits for irises. A samurai knot was forcing coarse black hair high up on the oni's forehead, and I suspected that it was covering knobby horns that had been sawed down to stubs. The oni's skin color was typical of a Japanese man, but that didn't mean anything. An oni's ability to bend light around itself means that it can be any color it wants, and they will often make themselves blue or red or green just for kicks and giggles.

As to the were-hyenas, they looked at me like one being with a dozen heads. They wore dark clothes, hoodies, oversized shirts, baggy and saggy pants, and gold spheres on necklaces or earrings. Some of Sig's gangbangers. They didn't appear to be a typical gang, though. Not just because they were culturally diverse—that's something that's starting to become more common as outcasts or younger-generation thugs from fringe territories band together to survive larger racially dominated gangs—the were-hyenas had some women in the mix too, and some of the members looked like they had grown up poor and some privileged. The outward age of the group looked like it ranged anywhere from sixteen to forty.

It made sense in a way. Of all the 'thropes common in America, were-hyenas are the least particular about who they hunt and have the strongest instinct to band together. When's the last time you heard someone described as a "lone hyena"?

Since I appeared weaker than the oni, the were-hyenas decided to show off by focusing on me in front of him.

"Get along, little doggie," one of the hyenas jeered, a short but thick Latino male who had a wide mouth. He was apparently their leader du jour.

"This can't be your turf," I observed. "Hyenas mark their territory by rubbing their anal glands all over everything."

His eyes bulged. "Wha'djoo say?"

"I said the only thing that smells like shit here is you," I shot back.

Okay, maybe I can't blame *all* of the trouble I get into in New York City on New York City.

My response wasn't quite as stupidly aggressive as it sounded, though. The supernatural world has rules, and if the hyenas attacked me now, they would either have to openly acknowl-edge that we weren't on their territory first, or disrespect the oni by acting as if we were.

Which is why the oni interceded, speaking up in a voice like a gravel pit. "You want fight, fight inside."

This pretty much made him the opposite of every bouncer I'd ever met.

"Let's do this," the lead hyena snarled, and he started to move toward the door, but somehow the oni was standing in front of him.

"Only three," the oni said. "You know rules."

The hyena leader looked up at the oni. Way up. "We don't like rules."

It suddenly got colder then, and I'm not just talking emotion-ally. The mist began to thicken and the temperature dropped drastically. What was weird was that somewhere in the back-ground, I could hear someone blowing steadily through pursed lips.

The oni moved without rushing while the hyenas were dis-tracted by the atmospheric changes. Sometimes, moving slowly is actually an effective offensive technique. The were-hyenas were faster than the oni, but the eye and the brain are pro-grammed to register threats as things moving rapidly toward them; someone moving a hand or foot slowly for a very short distance can avoid setting off any reflex reactions, can often step on a foot or grab a wrist before the target even realizes that there is danger. The oni's canned ham of a hand grabbed the leader's arm, and once he had a hold, the oni's other hand moved more quickly toward the top of the were-hyena's head.

The leader tried to squirm free and failed. He hammered a quick punch into the oni's torso, even snapped a kick into the oni's shin, but the oni didn't even grunt. Instead, the oni put its palm on top of the were-hyena's skull and twisted. The were-hyena's head rotated and its neck snapped with a sharp crack. The were-hyena went limp, and the oni picked it up and casually flicked it away into the mist with one arm.

The sound of impact was somewhere between ten and twenty feet away.

The were-hyena would heal, eventually, though spinal injuries are tricky. Even when the physical damage is fully healed, it can take the brain a while to believe it and start sending nervous signals again.

The other were-hyenas were pulling the triggers of the various firearms they had grabbed while all of this was going on, but the gun barrels were actually clogged with ice, the hammers frozen, bullets sticking to their chambers and magazines, sparks just not happening.

The were-hyena pack belatedly moved to attack physically, but one of them, a tall Caucasian with some serious sideburns and a goatee, was suddenly enwrapped by thousands of thin strands of growing black hair that shot through the doorway from inside the club. The hair strands must have had the tensile strength of spider silk. Some of the hairs were braided and had spiked metal balls at the end of them, but they were all elongating rapidly, spiraling like living things around the were-hyena's arms and legs and throat.

He was yanked into the club.

Another were-hyena, a female in the rear of the group, wasn't moving at all. In fact, she was frozen—motion-wise and temperature-wise. At some point, her skin had acquired the texture of ice. I only knew this because the were-hyena shattered into thousands of pieces, a feminine hand with long fingernails bursting through the were-hyena's chest from behind.

A Japanese woman walked through the place the were-hyena had just been standing, emerging from the mist. She was dressed in a flowing white robe and had long pale hair, her alabaster skin flushed with the warmth she had just absorbed from a living being. She was oddly beautiful and horrifying at the same time.

The remaining were-hyenas were already gone by this point. I could hear them off in the mist, grabbing their leader's body and dragging him off at a speed that was going to keep his spine from healing for some time to come. They had abandoned the guy in the warehouse for dead. That's another thing that separates hyenas from wolves—not only are they less selective, they're also less loyal.

I was left staring at the oni and the new arrival. I'd heard of yuki-onna, but I'd never actually seen a Japanese snow woman. Some stories consider them ghosts, and I could see why. Even with my senses, the yuki-onna was practically scentless. Quiet, too. If it weren't for her clothes, she would have barely made any noise at all. But she wasn't a spirit. Her heartbeat, slow as it was, had speeded up with the rush of heat she had just sucked out of her victim.

"Would you mind turning off the air conditioning?" I asked the yuki-onna, not trying to hide some shivering. "It was already cold enough."

She grinned. "It gets warmer inside."

I suspected her of speaking metaphorically.

"What your name?" the oni demanded.

I shrugged. "Do you want to make one up or should I?"

"Oh, I like this one's mouth," the yuki-onna purred. "Let's call him Down Boy."

She flowed next to me then, and suddenly her pelvis was rubbing against my left hip, her lips next to my ear. Bizarrely, her breath felt warm even though a magical icy mist had been coming out of that mouth a moment ago. "I can think of a few ways you could earn a name like that."

Suddenly, the yuki-onna was off me, shoved away by the oni's massive palm. "Go in, Down Boy," the oni rumbled as he stepped aside.

Yeah, I probably should have made up my own name.

"We are monsters. We are fang and claw and shadow. We are scream and nightmare and blood. But our claws have been clipped. Our manes have been trimmed. Our fangs have been filed down. We have been neutered and hunted instead of hunting. Blah blah blah blah...."

It was the kitsune talking, standing on the raised tines of a fork lift between two groups of massed monsters like some Moses figure parting a Dread Sea. She was letting her ass hang out in leather chaps beneath a green tube top tonight, and four fox tails were sticking out from the base of her spine. I was still listening on some level, but most of my attention was focused on my environment.

The warehouse was lit by torches and three chandeliers full of candles. The chandeliers were suspended by hooks that normally would have been used to move heavy pallets and crates, dangling from huge metal rails that crisscrossed the ceiling. The place would function during any magical energy surges that interfered with technology. The firelight also had a kind of primal effect. For a weird moment, I pictured that kids' story, *Where the Wild Things Are.* What was that line again? Let the wild rumpus begin, or something like that.

There were no crates or trucks or jacks in the large room, but at some point, there had been all of these things. You could still see the marks and outlines made by greasy treads and different degrees of light leaching. In the middle of the warehouse, two huge twenty-foot metal doors were built horizontally into the floor; when dropped down or pulled up, they would form a storage bay. Now, closed and locked, they made a workable fighting ring.

In the top southwest corner of the building, some fifty feet above the floor, there was a large rectangular window with tinted glass, presumably a control booth of some kind. I could sense a presence behind that window, a very powerful presence whose concentration and menace was a tangible thing. Almost certainly the man in the white overcoat who was almost certainly Akihiko.

I tuned back in.

"We. Are. Not. What. We. Are," the kitsune was saying. "It is men who are the monsters now."

There was an angry surge through the crowd and some actual growls. It was probably not a coincidence that the front doors to the warehouse were shut. The oni and the yuki-onna had spread out and slipped behind the edges of the group at this point. The woman thing with spiked balls braided in her hair—a harionago—was also watching, but she was crouched over the body of the were-hyena she had pulled into the warehouse. Dressed all in black, her long hair wove around while she chewed on the were-hyena's heart as if taking small bites out of an apple. I suppose another advantage to concrete floors and a water hatch was that hosing down the place and disposing of bodies would be a fairly simple process. The fish beneath the warehouse probably ate well. For now, though, the smell of death was in the air, and among some in this crowd, it would be an aphrodisiac.

"I'm no monster," one of the werewolves with a Gaelic lilt objected. He was a broad-shouldered but gaunt man. Dark-haired and scruffy, with a beard that looked like laziness instead of a personal choice. "And I'm no sheep."

"Oh, I know, you've all killed," the kitsune said dismissively. "None of you would be here if you weren't killers. But none of you would be here if you didn't know how to play it safe, either. How many of you have known someone who was hunted down by knights and ended for the sin of doing what comes naturally?"

Another ugly current passed through the ranks around me.

"I'd rather have a few knights than armies and laws." This comment was from the were-leopard, a striking black woman wearing black sweats and a pink tank top. The leopard woman's hair was shaved down close to her skull, which was far more practical for fighting, and she wore thick leather wristbands that were actually bracers. She smiled tightly without showing teeth, her arms sinewy and crossed over her chest. "Maybe you didn't notice, but the mobs these days have shotguns."

"That is a problem," the kitsune agreed. "This place is a solution."

"I didn't come here for a pep rally; I came here to gamble," a half-elf asserted. He was standing next to Sig on the other side of the room, a slender specimen in a light blue track suit. His hair was red, not blonde, and long enough to cover what were probably slightly pointed ears. His eyes were sea green, his lips slim and sneering, his nose sharp but elegant. He had the body of a swimmer or dancer. He would be as fast as I was but not quite as strong, and illusions and charms would pour out of his mouth like carbon dioxide. "I was told we could wager on these fights."

"This is strictly amateur night. The Crucible is for professionals." The kitsune nodded toward the tinted window in the upper corner. "If you want to use tonight as a tryout, that's your business, but money confuses things at this level."

Translation: This was about recruiting. Like giving someone the first taste of a highly addictive drug for free.

Suddenly, the kitsune jumped down from her perch and the creatures in front of me moved to the side. The kitsune stopped a few feet in front of me and snarled, though it was all surface. There was no rage pouring out of her skin. "What about you, Mr. Aloof? Mr. In-control? Mr. Watch-from-a-distance-and-gather-intel? When's the last time you felt fully alive?"

"When I beat the shit out of some random stranger in a warehouse," I said mildly. "Are we going to do this thing or not?"

She flashed a smile that was half angry and half amused. "You can't use any weapons other than what you were born with, and if anyone kills anyone on purpose, they're banned for life. Other than that, anything goes. Do you have a problem with that?"

"No," I said.

"Then you don't leave here until blood has been spilled."

"Right then, new boy is with me," the aswang stepped out of the group and forward. Apparently, the diaper thing that had been wrapped around it was a cotton gi that it wore when in human form. He yelled out cheerily for the whole group. "Let's go, wolfie."

The kitsune gave me an eyebrow with a question mark on it. "Sure," I said.

It wasn't an organized series of contests. The warehouse was huge, and we broke off into pairs and spread out while the onmyouji's crew strolled between us like referees. The bearwalker—a large and wide Scandinavian-looking tool with shoulder-length blonde hair tied back in a braid and biceps the size of cantaloupes—called Sig out. From the swagger in his hips and the smile on his lips, it was obvious that he was viewing this as some kind of mating ritual. He took off his shirt and made a big production out of flexing while he did so, six foot five and over three hundred pounds, most of it muscle.

"I'll be gentl—" he began to taunt, but he didn't finish, because Sig punched him in the face. Hard, and Sig is stronger than a were, even a bearwalker if not by much. She stepped into it and put her body weight behind the shot, and he went down flat on his back with an impact that rang the metal hatch beneath him like a gong.

I didn't see what happened then, though, because the three Irish wolves were apparently allowed to fight as a team, and they and the vampire they were attacking swirled between us right before the aswang attacked me. He came at me in human form, and apparently, he fancied himself some kind of martial artist because he was lashing out with open-palm thrusts. I faced him at a slight right angle and parried the blows easily enough, though occasionally, he tried to turn the movements into slashes and hook me with thick, talon-like fingernails. Then he got impatient and lunged forward for a flashy power move. I don't know what kind of move, exactly, because he never finished it. I stepped slightly inside the move's axis, putting my lead foot behind his while he ran his chin into my elbow. If his nervous system hadn't been fairly rudimentary, he would have been knocked out.

As it was, the aswang rolled to his feet with blood running down his mouth and several teeth missing.

"There's first blood. If you want to stay down, I'll let you," I called out. "Just saying."

Instead, the aswang used the reprieve to change shape again. He wasn't dumb enough to morph into a dog against something that smelled like wolf, so he changed into a birdman again, jaw elongating and hardening, claws thickening, feathers sprouting. It took it a few seconds, but I didn't try to stop the show. I wanted to make an impression. A second later, I showed the aswang why a flying side kick was a bad idea even when you were truly flying.

His body slammed into the floor so hard that even I winced.

"Seriously," I said, "if I have to put you down again, you're staying down."

Again, the aswang recovered quickly, so quickly that I had to wonder if his bones were extra flexible or hollow. His body had felt a little light. The aswang picked himself up off the floor and took off running away from me before launching himself into the air. I moved around in a small slow circle, tracking him as he flew around me. The aswang was violating other fighters' spaces but so high above them that they didn't register it.

Suddenly, the aswang's tongue lashed out from the air above, thirty feet of extending hollow tube with a spiked point aimed at my spinal cord. I spun, caught the tip of the tongue in my left fist, and stopped it there in midair, whirling and wrapping the tongue around my wrist, bringing all of my body weight and strength to bear while the aswang was flying in the opposite direction.

The aswang's tongue was ripped out of that beaked mouth by the root, and the tongue snapped back into something about nine inches long, lashing in my fist like a snake until I dropped it. The aswang was tilted off-balance and flew downward toward the ground then, and I charged him while he was madly flapping to correct his course and regain altitude. I know I just said that leaping kicks are a bad idea, but he was turned the other way when I caught him in the middle of his back and broke his spine. The aswang fell to the ground in a hot shrieking mess.

"HE WIPPED OUT MY TONGUH!" he screamed, but he couldn't do much about it, just writhed there, unable to move his legs. I can't say I felt remorse. The bastard had tried to drink my spinal fluid, and beings that have a history of hunting pregnant women aren't way up there on my pity list. Aren't even on it, actually. They're on another list altogether.

The kitsune wasn't too perturbed, either. Aswang are essentially normal during the day—in fact, daytime is the best time to kill one—but at night, their bodies are stronger, faster, and heal much more rapidly than any human's. He would be walking again before the sun came up. "Yes, he did."

She gave me a speculative glance but didn't make any further comment.

I watched the rest of the fights as they finished out.

The bearwalker was on his back again, halfway through a shift, sprouting black fur and gaining mass when Sig knee-dropped on to his stomach. His head jerked up and met her punch coming down, a hammer blow to his jaw/muzzle with all of her descending weight behind it. He didn't get up again.

The half-elf with a predilection for gambling was having problems. The vampire he was fighting was wide and big-boned, not only hefty but also carrying excess flesh, which was rare for one of its kind, and it didn't seem to care that the half-elf was darting around it, quick as a whisper. The half-elf sent a series of punches into the vampire's nerve clusters, but its nervous system was too shut down for it to care. It was when the half-elf tried an eye strike that the vampire finally reacted. His jaw tilted back, his mouth lunged upwards, and he caught the half-elf's outstretched fingers in his teeth. One quick snap and the half-elf's index and middle finger were gone.

The leopard woman was choking out one of the things I couldn't identify by taking the vines that had emerged from his skin and wrapping them around his throat, pinning him to the ground with a knee in his shoulder blades. Bark was beginning to form over his skin (a male dryad, maybe?) but it was too late.

A pale old woman turned out to be a viuda—a kind of South American cross between a vampire and a hag. I knew this because she released a puff of air into the other half-Fae's face, and her breath was toxic. He reeled, and then she was inside his reach and flaying him with three-inch-long nails that were apparently as hard and sharp as metal blades.

The trio of werewolves won their fight with the vampire, but only barely. All three had shifted, and there was only one standing when it was over, swaying amid a lot of blood splatters and tatters of flesh that weren't where they were supposed to be.

The half-elf tried to crawl away from his vampire, but it grabbed his ankle and dragged him back and began punching him viciously in the face while he tried to ward off the blows with increasingly feeble efforts, finally just lying there. The vampire didn't stop until the kitsune sharply snapped, "Robert," pronouncing it "Roh-bear." Her four fox tails were waving in a way that suggested anger.

It wasn't a good night for elvish cast-offs in general. The viuda finished the other half-Fae with a life-draining kiss. Her grey hair turned black and her ancient skin smoothed out, while he sagged and wrinkled like a paper bag having the air sucked out of it. What the hell. He was immortal and would recharge eventually. Probably.

I saw Sig standing there above her opponent, but I was staring at her in character, the way I would have if I didn't know her, so it was okay. She really did look like something out of legend.

When the combatants who needed more time to heal—or to find some healing from an outside source—were dragged aside and unceremoniously dumped against the west wall, the kitsune clapped her hands sharply. "Good!" Then she smiled. "Now let's move on to round two."

I didn't have to fight Sig, thank God. The leopard woman singled her out, though her smile was friendly enough in a savage sort of way. Me, I headed straight for "Roh-bear." He greeted me with a surprised and nasty snarl of a smile. I was weaker than him, alone, and hopelessly outmatched, and that was apparently just the kind of opponent he preferred.

Good.

"Are you going to set those?" There was something studied about the neutrality in the kitsune's tone. She was referring to the vampire's arms, both of which had been dislocated but not broken. "Roh bear" was also suffering from a shattered knee-cap, a spine that was intact but badly in need of realignment, two punctured eyeballs, three fingers that were realigning as we watched, a collapsed trachea, and a caved-in left temple. The blood sucking shit-heel lay on the ground gargling through a jaw that was still making snapping sounds while it relocated, his upper fangs lying on the floor some twenty feet away. He had tried that cute little finger-snapping bite on me, and I'd been waiting for it.

"No." I was pulling a heavy dark jacket on over a wool sweater and didn't see any reason to stop. "Are you?"

"Not unless he asks for help," she reflected distastefully. "Robert's been pushing the limits a little too much lately."

"I'm not too good at asking for help myself," I admitted, feeling her out a little.

"It doesn't look like you need it much."

I shrugged. "Everybody needs help sometimes."

This gave me another excuse to look at Sig, who, along with

the leopard woman, was helping the half-elf that "Roh-bear" had beaten to a pulp. We had been given another time next week if we wanted to come back, and most of the combatants who were mobile were making their way out. The half-elf was propped between Sig and the leopard woman's shoulders as he tottered out the door that the oni was holding open for them. Sig was obviously doing her social networking thing. I wondered if she had remembered to pick up the half-elf's fingers.

The kitsune didn't pursue my conversational gambit. "My boss wants to talk to you."

I looked at her narrowly. "Nobody said anything about a beat and greet."

Her smile was faint. "What's the matter? Don't like surprises?"

"No," I said. "I don't."

She nodded. "My boss doesn't, either."

I waited for her to elaborate, and when she didn't, I tried to pry a little more information out of her. "How do you know what your boss wants? I would have heard if anybody said anything to you. Nobody did."

I remembered Jerry Kichida's story. In it, a fox woman had spoken to Kevin's mother without using words.

Her mouth turned into a thin, flat line. "He has his ways."

Awesome.

～24～

LET'S SEE WHAT'S BEHIND
DOOR NUMBER TWO

It was a plain whitewashed stairwell that led up to Probably Akihiko's sanctum, complete with chipped concrete stairs, peeling paint on the stairway rails, and exit signs, but when the kitsune opened the door to the control room, there was another door behind it, a sliding paper one. What might have been calligraphy once had been overlaid with other signs and symbols until the calligraphy became sigils, carved into the wood and making a perimeter around the frame.

Oh, shit.

The kitsune moved the paper door open and revealed a hallway that split into three different directions, each formed by paper walls that were divided by black bamboo frames into row upon row of small uniform squares. The floor was covered with straw mats, lit from above by brightly colored red paper lanterns that hung from the ceiling.

More importantly, the three branching hallways I was staring at were already bigger than the control room should have been. In a proper universe, the east branch would be jutting out over the main warehouse floor, and the west branch would be extending out over the street. The hallways had to be traveling through some alternate dimension.

I did not want to go through that door. You know how some people have a fear of flying or enclosed spaces or the dark? Well, I apparently have a fear of Limbo that I hadn't known about until that moment. I recalled Jerry's story about his wife being shut off and trapped in an endless maze of doors and hallways, and I had to repress a shudder. The thought of wandering around an infinite loop of those uniform paper halls while my regenerating body slowly starved to death was more frightening than any monster.

"This doesn't smell right," I said.

The kitsune's smile was a tad bitter. "Go ahead. Leave." She didn't wait to gauge my reaction but walked down the west corridor.

The ghost corridor, my mind whispered while I watched her four fox tails bristle.

I followed her. The door I'd left open behind me slid shut, seemingly of its own volition.

There was another paper sliding door at the north corner when we turned, and I stopped and tried to listen at it, smell what was beyond it, but I couldn't hear anything through that thin paper barrier. Nothing at all, and I can hear things through two feet of thick concrete. I did smell incense, but it was a lingering smell rather than a fresh one.

I moved on to catch up to the kitsune, who opened another sliding door on the right. It opened into an east hallway that traveled some fifty feet and should have intersected the first main hallway and didn't. I could easily see how someone might get lost; the uniformity of the hallways was disorienting. There were no distinct vases or portraits, just row upon row of the same-sized squares and identical red lanterns. The new hall-way had several sliding doors on either side of it and ended in another.

The kitsune moved and opened the second sliding door on the north side, which opened into yet another long corridor with several halls and doors. At least she wasn't using any secret knocks that I would have to remember.

West. South. East. North 2. Wally saw Emma naked twice.

We took the second eastern corridor, and I felt like a termite burrowing behind the walls of the universe. She opened the first door on the south. West. South. East. North 2. 2nd east. South. Wally saw Emma naked twice. Both enjoyed seeing...a waiting room. A small table was in the center of the room, and on it a cup of fresh hot tea that smelled of roasted barley.

The kitsune didn't give me any instructions, just bowed once and sank down to her knees on a tatami mat, her bottom resting on her heels, her head lowered, her tails lying along her calves. It was a test of sorts.

I moved over to the kimonos hanging on the wall and the tabi beneath them. After a moment's hesitation, I took off my jacket and left it on a wooden peg.

"All the way, please." The kitsune was polite enough, but she wasn't asking.

I took off the rest of my clothes. The kimonos were cotton, not silk, and heavy enough to offer some protection against cold. The tabi were also made for outdoor use, boots whose tips divided into toe sections. I didn't know if that was a good sign or bad. I left the kimono open at the top and moved over to the table, sinking down into a lotus position. There was a small alcove with a hanging scroll that I badly wanted to look over, but I didn't want to give away too much. Akihiko had presumably left Japan because he had enemies there, and making it obvious that I'd been to the country might make him suspicious.

On the other hand, I had already demonstrated a working knowledge of some kind of blended martial arts system, and I wasn't showing up on Akihiko's psychic sonar if he had the gift, so he was probably curious as to why a werewolf was displaying knightlike characteristics or vice versa. If I acted like I didn't know anything about Eastern rituals, it would be suspicious. It was the Templar's fascination with Eastern traditions and philosophies that got them branded as heretics and mystics in the first place.

Not an easy balance to maintain.

At least, the tea smelled like normal tea. I recited my memory sequence as I sipped the hot liquid, though there was no guarantee the same route would work the same way twice. How hard is it to shift paper walls and doors around when they're forming wormholes through space?

I didn't see any signal, but eventually, the kitsune stood up and moved to the opposite sliding door. I rose to follow, and she opened the door to reveal another small square hall before another south door. The waiting area reminded me of a decompression chamber or a decontamination room. The kitsune slid open the next portal to reveal...a small, plain wooden door built into thin wooden walls. Fresh cold air and sunshine were peeking beneath and around its edges.

The ordinary door opened into the outside world, and suddenly we weren't in New York at night anymore. We were in the middle of the afternoon in Japan, facing a roji, a small outdoor waiting area enclosed by Japanese maple trees and dense hedges. The ground was covered with a fragrant moss, and a series of stepping-stones led to a small stone basin and a bench outside a bamboo gate. Beyond the gate was a tea house. The sounds of a distant sea were coming through the trees, and I could see nothing but open sky through bare branches.

Well, at least this explained how the onmyouji had gotten his oni servant across the ocean.

"This is quite a show your boss is putting on," I said, looking around. I'm sure my heart rate was up, though I managed to keep my face neutral and my tone level. "Is he planning to kill me or recruit me?"

The kitsune's pulse was steady. "It is not my place to say." She led me to the bench and bid me wait there, then went through the bamboo gate into the tea house.

I sat down at the meditation bench. There was a moss-free patch beneath the bench, and the ground was hard enough to use as a slate of sorts, but I had left my jackknife back in my pants, so I had to use a smooth pebble to write out my memory sequence. It was a pain in the ass, and I had to bear down hard. WSEN22ESSS. Wally saw Emma naked twice. Both enjoyed seeing several sexy... ryoji. I wrote the sequence backwards. SSSE22NESW. South, south, south, east 2, 2nd north, east, south, west. Sarah Smith secretly e-mails twenty-two notes every single Wednesday. I gave the story a little narrative just to help me remember. Sarah was an obsessive celebrity stalker.

I stared at the combination for a few moments, then scratched it out. The door we had emerged from was set in a Japanese garden shed, a small square building with a tiled roof and no windows. If I opened the door, would I find myself back in the extradimensional corridors or surrounded by gardening tools?

Hmmm. I sat there and thought about that, that and what I could use for weapons if it came down to it. If I did open that door and found myself in a gardening shed, there were possibilities there. And if I found myself back in the maze of paper hallways, at least I would have a narrow access point to defend. I could shatter the bench I was sitting on and use its wood components. The stepping-stones were flat and hefty and could be swung two-handed. The copse I was sitting in was on the edge of a cliff, if I was judging the sounds of water crashing below correctly. Perhaps if I could get past the surrounding trees, I could flip or push creatures off those cliffs...or climb or jump to a point where I could dive into the waters below if I got desperate...

This was probably not the kind of meditation that the bench I was sitting on had been designed for.

The door to the tea house opened, and the kitsune came down to the bamboo gate and bowed silently. I bowed back this time, and went to the stone basin, took the dipper there and poured water on my left hand, then switched hands and poured water on my right. It was as fucking freezing as water gets before turning to ice, but the Japanese take their purification rituals seriously. I put the dipper back in my right hand and poured water into my cupped left, using the liquid to silently rinse my mouth. When I was done, I spit the water back into my left hand, then held the dipper vertically and let the remaining liquid trickle over the handle.

The kitsune led me to a small door—the Japanese call it a nijiri-guchi, or "crawling-in" door—and I removed my footwear before entering the tea room. This kind of waiting drives a lot of Westerners crazy, but the traditions aren't just ceremonial. The quiet time allows for a cooling-off period if negotiations are tense, and the protocols allow a host to take security precautions without being rude. Removing one's outer garments in a waiting room makes it harder to smuggle in overt weapons, and putting on a kimono makes it harder to reach covert weapons quickly. Isolating the guest in a roji gives the host's guards time to verify that the guest hasn't brought anyone else along. And washing hands is still important today even if we are dealing with flus and colds more than plagues.

A hearth was built into the floor, keeping the tea house warm, and I walked around the tea room, observing the objects there. In each corner of the room, there was some kind of standing skeleton draped in a black house-guard uniform that looked like a Hollywood ninja suit. The only parts of the bone golems not covered by boots, uniforms, or gloves were their faces: skulls peeked out of the tight black hoods.

Fuck me if these skeletons didn't animate.

I walked up to examine one of the bone golems closer. The uniform wasn't draped loosely over bone—it looked as if the clothes were being filled out by a flesh-and-blood body. I took a deep whiff and smelled spider silk and latex and decay. Peering intently at the corners of the hood, I saw just a hint of yellow foam sticking out at the base of the jaw. This wasn't a traditional skeleton. This was a skeleton with a padded bodysuit draped around it and covered in a ninja uniform.

I guess it made sense. The bones would still move the padding around just like our bones move our meat around them, even if it was magic making the motion happen instead of muscle. The foam body would make it harder to shatter the enclosed bone, one of the things that makes animated skeletons fairly easy to destroy. And the thing would look more formidable when it moved, instead of looking like a set of clothes hung up on a bone rack, or the ultimate case of anorexia.

I thought about squeezing the bone golem's arm and decided not to push my luck.

The most striking and unusual object in the room was a massive aquarium with a giant clam inside it. A grown man could climb inside that clam. I walked up to the tank and stared at it through the glass, and a giant air bubble squeezed from the thing's slightly cracked maw, distorting and elongating. I glanced at the bubble, then did more than glance. The bubble shimmered and gave off different colors, and when I focused on those shifting colors, it felt like I was being sucked in; there was a slight rush of vertigo and a plunging sensation, like one of those movies that show you the perspective from the lead car in a rollercoaster.

I saw the kitsune staring at me, implacable but somehow sad, and then it was like my face was being plunged into a lake with my eyes open, but instead of water, my eyes were thrust through her chest. Bone and blood parted before me until I saw the kitsune's heart, but it wasn't a human heart. It was a dull, onion-shaped sphere that burst into flames, and then the flames exploded into bright sparks that reassembled into a katana. Something was reflected on the curve of the bright blade, and when I focused on it, the reflection expanded into a wall made of safety deposit boxes, kept expanding until I could see the number 1204 on one of them, inscribed in a tiny brass plate.

When I came out of the vision, my palms and forehead were resting against the glass tank. I realized that I wasn't breathing and felt a moment of panic because it seemed like I'd forgotten how. But then I pulled in a convulsive gasp and felt my heart thudding and sound filling my ears as I tore my eyes away from my reflection.

Had I just been blessed or cursed?

My host did turn out to be Akihiko. My nose told me that he was the man who had held the siren feather, and my eyes told me that he was the man I'd seen outside the warehouse.

The white kimono he was wearing didn't smell like cotton. It smelled like some odd combination of sweet gum and jellyfish, and I was pretty sure that it was alive. I remembered how Akihiko's white trench coat had moved oddly against the wind, and I wondered if this was the same...garment? Thing?

There is a brief period after the host comes into the room and makes tea where the guest is expected to ask questions or comment upon the objects he has been viewing. Kneeling at the low table and sipping the sencha tea, I obliged. "It that giant clam a chen?"

He smiled politely. "It is."

"I thought they were considered sacred," I mused. Some Chinese traditions hold that the chen are transformed dragons meditating on the ocean floor until the end of time. Was the presence of one in Akihiko's tea house a studied insult to the Chinese or just one more indication of how he used living beings for their utilitarian value?

"By some," he acknowledged.

"And is it true that the chen sometimes give visions?" I persisted. There was no point letting the onmyouji know I'd had one.

"That is indisputable," he told me, and a little smugness seeped out.

"And those statues in the corners." I nodded at one of the clothed skeleton statues. "Are those gashadokuro?"

His eyes narrowed, not quite imperceptibly. "You are surprisingly knowledgeable."

"Not really," I disagreed. "I was under the misapprehension that gashadokuro were giants?"

This time, his smile was thin. "My country's cultural preoccupation with giant monsters is quite real but not always practical."

I smiled back, but I wasn't amused, either. Gashadokuro are bone golems assembled from multiple skeletons. The Gashadokuro can animate upon their maker's command—bone puppets that the spirits trapped within them can direct. And one of the requirements for making gashadokuro is that the bones have to come from people who were starved to death.

When the onmyouji was finally ready to talk business, he didn't waste time. "Are you here to kill me?"

I sipped the tea and considered the question. "Not yet."

This was nothing but the truth. There was no way I was going to attack half-cocked in the onmyouji's place of power. As if to underscore the wisdom of that decision, one of the paper lanterns hanging from the ceiling briefly flared at my words, bathing us in a wave of bright heat.

A tiny flicker of annoyance crossed Akihiko's features— I don't know if it was at my response or because whatever flame-based being was in that lantern had just revealed itself. "I have several pieces of a puzzle. Perhaps you could help me fit them together Mr. . . . I assume Down Boy is not your real name?"

"You haven't given me your real name, either," I pointed out.

"This is true." He bowed his head slightly, though he kept his eyes on me while doing so. "You may call me Mr. Satou."

It was the fake name that his daughter had used most of her life while hiding from him, but I don't think my expression gave away the sign of recognition that he was looking for. "You may call me Mark or Mr. Powell. What are these puzzle pieces you mentioned?"

There were four sheets of rice paper set on the table before us. They were covered in Japanese calligraphy, but whatever words they formed weren't any kind of Japanese that I was familiar with. The onmyouji reached out and touched one of the sheets with his index finger. "Many years ago, I heard rumors of a gaijin werewolf who came to my country and acquired a set of swords from a master smith. Supposedly, this gaijin did so by hunting down and killing an amazake-babaa that was spreading disease throughout the smith's region."

At his words, the sheet of paper began to ripple and fold upon itself, gradually transforming into a crude sculpture that looked something like a bent and stooped figure in a Japanese-style headdress. Amazake-babaa almost always take the form of old crones.

The one I'd destroyed in 1971 certainly had.

"Sounds like a nasty piece of business all around," I observed.

"Indeed. Another puzzling piece is that someone is interfering with a private matter that I am involved with," Akihiko continued. "I have not discovered who yet, but events are threatening to spiral out of control."

He touched the second sheet of paper and it began to animate, twisting into a cone whose base was thinner than its top. Then, the paper sculpture accordioned in on itself so that greaves formed in its side. When it was done, the sheet of paper looked like a miniature whirlwind.

"Another piece is that I have heard troubling rumors." Akihiko touched the third sheet of rice paper. "Rumors that the knights who guard this country are forming an alliance with a large clan of werewolves. I find these stories... unwelcome."

The third piece of rice paper contorted and folded itself into a small long sword. It stood on its pommel, perfectly balanced.

"And then there is you," Akihiko went on, "who shows up at my establishment, a werewolf who I cannot see with anything but my physical senses. You then proceed to defeat at least one opponent who was much stronger than you. You seem to be both a werewolf and one of the geas-bound knights of this country, and that should be impossible."

The fourth piece of paper morphed into the form of a wolf with a series of rasping and scraping sounds that seemed mildly painful.

"I can't answer all of your questions," I said wryly. "But I think I can help you achieve a higher level of clarity."

He took a sip of his own tea for the first time. "That would be welcome."

"Imagine you are on a mountain overlooking a city," I invited. "And you see smoke where a fire breaks out. Then a little later, some distance away, you see smoke from another fire break out. And then later, another. Do you assume that one person is starting the fires, or that a mob is starting fires and these are the first signs of a much larger disturbance spreading and breaking out?"

He considered the question seriously. "It would be a mistake to assume either without more information."

I nodded and began to lie my ass off. "It is not impossible to bind a werewolf to a knight's geas. In fact, there are many of us."

"Explain." He forgot to ask politely, but I didn't press.

"You must know that a geas does not have a mind of its own," I said. "It is a thought planted into our minds with the force of a command, but it is not capable of thought in itself. If you planted a geas to go to Vegas in someone's head, unless you were specific, they might go by bus or by plane or by car or by motorcycle, depending on their means and preferences. And the command certainly couldn't tell them what to buy someone for their birthday, or offer an opinion on an upcoming election. Do you see?"

"Yes," Akihiko affirmed.

"And the geas that the Fae implanted in the minds of various secret societies across the world is just a compulsion to maintain the Pax Arcana. It doesn't tell people how in every specific circumstance. It can't. What the Knights Templar have done is taught their followers to believe that all sorts of other conditions are part of the geas, and because knights believe that, it is true. They believe that they are compelled to stay in the Templars to best maintain the Pax, and so they are. And they believe being turned into supernatural beings would compromise their geas, so their bodies shut down and kill them before such transformations can take root."

That was the real reason I had been hunted so relentlessly for so long. My very existence contradicted one of the beliefs that knights had been taught as scripture, and the order masters didn't want other knights to begin asking questions about what else they were taught that might be a matter of opinion. So, I had been demonized.

Akihiko sipped his tea again. "It is the same result. If geas-born knights cannot become werewolves, then werewolves cannot become knights, because the geas is passed down through the blood."

I nodded. "But the Templars have had a faction who believe that monsters aren't inherently evil since the 1920s. It was our version of a reaction against World War I. The other chapters call us Bug Huggers."

This was whopping lie number two, by the way. If I had been brought up by the Bug Huggers, my life would have been much easier. "For decades, my chapter has been marginalized and looked down upon, but we have persisted," I went on blandly.

Akihiko absorbed this thoughtfully. "And what does this have to do with the Knights Templar working with werewolves in this country now?"

I shrugged. "Once we believed that a werewolf's *curse* and a knight's geas were not incompatible, it was only a matter of time. The first member of my chapter to survive a werewolf bite was in 1937. We kept it a secret."

"You kept a secret from your own order?"

"The grandmaster commanded it." I allowed a hint of anger to enter my voice. This story was close enough to my own truth that it wasn't hard. "He said that the other knights weren't ready for that knowledge. If it wouldn't have caused more questions than it would have ended, I think he would have destroyed my entire chapter."

Akihiko did not seem to find this mind-set unthinkable or unlikely, but it was hard to tell whether he believed me or not. "And there have been others since? You are one of them?"

"At least a dozen over the last few decades," I lied. "And that doesn't count the secret societies from other countries who have had werewolf agents for centuries, like the Kresniks and the Benandanti."

Akihiko pointed at the four origami that had formed on his table. "And you are saying that these incidents are not the work of one individual but signs that a much larger truth is finally coming out of hiding."

"I'm saying that's where your rumors about werewolves working with knights are coming from," I clarified. "The Order got in a fight with a large werewolf pack calling itself the Clan last year. They sent those of us who were werewolves into the Clan to spy on them and make war. Instead, we made peace."

Some of the simmering menace beneath his thin veil of calm

peeked out. "And if this is such a well-kept secret, why are you telling me?"

I gestured at the origami sculptures. "You yourself said that you've been hearing rumors. The incidents are beginning to multiply. I imagine you are more well-informed than most, but it's only a matter of time before the ripples spread out to the supernatural community."

He betrayed his second hint of impatience. "None of this explains why you are here. I am not endangering your Pax. I am not drawing attention to myself. My Crucible gives supernatural creatures a healthy outlet for their base desires. Your geas should prevent you from harming me."

He wasn't wrong. But my geas didn't keep me from investigating, and my geas allowed for self-defense, and the wolf part of me considered protecting members of my pack as self-defense. I really do blur a lot of distinctions and bend a lot of rules just by existing. Emil Lamplighter, the Templar Grandmaster, had said as much when explaining why he wanted to kill me so badly.

Time for big lie number three.

"I'm not here for you at all," I said. "I'm after a rakshasa. It is cunning, but like most of its kind, it has a degenerate weakness for gambling."

"Ah." There was just a tiny nostril flare there.

Rakshasas are monsters who came to the United States from India, immensely difficult to hunt because of their ability to disguise their appearance. Their compulsion for gambling is one of the surest methods for tracking them.

"It will come see your contests soon if it hasn't already," I said. "I don't think it will be able to stay away from violent spectacle *and* wagering."

"Does this rakshasa use a name?" he inquired neutrally.

"It has had many," I said. "The last name it used was Nicole Matthews. It was running an underground poker tournament in Atlanta."

"I know of this rakshasa," Akihiko admitted. "It supposedly died in a fire. I assumed a knight had killed it."

"It didn't die," I disagreed. "The rakshasa knew I was sniffing around and killed all of its staff and faked its own death. It used the fire to destroy all physical evidence, and it worked. I lost its trail there."

Also a lie. I had come across and killed "Nicole Matthews" while trying to earn some gambling money off the grid. But I hadn't left any way to prove that. My story fit real facts that Akihiko could uncover for himself.

He pointed at the paper whirlwind on the table. Unsettlingly, it began to spin like a real whirlwind. "And my private affair?"

I shrugged and drank from the tea I had been neglecting. "How would I know? Is there some reason to think a werewolf or a knight is involved? If it's cunning folk business, I would think that your secret enemy would be another of your own kind."

That registered. He at least knew his secret enemy had gone into the Dreamtime and made protective wards. Hell, I almost believed what I'd been saying myself.

"We might be able to help each other," he granted. "Your original plan was to go undercover and fight in the Crucible, yes?"

"Not really," I lied. "I just came to the warehouse hoping to gather information. It would be easier to conceal myself by just watching the fights and mingling in the crowd. You won't even know I'm there."

He waved that away. "I have a proposition that may interest you."

"A deal with a cunning man," I commented unenthusiastically. "Wonderful."

"I could make a great deal of money on you," he informed me. "The odds given against a lone werewolf will be high at first."

"If that's what you're after, why not just rig some of the fights?" I wondered.

He gave me a flat stare. "That would be dishonorable."

He was serious. He was in the habit of sacrificing his own descendants to prolong his life, had killed his wife and bound her spirit, imprisoned his own daughter, starved men to death to make tools out of them, been cursed by his own ancestors, and he was worried about his honor. I recalled what Sarah had said about Akihiko obeying certain rules while perverting everything those rules were meant to protect or maintain.

Perhaps he picked up on some of my disapproval. In any case, Akihiko sweetened the pot. "Give me three fights, and in return, I will use all of my resources to make inquiries and keep an eye out for your rakshasa."

"Three," I repeated with even less enthusiasm. Why is it always three? Three days. Three bears. Three pigs. Three brothers. Three tasks. Three sisters. Three goats. Three fairy godmothers. Three blind mice. Three guesses. Three wishes.

"After that, the odds will go down anyhow," he explained. If I were really after a rakshasa like I claimed, and a man with connections to many different supernatural beings and an organized gambling ring offered his help at that price...shit. If I agreed, he would be able to surround me with dangerous predators while he kept an eye on me and did what he could to check my background out. If I didn't agree, he would know something was wrong with my story.

"I think we can reach an agreement," I said. Only time would tell who had gotten the better of whom.

And speaking of time, it didn't operate normally in that creepy-ass labyrinth. It had only been a few hours, but when the kitsune led me down those identical paper hallways and back out onto the waterfront, I blinked up at New York afternoon sun. At least half a day had passed. I looked at the kitsune.

"It happens," she said calmly.

∾25∾

A GOOD MINION IS HARD TO FIND

There's some kind of Asian were-woman watching this place." Gordon Porter signed. He was a knight if no longer an active one, one of those rare geas born who survive their sixth decade with all of their limbs intact. A greying hardcase, he leaned on a spiked truncheon disguised as a walking stick and ran a small alarm-installing company. Most of his employees were lay servants, which meant that they hadn't been born into the Knights Templar but had tumbled onto the existence of the supernatural under terrifying circumstances. When not eliminating, intimidating, or discrediting such people, knights like to make use of them—it both bolsters the order's ranks and helps them keep tabs on potential whistle-blowers.

Gordon was one of three (again with the three!) discreet contacts that I was maintaining with the Grandmaster of the Knights Templar, and the contacts had to be discreet. Alliance or no alliance, it was going to be a long time before any knights and I posed for a Christmas card together.

"She's a kitsune," I signed back.

"She knows we spotted her," Gordon replied silently. "And probably knows we're knights too. She's not just a natural tracker. She's developed some serious skills."

I just nodded. I wanted the kitsune to recognize Gordon and his people. Hell, I had rented a furnished apartment quickly in New York—which meant paying way, way too much money—specifically so that she could see Gordon's company at work. Akihiko was watching me full time now, and I needed to verify my ties with the Templars so that the lies built around that connection might sound more credible.

Gordon gave me a sour grimace and went back to helping his men secure the place. Since his most sophisticated alarms had a nasty habit of not working around magic, Gordon and his people also took other measures: sigils and wards that only showed up in ultraviolet light, holy symbols, medicine bags that prevented clairvoyant spying, and bug spray that kept out more than bugs. Finally, they strategically placed several white-noise generators so that no one with extra-sensitive hearing or directional microphones could eavesdrop from outside.

When the place was secure, Gordon spoke aloud. "Give it to me from the top."

I told Gordon everything I knew about Akihiko's operation in New York.

"This doesn't sound like an emergency." Gordon wasn't crazy about dealing with me, by the way. He was hard-core loyal to the Grandmaster, but we weren't friends.

"This cunning man is building up a cadre of enforcers and assassins from different monster types," I said. "And that kitsune out there was spewing some pretty serious anti-knight propaganda at the first meeting I attended too. I kind of thought the Grandmaster would like to have someone on the inside."

Gordon huffed. "You think we don't already know about

an underground fighting circuit for monsters? It's not our job to keep supernaturals from killing each other." Gordon's eyes were cold. "We've got real problems we're dealing with. Homeless guys in Boston are having prophetic visions while they die from a seizure, and we have no idea why. A jinn is running around New York like a bull in an explosives lab. One of your werewolves attacked the knights that he was supposed to be helping track down a boo hag. And more fucking people are seeing fucking shadow beings every fucking day and talking about it on the fucking Internet, and we have no idea if it's really some kind of shadow race or if these people are getting peripheral glimpses of supernatural creatures because the Pax is weakening. So why are you wasting my time with this shit?"

I tried to explain without mentioning Kevin or Sarah. "This guy's bad news Gordon. I'm investigating."

"Uh-huh." Somehow he managed to stay unmoved by my passionate eloquence. "What do you want, Charming?"

"I want you to get in touch with the yamabushi for me," I said.

Yamabushi are warrior monks and Japan's equivalent of the Knights Templar. Like the Templars, yamabushi started out as a society whose focus was on training a small number of elite warriors to impact a much larger population, and also like the Templars, the yamabushi fell in and out of political favor and had to become skilled at operating in secrecy. So skilled that they are as much legend as fact. There are still groups that operate under the yamabushi title publicly, and I'm not clear if there's a connection between them and the yamabushi that went underground after agreeing to the Pax Arcana or not. There are still groups who publicly call themselves Templars too, and some of them are splinter groups and some of them are parallel organizations and some of them are posers and some of them are fronts.

"That's not how this works," Gordon informed me. "I'm not your waiter. I snap my fingers and you come running, not the other way around."

I considered telling him that I was good at snapping fingers too, especially other people's, but then I remembered that I was asking a favor. "I just want a file or a conversation so I can learn more about this onmyouji. Akihiko lived in Japan for most of his life, and apparently, it's been a long, long life. There's no way the yamabushi haven't kept tabs on him."

Gordon considered this. "You're asking us to owe another group a favor. We take that kind of thing seriously. But I'll pass your request on. In the meantime, if the Grandmaster decides he wants this cunning man removed, I'll give you a call. If you take the cunning man out anyway, give me one." Then the son of a bitch handed me a bill.

"Really?" I asked.

"Details." His face was still stony, but there was a slight hint of a smirk in his voice. He hadn't given me a discount.

After they left, I used my phone to call Ben Lafontaine.

"Hey, Ben."

"What do you need now?"

"What do you mean, *now*?" I said, annoyed. Ben too? "I haven't talked to you for a month."

"Exactly," Ben grunted. "What do you want?"

"Did I forget to send you a birthday card or something?" I asked. "What's got your nuts in a knot?"

"I'm trying to hold the largest coalition of werewolf packs on this continent together, and werewolves aren't even a Chippewa tradition," Ben reminded me. "They came over here with the French Canadians. The only reason I wound up leading a tribe of wolfwalkers is because one of them got loose on my rez a hundred years ago, and all you white folk think the People know more about this stuff than you do. And now I'm trying to get knights to work with werewolves without treating us like trained dogs, and werewolves to listen to knights without biting their heads off, and the one man who knows what it's like to be a knight and a werewolf isn't much help."

It was the longest speech I'd ever heard from Ben.

"Hey, I've been teaching some of your pack leaders how to interact with knights," I protested.

"You did that twice." Ben sounded a little grim. "And you set the pack leader from Chicago on fire."

"Traditional teaching methods didn't seem to be working."

"He has been easier to deal with," Ben admitted. "But I know you want something because everybody wants something from me."

So basically, I'd caught him on a bad day and he was feeling grumpy and overwhelmed. It happens. "You're right, Ben," I said. "I'm coming back to Wisconsin to be your second in command as soon as I hang up the phone. That ought to make your life easier."

"You don't have to make threats," Ben grumbled.

"No, I think it will be great," I said earnestly. "It's not like the Templars resent me. And there aren't any wolves who blame me for the way their old clan broke up, either."

"Like you'd really leave that blonde. My people have a saying." Ben's voice was curt. "Shut your damn pipe hole if you're just going to blow smoke up my ass."

"Huh," I said. "I'm not sure, but I think that lost a little bit of its cultural richness in translation."

"My people's heritage can be difficult for an outsider to appreciate," Ben explained. "What do you want?"

"Does the Round Table have any people in New York City?"

"We have two packs there," Ben responded. "We had to weed the troublemakers out of one pack, and it's too small. We had to combine two other packs into one when a pack leader got killed, and it's too big. You should know this stuff."

"Hey, you need help with a fight, you call me." I was nettled, mostly because he was probably right. "You want somebody dead, or you want somebody tracked down or protected, I'm there. Anything involving Constance and you don't even have to ask."

Ben and I had both agreed to be godfathers to the Grandmaster's last surviving relative. It was one of the terms of the werewolf/knight truce, and it's complicated.

"Are these roaming charges?" Ben wondered.

He was right. Despite what I'd told the kitsune about everybody needing help sometimes, I have a hard time asking for it. "There's this underground fighting ring called the Crucible going on here."

"I know. A pack of were-hyenas tried to bite the people behind it and wound up getting eaten."

Huh. That was pretty up-to-date intel. It suddenly occurred to me that maybe I should have reported that to Ben myself. I really was a shitty pack member.

"I'm competing in the fights," I said. "I was wondering if maybe you could place some of your people in the audience."

"No," he said. "But maybe I can put some of *our* people in the audience."

My first impulse was to tell him to fuck off. My second impulse was to apologize. I swallowed both impulses, and they made uncomfortable lumps going down. "I'm not good at this, Ben. I don't know what I'm doing."

"You mean being part of a community?" he asked.

I sighed. "Yeah."

"And that's important to you?" he wondered. "Being good at things?"

"It is," I admitted.

"Because you grew up being judged by those knight assholes all the time and having a lot to prove."

"What's your point?" I snapped.

"There is no point," he said. "But being part of a real community isn't something you have to be good at. You just are."

"Then why have you been busting my chops about needing to do better?"

"Hmmm," Ben grunted. "Did I mention that my people's ways can be difficult for an outsider to understand?"

"I'm supposed to fight three times," I informed him through gritted teeth. "If you could pad the crowd out with some of *our* people a little more each time, it might not be noticeable."

"Oh, I don't have to sneak anyone in," he said. "A lot of our people have been going to the fights since they started."

"What?!?" I exploded. "And you made me go through all that?"

"Yes."

"You dog-breathed shit heel!"

He interrupted before I could gain steam. "You just make sure you kick some ass. A lot of werewolves joined our group because they wanted to fight knights. Now some packs are calling us traitors or weak because we made an alliance instead. We have members leaving us, and other werewolves who like the idea of pushing other monsters around are asking about joining us for the wrong reasons. Our people need good stories right now."

"I'll put on a good show, Ben." It was a promise I felt comfortable making. Fighting for my life is the one thing I don't find complicated.

∾26∾

THE TOWER OF BABBLE

A point in New York City's favor is that it has some of the best libraries in the world, and I found a building with a copy of both the *Konjaku Monogatari* and the *Nihon Ryakki* along with some more recent books on Japanese myths, fables, and folklore. I spent an entire afternoon researching and barely scratched the surface, but it was still better than trying to use the Internet—I didn't have to comb through the debris of links whose files could no longer be found, or sites that wanted my personal information, or blog after blog that basically repeated the same information that had been copied and pasted from some Wikipedia page over and over, or get halfway down a page and realize that I was reading something made up for a fantasy role-playing game. Even so, I didn't find any stories about Japanese cunning folk who specifically reminded me of Akihiko, but then, I had no idea how old he really was, and he had already proven that he was good at not making himself known to normals.

I had a little more luck regarding kitsune.

Sifting folklore and fables for useful information isn't an

exact science, but you get better at reading behind the meta-phors after a while. A lot of stories confirmed that kitsune could be good or evil, and the most powerful ones were always elders, suggesting that kitsune both valued family and got more powerful as they got older. It was also a consistent tru-ism that kitsune grew more tails as they aged, and I wondered if it was more than that, if kitsune grew a new tail each time they attained a new power or stage of development. All sources agreed that kitsune could grow up to nine tails, and I tried to count the number of different supernatural abilities kitsune displayed in the stories I was reading.

There were fables about kitsune carrying firebrands around in their mouths and starting fires, which might be a euphe-mism for breathing fire. I found stories about kitsune know-ing the future and stories about kitsune talking to people in their dreams. Some accounts featured kitsune who just seemed to have one human form, and others had kitsune who could mimic anyone they desired. There were stories where a kitsune could drain life force from someone else, or cast illusions, or put people in a trance if not outright possess them. That was at least eight powers right there, though I had no way of defini-tively ranking them.

I didn't find what I was really looking for until a statue of a kitsune and a mysterious gem at the Fushimi Inari-taisha shrine led me to a twelfth-century tale mentioning something called a hoshi no tama. It was an object that seemed to be linked to the kitsune's immortality, and supposedly, anyone who got their hands on one could control the foxes. As I kept reading, I found that in some accounts, the hoshi no tama were described like onions, sometimes like pearls. Sometimes like fiery gems.

And I was pretty sure that Akihiko was keeping the one that controlled his kitsune in a bank deposit box.

*   *   *

The group in the secret area in *Swords and Wards* was slightly different this time. Parth was there, and so were Sig, Sarah, Jerry, and Ted Cahill, all of whom had avatars who looked a lot like them.

I filled them in on my introduction to the onmyouji and the vision I'd had, and then we started kicking some ideas around.

TED: Who careris about this hoshitsnotama. You hadf a fhallucination.

JOHN: It was a vision.

SARAH: Don't forget the sword either. The spirits of Akihiko's ancestors are angry at him, and according to Jerry's story, they can work through that sword to get around Akihiko's magical defenses.

SIG: That's true. Itsa probably why hes keeping that sword with someone else. The last time Akihiko tried to hide it himself, the sword burnt his home down.

JOHN: Whichever we focus on, we need to find that safety deposit box.

PARTH: braithwaites is the only bank a wealthy supernatural being would use to keep something close at hand in NYC.

JOHN: I don't know. Physical distance doesn't seem to be a factor with those paper hallways Akihiko uses. He could have a bank anywhere.

PARTH: if A has properties in NYC and is generating income from interests in NYC he will have a bank in NYC trust me.

TED: I taekj it youf ahve a acounte in this splace?

PARTH: yes braithwaites has supernatural as well as technological dfenses. I can trace the name A bought the warehouse in and verify he has an account there if you like.

SARAH: I want to open an account of my own there. I want to see what kind of spells and wards they're using.

TED: Whoawhoa, whoa! WEre talking aobut robbing a banke now? Whey not just kill the guy?

JOHN: Because Akihiko gave me the chance.

TED: ???

JOHN: He wouldn't have if he didn't have some serious personal defenses. We need to scope them out.

SIG: Shenay says people who challenge him disappear.

JOHN: And even if we don't disappear, Akihiko might. With those doors he can run anywhere. If we blow our shot, we might lose him AND the advantage of surprise.

TED: Whosis Shenay?

SIG: A leopard woman. I like her.

SARAH: The point is, that family sword and the kitsune are the only two things we know of that can get through Akihiko's magical defenses for sure.

JOHN: There's another option too. That tea house he took me to is in a real physical location somewhere. If we could find it, I could fly to Japan and be waiting for him there.

TED: I like it. Go s straingt fromp oint A to point C. Cut out the vision bullshit.

JERRY: I want to be the one to kill him.

SARAH: He has the sight, Jerry. People like Akihiko and I are very difficult to kill with a rifle. If we don't get a precognitive flash of the bullet, we sense the person sighting on us through a rifle scope.

PARTH: i will keep tracing his shell companies and bank accounts and property holdings.

SARAH: And I can work on the bank.

TED: I can whistle with my nose.

JERRY: I still want to try to kill him.

JOHN: If you want to take a shot at Akihiko, you've got a warehouse location, Jerry.

SARAH: John...

JOHN: But we ought to plan it so that even if it doesn't work, it will make a big honking distraction that we can take advantage of.

SIG: You should get Choo to be your spotter too.

JERRY: My guard you mean.

TED: Incase you want t o do any exttra huntgin asshole.

SIG: Ted, STFU. And learn to type.

TED: You hut the fuckup. Its not just syour inhuman ass on the line if this guy goese ona killing spree.

JERRY: The only monster I'm focusing on is your onmyouji.

TED: Thats whatI'm talking about. He's YOUR onmyjoii numbnuts. I never hear boo from this guy unitl your family came to my town but your lumping us. altogether in your head.

JERRY: Only you. You are the thing that almost killed my son.

TED: That aws n accident. You almost killed Jon on purpose.

JOHN: And you don't see me whining do you? If Sarah trusts him, I trust him, Cahill.

SIG: Umm...what?!?

JOHN: She has the sight, Sig.

JOHN: And Jerry, Akihiko has supernatural guards. Choo knows more about evading them than you do.

SIG: EVERYONE JUST STOP FOR A SECOND.

SIG: Plan A. Jerry and Choo shoot the jerk. With an exit strategy.

SIG: Plan B. John and I keep gathering intel for the best way to kill Akihiko.

SIG: Plan C. Parth tracks down some of Aki's bolt holes and we ambush him there.

TED: Plan D. WE break into a fuckingt bank cos Wolft boy had a bad clam.

PARTH: i want to communicate with that chen when this is all over.

SIG: And we keep Kevin alive. Does that about cover it?

JOHN: Hope so. G2G.

SARAH: Wait!

JOHN: Can't. Kitsune.

SIG: Be careful.

That seemed a little un-Sig like. Or at least saying it in front of everyone else did. I couldn't respond; the kitsune really was standing at the entrance to the library's computer area, scanning the sea of heads bent over monitor screens, and I had already started logging out, or logging off, or whatever the hell you do with online games.

"You knights have some good code monkeys," the kitsune said quietly as I approached. "I broke into the last computer lab you used and took the entire CPU to my boss. He had some people try to open the hard drive and see what you'd been doing, and they went crazy. Something about viruses almost replicating inside their systems and programming code using Sumerian command words. I didn't really understand it all."

Was she being so frank because she had a certain degree of autonomy, or was she inviting confidences hoping I'd drop something? My guard? The soap? Some useful random tidbit? I contented myself by responding: "I don't understand that stuff either."

It wouldn't surprise me if everyone who downloaded Parth's online game wound up opening backdoors into their computer systems though.

The kitsune led me to an empty room set aside for children's storytelling hour, a large open space with curved, padded seats shaped like Ls. There were pictures of cute magical creatures and rainbows and fairy-tale characters painted on the walls all around us. I couldn't decide if that was ironic or just weird. She was dressed in a buttoned tan vest over a white shirt, light tan pants, and tennis shoes that were a little too practical to go with her outfit. A green winter coat was pulled over the ensemble. I decided to use subtlety to find out more about her.

"Can you breathe fire?" I asked.

She exhaled, just slightly, and a brief flicker of flame appeared and then went out. "Been reading up on me, Down Boy?"

"I like to know who I'm working with," I replied.

"Don't Knights Templar have lore masters and support teams and research analysts to do that sort of thing for them?" she wondered. "You act like someone who's used to doing all of his own leg work."

Damn it. Why couldn't she just be good at following people? Why did she have to be perceptive? "I'm not good at working with other people when I don't have to," I said truthfully. "Speaking of which, I still don't know your name."

"You don't need to," she said. "I'm not here looking for a date. I'm here because there's a Crucible tonight."

"Then I'll be there," I responded.

She didn't seem particularly pleased or disappointed. "The odds are seven to one against you tonight."

"But your boss is betting on me, right?" I pointed out. "It would help if I knew what I was fighting."

She smiled a smile that wasn't and gave me a slip of paper similar to the first one that she had given me.

"Okay," I said. "Can I at least bet money on myself?"

"My master encourages it. Anything up to thirty thousand dollars." The word *master* came with a slight increase in her pulse rate and a chemical tang of anger. "You just can't bet *against* yourself. Someone tried that not too long ago."

"And this someone is dead?" I speculated.

"No." An involuntary shudder of revulsion went through her. "She's not."

I didn't ask for more details. "He has your hoshi no tama, doesn't he? Mr. Satou?"

"That question is very rude." Her face wasn't sad or amused or angry. It was something, though. Maybe just tight from trying not to be any of those things. "And I wouldn't be able to answer you if I wanted to."

"I know what it's like to be compelled by an outside force," I offered. She just left me hanging there, and I finished lamely. "It sucks."

"My English is very good," she said. "But it isn't good enough to have this conversation."

"Do you get to read?" I pressed. "Make your favorite food for meals? Download apps for your cell phone? Go to movies? Have lovers? What is it that makes your life worth living?"

For a long time, I didn't think she was going to answer. She seemed to be struggling but also embarrassed to be visibly struggling. "The same thing that makes anyone's life worth living," she said finally. "Hope and stubbornness."

I started to ask something else and she interrupted me. "You seem to think you know why I'm here. Why are you?"

I was still trying to formulate an answer that wouldn't reveal too much and wouldn't be total bullshit when she said, "Never mind," and walked away. It only occurred to me later that the onmyouji had sent her to find out what she could about me, and yet she had left abruptly as if she regretted asking the question. Like maybe she didn't want to know any secrets the onmyouji could force her to reveal later.

If she had been waiting for the onmyouji to die for a long time, Akihiko's recent discovery of Kevin Kichida and his sperm donations hadn't likely filled her with joy.

Of course, she could just be playing me. After all, she was a fox.

~27~

FEE FI FUCK YOU

It was almost midnight and there weren't a lot of stars out or lights around when I found the normal human guards waiting for me in the deserted remnants of some kind of industrial park. Whatever factories had inspired this much pale concrete and peeling steel were probably in China or Mexico or South America now. The three guards were Asian, trim, dressed in loose black clothing that was formal but not overly so, and we were standing next to a dry riverbed. The concrete trench was maybe thirty feet deep and forty feet wide. I don't know if it had been built before some dam cut off its water supply or if it was designed to channel water in case of floods.

"Have money?" one man asked without preamble.

"I do," I said. "But I'd feel better if I knew who I was betting against. What am I fighting tonight?"

"Scorecard at Crucible," he told me.

"I was told to come here first," I explained.

He just looked at me blankly. "Have money?"

I was pretty sure he was just pretending not to speak much English, but since I was also pretending not to speak any

Japanese, I didn't take it personally. I took thirty thousand dollars from Mark Powell's bank account out of a beige backpack. "Where do I pick up my winnings?"

He seemed to find my presumption amusing. Handing my money over to a second guard, he said, "White van. After fight."

The last guard offered me a white cotton robe. "Take off clothes."

It was cold, but I stripped down to sweat pants and sneakers without arguing.

"No weapons in Crucible but what we put in," the guard said. "Or we kill."

I just nodded and donned the white robe. The last guard pointed down to a golf cart that was sitting at the bottom of the channel beside us. For some reason, it reminded me of that scene in *Grease* when they were drag-racing down the Los Angeles River riverbed. "Your ride."

Conversation didn't seem to be a priority, so I walked down the concrete embankment. It turned out that the driver waiting for me was one of the were-hyenas who had been showing their ass outside Akihiko's warehouse. I recognized his smell at the same time that he visibly recognized mine. He wasn't wearing gang-banging clothing anymore, though his suit was cheaper than the Asian guard's. He was thin and rangy and tough-looking, with wispy pale hair and skin that had seen a lot of scars before he developed the ability to heal them.

"What, you guys work for the man in white now?" I asked as I climbed into the passenger's side of the golf cart.

"It's not like you think." His expression and tone were sullen.

I gave him a neutral glance. "It never is."

"You're here, ain't you?" he muttered truculently.

"I'm here to fight for money," I answered. "And these people didn't kill my packmates in front of my eyes."

He snarled and drove. I wasn't trying to make enemies. I was just fanning the embers of whatever resentment and wounded pride he had going while it was still fresh. It seemed to me that if Akihiko had a weakness, it was the fact that so many of the beings who worked for him were slaves and conquered enemies. Was that just strategy on his part, or was domination what sent blood rushing into his cock?

The were-hyena wove the cart around the bits of driftwood and assorted trash littering the bottom of the channel without further comment. We didn't have to travel far—maybe the length of two football fields—before the channel curved into a bend. There was a lot of purposeless concrete infrastructure on the right, and riverbank and scraggly-ass woods on the left. I didn't see how Akihiko could police or enclose this place, but maybe that was the point. Maybe monsters wouldn't come to a place they didn't know without lots of exit options.

The stretch we came to had four large bonfires set in the bottom of the dry riverbed about forty feet apart. The bonfires smelled vaguely sulfurous and kept changing colors; one was red and two were green and one was purple but in the process of becoming blue as I stared at it. Right behind and above the bonfires was an old bridge crossing the riverbed, apparently prime seating for the fights that would take place below, because there were a lot of silhouettes leaning against the rails, not all of them humanoid.

The kitsune was standing between the flaming columns, waiting.

My opponent smelled like some kind of Fae. He looked like a gnarled and incredibly ugly old man—popeyed and lumpy-nosed and only standing a few inches over five feet tall—but looks don't mean much with the Fae and their genetic offshoots. Russet-haired, wiry, and shirtless, he flexed and stretched thin twisted-rubber-band muscles while he examined me from thirty feet away. There are a lot of Fae that appear short, but there aren't too many that look old, and he wasn't wearing a red cap or steel-toed boots, wasn't wearing anything except stretch pants.

A few minutes earlier, while encouraging the crowd to spice the fight up by throwing a little money on top, the kitsune had referred to the Fae as "Wee Willy."

We were standing between the four bonfires at the bottom of the overflow channel. The fires served to warm us and illuminate us, but they also kept me from being able to clearly see the silent observers looking down on us. There must have been at least a thousand shadowy forms, but they were only illuminated in patches and brief flickers. The bonfires' heat kept me from using infrared vision, and their pungent smell overpowered a lot of background scents. I couldn't tell if Akihiko was up there or not. Sig probably was.

The kitsune was holding a white scarf in one hand and a red scarf in another, and now she walked up to my opponent. "Are you ready, Llewyn?"

"Against one lone wolf?" Llewyn acted outraged "Who did this poor bastard cheese off, Chikako?"

The kitsune laughed. "He does have a mouth on him."

"I'll shut his feckin' cake hole for ya," the Fae promised. "But I should get somethin' more than seven-ta-one odds for it. How about a kiss?"

The kitsune blew Llewyn a kiss, and he pretended to grab it out of the air and press it to his lips, grinning widely.

She walked across to me next.

"Chikako?" I asked.

"Win this fight and maybe you can call me that too," she said. "Are you ready?"

"The odds are seven to one against it," I replied dryly.

She smiled a small but real smile. "At least it's not a fight to the death."

"Do you have those?" I asked.

The smile disappeared. "Yes."

"And accidents happen," I nudged.

"Yes," she agreed. "And so do not-accidents. Are you ready or not?"

"Here I come," I promised.

Chikako flashed me another of her speculative glances then, but she walked back to a midpoint between me and Llewyn and addressed the crowd. "YOU DIDN'T COME HERE FOR TALK. YOU CAME HERE FOR TOOTH AND CLAW! NO RULES. NO ROUNDS. NO ONE LEAVES UNTIL THE OTHER ONE'S DOWN."

The sound that came from the watchers above us is hard to describe. It might have been a communal snarl, or a rumble, or a grunt, or maybe all of those things in some kind of hungry harmony. She threw the white scarf and skipped nimbly out of the way while "Wee Willy" and I charged each other.

He was a bit of a boxer, and it didn't take long to figure out that he was as fast as I was and almost as strong. Llewyn liked to dance, and he weaved around, peppering me with punches, but he telegraphed them with his shoulders and it was relatively easy to sway back or block his blows. I had set up a steady beat to my own punches by this point, easy to anticipate, and he must have thought it was an unconscious rhythm or not thought about it at all, because when I broke out of the pattern and feinted an overhand right, it caught him off guard.

He panicked and overcompensated in a move that would have barely blocked the punch if I'd followed through with it, and I caught him with a left uppercut that rocked him back on his feet.

Nothing hampers footwork like being on your heels. I moved inside his guard while he was still recovering and jackhammered three short, stiff punches into his torso. He doubled over, and I might have finished him then, but a weird thing happened. He lashed out, and I stepped back just enough so that I could move in when his punch went by and left him open. But the punch didn't go by. The feeble backhand connected when it shouldn't have. And it wasn't so feeble.

Most of a knight's training consists of learning how to fight beings who are physically stronger, and I automatically let the blow knock me back instead of trying to resist it, dispersing some of the impact. That was probably a mistake, because when I moved in again, Wee Willy was eight feet tall and still growing.

He was a spriggan. Some people say that spriggans are what giants evolved into when blending in became the only way to survive, and some people say that spriggans are actually mediums... that they can allow the spirits of dead giants to move into their bodies and shift the furniture around, so to speak. I just think they're pain-in-the-ass Fae shapeshifters myself.

The spriggan wasn't just growing taller; his muscles and torso were thickening. The mass was slowing him down a little, and he was still a bit cross-eyed from the brief beating I'd handed him, so I managed to step in and hit him with a right, but it didn't seem to have much effect. He forced me back with his now-longer reach, and by this point, he was ten feet tall.

The watchers weren't restrained any longer. They were screaming encouragement to the spriggan, growls and snarls and hoarse yells and high shrieks. I suspect even those watchers who had bet on me, if there were any, were caught up in the frenzy.

He was twelve feet tall and moving slower when I ducked under a looping overhand and got inside his reach. I used his bent knee as a stepping-stone and jumped, propelling myself straight up between his arms and slamming my knee into his throat. It hurt him, but he tucked his chin down and drew his arms in and caught me in a bear hug. The only thing that kept my spine from breaking was that he was gagging, unable to pull wind down his trachea, and his arms were around my butt, not my lower back.

We both moved fast. He was loosening his grasp just slightly, pulling my body down lower, when I gouged the tips of my stiff hands beneath his thick eyelids. He howled and loosened his arms further, just for a moment, but we were both covered in sweat by this point, and he might as well have been trying to hold on to an eel. I moved my hands under his jaw and pushed myself down, sliding out of his embrace and dropping to the ground at his feet.

He tried to kick me like a soccer ball then, would have driven my ribs out through the back of my shoulder blades if his foot or knee had connected, but I rolled to the side and between his legs, coming to a crouch behind him. I twisted my whole body and drove an elbow into that sweet spot behind his right knee, that reflex point that makes legs buckle at the slightest tap. He dropped down to that knee, and I rose up to my feet behind him, twisting and getting an arm around his throat.

It wasn't a traditional choke hold. I couldn't get the hand of my encircling arm all the way around that thick neck and the base of his skull, and actually had to lock one of my wrists over the other to pull tightly enough. But he still hadn't managed to get a breath in through his throat, and it was enough. He tried to pull my arm off, but his fingers were too big and our flesh was too sweaty and my forearm was pressed so tightly into his own flesh that he couldn't get a grip. He tried to headbutt backward, but I felt the muscle movements and vibrations through my arm and swayed aside. He tried to reach a hand back over his shoulder to grab me, but the new thick slabs of muscle in his arms actually limited his flexibility there, and I managed to slide around his neck while still maintaining pressure. When he tried to position his other knee to stand, I kicked the back of that knee too, and this time, he went with it and threw himself backward.

It was like being caught under a falling tree, but I held on while the weight and impact resonated through every bone and tendon in my body. Hell, I squeezed tighter, ignored the black patches in my vision, and focused everything I had on maintaining the choke hold. Now he really couldn't reach me because I was pinned beneath him.

The spriggan went limp. Yeah, right. Nice try, elf boy. I used the sudden lack of resistance to squeeze even tighter. He began to thrash around in a reflexive panic then, rolled onto his side, dragging my body up and behind him like some kind of streamer or banner made out of flailing legs. Finally, his instincts took over and he did the thing his lizard brain was screaming at him to do when the pressure around his throat was too tight. He began to shrink. I'd been waiting for it and cinched my arm in tighter, and when he didn't get the sip of air he was looking for, he kept shrinking, and when he realized that he'd given his only remaining advantage away for nothing, it was too late.

The next time he went limp, it was for real.

I slowly, painfully stood up and did my best to stretch

while the kitsune walked over and threw the red scarf on top of the spriggan's body. The shadowy watchers weren't screaming encouragement or appreciation. If anything, they seemed caught in a sullen pause. They wanted blood, not oxygen deprivation, and a lot of them had probably lost money. But nobody was storming down the concrete slope of the trench to vent their frustrations out on me, either. Given what I knew about Akihiko, his methods of crowd control were probably brutal, effective, and well established.

"You can call me Chikako," the kitsune said.

~28~

NO, YOU CAN'T HAVE ME
FOR LUNCH SOMETIME

There was a kind of dark carnival atmosphere at the Crucible when I finally came back. I had been told to wait until the next fight was over so that anyone who lost money betting against me could have time to cool down, and I had seen the logic in this. So, I'd changed into some warmer clothes, retrieved my backpack, then stretched until another were-hyena—a young, gaunt male who I'd never seen before—came to fetch me. I soon realized that there was a lot more going on at the top of the dry riverbed than I'd been able to see from the bottom.

My first hint of this was another of Akihiko's gashadokuro, the same padded black uniform draped over a skeleton, only the skull face visible through the surrounding black hood. I gave the bone golem a wide berth. Somewhere, a fiddle played in the background. It seemed oddly appropriate.

There were more booths and cars pulled up on the river embankment side of the trench, and I encountered a half-elf lounging on the outskirts of the throng beside a blue Honda Fit. The car's hatchback was open to reveal bags of blood clearly labeled by type and kept warm by a space heater. The half-elf had a lot of tattoos peeping out, which I wasn't used to seeing among the Fae (they have to plan centuries ahead), and he was shivering in some kind of brown sweater-shirt and a multicolored stocking cap. A half-smoked cigarette dangled limply from his mouth. It was really too bad that he couldn't grow facial hair. Some stubble would have completed the slovenly hipster elegance he had going. All half-elves look young, but this one seemed young, and maybe he was.

I nodded at the plastic packets of blood. They were linked together by perforated strips so that you could hang a whole string of them over your shoulder like a bandolier or tear one off like a juice pouch. "Are you selling those?"

The half-elf shrugged unhappily. "Trying. Most of the vamps stayed away tonight."

I nodded judiciously and blew a big, misting breath to make a point. "They're cold-blooded." This was nothing but the truth. One of the reasons there are so many werewolves in the Midwest and Alaska is because we don't like vampires, and the bloodsuckers usually avoid cold places with lots of distance between dense population centers.

"Live and learn," he muttered, looking away and clearly wishing I would move on. I obliged.

The next way station I encountered was a barbecue set up by a ghoul in ratty layers of cast-off clothing. He probably did most of his hunting in homeless shelters and subway tunnels and abandoned buildings. Roughly a million people go missing in the United States every year, just vanish and are never accounted for, and those are just the legal citizens. The disappearance rate among people who don't have green cards or IRS records or checked boxes on a census form is much higher, and ghouls tend to go for easy prey. They are the low-hanging fruit of the supernatural world, little more than sentient zombies or cannibals. I have no idea how their name got bastardized from the Middle Eastern ghuls; the two species have nothing in common.

In the dark, this particular ghoul could still pass for human though it had shitty teeth and greyish skin and was selling lumps of meat on skewers. Some of the meat was raw, some of it roasted, all of it human.

"I lost three hundred dollars on you, Down Boy!" the ghoul yelled, but he was giggling as he said it.

"You should have spent some of it on a toothbrush," I called back.

Our exchange had drawn attention my way, and I could feel cold if mostly neutral gazes around me as I slipped through the edges of the crowd. The throng was mostly made up of were-beings, cunning folk, and elvish castoffs, but there were enough other kinds of scents that I found it a little disorienting. It was the olfactory equivalent of being surrounded by a hundred television sets all broadcasting from different channels. I didn't see or smell Akihiko, but I did spot a white van in the deserted industrial park across the bridge.

I worked my way across the bridge and around a booth where various beings had gathered to watch an argument between some kind of nymph and a gorgon. The gorgon was apparently telling fortunes for ten thousand dollars a pop. Expensive until you considered that her predictions were probably the real thing. The gorgon was dusky-skinned and wearing mirrored sunglasses over her bony nose. Greenish scales—a gorgon's primary defense mechanism—had emerged and begun to cover her skin. Her dark hair, while not literally made of snakes, wove about her skull as if alive.

The nymph was unspeakably lovely, with skin made rosy in

the cold. Long, sweet-smelling nut-brown hair cascaded over the swells beneath her pink ski suit. "I want to know where Lelika is!"

"It doesn't matter where she is," the gorgon said stiffly. "You'll never see her again."

It suddenly got windier as a breeze blew past me and visibly swirled around the gorgon, rocking the booth she was sitting behind and causing her dangling earrings to sway violently. All nymphs have elemental affiliations, and this one must have been one of the aurae.

Unfortunately, the breeze also blew the gorgon's sunglasses off while the nymph was trying to stare her down. I had a brief impression of blind milky-white eyes devoid of any pupil or iris.

A moment later, the nymph hit the ground. She wasn't really turned to stone, just paralyzed into a state of near rigor mortis that would last until her neurons came back online.

"Is there a problem here?" It was an icy voice that burned and cracked. The yuki-onna. Suddenly, the crowd around me disappeared like water down invisible cracks and I found myself in front of the snow woman.

"She didn't like her fortune," the gorgon said calmly, picking up her sunglasses.

The yuki-onna kicked the nymph experimentally in the stomach. Her foot disappeared into the pink padding with a heavy thud, but the nymph didn't make a sound. Then the yuki-onna looked up at me. "Is that true, Down Boy?"

"Who are you talking to?" The gorgon seemed alarmed for the first time.

Gorgons are technically blind. The eye they see with, their psychic or "third eye," is entirely separate from their physical body, and they can't see knights at all.

"It's true," I said.

The yuki-onna cackled, all bitterness and malice and glee. "Only a fool wants to know their fate."

"Is that a—" the gorgon was facing my direction, and she choked as the yuki-onna reached out and touched an index finger to her throat, her vocal cords suddenly frozen.

"You've said enough for tonight," the yuki-onna advised in a vicious parody of kindness.

The gorgon could clearly see her own possible future. She stood up and began folding her table and chair with alacrity.

Placing a companionable hand around my arm, the yuki-onna led me toward the white van. Her flesh was warm and her skin robust, and I wondered whose body heat she had consumed recently. "Come along, Down Boy. We never did get to discuss all of the possibilities of your name."

It is said that yuki-onna mix arousal and killing in odd ways, though you have to take the Japanese sexualization of female monsters with a grain of salt. Actually a bag of salt, if only because there's so much of it. Sometimes, the stories make the yuki-onna beautiful, and they will fall in love with a man and be a faithful wife until something tragic happens, but in most of the tales, yuki-onna are straight up predators. In some stories, yuki-onna have sex with men and leave them drained of semen and body heat. In others, they have sex with men normally and *then* kill them normally. Or they kill men and *then* have sex with them. The stories I find the most disturbing are the ones where the yuki-onna are hideous and force men to have sex with them against their will by, well, freezing the men . . . stiff.

"It'll never work out," I told her. "We have very different ideas of being in heat."

Her fingernails pressed into my bicep, but her other hand patted my forearm companionably. "Aren't you clever?"

"No, but I am quick." I tried to keep my voice neutral and inject a little if-I-even-feel-a-chill-I'm-crushing-your-throat-before-you-can-blink-bitch into it at the same time.

She cackled—or maybe, in her case, crackled—and made sure to brush her hips against mine as we walked. It was a pretty fearsome assemblage, but the crowd parted in front of us like leaves in front of a very cold wind. We reached the van, a large white vehicle whose sliding side door was open, and I finally got one of the scorecards to the night's fights. The sliding door reminded me uncomfortably of…wait a minute…I looked closer. Scratched faintly into the paint around the door were the same kind of sigils I'd seen on the sliding paper door in Akihiko's warehouse. Son of a bitch.

The assclown had made himself a rabbit hole on wheels.

"This is Down Boy." The yuki-onna was talking to a bald Asian man sitting at a folding table in the van's interior. She was speaking Japanese, so I had to remember to pretend not to understand. "You have some money for him."

I wordlessly unshouldered my backpack and handed it over. He took it with a grunt and told someone in the back of the van to get two hundred and forty thousand dollars. It wasn't as much as it sounds like. Our group splits all the money we make along the way evenly, which meant that I was currently dividing any winnings eight ways.

The yuki-onna loosened her grip on my arm. "You don't have to worry about anyone stealing your prize money here."

"I know," I told her, and she made that sort of amused hostile sound again and leaned over to kiss my cheek before releasing me. The kiss burned like dry ice.

I was still watching her leave—just to make sure she really did—when the fat Asian man in the van got impatient. "Do you want to bet on any other fights?"

I glanced down at the card and found Sig's fight; she was listed as Britte the Hittah, and the card listed her vital statistics and mentioned that she was a valkyrie with an exclamation point. She was fighting someone named Big Bertie who the scorecard said was a siren, maybe the same one that Alyssa had gotten a feather from. The odds against Sig were three to one.

"Well?" the man repeated.

I would have liked to have put some money down on that fight, but... "No." He handed me my backpack and told me to stop blocking the van.

"Down Boy!" I was really going to have to see about changing that name. I turned and saw the half-elf who had gotten the snottiness beaten out of him at the warehouse. I could smell that he'd been around Sig recently, but I wasn't going to show any undue interest in that. His bruises and abrasions had already healed, or been healed, and he was dressed like a riverboat dandy or a pimp. Long red hair dangled beneath a broad-brimmed white hat, and he was carrying a walking stick with a heavy brass knob. The cream-colored all-weather coat was open to reveal a white dress suit and a pink carnation. "I made a lot of money off of you tonight."

"Glad to hear it." I nodded at his outfit. "I see you're all dressed up for the dance."

He flashed a breezy smile and made a point of smelling the pink carnation. "But not all alone for romance."

I smiled. "I'll take your word for it."

He stuck his hand out. "Aubrey Dunne."

I shook it. "Just call me Mark."

He nodded toward the edge of the dry riverbed and began walking. "We're missing another fight I have money on. Come on."

We moved around another one of the motionless bone golems. It was the ninth one I'd seen.

"I never did thank you for settling with that mothersucker who humiliated me." Aubrey's eyes glittered for a moment. Elves, even half-elves, have long memories, and that's not just a turn of phrase. Some Fae deal with the burden of immortality by completely immersing themselves in the endless now, but others think long-term like it's another language. Piss the latter kind of elf off, and it'll set a revenge plan into motion that you won't see coming, because it'll hit you ten or twenty years later, if it isn't aimed at your great-grandchildren.

Aubrey seemed to fall somewhere in between those two categories.

"I didn't do it for you," I remarked. "I was trying to get some attention."

"Well, you got mine," Aubrey said easily. "In fact, I think we could make a lot of money together. I was thinking of using this place as a model and trying to set up a traveling underground fight circuit."

Aubrey had recognized my reference to a Marty Robbins song about a white sports coat and a pink carnation earlier, so he was probably at least as old as I was, but here he was, talking about becoming Akihiko's competition out loud, on Akihiko's turf, in a place full of beings with enhanced hearing. This after almost getting beaten into paste. Either Aubrey was one of those eternal fools, or he liked to give his long, jaded life a little extra spice by living recklessly.

When we got to the edge of the riverbed, we joined the leopard woman who had helped Sig carry Aubrey out of the warehouse. Naturally, the person fighting was Sig.

〜29〜

AIN'T NO THING BUT A CHICKEN WING

Sig's opponent was beautiful. The siren's olive skin was flawless, and her jet-black hair snapped and flashed around her face like it was part of some kind of dance. Her body looked strong and lithe, shoulders and arms and abs on display, her breasts barely contained in a halter top. I mean, yeah, her legs were covered in yellow-gold feathers, the haunches thick and the knees strangely jointed, ending in big gnarled bird claws with long talons. But hey, you can't have everything.

Hide the lower half of her body behind some rocks and she'd be a ten. Maybe an eleven. Any sailor would go crazy for her.

"How much do you want to bet that they always have at least one girl-on-girl fight?" Aubrey chuckled.

"No, thanks." Those clawed feet were causing Sig problems. The siren had studied some kind of martial art that emphasized foot fighting—savate, I think—and her legs didn't quite bend in ways that Sig was used to. Those legs were at least as strong as Sig's were too, maybe stronger. I knew from experience that the siren's human torso was weaker, but Sig was having a hard time reaching it. She had gashes all over her forearms, some of them deep enough to be more than an inconvenience if the fight went on much longer. Sig is tough, but she doesn't regenerate like I do.

"Come on, Britte!" the leopard woman yelled.

"Damn it," Aubrey cursed. "I have money on her."

The siren opened her mouth and screamed into Sig's face. It wasn't a hypnotic scream, but it wasn't a human one either, and its high, piercing note had my skull ringing. Sig was in obvious pain; she staggered back and dropped her guard, and the siren moved into some kind of high kick. I don't know if it was going to be a roundhouse kick or an axe kick because of the odd way the siren's legs were jointed, but it was arcing above her waist, a real showstopper, and it would have finished the fight if Sig had really been as disoriented as she was acting. Instead, Sig punched the siren in the throat while she was still bringing her leg up and around.

There wasn't going to be any more of that screaming nonsense.

Sig grinned, and I knew her well enough to know that she was trying to make the siren angry. It worked. The siren tried to stomp down on Sig's lead foot with those bone-crushing, sharp claws of hers—it was probably another one of her winning moves—but when the siren tried to drive those piercing talons down through Sig's right shoe, Sig slipped her foot out at the last moment and brought it down over the siren's claw instead.

Those talons drove into the concrete and anchored there.

The siren squawked in anger and surprise, and Sig leaned in and put her body weight on the foot, keeping the siren trapped. Then Sig was inside the siren's guard and they were just boxing, not kickboxing. Sigs arms were longer and stronger than the siren's, and she hammered a blow into the siren's midriff, then into the siren's face when she lowered her forearms to protect her torso, then back to the body.

"YAYUH, BABY!" the leopard woman cheered.

I didn't see the end of the fight, though I expect it didn't last for more than a few seconds after that. Something was happening behind me.

Beings were edging past me. These were predators and they kept their dignity, but they were still trying to get away from something, like animals fleeing a forest fire. The source of their alarm was clearly behind us. I turned and began edging against the crowd. The sound of rattling bone and rasping steel made a counterpoint to the yells as bone golems animated and converged on the area in front of me.

Several were-hyenas were attacking Akihiko Watanabe. Akihiko's decision to end the tension with the hyena pack by co-opting them into his organization had been bound to involve some eruptions, but I had been hoping to guide those disturbances and take advantage of them. Instead, I stepped around a hyena who had been beheaded. I never did find out how.

What I did find out was that Akihiko's coat was indeed a living, pliable being that looked like white putty in its natural state. It slid and spread out and billowed off of his body like an inverse parachute and intercepted a knife that was flying through the air. The knife got lost in the being's rubbery flesh, and the creature continued onward and enveloped the were-hyena who had thrown the knife. For a second, the were-hyena looked like nothing so much as a man who had suddenly, comically, had a bedsheet thrown over him, but then the pliable mass continued to writhe and wriggle and the were-hyena's convulsions became more frantic. The thing bound the were-hyena, choked him, slid down his orifices, and he went down still vainly thrashing.

Another were-hyena, a Latina female, tried to charge Akihiko's back, but something emerged from his shadow to intercept her. Whatever it was, the thing was dark and vaguely humanoid, with red eyes and tusks. Strands of living darkness flowed down from its top and traveled over the length of its body, a cloak made of living inklike hair. It was too late for the were-hyena to stop her leap. She flew into the shadow being's mass, was caught in an impossible violent swirl of motion and darkness, and then the thing sank back into Akihiko's natural shadow and disappeared again, leaving the were-hyena's broken body on top of the ground behind it. There was a gaping hole in the were-hyena's chest where her heart had been removed.

Another were-hyena was coming at Akihiko from the side, and the onmyouji calmly puffed on his cigarette. A flaming sphere flew out of the cigarette's tip, burned and roared and expanded dramatically into life. The ball of fire was the size of a small meteor when it struck the were-hyena and threw it backward. The were-hyena tried to roll to the side, but the ball of fire—probably the flaming spirit that had been hiding in one of Akihiko's paper lanterns when we first met—continued to expand, immolating its flesh. There was a name for that kind of ghost—bakechochin, maybe.

The last two were-hyenas involved with the attack tried to leave, but one was pulled down almost instantly by several gashadokuro that swarmed over it like piranha, swinging curved blades inhumanly fast.

The other was killed by Akihiko himself. A slender silver blade appeared in his hand, and even from a distance, I could see it was covered in runes. Akihiko hurled it, and six other similar blades flew out of slits and sheaths in his clothing, paralleling the original blade's trajectory. The effect was something like buckshot. At least four of the silver blades sank into the were-hyena's body, and it collapsed. The smell of wolfsbane cut through the sharp coppery scent of its blood while it twitched.

I wondered if he had prepared that little trick for me.

The event didn't seem like an opening or an ideal time to attack. Not unarmed, not with the rest of the onmyouji's henchmen rushing in from all directions and a crowd whose reaction would be hard to anticipate. So I stepped aside as another gashadokuro clattered by and stayed back.

That was when I saw Sarah White standing in the crowd across from me. I knew she had come to the city to check out Akihiko's bank up close, but what the hell was she doing at the Crucible? I didn't let my gaze linger or try to maintain eye contact with her. No significant glances. No warnings. She stayed still.

Akihiko did make eye contact with me, though. Our stares met, briefly, and he nodded sharply and held up two fingers. It wasn't a peace sign. I had two more fights according to our agreement. I nodded back, wishing I only had one fight left so I could give him the finger.

When I let my eyes return to the crowd, Sarah was gone.

At least I had learned a few things about Akihiko's personal defenses.

∿30∾

NOTHING NEVER HAPPENS

The following days acquired a patina of routine as I tried to become a regular part of the onmyouji's world. Akihiko wasn't going to let a knight who he couldn't psychically read or predict run loose on his own territory, and accepting that the kitsune was going to follow me was my price of admission for being part of the Crucible. Akihiko never actually verbalized this, and I never formally agreed to it because acknowledging that particular reality would have caused one or the other of us to lose face, but it was true just the same.

It became a kind of game. I rarely saw the kitsune though I would occasionally come across her scent trail when I doubled back, and at least once a day she would make a point of letting me catch a glimpse of her sitting across from me at a café or standing behind me in a taxi queue, not that she needed a taxi. Chikako had a team of were-hyenas helping her follow me, and they were a lot easier to spot than she was. One of them was on a motorcycle, one of them was driving a pizza delivery car, one was on foot, and several more were jumping across surrounding rooftops as they watched me through field glasses. We didn't speak or interfere with each other, and we all pretended not to care that the other side was out there. That would have been against the rules.

One time when the kitsune sat across from me at the park, I lowered the paper I was ostentatiously reading to show her that I was wearing one of those pairs of novelty glasses with a fake nose and moustache beneath them. Other times when I knew she was in hearing distance, I would speak cryptic code phrases into burritos I'd gotten off a food truck, or lean over and say into a nearby parking meter: "There are fireworks in the picnic basket. Repeat, there are fireworks in the picnic basket." I don't know if she was amused or annoyed.

Because I was being followed, I had to research Akihiko and his operation in plain sight while doing the sorts of things I would be doing if I really was hunting a rakshasa. I went to the warehouse a few times under the pretext of asking Akihiko if he'd heard anything, and I used these visits as an excuse to study the warehouse's security whether Akihiko was around or not. I also made the rounds hunting down pit fights and gambling dens and poker games and various contests that waged animals against each other in cruel ways. Because, you know, humans suck. Whenever I encountered supernatural beings who gambled, I asked them questions about the Crucible under the pretext of finding out if a rakshasa had infiltrated it.

I wanted to know more about the physical location the Crucible was being held in too, and the larger context of aqueducts, canals, spillways, sewers, estuaries, and overflow channels that formed the system it was a part of, so I copied blueprints of the city's infrastructure—something any hunter might do—and secretly mapped out the waterways in increments. And when I researched books on Eastern mythologies, I made sure that some of them focused on Japanese as well as Indian folklore.

I discovered that the creature pretending to be Akihiko's coat was called an ittan-momen, and the shadow thing was called an otoroshi, though specific information about these creatures and their motivations or weaknesses was proving hard to find. I wasn't wasting time—I was laying the groundwork for any number of options or scenarios—but it was slow going.

When Akihiko made his next big play, I wasn't even aware of it.

The person who had a front row seat was Ted Cahill.

Max Selwyn, one of Kevin Kichida's best friends, went missing. Ted Cahill knew this because he was the sheriff of the town where Max Selwyn and Kevin lived, but also because Cahill had a short list of Kevin's friends that he was keeping an eye on. Which was how Cahill wound up standing in the old house that Max shared with four other students off campus even though no one had officially reported Max as missing yet.

The same girlfriend who had called Tatum's sheriff's office just to make sure that Max wasn't hurt had been Skyping with Max thirty-two hours earlier when their Internet connection was disrupted a bit after midnight. As far as Cahill could tell, Max had promptly stood up and left the room without turning off his computer or his lights. Then he left the house without taking his wallet or his car keys or his cell phone.

Max had walked downstairs, past the living room and out the back door in the kitchen area. The last person to see Max Selwyn was Max's housemate, Sam Testerman. Sam saw Max go by in his peripheral vision, and maybe Max had seemed kind of out of it, but Sam didn't think much about it. Sam had been wearing a headset while playing some alien-invasion videogame, and he'd been kind of out of it himself.

The other two boys in the house had been asleep. The only odd thing—maybe nothing—was that one of them had mentioned having really intense and crazy dreams that night, and the other roommate had blushed when he heard that. Blushed and admitted to a similar experience under Cahill's special brand of hypnosis. While tranced, both boys recounted waking up to discover that they'd had explosive orgasms during the night. One remembered beautiful singing in his dreams.

Singing? Cahill recalled hearing somebody say something about a siren feather, even though he thought sirens were mermaids. Sirens sang and hypnotized people, though; he remembered that much from the *Odyssey* in the ninth grade.

Wandering outside, Cahill checked out the backyard, not that there was much of it. More interesting was the narrow back alley, a barely paved unlit strip where neighborhood residents could set their trashcans for pickup. Cahill followed Max's scent trail until it abruptly stopped at a point where somebody could have had a car idling with its lights off. No signs of blood or scuffling. No neighbors who had heard screams or yells. If Max had gotten in a car under some kind of hypnotic compulsion, it would explain why there weren't any signs of a struggle.

What it didn't explain was what Cahill was supposed to do next. Max didn't know where Kevin was. Akihiko probably didn't expect Max to know where Kevin was. Akihiko had kidnapped Max in order to draw Kevin out of hiding. Kevin was supposed to be staying off of any social media accounts or e-mail providers just to prevent these kinds of head games, but he was a smart, curious kid and had access to the Internet. If Cahill wanted to control the information flow, he probably didn't have a large window.

Cahill had to take a sick day and drive to New York City to do it, but he found a physical location where people who worked for Kevin Kichida's service provider were situated. After five minutes of conversation, he used a mental compulsion to make some kind of jumped-up clerk give him Kevin's message service password. Then Cahill made the office drone forget about it.

Cahill proceeded to check the phone messages on Kevin's account. One in particular was both simple and strange: "This is your grandfather. I do not like the people you are associating with, Kevin. They are a bad influence. Look at the trouble they got your friend Max into. He is in so much pain. Why don't you leave these troublemakers?"

The message was from a cloned phone, the burner number already smoke. No contact information. No directions for a time or place to meet. But then, if Kevin ran away from the people who were hiding and protecting him, Akihiko could find him easily enough. And if Kevin didn't run away, the people protecting him couldn't follow Akihiko's message back to him.

Cahill deleted the message off Kevin's account.

Max was taken. Dead or prisoner, nothing was going to change that. We were after Akihiko anyhow, and nothing was going to change that, either. I don't know that Cahill decided to say to hell with Max, exactly, but Akihiko had made a move to put pressure on us, and the best way for Cahill to counter that move was to make sure we didn't even know about it. No knowledge, no pressure. Cahill would work on tracking down Max himself.

It's an easy thing to do when you're freaked out, to try to control situations and not burden other people with information that will just make things harder on them while you're handling everything. Information that might even make them worry and fret so much that they ask you a lot of questions you don't have time for, or make you anxious or defensive when you need to focus. Hell, information that might even make other people do something stupid that will fuck things up before you have a chance to work it all out. Keeping things that you're dealing with from people who might be affected can seem like a practical and protective instinct at the time, not like a lack of trust or a tendency to be controlling. I have been known to err on that side of things myself on occasion though I'm working on it.

All that's just a guess, mind you. I can't honestly say if Cahill's decision to conceal knowledge from the rest of us was coldly rational or passionately irrational. Did his decision come from an inability to empathize, or was it all snarled up in love or need or desire? Was he convinced that Molly would do something noble and impractical, or that Sig would reveal herself while undercover, or that Kevin would sacrifice himself? It brings me back to my original question, really. Did Cahill's decision result from having changed too much, or from not having changed enough? Was he inhuman or too human?

∽31∾

BANK SHOT

Cahill wasn't the only member of my team who was keeping busy.

Late one night, I found myself walking down a dark and strangely generic street. There were street lamps, but they were isolated little bright points, not radiant bridges of light, as if the darkness were squeezing them down to their nubs. There was no one else around, and I was wondering about that when Choo's van stopped beside me and the side door opened. There was nothing to be gained by hesitating and a lot to be lost, so I climbed in and found Sarah White sitting in the back, drawing on a sketch pad.

She didn't look up from her efforts. "I was hoping you'd find me."

This seemed like an odd statement since the van had found me, but I just sat down in the seat next to her wordlessly. The van started again, and it didn't seem at all unnatural that no one was driving it, Sarah looked up for a moment anyhow. "Oh, we're in the van? I thought I was still in Wagyl."

I struggled to almost make sense of that.

"We're in the Dreamtime, John," Sarah murmured as if I'd asked. "Now give me a moment. I want to put the finishing touches on this."

The Dreamtime? I sat there numbly and looked at the sketch pad. It was Akihiko, not just a physical rendering, but a picture that revealed his inner qualities: obsessive determination, ruthlessness, calculation, selfishness, smoldering anger, and beneath it all a gnawing fear that would never admit to its own existence or tolerate not feeling in control.

Those thoughts seemed too heavy to think. That pissed me off, and staring at the menace in Akihiko's eyes, even on paper, added a growing sense of urgency to my attempts to snap out of it. When I finally spoke up, it was like tearing a scab off of my mind. "What's the point? Won't that drawing be gone when you wake up, anyhow?"

Sarah seemed both pleased and irritated at my interruption. "I'm not technically asleep, I'm in a trance. My physical body is sitting in a canvas chair, drawing this picture on a real sketch pad right now. So be quiet for a minute, but don't let your attention wander."

It was hard, bringing myself to a fuller state of awareness without waking up entirely. I kept feeling myself getting pulled in different directions, starting to go somewhere and stopping, as if my consciousness was a manual car being driven by someone who didn't know how to use a stick shift. I anchored myself by watching Sarah.

Her trance must have included some kind of total recall, because she captured Akihiko down to the smallest details. A mole on his neck. A small white scar on his chin. The van stopped at the same time Sarah did, and the sketch pad in her lap disappeared. "All right, let's go."

The van door slid open, and we were parked in front of a bank. Oddly enough, it was daylight.

"Braithwaite's," Sarah said.

"Are we really here?" I asked stupidly.

She just looked at me long enough to convey what a pointless question that was and got out. I followed.

"How is this possible?" I asked. "I didn't take any of your drugs."

"You're a natural," she said. "It runs in your family."

"What?" That got me focusing a little more sharply.

"Your ancestors didn't get the name Charming for their good table manners," she said. "They were experts in the making and breaking of charms."

"They were witchfinders," I said. "Not witches."

"Lines blur," Sarah said. "I've been talking with your friends. Your gift for languages...your fascination with lore...the way you put information together intuitively...your ability to put yourself in other people's places...these qualities are more common among my kind than yours."

A cunning man named Phoenix had once said something like that. I hadn't responded to him, and that had worked out pretty well, so I didn't say anything to Sarah either.

Braithwaite's was a dark building, the stone so smooth and polished that our reflections were visible in its surface. There were no windows in the first floor. The only glass at street level was in the doors of the front lobby, and that glass was stained so darkly that no one could see through it. Sarah walked up to a revolving door holding a key. "This bank is run by a family of zmeu. Do you know what that means?"

Even dream-dazed, I did know. Ever wonder why dragons are always kidnapping virgins in the old stories? It took a lot of effort for dragons to shape change into human or human-like forms, and even more effort to sustain those forms, but sometimes they managed it long enough to impregnate human captives. The result was zmeu, half-dragon, half-human children who could move about humanity unnoticed. Zmeu were the dragons' servants, managers, ambassadors, and spies, and when dragons went into a hibernation state near the earth's core a thousand or so years ago, some zmeu hung around.

I summarized concisely. "It means we're fucked."

Sarah grimaced. "I hope not. Come on."

We emerged into a large lobby full of people. It looked like a regular bank to me. A regular security guard. A regular desk with different forms that people could fill out. A regular row of tellers with regular customers lined up in front of them. A regular series of offices on one side, a large mirrored wall on the other. At the back of the building, beside the teller cages, were a regular-looking staircase and elevator.

"I'm going to walk you through this," Sarah said, and apparently that wasn't just an expression, because she walked through the large mirror on the west wall.

After a moment's hesitation, I followed her and wound up in an identical lobby.

"Normally, you have to get one of the associates to bring you here, but this is my dream," Sarah explained.

I looked at the mirrored wall from my new angle. Everyone was reflected in the mirror except for Sarah and me and a number of extra guards. "Where are our reflections?"

"You don't understand. We're in the mirror. The people around us are the reflections." Sarah passed a hand through a woman in a courier's uniform. "You can do this in real life too, not just my dream. Look. You can still see this woman standing in the lobby we just left."

I didn't look. "What?"

"We're in a mirror dimension formed by the magic mirror in the lobby," Sarah said patiently, as if that somehow made things clearer. "You'll never be able to burrow into here from a neighboring building or a sewer tunnel. That's why I brought you here. If you really want to get into Akihiko's safety deposit box, I'm going to need a certain number of things from you."

"Let me guess," I said. "Three things."

"I..." Sarah frowned. "Yes."

It belatedly occurred to me that I was so out of it that I hadn't checked the ceiling, and knights are always supposed to check the ceiling. I looked at the wall above the large mirror. Twelve gargoyles sat on stone perches that emerged from the wall, and even though they were motionless and stone-skinned, somehow I didn't think they were statues. My eyes kept traveling up without encountering a ceiling. Thirty feet up, the room became impenetrably dark, but I thought I saw signs of spider webs curling around the edges of shadow. I heard a noise, or technically, I suppose I heard Sarah's memory of a noise, but something made a skittering sound up there.

I cleared my throat, or dreamed I cleared my throat, or cleared my dream throat. "So. Three things."

"Yes," Sarah said. "And they're all very dangerous."

"Oh, well, forget it, then," I said.

She looked at me.

"I just wanted to see what that would feel like," I explained. "Go ahead and lay it out for me."

"We'll never break our way into here physically. We need to trick our way in. That's why I had to go to the Crucible." Sarah shivered at the memory. "I know a way to change Kevin's body into the exact image of his grandfather's, even down to his retinas and fingerprints, but I needed to see Akihiko for myself."

"I've never even heard of a shapeshifting spell that power-ful," I protested.

Sarah smiled distractedly. "It only works with people who share the same DNA. I'm going to liposuction some of Kevin's fat off and turn it into soap, then carve the soap into a likeness of Akihiko. If I do it right, Kevin's flesh will shift and contort as I go along."

I'm pretty sure I wrinkled something. "I didn't think you were that kind of witch."

"You think I like it?" she snapped. "You brought all of this to my door, remember? I'm a baker!"

That was one hell of an oversimplification, but I didn't argue. "So, you need some identification good enough to get Kevin in the door?"

"No, your friend Parth says he can supply that." Sarah hesitated. "The first thing I need is a personal possession of Akihiko's. Not just something he's touched, something he owns and values. I need it to complete the spell. I know that's going to be almost impossible with—"

"No, it's not," I interrupted, and showed her one of the silver knives that Akihiko had thrown at the Crucible, one of the two that hadn't hit a target.

"You grabbed one of those? That's fantastic!" Sarah looked enthusiastic for the first time. "Leave it in the drop box tomor-row morning."

The drop box in question was a mailbox that belonged to one of Parth's New York properties.

I was sharper but still having a hard time thinking straight. "Why not just take the knife now, Sarah?"

"John, you're not holding the actual physical knife." Sarah sounded exasperated. "Dreamtime, remember?"

As soon as I realized that I'd conjured the knife mentally, it disappeared. Sarah smiled and took my hand. "Come on, John."

Things got a little blurry then, but she led me past some guards and gates and vaults, none of which stopped us, and down a set of stone stairs lit by torches. Our shadows weren't acting like they completely belonged to us, and stone faces emerging from the walls were chanting in a language I didn't recognize, menacing-sounding words that hissed and slithered out of the dark open holes below their noses. "Usually, I can sense wards and charms around me like a net," Sarah said. "But there are so many protecting this place that the pressure felt like pressing against an iron wall."

The stairs led to a stone wall with a giant dragon's face carved in it, the jaw protruding a good ten feet into the hallway. As soon as we reached the bottom of the stairs, the stone began to turn green and the bricks began to resemble scales. What resulted wasn't organic, but it wasn't exactly unalive, either. Those huge eyes opened and pupils made out of impossibly large rubies stared at us balefully. The nostrils in the dragon's snout actually widened as it smelled us.

"This is the second thing I need from you," Sig said. "Everyone who purchases a safety deposit box in this bank chooses an individual word or magic phrase. Say the right phrase and the mouth will open to a room. Say the wrong phrase, and the mouth will open to flaming breath and gnashing fangs."

"What's your phrase?" I asked.

"Crappuccino."

As soon as Sarah said the word, the stone mouth opened wide enough for us to step through, but Sarah didn't move. She looked at me to see if I got it.

"You need Akihiko's phrase," I said.

"Yes." Sarah frowned. "I know that seems impossible."

"Maybe not," I said. "Sig's good at getting her hands on information that nobody should know. It's that whole connection-to-the-dead thing."

Sarah seemed doubtful, but she didn't argue. Instead, she stepped over the bottom fangs of the dragon mouth entrance and led me into a massive room filled with safety deposit boxes.

When we got to her specific safety deposit box, she showed me a key. "This is the third thing I need from you. Akihiko will have a key like this one. We need it. Even trying to pick one of these locks would result in..."

"Death. Agony. Disfigurement. I get it, " I said. And I did too. I'd been gradually adjusting to being in the Dreamtime, and my mind felt cleaner and quicker. "But even if I did manage to pick his pocket, wouldn't Akihiko notice the key was missing?"

"No." Sarah sounded pleased with herself. "You'll substitute mine for it on his key ring."

I frowned doubtfully. "He's a psychic, Sarah. He won't sense me, but he'll sense you all over that key the minute he brushes against it."

The reason she was pleased with herself became clearer. "Do you remember what I told you when you brought Kevin to me? His aura has been overlaid with Akihiko's. It's part of the magic trade Akihiko is trying to make with the universe. I wouldn't dare try to slip Kevin into this place otherwise, shaping magic or no shaping magic."

"I remember," I said slowly.

"I'll give this key to Kevin to hold as soon as my transfiguration spell is complete. He'll leave Akihiko's own scent and psychic impression on it. If Akihiko looks at or touches this key, he won't sense anything off."

Okay, that was clever. I felt a wave of genuine admiration for the woman standing in front of me.

Clapping my hands sardonically turned out to be a mistake, though. I woke up with a feeling of panic and disorientation, like coming out from under a wave that has sent you tumbling head over heels through dark water.

I was so out of it that it took me several seconds to realize that there was someone in my apartment.

~32~

OH, BROTHER

There was a warrior monk waiting for me in my living room. I knew he was a monk because he was sitting with his legs extended parallel to the ground while he balanced his entire body on the tips of his fingers. I knew he was a warrior, because why else would he be in my living room?

It had been a long day and an odd night, and he had gained some pretty major cred at my expense by breaking into my apartment without me noticing. The Japanese are terrible braggarts by the way—they just do it by acting as if their accomplishments aren't worth mentioning. So I got a few cool points back by ignoring him while I went to the kitchenette. He was a fit man who could have been anywhere between thirty and fifty, with skin that was seamed but taut. Around five nine, he was unusually bulky in his musculature for a monk. Maintaining the health of the cranial/sacral connections along the spine is all to people who really view their body as a temple, and lifting weights is too unnatural and inorganic and hard on the joints for most of them. Completely hairless, this monk was dressed in comfortable street clothes that were so tight, he might have been French if he wasn't obviously Asian.

"Do you want some coffee?" I asked.

"Some tea would be nice, if you have it." He lowered himself and folded his legs into a sitting position. It looked natural and simple and excruciatingly painful.

"Is honey vanilla chamomile all right?" That tea helps me sleep for some reason. "It's the only kind I've got."

I could tell that this wasn't all right, but I could also tell that he didn't want to unbalance his aura by going off on a rant about American tea. "Perhaps water, then."

I did a few breathing exercises and some brief stretching while I prepared the beverages. If he was expecting a ceremony like the kind Akihiko had prepared for me, his next big showy limber position could be fucking himself. When I was done, I brought him a glass of water and sat down across from him with a mug of coffee. "My name is John. John Charming."

He took a small, polite sip. "You may call me Brother Takeshi."

It was a warrior's name. "Are you here because I asked for help from the yamabushi?"

He agreed that he was, not wasting any motion or time. "Your friend Gordon says constance is a virtue."

Constance was the name of my goddaughter, and maybe seven people knew she existed.

"Calling Gordon a friend might be an exaggeration," I said.

"He asked me to contact you nonetheless."

I nodded. "You didn't have to come here. All I was expecting was a folder or a flash drive."

"Expecting things is a natural mistake," he responded graciously. "What may I do for you?"

"I'd like to know everything you can tell me about Akihiko Watanabe."

"Ah." A slight exhalation. "Perhaps it would help me know where to start if you told me what you know."

I nodded. "I'm afraid you're going to have to prove you are what you say you are first. It's just possible that Akihiko planted you here."

He smiled faintly. "How do you suggest I prove that?"

"Stand up." I set my coffee aside and stood fluidly. He mirrored my movements, and I slapped him fast, inhumanly fast. It startled him, which was probably enough to prove that he wasn't from Akihiko all by itself. Gordon wouldn't have told him I was a werewolf. Akihiko would have.

"Not expecting things is a natural mistake," I told him, just to see how balanced his chi was.

He went completely motionless. Motionless but somehow conveying power or building tension. Reality seemed to condense and compress around him. It was like staring at a snow globe in a way. Cheesy, plastic, cheap, there's nevertheless something fascinating about those tiny spheres, that idea of looking into a moment of stillness perfectly captured, complete in itself. Watching him was like that.

When he slapped me back, he was moving faster than a human too, though not faster than humanly possible. There are all kinds of stories about yamabushi being able to harness their internal resources to accomplish nearly supernatural feats, exhibiting strength and speed far beyond normal human capacity. Supposedly, they can do things like go into trances that speed up their healing, focus their senses, achieve states of deathlike hibernation, win any dart match or game of Twister, predict the endings of movies, rap on demand...Okay, I'll shut up now.

I smiled and sat down on the floor again. "Thank you."

After a moment he joined me. "It was nothing."

"Would you like me to talk to you in Japanese?" I asked. "It's been a while."

"That is not necessary. My English is excellent."

"You've been here for a couple of years," I observed. He was saturated with the smell of New York. The city was coming out of his pores, though that didn't seem like something I could mention politely.

"Yes."

"Watching Akihiko."

"Yes."

I proceeded to tell him my story then, or at least the highlighted version. When I was done, he disappointed me. "I can't tell you much that would help you."

"Can't or won't?"

"I cannot," Brother Takeshi said regretfully. "Akihiko Watanabe has lost all balance. He is unable to see beyond his own fears and desires, and his only concept of morality is selfishness. I could tell you about people he has killed, laws he has broken, traditions he has perverted, but that would only confirm what you already know. What you are really after is knowledge that will help you kill him."

"That's true," I admitted.

"If my order had decided to kill him, he would be dead," Brother Takeshi said simply. "He is a monster, but he is a careful monster. He is adept at staying within the boundaries of the Pakkusu Arukana so that it protects him rather than confines him."

"He left Japan," I pointed out. "You followed him here. This suggests that you were close to taking action or finding out something that would allow you to take action, and he left to avoid that."

He sighed deeply. "Perhaps you should know something. I loved Etsuko Watanabe."

Again, I was tired, and I had never heard the woman's real name. I stared at him blankly.

"Akihiko's wife," Brother Takeshi added with the slightest trace of anger.

Oh. I suddenly remembered something Jerry Kichida had said while telling his wife's story. When Yuna's mother went missing, Akihiko told his daughter that her mother had run off with another man.

"I was young, and my Order assigned me to investigate Akihiko." Takeshi's breathing was slower, deeper. "I thought his most vulnerable point was his lonely wife. Do not misunderstand me. I did not intend to seduce her. I befriended her."

"Did you . . ." I stopped.

He didn't have any problem finishing the thought. "We never consecrated our love. Does that matter?"

"I don't know," I admitted.

"I know what Americans think of martial arts," Brother Takeshi said. "I've seen some of the movies that travel from my country to yours. A man who studies the way is a man of peace. Then bad people take everything. They kill his family. Rape his woman. Destroy his dojo. Finally, he can take no more and explodes."

"Our westerns sort of operate on the same principle," I said.

"The woman and the family and the dojo only exist as an excuse for the hero's violence." Brother Takeshi was staring at me intently. "The movies do not really care about love or honor or discipline. All they really value is the justification of rage."

"I'm not sure what you're saying," I said.

"My Order forbade me from killing Akihiko Watanabe unless he violated the Pakkusu Arukana," he said. "For the sake of my own spiritual well-being."

"Oh." That seemed a bit inadequate. "But they still have you monitoring him?"

"Yes." His face was stone. "I am highly motivated."

"That is one hell of a penance," I said with feeling.

"It is not a penance. It is a journey. And it has not been an easy one." Something loosened in him then, and he sighed. "Understand this. Akihiko Watanabe is an abomination. He is a perversion of everything that is timeless and honorable and harmonious about my country. He offends my sense of order just by existing. But I am not a judge or an assassin."

"There seems to be something contradictory about all that," I noted.

He almost smiled. "I told my master the same thing. He replied that the search for harmony is the struggle to balance contradiction."

I remembered to sip my coffee again. "I seem to wind up getting in a lot of fights."

Not sure why that was relevant.

"That does not surprise me," he told me.

I took another sip of coffee. I needed it. "I'm also good at seeing patterns. Always have been. When I stare at something long enough, eventually something reveals itself, and all the assorted little bits and pieces start to align."

"I believe you," he granted. "Although such patterns are just one small part of an even greater design."

"Maybe so, but something is starting to emerge with this man," I said. "He's been getting more and more into necromancy. He wants to prolong his own life at any cost. He's interested in confining spirits to objects. He's interested in the way kitsune become immortal by placing an essential part of themselves in a star ball. He spits on the immortality that one achieves through family and honor...has in fact sacrificed these things for a more material and obscene kind of immortality. This is all true."

In some indefinable way, his focus became sharper. "Yes."

"And it's all leading to some great perversion of the natural order of things," I said. "It reminds me of stories of Koschei the Deathless, the first lich. We are observing the beginning stages of some horrible birth in progress."

"I agree," he said. "But that does not change my Order or my orders."

"You've been observing him for a long time," I said. "Akihiko has to take his clothes off sooner or later. He probably gets laid. Goes to bathhouses. Visits other Japanese individuals of import and dons new robes. Practices martial arts and gets sweaty. Plays handball with prospective business partners. Swims in lakes or pools. Something. With those sliding doors of his, he could go anywhere he has established a portal, and you must know some of the places he goes."

"I do." There was a world of intensity and suffering in those two words.

"Do you know of a key that Akihiko carries on his person?" I asked. "A safety deposit key to a bank called Braithwaite's? We think he's keeping a family sword that channels the spirits of Akihiko's ancestors there. The hoshi no tama that he uses to enslave his kitsune too. If someone could get that key and replace it with a duplicate..."

Brother Takeshi didn't say anything.

"It would be information-gathering, not assassination," I continued. "The spirits in that sword have something they want to express, and we also have the family heir that they would be willing to talk to. For that matter, the hoshi no tama would free the kitsune, and she is a key witness to his secrets. You're looking for proof. If anyone or anything will unlock the proof you're looking for, it would be that sword or that object."

My guest held up a palm to stop me talking. I obliged. I honestly don't know how long we sat there. It could have been anywhere from five minutes to half an hour. It was a very intense silence.

Abruptly, Brother Takeshi said, "Don't talk to me anymore. I cannot get you the key you are asking for. It is on a chain that Akihiko wears around his neck and under his clothes at all times. But I can get you a copy of the chain."

"Then that will have to do." I stared at him some more. He didn't give any sign of leaving. "Aren't you going to move?"

He gave me a look that clearly said, *What part of not talking to me anymore don't you understand?* "When the time is right."

The story of his life.

Well, he'd gotten into my apartment without raising any alarms or leaving any sign. Presumably, he could leave it the same way. I got up and went over to the kitchen counter and got a Post-it note and wrote down the address of Parth's drop box. I took the slip of paper to him, and he took it wordlessly.

"You can drop a copy of the chain there," I told him.

Brother Takeshi didn't respond. Sad, shaken, slightly awed by his story, I left him there.

I thought about what Brother Takeshi had told me while I took a shower, stayed under the hot jets for a long time, and tried to let all the information and emotion floating around in my cranium find some natural kind of balance. Maybe the harmony he'd talked about. His story had some parallels to mine that were a little unsettling, and some differences too.

When I got out of the shower, Brother Takeshi was gone.

∾33∾

HAPPY RAILS

Shaking the kitsune off my trail took some delicate timing, and I only managed it because she was following me at a discreet distance and New York subway users tend to stay in their own bubbles. I milled around near some stairs leading to a subway platform until my enhanced hearing picked up the distant rumble of an approaching subway train, then walked down, knowing the kitsune would emerge from the crowds and follow me. Hell, she was probably on a smartphone looking up the subway stops and sending the were-hyena on a motorbike out to the next one just in case. I had one hand in my pocket, not because I'm an Alanis Morissette fan, but because I was holding a washcloth that I had rubbed all over my unshowered body that morning.

As I was walking down the stairs, I moved behind a female tourist who was dragging one of those rolling suitcases clanking down the stairs. She had a huge shopping bag looped around her elbow, and I dropped the washcloth into the bag as I moved behind her. When we got to the bottom of the stairs and rounded a corner, I took a chance. No one was looking at me, and I jumped seven feet and moved behind a pillar, breaking my scent trail. Hopefully the kitsune would follow the tourist now.

With my back pressed against the pillar, I watched the tourist disappear into the throng of commuters as the subway train pulled in, then saw the kitsune appear behind her. Chikako was looking about but not too overtly. I edged around the pillar until I was completely hidden from her view. The kitsune probably suspected some kind of trick, but she thought I was hidden in the crowd boarding the train and kept following the scent trail left behind by the washcloth. She followed it all the way onto the subway train and probably stayed by her door, looking out the windows in case I tried to jump out of some car further along the tracks at the last minute. She was still on the train when it took off.

It was a lot of work just to leave Akihiko's silver blade off at our drop box, but it got the job done.

~34~

NOTHING COULD BE FINER THAN TO MEET HER IN A DINER

I met Aubrey Dunne for brunch at a French bistro. Well, half bistro and half cafeteria. You slid a tray along a metal rail while picking things out of glass cases, but the soups and the bread were reasonably fresh, even if the dishes involving eggs had to be microwaved. The place was nestled between working-class and pseudo-bohemian neighborhoods, and even though it was bustling, the air had that lack of tension that only comes with a sense of community or mild despair. A plump woman was singing jazz accompanied by a craggy guitarist. The duo were all right, and the food was pretty good too.

The place didn't have booths, but there was one solid fifty-foot-long red seat set against the far wall, and tables were placed across from it at random intervals. I found Aubrey at one of them. Sig was there too, and the leopard woman she'd made friends with. Both women had the kind of carrying cases people used to carry pool cues in before they started making cues that could be disassembled.

I wasn't thrilled at forming a public association with Sig, but at least it had occurred naturally.

"I saw you at the Crucible the other night," the leopard woman said after she'd introduced herself as Shenay, no last name. "Damn, where'd you learn to fight like that?"

I yawned theatrically. "I was out late. Can we just pretend I said something clever that didn't offend you and didn't tell you anything about my past?"

Shenay made an *ooh* sound. "A man of mystery."

"Hold on, I'm good at this game." Sig's mouth was hidden by a big mug of tea, but I could picture the faint smile from her tone. "He's the ex-member of a boy band. He couldn't handle growing up and losing everything, so he started adapting his dance moves into a new kind of martial arts. One night, he heard a strange howling noise..."

Sig and I have a lot in common, but taste in music isn't one of them. She spends a lot of time in dark places and likes to listen to lively bouncy dance music that I don't really mind but find largely interchangeable and forgettable. I like big band stuff that she basically thinks of as pleasant background noise or folk rock that she describes as whiny guitar people. When we ride together, we compromise by listening to alt rock or audiobooks.

Shenay made a *pffmmph* sound. "More like he's a MMA fighter who has some kids from before he became a 'thrope, and he doesn't like to pay child support."

"No, wait, I've got this," Sig addressed me directly. "You were one of those professional dog walkers. You had about fifteen dogs wrapped around you while you were moving down the street one day, and suddenly you realized that this little Pomeranian was looking at you funny..."

I smiled at her, but like she was a stranger who was messing with me, the slight grin crooked and quizzical instead of warm.

"It's more likely he was in some branch of the Special Forces when he became a werewolf and had to desert." Aubrey grinned. "No further explanation necessary."

"Actually, I'm hiding from my abusive girlfriend," I interrupted. "She's a were-moose."

Aubrey laughed. "There's no such thing as a were-moose."

"The hell there isn't," I said. "Her voice scrapes the wax right out of your ears. Her breath curls your nose hairs. I swear to god, when a man looks into those bloodshot, bugged-out eyes, his manhood shrivels up like a leaf in a bonfire."

"If she's that bad, why did you have sex with her in the first place?" Shenay was cracking up.

"I haven't yet." I shuddered. "But only because I'm faster than she is."

"Sounds like you should keep running," Sig said a little grimly.

"I didn't catch your name," I told Sig. "But I did catch you staring at me when I walked in."

"My name's Britte." Sig gestured at me with her mug of tea. "And I was trying to figure out if that's your human form."

I left that one alone and nodded toward the pool cue carrying cases. "So, what's with the baggage? Are you two pool players or something?"

"There's a weapons practice at the warehouse this afternoon," Aubrey answered.

First I'd heard of it.

"They're stepping up their schedule," Shenay complained. "They used to wait at least three weeks after a Crucible before having another fight, and they only practiced after midnight.

Now we're having another Crucible tomorrow night, and we're practicing during the day. I had to take off work for this."

I filed that away and wondered if I was the reason Akihiko was increasing the pace. Maybe he had changed his mind and wanted to get my three fights over with quick, or keep me off-balance. Or maybe everything wasn't about me, as unfair as that seems sometimes. "What kind of work do you do, Shenay?"

"I work at a television station," Shenay said. "I'm a producer's assistant. But not an assistant producer. They're very clear about that."

Aubrey clearly didn't give a wet fart. "Anyhow, the girls like to play with spears and staffs." He made this sound dirty and did it loudly enough that the people at the table next to us, an older couple, could hear him.

I leaned over to our neighbors and whispered, "Renaissance Faire types." The woman nodded with a tight not-quite smile. The man grunted uncomfortably.

Shenay wasn't outright offended, but she wasn't amused either. "I'm not playing. And I'm a woman, not a girl."

"It's hard to keep up with politically correct bullshit when you don't age," Aubrey said dismissively. "Mortal terminology keeps changing, and humans just stay the same."

"So do immortals who don't want to grow up." Sig doesn't have much patience for existential poses. God knows she punctures mine from time to time.

"Maybe so, but believe me, my dear, I am fully aware that you're a woman, not a girl." Aubrey reached out and took her hand, stroking her wrist. "And you can even spell *womyn* with a Y if you really want to."

"I can spell it with your teeth if I really want to," Sig pointed out.

Aubrey laughed lightly and removed his hand. "I've had enough fighting, thanks. I only went to the warehouse to establish a connection with the Crucible."

I tried my coffee. It was okay. "Speaking of weapons, nobody told me about this weapons practice. Is there some kind of newsletter I don't know about?"

"It's more of a grapevine," Sig said quietly. "Shenay here's been going awhile."

"They're probably saving you for unarmed combat," Aubrey chimed in. "They'll be able to keep the odds higher that way."

Sig changed the subject just a tad clumsily. "I'm a little surprised the security was so lax at the last Crucible. There's no way to secure a place with that much open space."

"It's protected by magic," Shenay said. "I was carrying a knife on me the first time I tried to go to the Crucible. I got to a certain point and just stopped. I couldn't take a step further."

That made sense. Dammit.

"So, how did you find out about the Crucible?" I asked Shenay. "Do you want to fight for money too?"

She rolled her eyes. "Naw, I don't want to fight for reals. I'm just tryin' to understand this new life of mine. I can spend it hiding in my room, or I can try to figure myself out, maybe meet some people like me."

I nodded. Were-leopards feel a strong imperative to find a mate. I wondered if she had put that together, was thinking directly in those terms, or was acting under compulsions and instincts she didn't fully understand.

"What about the leopard who bit you?" I wondered.

Shenay considered telling me to mind my own business, but she'd implied she was lonely. "I was on a mission trip to Nigeria. I got scratched by a crazy man with long nails and yellow eyes. Next thing I know, I'm walking around in some crazy fever like I'm on steroids and PCP all rolled into one. Somebody's cousin made eyes at me and patted my ass about a week before the first full moon, and I went off. They had to send him to the city to a hospital. My church had to pay all kinds of money to get me out of Nigeria before I wound up in prison. And then...well..."

"Shift happens," I said.

She laughed at that, if a little bitterly. "I like that. Shift happens."

"So, you're religious, Shenay?" I inquired mildly.

"I used to be," Shenay said. "I'm not so sure now."

"I'm kind of the opposite," Sig said. "I never used to believe in anything. But now...well, I don't know. I've seen people who get strength from believing in a higher power."

Sig's been going to AA meetings, and I wondered if she'd been to any while undercover. How much I missed her hit me all at once. The intensity was unexpected, and I had to glance down and focus on my food. I was around people who could smell acute emotional shifts, but a conversation about God or ultimate meaning could account for some spiritual turbulence.

"People get strength from believing, sure." Aubrey was being dismissive again. "If you give someone a sugar pill and convince them they're taking a painkiller, they feel better. They call that the placebo effect."

"Some people call that magic," I pointed out.

"The strength is real, whatever the source," Sig said. "And they need it."

I would have liked to hear more, but I wanted to have that conversation with Sig, not Britte, and not here. So, I let Aubrey bring the topic back to gambling again. While he was rambling on, I caught a glimpse of the kitsune staring at us through the front window of the bistro. She wasn't trying to hide, and when

I made eye contact, she actually waved. I didn't see any point in clueing the others in to her presence, so I returned my attention to the table and lifted my coffee cup to my mouth, smiling a small smile that only the kitsune could see. When I glanced over again, she was gone.

I'd been seen hanging out with Aubrey at the Crucible. I really hoped that after losing me at the subway, the kitsune had gone ahead and grasped some straws and tracked down the only mutual acquaintance we had.

An alternative was that after losing me, she'd decided to find Sig.

∾35∾

SAY
AGGGGGGGGGGGGGGGGGHHHH!

This isn't even close to funny," I gasped. I was back in the dry riverbed, facing a large iron cage that contained something that looked like a gorilla. It was at least seven feet tall with disproportionately long arms and thick, dark, matted fur that smelled god-awful. In fact, the stench was so thick and putrid that I had to spend the first few minutes vomiting while the thing was driven up to the arena area on a forklift. That smell was one hell of a defense mechanism. The kitsune was wearing a bandana tied around her nose and mouth as if she were robbing a stagecoach, and I could smell that it was lightly soaked in lavender. When my stomach was empty, I pulled off my T-shirt, rubbed it in my own spew, and made a makeshift face mask.

It was gross, but it was better than trying to fight doubled over.

"This isn't right," I said.

"Take it up with the management." The kitsune's face was a closed cipher again.

I looked around. There weren't any spectators on the bridge behind me tonight. They had been replaced by snipers wearing gas masks. Somehow, I doubted they were there to keep my opponent under control. Apparently Akihiko was raising the stakes. Was this because I'd ditched the kitsune for a few hours, or was he just squeezing to see what would happen?

The thing I was supposed to fight had a belly that was large and distended. The belly had to be; in the middle of that enormous stomach was a gigantic mouth. I knew this because the mouth was snapping hungrily, huge fangs visible. The kitsune was standing in front of the cage unfazed, preparing to unlock the end of an arrangement of long thick chains that were wrapped around the beast.

"This isn't supposed to be a death match," I said.

"Then don't kill it," she said, and unlocked the padlock. "That seems simple enough. Or you can leave the Crucible now and never come back."

It was a mapinguari. I'd heard of them, but only because I'm anal about researching monsters and because the mouth thing was unusual even among supernatural beings. The creatures are extremely rare, living in depths of rain forests that South American cunning folk have protected from deforestation with a variety of Turn Away wards, dimensional pockets, and glamours. How had Akihiko gotten it past...oh, right. The onmyouji's sliding doors.

By way of answering the kitsune, I faced the crowd and lifted up my hands as if asking for applause. "I GOT THIS!" I yelled. "YOU THINK I DON'T GOT THIS? I TOTALLY GOT THIS!"

I really didn't care about posturing or the performance aspect one way or the other. I just didn't want any werewolves that Ben Lafontaine had sent to interfere.

"LISTEN TO THAT WOLF HOWL! HE'S GOT THIS!" the kitsune yelled, and gestured at my opponent. "OR MAYBE THIS HAS HIM. WHAT DO YOU THINK?!?"

The crowd let her know exactly what they were thinking. Surprisingly, it didn't have anything to do with the nature of particle physics or a thoughtful discussion of the essays of Montaigne.

The kitsune stepped back beyond the cage and threw a white scarf down. No more introductions. As if by magic—no...definitely by magic—the doors to the iron cage flew open, and the watching crowd roared.

So did the mapinguari. It staggered out of the cage and expanded its massive chest and brought those long hairy arms, swollen with thick muscle, upward and outward. The iron chains looped around the thing swirled and hit the concrete with a loud clatter as it raised its arms and screamed a challenge.

I didn't wait for the scream to end. I charged it.

The move startled everyone, even the mapinguari. For a moment, it actually looked puzzled and stepped back, dropping down to the ground in a more guarded stance that brought its knuckles to the concrete as it took a step back and growled. But I didn't complete my charge. I grabbed the edge of the nearest chain and darted back, pulling it after me, the iron hissing against concrete.

The rules were that I could only use weapons that the Crucible provided in the arena. If anybody had a problem with what I was doing, the kitsune was free to ask the mapinguari to stop while judges conferred.

My bluff angered the creature. It came loping after me then, but there were three vulnerable places on it not covered by hair so thick that it was practically armor, and one of those places were the thick sausage-like pink toes sticking out from all that hair at the bottom of its legs. I went into a whirling movement that brought the tip of the chain lashing into those large feet. It didn't stop the creature entirely, but it did slow its momentum again as it jumped back, and I kept turning into the whirl, bringing the chain slashing up between the mapinguari's arms and into its face while it was distracted.

The mapinguari tried to grab the chain, but it only batted the end aside as I danced backward, moving lightly over the concrete. I didn't stop until I was directly in front of the southernmost bonfire. The heat from that massive blaze began to cook my flesh, but I did my best to ignore it. The fire offered my only chance, and I could heal from burns. I couldn't heal from a torn-off head.

Thinking I was getting away, the mapinguari screamed its rage against the wrongs of the universe and pursued me, the man who had come to represent them. It saw in infrared, and its eyes, already watering, were having a difficult time spotting me against the backdrop of the fire. It slowed down as it approached that solid wall of heat. The mapinguari's arms were longer than a human's, and it sent out two long, probing swipes, not full power but still strong enough to crush bricks. One of them tore a piece of scalp off the top of my head. As the smell of my blood filled the air, the mouth in the monster's cavernous belly began snapping hungrily.

I had to shut that large, unnatural maw.

I began to swing the chain towards the mapinguari's eyes again. It was expecting it this time, was still hurting from the last lash, and it unleashed an overhand swing that would have torn the chain out of my hands if it had connected. But the swipe didn't connect. I pivoted my hips and brought the chain crashing down between the snapping teeth in the mapinguari's stomach instead. Some of those teeth broke, and some of them clamped down on the thick metal of the chain painfully, full-force. The mapinguari screamed and retreated again, and this time, it dragged the chain with it, that bleeding mouth clamped around the chain's end.

I didn't pursue my advantage, if that's what it was. I stepped outward just enough to escape the heat of the bonfire a bit and waited. The back of my legs and the flesh over my spine were covered in blisters. The mapinguari roared, and I roared back, and it came at me again, faster this time, enraged but still half blind and keeping that large wounded middle mouth shut to protect itself. It was the only chance I was going to get. I was shorter and it was half blind, and the mapinguari overbalanced itself just slightly, lowering its swing. I grabbed that downward wrist and turned into its motion, moving with it, adding my weight to its weight, sliding my back into the mapinguari's torso and screaming while I dropped and rolled its humanoid form over my ravaged back. The only reason it worked was that I'm not human and have been turning the power of larger, stronger opponents back against them my entire adult life.

My back foot skidded over the concrete beneath the unaccustomed weight, but the mapinguari's massive body still crashed directly into the bonfire and collapsed wood and flames all around itself. The beast scrambled and flailed over the shifting wood beneath its feet and fell again, screaming and burning. Whatever putrid bodily oils were coating that matted fur and producing that toxic stench, they made the creature more flammable. The mouth in its stomach must have opened again at some point, because when I got a glimpse of its torso, the maw in the creature's middle was on fire and belching smoke.

The mapinguari managed to stagger and stumble and crawl out of the flames, and I was waiting for it when it did, the second chain in my hands, the padlock snapped around the chain's end like the head of a flail. Thankfully, the fight didn't last long after that. I collapsed as soon as the mapinguari's skull was crushed.

It had been a mercy killing.

The crowd was utterly silent. Nobody came to help me up. Eventually, I did it myself.

∾36∾

GO FISH!

I hate burns. They heal slower than other wounds, and they hurt worse while they heal. The dead flesh screams while it comes back to life. I let my were-hyena guide—a different one—drive me back to my clothes and my backpack, but I didn't wait out the next match this time. I wanted to see if Sig's match was as deadly as mine.

The same Asian fellows who had given me instructions at my first match tried to lay down the law about me waiting until the second match was over, but I wasn't having any of it. We were all insisting that we couldn't speak each other's language, and when one of my guardians got impatient and palmed a Mace canister that smelled like wolfsbane, I snatched it out of his hand, gave him a gentle slap that hurt me more than it hurt him, and put the canister back in his hands before he was done blinking.

Another guard started to reach for his weapon and found himself staring at the semiautomatic I'd just taken out of the first guard's holster.

The air became cold almost immediately, and for once, it

felt good. The yuki-onna's voice cracked and splintered from somewhere in the mist that had suddenly formed behind us. "Haven't had enough fighting for tonight, Down Boy?"

I understood how she killed her scent, but how did she move so quietly? "I'm not trying to dishonor anyone," I said, putting the firearm back where I'd gotten it with no sudden movements. "I didn't make any big defiant gesture in front of the crowd, despite the way your boss is holding up his end of our agreement. If you want a war with the Templars, just kill me now. Straight up. No bullshit."

She hummed, more a hungry sound than a contemplative one. When I turned around, I saw that she was pale-skinned again, almost as white as the robe that flowed around her. It must have been her dinnertime. She certainly sounded hungry when she said, "I didn't think you were this excitable. If you have rules or concerns about the fights, you should have mentioned them beforehand."

"I have no way of making an appointment with Mr. Satou," I pointed out. "No phone number or set location or schedule. Would you like to give me one?"

She giggled, half girlish and half ghoulish. "How about I escort you to the Crucible instead?"

"Fine," I agreed. "But keep your hands to yourself this time. I'm a bit jumpy."

The yuki-onna pouted but acquiesced, gliding slightly beside and in front of me without touching as we began the trek back to the arena. She set a brisk pace without seeming to rush. It hurt to keep up, but I did.

"Are you doing this because you don't care if your boss gets a little pissed?" I wondered. "Or are you doing this because phones and radios don't work here and you don't want to kill me without his say-so?"

She spit, and a hailstone cracked against the concrete beneath our feet. "I am here because the food is good, the risk is low, and I get lots of entertainment."

That didn't precisely answer my question, but I went with it. "I amuse you?"

"It always amuses me when the fish think they are the ones fishing." She turned and gave me an exaggerated wink. "Like you and your new friend, the half-elf. You pull against the line between you and the onmyouji and think you are reeling him in. You don't feel the hook in your own mouth."

"And you've seen a lot of others like me," I clarified.

"Countless." She made that humming noise again.

"You know, I had a refrigerator that made that noise once," I said. "I replaced it."

She laughed again, and the sound made the crowd that we were approaching make room hastily. The yuki-onna put her palms together, extended her fingers, and moved her hand frantically from side to side. "Wriggle, little fish. Keep wriggling."

For a moment, I saw a large distorted blur against the backdrop of a torch. The oni, Akihiko's personal invisible ogre, shadowing us. It would be like having an imaginary friend who could rip limbs off people or medium-sized trees without breaking a sweat.

The same half-elf who had been selling blood the other night was packing up a stand that had been selling lavender-scented bandanas. He must have made a profit tonight. Most of the beings there had an enhanced sense of smell, and the stench of burning mapinguari was still in the air, stomach-twisting and fetid. The bastard was charging forty dollars a bandana, and they were worth it. I had discarded my vomit covered T-shirt.

"Your bookie has my cash right now. Can you loan me forty dollars?" I asked the yuki-onna.

She made that crackling laugh again. "Alvin, give him one of your handkerchiefs."

Alvin? One of the many names for those Fae who look human is Alvar, and I suspected the handle was one of the yuki-onna's disparaging nicknames. If it was, "Alvin" didn't object. He was too busy hastily giving me a bandana. No money changed hands, and I kind of doubted any ever would.

The bandana helped. I tied it over my nose and mouth slowly, my back protesting when I had to flex my arms upward and behind my head. The surface of the skin was healing rapidly, but the nerves that were coming back to life weren't happy about it.

It wasn't until then that it occurred to me that I didn't see Aubrey anywhere. It was hard to think through the pain, but I didn't hear him. Hadn't smelled him. And the yuki-onna had made a point out of mentioning his name. I turned to ask her about that, but she was gone.

I drifted down to the trench and found Sig in the Crucible arena. It was a weapons match, and she was fighting a gasha-dokuro, one of the more traditional giant economy-sized ones without a uniform. You have to understand, it wasn't a real skeleton. It was a sculpture made out of different fused bones, its connecting points a series of smaller elbow and knee joints and hip and arm sockets working together. This gashadokuro was about the size of a small house, and its skull had once belonged to an elephant.

How many people had been starved to death so that their spirits and bones could infuse that thing?

Sig was armed with a spear, and the gashadokuro was armed with a wrecking ball and chain that someone had taken off of a crane, whirling the iron sphere over its head as if it were a tetherball. She ducked once as the ball went over her head, stepped forward, and leapt over the chain the next time the ball came around, and then the fight was over. Sig threw her spear through the gashadokuro's skull, and the statue began to disassemble. First, its left leg collapsed in a small avalanche as bones began to scatter and fall in a ripple effect, then its right arm dropped wholesale from its shoulder socket and shattered into a thousand separate bones on the concrete. The wrecking ball flew off to the side in a splatter of cement chips.

I didn't allow myself to smile or even dwell on feelings of pride or relief, not then, not there. A lot of the crowd seemed puzzled and sullen, and the kitsune made a point of checking Sig's spear, but she wasn't going to find any sigils or glyphs. Sig hadn't just been fighting while she was dancing around that monstrosity. She had been talking. However many unhappy spirits had gone into the making of that bone golem, Sig had managed to break the ties binding them, gotten them to form a union and go on strike. I turned and walked away, toward the van where my money was waiting.

Again, it struck me that Akihiko's weakness was that he didn't have followers or family. He had servants and slaves. There was no one who was going to defend Akihiko out of love or loyalty. One sign of vulnerability, and his entire empire would start collapsing into fragments just like that giant skeleton.

It was just a question of finding the right weak spot at the right time.

I crossed the bridge—the snipers were gone now—and found the onmyouji near the van. Akihiko was wearing his white definitely-not-a-trench-coat and smoking his much-more-than-a-cigar and calmly talking to a burly pale vampire who was wearing a winterized version of gang-style clothing. He had multiple layers beneath a hoodie, gloves with metal studs embedded in the knuckles, a black bandana visible beneath some kind of stocking cap, and hiking boots that had never been in any kind of wilderness that wasn't paved over with concrete. The vampire probably looked like sex on legs to anyone who was susceptible to the mental broadcasting he was putting out, but to me, he looked like a big greasy grub with limbs and teeth.

I used my hearing to listen in on them while I collected my winnings. Akihiko was saying, "You could use the Crucible to discipline your more unruly hive members, Alfonse."

"I deal with my soldiers myself," the vampire responded.

"Then you could use your best fighters to increase your hive's prestige," Akihiko countered blithely.

The vampire showed a little fang. "I want to impress some fool, I blow one down."

He was definitely trying to sound gangsta, whether naturally or by design. It wasn't the first time I'd seen a vampire hive or a werewolf pack structuring itself like a gang—the violence, secrecy, and mobility of the lifestyle make it ideal for supernaturals trying to stay off the grid—but vampire leaders tend to be centuries old, and they take pride in that. When talking to peers, they usually sound more like a Lord Byron than a gang lord, no matter how they're dressed. Either this Alfonse was relatively young, or he was rejecting that standard for a new one.

That was all the world needed: fangstas.

The harionago stepped in front of me as I drifted over. Her long black hair writhed down her body rather than hung limply, braids with metal spikes sinuously winding and unwinding around her like snakes. I wondered, irrelevantly, what the yuki-onna called her. Harriet? Dreadlocks? Braidy?

"Ah, well, it was just a thought," Akihiko told his companion blithely. "Would you excuse me for a moment? I want to congratulate one of my fighters."

"The wolf." The vampire said this the same way he might

tell someone that they forgot to flush, but Akihiko had already left his side to come greet me. The harionago stepped aside.

Akihiko and I stared at each other. What had he been doing all day? Casting divining charms? Researching me the same way I'd been researching him? Kidnapping and torturing Aubrey? Making arrangements for the mapinguari? I still didn't have a handle on the man. I could smell anger coming off of him, and his politeness was starting to fray around the edges. Maybe he just wanted any uncertainties in his life removed, and I was one of them.

"Mr. Powell," he said. "I have to tell you, I haven't had much luck locating that person we discussed."

Did he mean the rakshasa I was supposed to be hunting, or Kevin Kichida? The ambiguity was probably deliberate.

"You didn't tell me that I was going to be in a death match, either," I said.

His eyes narrowed. "You didn't have to kill that beast. I could have gotten many more fights out of it."

"It was trying to kill me," I said softly. "Were you?"

Akihiko waved his cigar dismissively. "I would have lost money if you had died tonight. A lot of money. I needed to do something a little more extreme to get ten-to-one odds against you after the last Crucible, and you said the creature you are after is attracted to violence and spectacle. I decided to help us both out. What is the expression? Win-win."

Uh-huh. At the very least, he was trying to not-so-subtly encourage me to pack my bags and get the hell out of there if I really was just a knight who happened to be annoying him. As if to drive that point home, Akihiko added, "But you're a guest here, not a prisoner. If you don't like my games, you are free to leave."

"I promised you three fights," I reminded him.

"Yes, you did." He smiled around the cigar clamped between his teeth, a fierce and brief smile, though he didn't seem to enjoy making it.

"So, when is the next fight, anyhow?" It took a lot of effort, but I didn't flex my shoulders or wince.

His face went opaque. "I don't like to give much advance warning or keep to a regular schedule."

"That sounds like a man who has enemies," I commented.

"Any man who doesn't have enemies isn't a man," he observed. "You know this. You have had all kinds of enemies, I think."

"What kinds of enemies do you have?" I persisted.

"Only two kinds." He made that fierce baring of teeth again. "Dead ones and soon-to-be-dead ones."

I pretended to mull that over. "That's pretty tough talk. Weren't you a priest once?"

He nodded, but to himself, not in answer to my question. "Have you been checking up on me, Mr. Powell?"

"I have. You're an interesting man." Blatant flattery, but it was worth a try. Most sociopaths like to talk about themselves. It's the narcissistic part of their disorder. Psychopaths are the ones who are so completely isolated in their own skin that they could care less if you understand them or not.

"You are interesting as well." He said this with the air of someone being gracious. "You know, I thought about becoming a werewolf once. To stay young and heal from most injuries. What a magnificent thing."

"But the hours suck," I pointed out.

He waved that off impatiently. "I decided I did not like the odds against surviving the first full moon. Or the constant struggle with foreign instincts, either."

I shook my head slightly. "You don't like to lose control, do you?"

"Does anyone?" he wondered. "It was the discipline and ritual of religion that appealed to me, to answer your original question. The idea of re-creating the same ceremonies and traditions that had been performed for thousands of years, so that I was in effect helping make something that was immortal... being part of something timeless and beautiful... that was a kind of drug when I was a young man."

"So, what happened?" I asked.

His mouth tightened. "I stopped being a young man."

"That does tend to happen," I said.

"To ordinary men. That is when I realized that I was simply doing what everyone else was doing," he elaborated. "Trying to be immortal and failing. I realized that if I really wanted to honor the... I suppose you would call it God... if I really wanted to honor God, I would have to try to be more like him."

I might call the force he was talking about God. I wasn't sure I would call that force "him." And even if we agreed to use the same word, I was pretty sure the underlying meaning to the universe I believed in but didn't understand wasn't anything like whatever Akihiko was talking about.

"You decided to become immortal," I summarized.

"Not just immortal," he said. "Timeless. So powerful that just my existence would cause others to be an echo or expression of me. A man has to have a goal, yes?"

"And you decided that being a priest of whatever religion you're being so coy about was a weak substitute?" I probed. It would be a lot easier to try to track him down through history if I could narrow him down to Shintoism or Buddhism or some more obscure religion.

"All religions are a stepping-stone," he asserted. "We are all driven to become part of something bigger than ourselves. But the things we experiment with are traps if we don't grow and move beyond them."

"What kind of things?" I said.

"Everything," he said. "Fame. Religion. Art. Family. Fortunes. They are all things we try to build or be a part of so that some part of us will live on after we die."

I shook my head then. "I don't think family is a trap. That's one of the worst things about being a werewolf. Constantly being driven to have a family and not being able to have children."

He tapped the side of his head. "That is because you are trapped in here. You are Catholic, yes? Your God sacrificed his son."

And there it was. The left turn from Self-Obsessed Asshole to Batshit Crazy.

"Sacrificed an aspect of himself, as I understand it," I said. "And not for selfish reasons."

"Abraham's trial—the way he proved his godliness—was through his willingness to sacrifice his son," Akihiko pressed on. "And David failed his test of faith when he was unwilling to accept the loss of his son, Absalom. Abandoning mortal attachments is one of the final steps toward understanding divinity. Do you read your own Bible?"

"I'm actually a lapsed Catholic," I said. "You should really be having this conversation with a priest or a rabbi."

Again, that mirthless smile. I wondered how long it had been since he felt anything like joy. "But I told you. I have moved beyond priests."

And then he moved beyond me, at least physically. He abruptly turned and strode off into the night, his shadow stretching and lingering and deepening behind him in a way that was entirely unnatural.

~37~

I'M PRETTY SURE THAT'S NOT WHAT ALL OF THOSE FAIRY TALES MEAN BY A HAPPY ENDING

That's good," I sighed. Sarah was massaging my back. I was lying facedown on the same bed above her bakery where I'd recovered from having my mind blown, so to speak.

"You and I have very different definitions of good," Sarah said a little tartly. "Akihiko tried to kill you tonight, didn't he?"

"He definitely risked killing me tonight," I murmured sleepily. "But I think he's really just turning up the pressure to see if I'll run away or reveal something."

Sarah's hands paused and then resumed kneading. "I'd love to run away."

"Of course you would." I stretched, and none of my skin hurt. "A lot of people in your position would be turning the rest of us in to Akihiko right now, trying to make a deal for their own safety or for money. It wouldn't work, but they'd try it."

"I would never do that!" Sarah's hands pressed more firmly. It still felt good.

"I know you wouldn't." And I did know.

"But if I thought the Kichidas would go along with it, I would be very tempted to help them forget all of this and hide them the same way Kevin's mother did." I don't know if Sarah was admitting or complaining there. "But Kevin's visit to the sperm clinic ruined all of that. Neither of them would be able to live with the idea of Kevin's future children being raised by a man who basically eats his young. I don't think I can either, to be honest."

"I'm always bringing trouble to your doorstep, aren't I?" I half grunted and half groaned while she put her weight on an elbow and ran it along my shoulder. "I'm sorry about that, Sarah. I really am."

"You saved Courtney's life the first time we met." Sarah's efforts eased up again. "And I think if I ever need help, you'll be a good friend to have whether you owe me a favor or not. That's not a small thing."

I was feeling too comfortable to feel uncomfortable, so I switched topics. "So, how's everything with the kids, Mom?"

"Kevin is a walking, talking replica of Akihiko now." Sarah made a fist and ground it into my spine. "It's upsetting his father. We need to find something for Jerry to do soon, or he's going to do something stupid on his own."

"Hmmm." It was the most intelligent comment I had to offer.

"Your friend Choo is worried that his normal life is falling apart while he stays here, but he's too decent a man to leave you all in the middle of a bad situation, so he's becoming more withdrawn as he feels stretched tighter and tighter," Sarah continued. "He's trying to bury his feelings working out a way to kill shadow beings."

"Good." This time, I just grunted. "Well, bad too. But good."

"I think your friend Molly is actually peaceful, but it's hard to tell," Sarah said ruefully. "Her faith makes her as hard to read as your geas. She's reading and rereading the book of Thessalonians and acting like a cruise ship director trying to keep everyone's spirits up."

That sounded about right.

"I haven't heard much from your battle goddess." Sarah flattened her palms on the base of my spine and put her weight on them. "But she doesn't seem to be any closer to discovering Akihiko's secret phrase. She says she's having a hard time finding the right ghosts to speak to because Akihiko's warehouse is warded against spirits, and there are too many random ghosts around the docks in New York."

My battle...Sig?

"You're tensing up," Sarah said matter-of-factly.

I pushed my torso up on my elbows and looked around. For the first time, it seemed odd that I was there, that Sarah and I were together, that I was getting a massage. "What am I doing here?"

"You probably passed out," she said. "You did a lot of healing and didn't eat enough."

I...what? "Are we in the Dreamtime again?"

"Yes," she said. "Lie back down. Your body is a metaphorical representation here. You don't just have physical damage, you know. Emotional scars are a real thing."

I twisted around on one elbow and half sat up instead. "You're massaging my emotional scars?"

"Every time you damage yourself like this, your brain makes neural pathways to messed-up places." Sarah was standing beside the bed in a white nightgown that looked comfortable and soft and clung to her. She was lovely. "If you weren't into meditation, you'd be an emotional and physical wreck by now, healing ability or no healing ability. But there are still a lot of pathways I'm trying to smooth out."

I swung my legs over to the edge of the bed. "I came here?"

"Yes." She was trying not to smile. "But I'm pretty sure it's because your mind knew I could help you. Your back looked like a nightmare. And that's not just a figure of speech."

"Don't you have wards to protect your dreams against intruders?" I demanded.

"They don't work on you," she reminded me. "You're a knight. Besides, we need to talk."

I looked down at myself for the first time. I was naked. Again. Shit! I pulled a sheet over my waist.

Sarah did laugh then, a compressed, muffled sound. "Your virtue is safe with me, John."

"This Dreamtime crap has to stop," I said. "How do I turn it off?"

She stopped laughing then. "I don't think you can."

"What?"

Her voice was not without sympathy. "You know how our world works."

And I did. Watch that first step. It's through a looking glass. "Well, that's just great." Sarah didn't say anything, and I added: "I don't think Sig would like the idea of me popping up in your bedroom in my dreams."

I wasn't crazy about it myself. My rules about sex and love are pretty simple. One woman at a time. No sleeping with anyone while they're high or drunk or emotionally unstable. No making promises I can't keep just to get in someone's pants. And I realize that not everybody comes from the same place or has been through the same things. I know we all have different needs and issues. I'm okay with different people having different rules and all that, but my rules make sense to me, for me, and anybody who has a problem with that can go have sex with themselves or whoever else they can get to help. But somehow, even with simple rules, things get complicated.

"I'm not interested in you, John," she told me.

"That's good to know," I said. "And ouch."

Sarah laughed a little and moved to sit on the opposite side of the bed. "It's not like that. It's like... do you know how sharks never stop moving? How they just stay in constant motion, wandering and killing until they die?"

I thought about the yuki-onna and her talk of fish. "I do know that, actually. So what?"

"You're a shark, John. Or you've been living like one for so long that it's the same thing." She said the words simply, without judgment. "I like you in spite of that. But I don't want to live like you, or with you. And I don't try to break up relationships."

"You're not getting it," I said. "I'm not upset because I think you're trying to seduce me. I'm worried that my subconscious might be hitting on you."

"Oh." She laughed again. "I really think your subconscious brought you here because I'm the only other person you can communicate with this way right now, and you're just learning. But you know, we never do learn to totally control our dreams. They wouldn't be dreams if we did."

"Awesome."

Suddenly, Sarah was dressed in a suit of armor instead of a nightgown, her face hidden behind a helmet. "Does this help?"

"Cut that out," I said irritably. I had been trying to will some clothes on myself and couldn't manage it.

Sarah became herself again, but she was wearing thick flannel pajamas instead of a nightgown. "Relax. We can't choose who we really love, John. But we can't really love without making a choice, either."

"Thanks, Sarah." I did something with an "umble" in it. Mumbled, grumbled, fumbled, bumbled, rumbled. "So, what else do we need to talk about?"

"Killing Akihiko," she said grimly.

Okay. We did need to talk some more.

"Did Brother Takeshi drop off the chain you needed?" I asked.

"Yes," Sarah sighed. "And Kevin has been wearing my key and that chain around his neck. If we can switch it for Akihiko's set, he shouldn't be able to sense a difference."

"And you said that Jerry Kichida and Choo both need something to do?" I said.

"Why do I already not like where this is going?" Sarah wondered.

Well, I didn't like our choices either, but the second Crucible had been a clear sign that we were running out of time. "You should put the chain and the key in the drop box," I said. "I'm going to need them. And a big distraction too."

And then we talked some more. And then I woke the hell up.

⌢38⌣

PLAN A

It was midmorning, not night, but I was on the same roof where the aswang had spotted me while flying by in the form of a giant black bird. I was watching Akihiko's warehouse again, sitting and smearing thick globs of goat cheese on some authentic New York City bagels, occasionally sipping from a water bottle. "You can have some of this if you want, Chikako," I called out.

I was bluffing—I hadn't heard or smelled anything—but I had been there for a couple of hours and figured I had to have been noticed by now. And sure enough, the kitsune came around the air vent she was crouching behind and joined me. There were no fox tails trailing behind her, and she was dressed in some kind of black insulated stretch pants and a running jacket, her hair bound up in tight swirls around the side of her head. "That is kind, but no, thank you."

"I thought your boss would be here by now," I said. "Weapons practice for the newbies started an hour ago." I had watched the security around the warehouse increase as Akihiko's people swarmed over it like ants, watched Sig and Shenay and other beings arrive, but I hadn't seen any sign of Akihiko. Of course, with those sliding paper doors of his, Akihiko didn't have to go outside to arrive or leave, but I thought my chances of spotting him were pretty good anyhow. For one thing, Akihiko couldn't have dimensional portals everywhere, and as Parth had reminded me, he had business interests in the city. For another, the kitsune seemed to be keeping in touch with him telepathically, and I thought he might just get curious and come see me.

Chikako folded her legs and sat down beside me. "Why do you want to see him?"

I wiped my hands on a bagel wrapper. "I went by the address that the gambler, Aubrey, gave me this morning…but I guess you know that. There was nobody there, but I smelled Akihiko's scent all over the place. And your friend the yuki-onna made some comments about that half-elf and me being friends last night. I just wanted to make sure there wasn't something weird or paranoid going on."

Chikako looked up at the sky. "It's strange. I thought I spoke English well."

"You do," I said.

"Really?" She shook her head. "This is a place where monsters fight each other. I have been sent to watch you. You know I have been sent to watch you. And it sounds as if you are asking me if something weird and paranoid is going on."

I laughed quietly. "Even more paranoid and weird, then."

"Ah," she said. "The sky is nice."

Meaning she wasn't going to talk about Akihiko or Aubrey anymore. "It really is," I agreed. "But the air is a little crisp and cold for my taste."

"So go someplace warm," she said. "You are free." Definitely a hint of bitterness there.

"A little more free than you maybe, but I have my own kind of magic binding me," I reminded her. "But if there's a particular movie you'd like to see or place you'd like to eat, I'd be glad to go there so you can follow me."

This time, she laughed. "This is one of the oddest conversations I have ever had."

"It's not even in my top ten," I admitted.

We sat there in a strangely companionable silence for a time, until a black limo appeared down the street from Akihiko's warehouse. I was already moving down the fire escape on the side of the building by the time the vehicle pulled up. Chikako followed me.

There were four people in Akihiko's retinue when he came out of the limo: himself, the harionago who seemed to function as his primary valet/bodyguard, and two of his black-suited human flunkies, all of whom seemed to be Japanese. The parking space was perhaps thirty feet from the warehouse entrance, and Akihiko stood when he got out of the car and waited for me to approach.

Then he stiffened. Suddenly, Akihiko swayed slightly and the bulletproof window next to him cracked. Akihiko stepped to the side, not seeming to hurry, and another bullet smacked off the ground somewhere beyond the car. Akihiko was prescient, just like Sarah had feared, or so psychically sensitive that he could sense Jerry Kichida's intent before Jerry pulled the trigger.

A lot of things happened then. The human guards pulled out weapons. The harionago's hair lengthened and whirled impossibly about as she faced the direction the bullets were coming from, which was good, because it triggered the Pax Arcana. Any normal civilians and bystanders would look right past the events around Akihiko without registering them now.

Nearby cell phones and security cameras would stop working. The warehouse door opened, and the entire wharf seemed to vibrate as the oni charged outside, massive, heavy, and invisible. Were-hyenas began to appear from around corners and alleys, running toward the direction of the gunfire. And Akihiko continued to do his minimal evasive movements as bullets cracked around him, but he didn't seem particularly worried or hurried as he did so, perhaps even hoping to keep the sniper fixated on him while his guards homed in on his attacker's location.

Well, I had given Jerry Kichida his shot, just like I promised. Several of them, in fact. Now it was my turn.

Distracted, Akihiko didn't sense me coming. After all, the reason Akihiko had his best tracker following me in the first place was that my geas functioned as psychic repellant. The last thing Akihiko wanted was *me* sniping at him from some distant roof, and if he hadn't known exactly where I was, he probably never would have been in the open like this in the first place. It was why killing Akihiko without dying ourselves was proving so complicated. The kitsune yelled out a warning from behind me, but I was moving faster than humanly possible now, and I darted between the guards and past the harionago while they were looking for the sniper. Then I was lunging into Akihiko, yelling, "GET DOWN!" I knocked him over the hood of the limo, and we slid to the ground on the other side of the bulletproof vehicle, away from the sniper fire.

A bullet took some meat off the outside of my shoulder as we went. Dammit, Jerry! Why was he still firing? He was supposed to be getting the hell out of there.

The onmyouji and I rolled gracelessly onto the ground and then I couldn't see anything. The onmyouji's coat, or rather, the ittan-momen that was pretending to be his coat, slid off of Akihiko and engulfed me. The white pliable flesh stretched and wriggled over me, like gum or tar except that it was slimy rather than sticky. My nails elongated and became claws, and I managed to rip an air hole over my mouth while I writhed and struggled, then tore slits out for my eyes to see through, repeating the process as the openings sealed again.

I hadn't known I could do that.

Then the ittan-momen suddenly flowed off of my face, though it continued to bind my body like a straitjacket. I was on the ground, thrashing on my side, and Akihiko was sitting against the limo, bent slightly so that his head was beneath its windows. There was still sniper fire going on, though I couldn't hear any bullets ricocheting or impacting near us. What was Jerry Kichida waiting around for? For that matter, what was he shooting at now?

"Did you just draw me into an ambush?" Akihiko demanded. Somewhere beyond us, a muffled explosion went off.

"If I wanted to kill you, that would be a knight firing at you, or there would be a knife sticking out of your throat," I gasped. Of course, I'd be dead too, but the truth of my words was indisputable. "I was trying to save your life."

It was only then that Akihiko noticed that a key on a chain had become dislodged during our tumble. The key was hanging outside his shirt instead of beneath it. He hurriedly tucked the key away so that it was concealed again. Or at least, he thought so. The key and chain were actually the ones that Sarah had put together.

∽39∽

DOWN ON THE ROOF

The ittan-momen receded off of me like melting ice, if ice were room temperature and the texture of snot. The jellied mass slid and quivered back over Akihiko and resumed its habitual shape, molding itself around his arms and torso until it looked like a white trench coat again.

"Why would you try to save my life?" Akihiko wondered.

"Our business isn't done yet," I snapped. Rolling into a crouch against the car, I added, "Besides, you're a supernatural being, and you haven't violated the Pax or directly attacked me."

I saw the impact of those words on the onmyouji. If they were true, I had just gone from potential assassin to additional security. Akihiko's eyes widened and his back straightened as he indicated my shoulder with a brief movement of his chin. "You are wounded."

"It's nothing." The wound stung, but the bullet had sliced through the flesh on the outside of my arm without doing any significant damage. "Do you know who shot me?"

"I will soon," Akihiko said grimly.

"Screw that," I said. "I'll find him myself."

Akihiko yelled something, but I had already moved around the car and was jumping over the trunk at that point. Jerry's prolonged shooting worried me. Blowing whatever cover I had left to save his life wasn't part of the plan, but if I had to, I would. I charged down the wharf and turned into a back alley, where I caught intermittent whiffs of fox. Akihiko's best tracker was after Jerry, and the kitsune was moving fast.

I turned into another alley and ran with a wolf's speed past someone who may or may not have been homeless. By the time she even managed to call out, I was gone.

As I got closer to Jerry's firing point, my ears began to ring, then hurt. Someone had set off a Long Range Acoustic Device. The high-frequency sound was enough to mess with my hearing without being audible to normal human beings. One of Choo's calling cards.

I ran across a street and found the first dead 'thrope, a were-hyena lying in a long, straight alley. The 'thrope's head was gone, and it wasn't lying around somewhere else, either. The head was just gone. The splatter suggested that the skull had exploded from close contact with a high-caliber bullet. As I approached, something invisible scooped the body up and slammed it into a nearby Dumpster.

I swerved around the area just in case the invisible oni considered me another mess to be cleaned up. The sound of two unmuffled gunshots overrode the sonics in the background for a moment, and then there were several more gunshots. I jumped to the top of a metal fence to a windowsill to a fire escape. My right shoulder was still hurting, but I ignored it and picked up the kitsune's scent again as soon as I hit the metal landing. At least two more people caught glimpses of me through windows, but that kind of thing has been a lot easier to get away with ever since parkour started catching on. I had more important things to worry about.

Like, how good was Jerry and Choo's exit strategy?

I ran across a rooftop, veering and finding angles and cover as I moved, laundry hanging across a clothesline, a sloping roof, a small garden of some kind, a water tower, and everywhere I went, I crisscrossed the kitsune's scent trails. I passed a sobbing were-hyena whose knee was shattered, another one who was unconscious and trying to breathe through a chest cavity and lungs that hadn't regrown yet, and a human corpse, some old man whose neck was broken. Probably killed by one of the passing monsters just to keep his mouth shut.

Why had Jerry Kichida stuck around so long? Had Jerry let his emotions interfere with his professional judgment? Or had he figured that he could at least weaken the opposing forces if he couldn't hit his primary target?

I was hot on the kitsune's scent and heading toward the edge of the roof when I saw a broken window in an abandoned warehouse across the street. The kitsune must have leaped at least forty feet. It was broad daylight, traffic sounds in the street below though it was a side street, and my legs began to lock up and buckle. My geas wouldn't let me jump after her. Not under these conditions. Too visible.

Cursing, I kicked open the door to a stairwell top and took the stairs five at a time, four flights' worth, and when I emerged from the building and ran across the street, I did it fast, but not impossibly fast.

A cold fog was filling the street, slowing traffic and obscuring the view. Apparently, Akihiko's pet snow woman was getting into the act too. I picked up several were-hyenas' scents and followed them through the fog, then found the bottom of the building that the kitsune had jumped into. There was an open door swinging where someone had kicked it in, and I escaped the yuki-onna's icy mist and ran into a large, empty storage area, past two more dead vagrants whose throats had been torn out.

I followed the were-hyena smell to a stairwell that reeked of cordite—and found the were-hyenas' bodies in front of a door they had kicked down. Burnt and bent forks and knives were all over the place. It was real silver silverware that had been packed into some kind of homemade nail bomb.

Another one of Choo's favorite tricks.

Somewhere up the stairwell, I started to breathe hard, but I caught the kitsune's scent again and kept running. I burst out on another roof, higher than any other roof around for a good ways, and followed the kitsune's trail until I started choking and sneezing, my eyes watering painfully. Someone had dusted the area with chili powder and ground pepper! Now I couldn't hear or smell, could barely see. Dammit, Choo!

I still managed to spot a zip line that Jerry and Choo had set up near the edge of the roof, on the side farthest away from the warehouse. I staggered toward it, wiping and blinking my eyes, and saw that the line led to a slightly shorter building some forty feet away.

Jerry and Choo were gone, but one of the zip lines hadn't been used, and there was a dropped rifle on the tarmac. Knowing what I was going to find, I peered over the edge of the roof, but I was wrong. There weren't any bodies below.

I didn't have a harness or gloves, but I grabbed the lower half of the pulley hanging beyond the edge of the roof and took the zip line down to the adjoining building, only using one hand on the upper half of the brake. My shoulder barely complained at all; it was my sphincter that tightened. But when I got to the edge of the neighboring roof, I dropped just past the parapet without mishap. And landed among corpses.

The bodies had been stacked against the edge of the parapet so that they wouldn't be immediately visible from higher elevations. One of the dead bodies belonged to the siren that Sig had fought in the first Crucible. The siren's feathered legs were concealed in wide blousy cargo pants, her clawed feet covered by long boots with huge rubber heels that probably had rear talons driven through them.

The second corpse was the aswang. He was in human form, his head separate from the rest of his body. The head was lying on its side, its eyes open and seemingly staring at the bullet holes in the aswang's chest in horror.

The third corpse was what used to be Jerry Kichida.

~40~

A HELL OF A THING

Most of Jerry Kichida's face was missing. And sitting next to Jerry's body was Chikako. The kitsune had her back against the concrete rail, four fox tails curled on the ground beside her hip.

"Well, hello there," she said. The words were playful but her tone and face were flat. "Aren't I supposed to be the one following you?"

"Some asshole shot me." I focused and shut down the emotions going through me as if I were tamping down gunpowder.

"So, you really didn't know anything about this?" She was watching my eyes intently.

"No." Maybe I fooled her or at least created doubt. The rage and aggression pheromones I was releasing had other good reasons for being there. "I didn't have anything to do with any of this. But I can't help noticing that your boss seems to get attacked a lot."

"Yes, he does." Her voice and face were covering up stronger emotions too. "But he always survives. One of the people involved in this got away, but it won't be long before we find him."

"What happened?" I asked.

Her eyes and nose were still running from the chili powder and red pepper, and she wiped her nose across her sleeve. "There were two of them. Normal humans, if you can believe that. I think the birdman grabbed one of them—the shooter, I think—and lifted him into the air, but the man pulled out a handgun and shot the aswang in midair, and they came down on this roof. Then I think the black man cut the aswang's head off with something while the birdman was stunned."

"Okay," I said.

"I don't know how far they got before Kris jumped across the roof and called them back," Chikako said tonelessly.

"Kris is the siren?" It was odd, for a moment, knowing that the siren had been a "Kris," that the kitsune had known her well enough to use her proper name, that the siren had lived in an apartment, listened to music, maybe ordered a lot of takeout, surfed the Internet, and so on. Or maybe Kris ate worms and listened to the tape-recorded screams of small puppies. What did I know?

"Yes." Chikako stood up and pointed at the siren's nails. They were covered in gore. Jerry's gore. "The one doing the shooting was wearing Kevlar, so Kris tore half his face off instead of gutting him. But his friend was strong-willed."

"What do you mean?" I asked.

The kitsune had one hand closed in a fist, but she took the other and fished in her pocket and came out with a suppressor. "She must have stopped singing while she was attacking the sniper. The black man couldn't make himself shoot Kris, but he shook off the trance enough to unscrew the silencer on his gun and fired it right next to his ears. He deafened himself so that he couldn't hear her song anymore. Kris realized what he was doing and charged him, but he shot her in the chest. She doesn't heal like you do."

"And you thought I had something to do with this?" I demanded. "If they had been knights, they wouldn't have been affected by siren songs."

She considered this. She had seen me working with knights. It did seem strange that I would use a sniper who wasn't one.

I went on. "How do you know any of this? How do you know the other man was black?" She unclenched her fist. There was a black and bloody scrap of flesh in it. "He left part of his earlobe behind."

Sarah was going to have to do some serious warding around Choo now.

"He got away in a taxi," the kitsune continued. "It was going too fast for me to follow, and there was mud smeared over its license plate. He must have stolen a cab. Or hired one. Or made a car look like one."

Huh. That was smart. There would be no way to track down one taxi cab in New York City. It would be like looking for a grain of salt in a snowfield.

"I didn't want to run blindly down the stairwell after the man," she admitted. "Not after all those booby traps."

"That's probably smart," I commented.

"My master is going to beat me for it. Maybe burn me." She said this matter-of-factly. I had no idea how to respond. I wasn't going to openly admit to being Akihiko's enemy, and saying "Sucks to be you" didn't quite seem to cover it.

Sirens began to sound in the distance, the police kind.

I've never been the kind of person who pretends to like someone just because they're dead. I didn't know Jerry Kichida well—tension and caution and distrust had kept us both kind of emotionally constipated the whole time we'd talked—but he'd loved a woman, and truly, as far as I could tell. He had fought for his country and his family. He had also taken out at least six supernatural creatures. Jerry Kichida's legacy wasn't going to be a failed attempt to protect the son he loved.

I wouldn't let it be.

The kitsune's eyes unfocused for a moment, but the next time she looked at me, they were perfectly clear. "My master wants you to know . . . the next Crucible is tomorrow night."

ᴄᴠ41ᴄᴠ

REQUIEM

Sig was in the middle of weapons practice while Jerry Kichida was shooting at Akihiko. When the oni ran outside and everyone started gravitating toward the front of the warehouse, she took the chance that she'd been waiting for. There were faint letters and sigils etched into the smooth concrete walls all around the warehouse, ten feet above the ground and hard to see unless you had phenomenal eyesight. Sig took the tip of her spear, wedged it against the edge of one of those letters, and shoved the metal tip hard enough to form an additional groove into the concrete.

Not much of a change at all. Like changing one word or adding a random comma. But magical inscriptions are the most unforgiving legal contracts there are.

The harionago burst into the warehouse, braided strands of her hair waving about threateningly as she screamed at people to flatten against the wall. Then guards came through the entrance and ushered Akihiko through the practice area. Sig took the end of her spear and prodded the unconscious form of a were-something that was bleeding out on the floor.

"Wake up." It didn't respond, but she didn't really expect it to. What Sig really wanted to do was get a good bit of its blood on the wooden spear butt that had been sharpened for vampire impaling.

There were three long white scrolls or banners hanging from the walls, red words trailing across them in symbols that Sig couldn't read. The words were written in dried blood. Sig took the bloody end of her spear, and as she moved among the crowd of supernatural beings milling against the wall, she made three small smears. Very strategically placed small smears.

It was time to let the ghosts in.

Only one person noticed what Sig was up to. Shenay, who had gone looking for "Britte" when she realized that her friend wasn't by her side. Sig looked up from the last banner and found Shenay staring at her.

"I . . ." Sig started to say, and Shenay quickly held up a hand and shook her head.

"I don't know what the *hell* is going on," Shenay said, a sentiment that none of the beings with enhanced hearing around her could disagree with. "And I don't want to know. As soon as they let us out, I'm gone, and I'm not coming back."

And she was. And she didn't.

Akihiko and his entourage had already disappeared when the ghosts began to appear in the warehouse. The supernatural beings in the room sensed the spirits, but they didn't know precisely what they were sensing, and the tension ratcheted up another notch. Several beings began to unsheathe their claws and fangs and horns and tentacles. The guards weren't going to be able to constrain them much longer without outright violence breaking out.

Sig didn't pay attention to any of that, though. She was staring at the ghosts. They were Chinese and had died traumatically. Most of them couldn't speak, and those that could didn't speak English, but they began to communicate with her through... I'm not sure how they communicated with Sig, to be honest. Gestures, perhaps, or brief contact or psychic flashes or emotional surges or all of those or more. Sig is never very specific about such things.

Whatever the mode of communication, Sig gradually came to understand that there was a reason Akihiko had set up operations near a waterfront. He was taking advantage of human smuggling operations that brought illegal Chinese aliens into the country in shipping containers. Akihiko didn't have to hunt for victims whose skeletons and tortured spirits could be used to make his bone golems—they came to him looking for jobs and shelter and hope. The illegal aliens had no legal record of their existence, no rights, no papers, no power, no authority, and Akihiko paid for them, took them prisoner, and starved them to death.

If Sig had any reservations about killing the onmyouji, they evaporated. It was possibly the worst moment for the harionago to appear and tell Sig that Akihiko wanted to see her.

Cahill was in or around the Clayton Inn in Tatum when Jerry Kichida died. He was there because he'd figured out who Akihiko's man on the ground in Tatum was. After all, somebody had found out about Max Selwyn and his relationship to Kevin, then scouted out where Max lived. Somebody was still poking around, trying to find out who had foiled the attempts on Kevin's life. And Cahill had tracked someone who was asking very specific questions under the guise of being a news blogger to the Clayton Inn.

And maybe it was racial profiling, but when Cahill looked at the guest register, he saw a Japanese name, just one, and it turned out that the man was paying in cash. It also turned out that he was a hard-looking man, compact and solid-looking, with a flat stare and a large burn scar on his cheek.

Cahill watched the man eat at the hotel restaurant, but he didn't follow him when the man left. There was time for that later. Cahill just waited for his moment, stood up, and took the glass the man had been drinking from.

Akihiko was proving a hard nut to crack. Cahill had learned his lesson about trying to mentally dominate people who might be psychic or warded, and it wasn't something he was going to try lightly. But maybe running the prints of a man who worked for Akihiko would provide some useful information.

Kevin Kichida was screaming and holding his face. He knew. He knew the second his father was wounded. He yelled at Molly to stop the van, and when Sarah reminded him that leaving the wards she'd made for him might tell Akihiko where they were, Kevin screamed that he didn't care, that he wanted the fucker to find him. Molly touched his arm then, and Kevin shook her hand off and demanded to know why they had let Jerry go, what the hell they were doing just driving around while his father was dying.

I'm glad I wasn't there. I would ten times rather fight for my life in the Crucible.

∽42∾

THE PLUS SIDE OF WORKING WITH OTHER PEOPLE

I will say this in favor of New York City: There's a way to get a burner phone in any given three-mile radius if you know the kind of places or people to look for. I called Ben Lafontaine. "This is just a social call, Ben. I have absolutely no favor to ask you at all. None. Not me. Nope."

He didn't laugh. "I heard about your fight with that gorilla thing. What's this *Down Boy* stuff?"

I got to the point. Or, at least, a point. "I've been studying the layout of the riverbed where the Crucible is held. Akihiko has warded the area so that no one can bring a weapon into it without running into a mental compulsion, but those wards don't bother me."

Ben saw the ramifications at once. "You want to plant weapons inside the zone for our people to use?"

"Actually, yeah, but I don't have time to slip surveillance *and* get to a weapons cache *and* plant the weapons at the edge of the woods inside his wards."

"I can get some of our people to hide some guns and knives

near the place so you can pick them up," Ben said. "But the shadows are getting a little dark here, John. Letting the world know that the Round Table is strong and that we protect our own is good. Starting a blood feud with umpteen different supernatural races is bad."

I heard what he was saying. Ben was my friend and sort of my leader, though we both knew what would happen if Ben ordered me to abandon Kevin Kichida to his death, especially now that my friends' fates were inextricably tangled up with his. What Ben definitely wasn't was my flunky. "I'm not planning on attacking Akihiko at the Crucible," I said. "I'd much rather isolate him. I'm planning for what to do if he attacks me."

"Just so long as you understand, if you die in a straight-up fight, you die," Ben told me. "You're entering this fight on your own free will, and I've got responsibilities to all our people."

"I get that," I assured him.

"But I wouldn't mind having them armed," Ben admitted grudgingly. "Having an outsider take over a pack of 'thropes doesn't set a good precedent, even if they are hyenas."

"Then leaving weapons in a car parked near the woods would be good."

Ben actually laughed then. "I've been asking around about that riverbed too. Want to hear something crazy?"

I did.

It was.

I was still digesting what I'd learned when Ben asked, "What's wrong with you? You sound like you've already lost."

"I got someone killed today," I admitted.

"What happened?"

I told him about Jerry Kichida and how part of me couldn't help wishing that I was working on my own again.

"It sounds like you couldn't have stopped him," Ben said

finally. "He wasn't just trying to save his son. He was trying to save his idea of his son."

Normally, I could have followed along, but I was having a hard time shaking my brood off. "What do you mean?"

"This Jerry couldn't accept his son becoming a part of our world to survive it," Ben explained. "That's what got him killed."

"I can understand his thinking," I said.

"Me too." Ben sighed. "But it's still wrong. You can't make people do what you want them to do, or feel what you want them to feel, or be what you want them to be. That's hard to accept anytime, but it's especially hard if it's your kid."

The words were saturated with sadness, as if they'd been soaking in it for a long time. "Are you thinking about Catherine?" I asked. Werewolves can't have biological children, and Catherine was Ben's adopted daughter.

"And her brother, Gabriel, too," Ben confessed. "Do you know how they became werewolves?"

"No," I said.

"They were two Indian kids in a Catholic orphanage in the fifties," Ben said. "And the orphanage took in a stray kid who happened to be a werewolf. Catherine and Gabriel were among the few who survived when the wolf shifted on the first full moon."

"Shit." It was an inadequate statement, but I don't know what an adequate one would have sounded like.

"That orphanage had already damaged them worse than any werewolf could when I found them," Ben said. "The priest who ran the place didn't have much love in him."

He stopped talking, but he wasn't finished, so I waited.

"I took them in, but Gabriel was like a wound gone bad. He had so much bitterness trapped inside him. And Catherine wanted to find something to replace the God that the priest kept promising her and beating her with at the same time. It's why she fell for Bernard's lies."

Catherine had married Bernard Wright, a charismatic were-wolf leader who turned out to be more like a cult leader or a terrorist than the prophet he pretended to be.

"And I knew better, but I let myself get pulled into Bernard's clan trying to protect her from her own decisions," Ben said. "And I pulled my whole pack along with me."

I suddenly understood why Ben had taken Bernard's place even though he didn't want the job. Ben was trying to atone.

"So, this Jerry Kichida messed up, but he didn't mess up too bad," Ben finished. "He meant well, and nobody paid for his mistakes but himself."

For some reason, I began talking about Brother Takeshi. About how he had loved and lost and how his order had commanded him not to act on his emotions for his own spiritual refinement. "I know I keep putting myself in situations where people are going to die," I said. "And I know I mess up sometimes. But they're messed-up situations where people are already dying anyway. I don't think I'd make a very good Japanese monk, Ben."

"Everybody has their own path. About twenty years ago, I met a white woman who was really into the idea of sleeping with an Apache warrior," Ben began.

"But you're not an Apache," I pointed out.

"Shhhh," he said. "Anyhow, this was a woman who walked many paths. Tai Chi. Crystal healing. Tantric sex. Herbal teas."

"Was she into Japanese monks?" I wasn't seeing the connection.

"Probably," he said. "But she told me something that stuck. She said that when you died, the angels..."

"Not the Great Spirit?" I interrupted.

"Let me talk," Ben said, momentarily irritated. "She thought people who believed in the Christian god were stupid, but she talked about angels a lot. She was complicated."

"Just searching," I said. "Like everybody else."

Ben didn't let himself get sidetracked again. "The thing she said that stuck was this: She said that when you die, the angels won't ask why you weren't Moses or Gandhi or Martin Luther King or Mother Teresa. The only thing the angels are going to ask is why you weren't yourself."

It was good, having friends.

∾43∾

GHOST OF A CHANCE

I'm not sure exactly when this happened, because time tended to dilate and contract in the endless paper corridors that Sig followed the harionago down. She had traveled to Japan and found the waiting process to interview Akihiko a lot more trying than I had, but at least the onmyouji hadn't been back to New York yet. His questions had nothing to do with ghosts or his sabotaged wards.

"You have been talking to the werewolf who calls himself Down Boy." Akihiko made it sound like an accusation.

I imagine Sig gave him the look she sometimes gives me when she is dealing with strong emotions; it is an empty expression, but currents run under her skin like water and electricity and steam coursing beneath a quiet city street. Sig feels things, and feels them deeply, and she took the fate of those Chinese spirits she had encountered personally. She wanted to kill this unspeakable asshole right there, but between the harionago, the four bone golems, the pliable thing Akihiko was wearing as a robe, whatever guardian lurked in his shadow, and the fiery spirit in his lantern, Sig would be outnumbered eight to one before she even reached the onmyouji himself in his place of power.

Sig was also suddenly very glad that Shenay had mentioned going far away. Unlike Aubrey, Shenay had been a known commodity at Akihiko's warehouse for some time, even before Akihiko discovered that his grandson was alive and a sperm donor. But Sig had lived with Stanislav Dvornik, a man who dealt with horrible things—a man who had saved her from horrible things. She had stayed with Stanislav longer than she should have after he became increasingly bitter and paranoid—and she knew that once a man reaches that point where he is willing to kill people to remove *possible* threats, the things he perceives as threats start multiplying.

"This is the part where you say something," Akihiko reminded her.

"Do you want me to kill the werewolf?" Sig asked.

The question took Akihiko off guard. The whole faux action fuck doll persona is a role that Sig falls into easily, just like I channel my inner smartass. We are more than that, but when dealing with things that are overwhelming, emotional complexity is not your friend. Sig was very aware that she could die in that tea house. She could be killed and her body discarded like a sock with a hole in it. She might even become like one of the ghosts who haunt her, a prospect she probably finds more terrifying than honest-to-God death. But Sig really is brash and brave and fierce even if she is other things, and she grabbed hold of that part of herself and focused on it as if it were the sum and total of her being.

It was Akihiko's turn to stare. Sig had just gone from being a possible annoyance that he was considering removing to a possible asset that he should consider using. "You would be willing to kill him if I asked you to?"

"No," Sig disagreed. "But I'll kill him if you pay me to. Besides, I don't like the way he looks at me."

Akihiko found his ground again. "He is interested in you?"

"No," Sig corrected. "He wants to sleep with me."

"Would you be willing to let him seduce you?" Akihiko inquired softly. "So that you could be closer to him when the time is right to kill him?"

I imagine Sig's eyes narrowed. That, too, is a look I know well. In any case, she said, "My sword is for sale. My body is not."

Akihiko examined her boldly then, allowing his eyes to examine her body, if only briefly. "That is a shame."

Sig marshaled her anger and redirected it. "And even if I was willing, I could never fool a werewolf that way. They smell feelings, and I'm a lousy actress."

Akihiko waved this off. "All women are skilled at deceit."

As if Sig didn't have enough reasons for wanting him dead. "Whatever. To answer your real question, I don't have any friends here. I don't want any friends here. I don't know who I'll wind up having to kill yet."

"A wise choice." Akihiko smiled thinly. He then proceeded to ask Sig questions about our conversation in the diner, and he was not as formal as he had been with me, perhaps because Sig could not possibly have the Knights Templar backing her, or perhaps because she was a woman.

Sig balked. "Why should I tell you anything?"

"You won good money at *my* Crucible the other night, and you will have a chance to win more if I don't take a disliking to you." Here the room darkened, and Akihiko's body suddenly seemed limned with a light that did not come from the sun, from any source that Sig recognized. The steam from the pot of tea between them began to coalesce into the shape of a coiling serpent. "And besides...I am asking politely."

Sig allowed herself the luxury of being cautious after that, and she more or less played back the entire conversation we'd had at the diner, minus the part where Shenay told us about how the Crucible was warded against weapons. If nothing else, Sig figured she was buying Shenay time to get gone.

It was possibly Akihiko's unwillingness to view a woman as a primary threat that led him to finally send Sig away. She was both grateful for his oversight and determined to make him pay for it.

"Your boss is a pig," Sig said to the harionago as she was escorted away from the tea house, hopefully back to New York.

"He is iron." The harionago had real admiration in her voice.

"Your boss is pig iron." Sig saw the harionago stiffen, but Akihiko's bodyguard didn't turn around.

Which was just as well. As they came to a fork that branched into two different hallways, Sig saw something out of the corner of her eye. A faceless woman standing in the center of an adjacent hallway, staring at her despite a lack of eyes with which to do so. Jerry Kichida was there too, almost as faceless as the noppera-bō, though her head was smooth as an egg and his features were a red ruin. It was the first sign Sig had that Jerry was dead.

And if that was Jerry...was Sig also staring at the shade of Akihiko's wife? Kevin Kichida's grandmother?

Sig said nothing, and the harionago continued to lead her around bends and through doorways. The noppera-bō and Jerry Kichida appeared in Sig's peripheral vision twice more, somehow moving rapidly without seeming to rush, traveling ahead of them down parallel hallways without a sound or scent. The harionago seemed completely oblivious to the ghosts, perhaps because they were keeping their distance.

When they reached the hallway that led directly back to the

warehouse, the branch that split into three different directions, Sig got her final surprise. A phrase was written on the door in blood, maybe Jerry's blood. In any case, it was blood that the harionago could not see.

Shinbo Suro

And Sig knew, knew it in her DNA, that Kevin's family had just given her the phrase Sarah White was looking for, the words that would help unlock the onmyouji's secrets.

PART THE THIRD

The Last Day

∾44∾

LISTEN, ABOUT THAT "ANAL GLAND" CRACK TWENTY CHAPTERS AGO...

It was two were-hyenas following me after midnight, not the kitsune. That bothered me. Akihiko might be an obsessive, narcissistic, ruthless, high-functioning sociopath, but he was a *smart* obsessive, narcissistic, ruthless, high-functioning sociopath, and the reminder that he wasn't just sitting around being predictable while I made my own plans and preparations gave me a few qualms. What task was so important to him that his best tracker wasn't watching me any longer?

In any case, I had borrowed a page from the kitsune's book and was crouching with my back against the parapet of a roof when the were-hyenas leaped over it. Over me. They were both young-looking, one white and male with short, curly, sandy-brown hair and a long lanky body, the other short and African-American and female. They were intent on catching up with me, and they kept going for twenty feet before they realized that my scent trail had ended. It wasn't until they slowed down that they realized I was running lightly behind them, keeping the same rhythm so that our footsteps and the vibrations they sent through the tarmac matched.

It bears repeating that even creatures who regenerate can be knocked out if their brains slosh against their skulls violently enough. Some creatures have smaller brains, or stronger neck muscles, or less-developed nervous systems, or faster recovery time, but even then, it just becomes a question of how much more force is necessary.

The male yelled and started to whirl as I snatched the semi-automatic he kept holstered at his back and smashed it against the side of the female's head. I had no choice; she had faster hands than the male and was reaching for her own weapon. Between my greater strength, height, and the precise application of the metal gun butt against the side of her temple, the female went down and stayed down.

The male's mind didn't work as fast as his physical reflexes. He completed his turn while I was still following through the motion that took out the female, and he had a moment where he could have hit me or kicked me. The problem was, he wasted that moment reaching for the gun that was no longer behind him, and by the time he realized whose gun was in my hand, his moment was gone.

So was he, though I had to be a lot less gentle and quick.

I stared at their unconscious bodies, trying to figure out if the kitsune's absence was a good or bad thing. She would have been a lot harder to trick, probably a lot harder to take out, and she had that weird telepathic bond with the onmyouji, so that was in the plus column. On the other hand, removing her would have taken one of Akihiko's major playing pieces off the board.

As the options and ramifications and consequences and possibilities tumbled around in my head like drying laundry,

I began to see a possible way to turn this development to my advantage. I walked over to the side of the roof and began looking for a good car to steal.

The next time I picked up two were-hyenas' scents, it was in the wooded area outside Akihiko's riverbed arena. I had located a few human guards by sound and smell too, but they seemed to be stationary, probably set up in tree stands with hunting rifles, and they were easy to avoid. As soon as I figured out the were-hyenas' patrol pattern, I carefully crossed their trail and left a scent for them to follow. I stayed ahead of them but close enough to overhear if they started talking to anyone else.

The pair of them found the Ford Escort I'd parked near the riverbed bank. The Ford Escort that was loaded with the weapons Ben Lafontaine had provided. By the time the guards realized that I wasn't in it, I had looped around and come at them from the side with a double-barrel shotgun. "This shotgun has shells loaded with small silver prayer beads," I lied. "I pull a trigger and you're both gone."

That didn't stop them from whirling and training their own guns on me, but it did stop them from firing. One of the were-hyenas was the short but stout Latino male who had accosted me at Akihiko's warehouse. The other was an average-sized kid whose heritage seemed to be Polynesian and something else, maybe African or Latino or Native American. The latter looked like a teenager, but that was because of a blank expression as much as his slender frame and smooth features.

"It's you," the stout one said, as if I needed reminding. "Down Boy. What you want, fool?"

"I want to know what to call you," I said. "You're the one I need to talk to, right? Of the two of you, I mean?"

"Yeah," the stout one said levelly. And when I didn't respond, he added, "Gustavo."

"I think we can help each other, Gustavo." I told him. "Your pack is dying. I've seen at least ten of you die with my own eyes."

"Fuck all that," he snarled. "Whadjoo do to Trip and Tasia?"

"Are those the two that were following me around tonight?" I asked.

"Yeah." He glowered.

I indicated the Ford. "They're alive and in the trunk of my car. As a peace offering."

"Gimme the keys!" he commanded.

"The trunk's unlocked," I said. "See for yourself."

Neither of them moved.

"Ten of you," I mused. "And your new master must have killed even more than that when he was taming you."

The younger-looking one muttered something I couldn't hear even with *my* ears. Gustavo got even angrier. "Watch your mouth."

"I'm not your enemy," I said. "It's the man in white who's going to keep using you up until you're gone. You know that, right?"

"What you want us to do? He can find us anywhere." The kid's words had a whining quality.

"Shut up, JJ," Gustavo snapped.

"I get it," I said. "You just keep doing what he says, and your pack keeps dying a few people at a time, and you're just hanging on, hoping things will calm down or somebody else will come along and kill him for you because you don't know what else to do."

"We took on the man in white when nobody else would," Gustavo snarled. "Where were you and all your trash talk then?"

"I was just getting here," I pointed out. "What matters is, you have a choice to make. You can pull that trigger and hope I don't pull mine. Or you can let me go and contact your boss and tell him what just happened. Or you can try to follow me again and hope I don't double back and kill you. Or you can not tell anyone anything. Just stay out of it and watch and hope I stir up some trouble that your pack can take advantage of later."

"So, what I hear you sayin', we gettin' the fuck stick no matter what," Gustavo sneered.

"Exactly." I lowered my shotgun. "So, what do you have to lose?"

Gustavo's eyes widened. He thought about firing then. The moment hung poised there, heavy and silent. I had definitely been hanging around Sig too much. This was the kind of thing she would do. Thankfully, JJ tipped the balance.

"The vampires..." JJ began.

"Shut up!" Gustavo rapped out, and JJ did.

"Vampires?" I repeated softly.

Gustavo fumed about it, but he told me anyway. Whatever his reasons were, it was a good sign. "There's a big vampire gang callin' itself the Rips."

The Rips? Was that supposed to be like the Crips, or was it some lame play of words on RIP? I remembered the last Crucible, where Akihiko was chatting with some vampire who was doing the gangsta thing. "Are you talking about the vampire hive headed by some guy named Alfonse?"

"Not no more," Gustavo said scornfully. "Alfonse wouldn't play nice, so the man in white made a deal with Alfonse's second-in-command. The man in white took Alfonse out, and now the Rips have a queen instead of a king."

"And what did your boss get out of it?" I asked.

"The Rips are gonna help guard the Crucible on fight nights."

Well, at least I knew how Akihiko had been spending some of his time now: beefing up his security.

"Meaning he doesn't really need you anymore," I observed.

Gustavo regarded me sullenly. "What you plannin'?"

"It's not just me. A bunch of people are tired of the man in white." I wasn't giving away any information that Akihiko hadn't already guessed. He'd told me about rumors of werewolves working with knights himself, and there was no way he wouldn't be keeping an eye out for werewolf threats in the crowd. It was one of the reasons I wanted to even the odds so badly. "I've got a lot of guns in my car there. I'm going to hide them inside the edge of the Crucible's boundaries."

The guns were lightly doused in some kind of sandalwood aftershave. Ben's people...our people...would be able to locate them easily among the trees as they drifted into the area, at least if they knew what they were looking for, but the woods were full of so many scents from so many creatures and cunning folk with special wares that no one else would find the odor peculiar.

Gustavo's nostrils flared. "The wolves are makin' a move?"

"Among others," I said. "But I need you and yours to look the other way while I plant these weapons."

"We do, we die," Gustavo snarled.

"You're dying anyway," I said bluntly. "But I'm not asking you to fight. All you have to do is sit back and watch. If you think we don't have a chance, go ahead and help Akihiko kill us. But if you do see a chance...well...it might be your last chance."

"Let me see your knife." Gustavo lowered his weapon and held his hand out.

Curious, I unsheathed the knife at my side and handed it over hilt-first.

Gustavo examined the blade critically. "This is real, JJ. This a knight knife. That silver steel shit."

JJ lowered his gun and bent closer to see, and Gustavo stuck the tip of the knife beneath JJ's jaw. "You don't leave my side, JJ. Not until after tonight. You get me?"

JJ croaked.

"I don't think he can nod," I said.

"No way JJ keeps this quiet unless he's with me," Gustavo explained expressionlessly.

"It's your pack," I said.

That hit him so hard, it left an aftershock of tightened muscles in his face and shoulders. Gustavo swallowed. It hadn't been his pack for a while, and his pack was all he'd had. Like a lot of tough guys, Gustavo rode out the strong emotion and pretended it never happened. He released JJ and looked at the knife again. "So, it's true. Wolves and knights."

"It's true," I admitted. "You have a problem with that?"

Gustavo handed the knife back to me hilt-first. "Not tonight."

∾45∾

THIRTY-DOLLAR SANDWICHES

It was maybe five in the morning and Sig was freshly showered and heavily armed when she opened the door to her one-floor hotel. We'd exchanged a few words in Parth's computer parlor, but nothing too involved. Now I shut the door behind me, pulled her in close, and kissed her. It took a moment for her to kiss me back, but when she did it was long and wet and warm.

We finally separated with a gasp, and I said: "It's good to see you. Can we talk here?"

"Yes," she said, and I trusted her enough not to demand details. She put her palms on my chest and pushed me back, just a bit. "What's wrong?"

"Nothing specific." I gave her a squeeze for good luck and released her reluctantly. "Generally speaking, everything. We need to go."

She gave me her measuring look but also gave me another kiss, a quick one, and turned around and went back into her room without wasting any more time. It was another thing I liked about her. She was wearing a blue T-shirt that said *Your Life, Your Choice* and peach-colored panties, and the first thing she did was set her SIG Sauer on the corner of her bed so that she could don an old-fashioned shoulder holster rig. "What happened to us keeping our distance?"

The hotel she was staying in wasn't a chain, and it wasn't a homey bed-and-breakfast–style place or a classy independent, either. The room was pretty basic. Cleaned but not spotless brown carpeting. A single-sized bed with light green covers. A small bathroom with a shower. A bar to hang clothes on instead of a closet, and a large recessed window whose ledge doubled as shelf space. The television set was the lone luxury. "Things are happening. I have a pretty strong feeling that we're safer together now."

I was momentarily distracted when Sig bent over her small rolling suitcase. She glanced over her shoulder, saw me looking, and snorted. "Where's this feeling coming from?"

My answering smile was unapologetic. "That thing with the mapinguari and the gashadokuro...the way he called the next Crucible so soon..." I fumbled for the right words, couldn't find them, and settled for "Akihiko was pushing it even before he got sniped."

"I know." Sig sat down on the bed and rolled back slightly so that she could straighten her legs and pull some black jeans on. "I confused him when he asked me questions, but I guess he's found out that his warehouse is full of ghosts by now. He'll know that's on me."

"That's about how I figure it too." It really was good to see her. I'd talked to Sig without smelling her, and smelled her without being able to really talk to her, and the dream with Sarah had bothered me. "I don't know what he suspects, but he knows enough not to want us around any longer."

"Could you find me some clean socks?" Sig was putting on a black leather jacket that I'd never seen before. Then, picking up the original thread again: "We could just leave and work this from the outside now."

"We could," I reflected. "But we wouldn't be any closer than when we started. And I don't think we're going to catch Akihiko anywhere but at the Crucible from now on."

"You're probably right about that." Sig's suitcase was mostly dirty clothes. I would have told her to just leave it behind, but Akihiko could use her personal possessions for all kinds of scrying spells and curses, and Sarah wasn't here to help us with wards. "He's not going to feel safe again until all his questions have been answered."

"Or removed." I tossed her a dark pair of hiking socks. "If Akihiko wasn't worried that outright murdering me would drag more knights into this, I'd probably be dead already."

Sig sat on the bed again. "I'm not so sure about that. I think he's been planning to kill you or chase you off on the third night all along. He really has been making a lot of money off of you. And he likes playing games."

I stroked her back while she pulled her socks on. Her muscles were tense. "Maybe that's why he's been increasing the danger in increments. If I die in a fight now, it's not like anyone could claim I was unaware of the risks."

Sig jumped up and began looking for footwear. "So how does any of this make you being here less dangerous for me?"

"I figure you're on his things-to-do-before-the-Crucible list now. If I openly declare you my territory and stay by your side, Akihiko will wait until he's ready to take us both out."

"You're declaring me your territory?" Sig paused in her efforts to pull on a pair of combat boots and looked up at me.

Uh-oh. "I'm trying to think the way Akihiko thinks," I mumbled, gathering loose items and tossing them in her purse. "So I can use it against him."

"Uh-huh. Because that whole marking-your-territory instinct doesn't come naturally to you at all." But Sig wasn't really offended. She came over and kissed me again, briefly but hard, then looked at me and said, "Just so you know, if you pee anywhere near me or on me, it's a deal breaker."

I sputtered, and Sig stood up, grabbed a tote bag off the floor, and went into the bathroom. "Well, right or wrong, we're together now. Where do you want to go?"

"Anywhere, so long as we keep moving." What I wasn't telling Sig was that it would probably drive Akihiko crazy when we disappeared off his radar, and I wanted to keep him distracted trying to locate us. Sarah would be orchestrating her move on Akihiko's safety deposit box soon, and it would really suck if he located Kevin and the others this close to the finish line.

The reason I wasn't telling Sig that was that even though cunning folk can't spy on me magically, and it's really hard to bug women who can summon spirits that disrupt electronic signals, it was remotely possible that Akihiko might have some other way of monitoring us. Neither of us had mentioned the other's real name. Neither of us had mentioned Kevin Kichida. We hadn't said anything about wanting to kill Akihiko. Basically, nothing we had said included any information that Akihiko wouldn't figure out the moment he realized I'd joined her. Whatever else Sig and I were, she was my partner, and she was a good one.

Sig emerged from the bathroom. "Well, you just gave me an idea. Did you drive here or call a taxi or what?"

"I thought we'd take the Volvo," I said.

She tried to recall what I was talking about and frowned. "What Volvo?"

"The one the two Asian men who were watching your hotel room were sitting in."

She smiled faintly. "They're not driving it anymore?"

"Not unless there's a steering wheel in the trunk."

I had to wonder again though...where the hell were Aki-hiko's main supernatural servants. The oni? The kitsune? The harionago? The yuki-onna? What were they...or, more to the point, Akihiko...up to?

I took Sig from that car to a wharf, where I convinced her to set her luggage on fire, and then we threw what was left into the salt water. Next, we found a train crossing where we hopped on the side of a locomotive for two miles, jumped off near a ferry, walked over the iron rails for a bit before getting on the boat, crossed some water, milled around in a crowd, climbed down a small stretch of power line conduit, came up near a cathedral that we passed through, and caught a taxi from there. As the cab was driving off, I leaned over and whispered, "Will you try green eggs and ham *now*?"

Well, *I* thought it was funny.

For her part, Sig took me to the Waldorf Astoria. The lobby of the luxury hotel was as big as some train stations, and we passed through gilt-edged, dark, gleaming columns and flank-ing sculptures. There was also a nine-foot lobby clock that had really ornate filigree. I would have liked to stop and study it more closely. It was my first time in the Waldorf, and I had to admit that it was impressive.

"We don't exactly blend in here," I pointed out. There were people dressed casually around us, but not in layers of T-shirts, flannel, and hoodies. The comfortable shoes people were wear-ing weren't designed for any activity more strenuous than walk-ing briskly, either. "Did you get some info from a dead person that I don't know about?"

"I got some info from Shenay who got it from Aubrey while he was trying to get in her pants." Sig smiled and gave my arm a squeeze. "You always like to be mysterious and hold little surprises back. Suffer."

I gave her a look but shut up.

It took some negotiation with a concierge staff that acted like they were border patrol guards, and Aubrey's name was dropped, then some messages were passed, but eventually, Sig arranged to meet a woman named Holly Blake for brunch in a room that had the word Oscar in the title, some kind of restaurant whose aromas made my stomach growl. Holly's name sounded vaguely familiar, and I kind of got the impression from the staff that the only reason we got as far as we did was that Holly often had strange visitors.

"Holly Blake," I repeated. Sig just smiled and kept looking at a menu that had thirty-dollar sandwiches on it. Maybe they were magic sandwiches. It was as likely a reason for being there as any other I could come up with.

A half-elf came in and scanned the room, identifying us as the things he was looking for almost immediately. He was some semi-humanish offspring of the dokkalfar, or maybe the svartalfar (I've never really been clear on the distinction between the two). A dark elf with pale skin (*dark* refers to these elves' violent nature and their tendency to live underground, not their coloring). His thin white hair had been shaved off, leaving his skull completely bald. He didn't have sunglasses, but the contacts that made his eyes look like a normal brown probably filtered light for those sensitive red pupils. The guy definitely stood out in the room, but he wasn't blatantly inhuman, a five foot eight albino moving with power and purpose.

He scanned the room again, then came and sat down at our table without saying a word.

"Hi," Sig offered.

He didn't say anything.

I put down my menu. "Maybe you could help me out. Are the sandwiches here magic?"

He still didn't say anything.

Then a lot of my questions dissolved in an invisible cloud of apple, rose, and jasmine. Holly Blake was stunningly beautiful, her honey-brown hair curled in tiny ringlets around green eyes and a lush mouth. She was all lovely swells and hollows, and her body moved under a light green dress like ripples across a lake. Instead of dripping water, though, she dripped sex.

Holly Blake was a nymph. An anthousai, probably, from the way all the hyacinths in the room sighed and released a subtle wave of fresh scent. Or in plain English, a flower nymph.

"That's her," a woman thirty feet behind us whispered in a way that suggested she was speaking out of the side of her mouth.

"The woman who writes those romance novels?" her companion whispered back, and then I stopped paying attention to them because the dark elf was rising and pulling out a seat so that Holly could sit down.

Holly's eyes traveled over us with frank intimacy and appreciation. It felt like I'd been visually fondled. "Well, you two are a striking pair."

"Thank you for having lunch with us." Sig was so polite that I decided to suspend any flippancy for the time being, if only until I figured out what her play was. Good partnerships work both ways.

"Well, I'll be having tea, at least." Holly smiled a luminous smile. "We'll see about lunch. And then see about after lunch. Steely blue eyes and firm asses will get you far."

"What she's trying to say," the dark elf translated, his voice raspy and surprisingly deep, "is that she wants to know why you're here."

"We're here about your son," Sig told her. "Aubrey."

That's when I knew I really was in love.

～46～

WE DID THE MASH. WE DID THE....WELL...YOU KNOW.

The moon was three-quarters full, casting long and deep shadows as Sig and I made our roundabout way to and through the dry riverbed where the Crucible was held. The night air was crisp and cold, heavy with the smell of roasted goat and toasted corn. Somewhere, bagpipes were playing. Nobody tried to separate us or lead me off to a prep area at the checkpoint.

"You're scheduled for the fourth round," a human guard with more fluent English than the others I'd met informed me. "You don't have to report in until the second fight is over."

I knew Akihiko would have some surprises of his own. Opponents don't just stay static while you make plans and set events into motion, but I definitely hadn't expected this: No one seemed to be paying any particular attention to Sig or me at all. Neither the guards nor any of the supernatural creatures around us gave any indications of unusual hostility, though one of the were-hyenas was keyed up and pumping tension into the atmosphere. Sig and I drifted into the Crucible on a tide of random spectators.

The air of normalcy was creepier than a blood-red moon or flaming skulls set on spears would have been.

Booths were being set up, and Sig and I paused to watch some kind of reverse limbo contest. A couple of gypsies had rigged a pole vault bar and were inviting various supernatural competitors to jump over the crossbar without benefit of a pole, periodically raising the height. One of the gypsies was an old man playing the theme to *Hello, Dolly!* on a guitar. I don't know if it was the only song he knew or the only English he knew or if the wine on his breath had something to do with it or what, but he kept yelling "rock and roll" at random intervals even though the song wasn't.

Sig reached out and squeezed my hand. "It reminds me of Paris."

That was a place I'd never been. "Why?"

"The streets around the big tourist areas at night," she said. "You'll see."

And then she abruptly shut her mouth. It really wasn't a good time to think about the future or lack thereof. It really wasn't a good time to be tying each other's hands up either, and I gently eased mine out of her grip.

We left the contest while something with mandibles was clearly winning.

A nix who kept changing her appearance was selling something she called moonshine for twenty thousand dollars a cup, and from the way the pale liquid was glowing, I'm not entirely sure that the drink's name wasn't literal. I looked around, but I didn't see the entrepreneurial half-elf I'd talked to on the two previous fight nights, at least not yet. I wondered if maybe word that a bad moon was rising had gotten out on the half-elf grapevine.

Some redcaps were getting in a craps game run by a bocor,

and I don't think the dice were carved from ivory. It was hard to know who the bigger idiot was, them for thinking they could win or him for thinking they would lose gracefully. If I'd been a sheriff or a bouncer, I would have broken it up.

"This is almost pleasant," Sig observed in a tone that was also almost pleasant.

"Almost," I agreed.

The gashadokuro standing motionless among the gathering crowd weren't quite as spread out as they had been on the previous two Crucibles, and since I didn't see any areas free of the damn things, that meant there were more of them.

There was also an increased number of vampires even though the weather hadn't gotten any warmer. I'm pretty good at spotting weapons under clothing—the bulges, the constricted movements, the odd alignments, the ripple and sway of fabric… and not only were there more vampires around, the pasty-skinned, greasy mothersuckers were armed. It looked like Gustavo and JJ hadn't been lying about Akihiko recruiting new muscle.

There were also more cunning folk of Asian ancestry milling about, or at least Asian males dressed up as cunning folk, and many of them were suspiciously young, fit, and hard-eyed.

It was the first Crucible where I wasn't fighting in the opening match, and I actually got to see the schedule of announced fights. Sig was the third fight, listed in a weapons match using bo staves. She was up against a trauco whose fighting name was Jungle Jim. I was the fourth fight and scheduled to go toe to toe with a suiko called Gill Billy. Both fights were even odds.

A suiko? They're tough, but those fishbowl heads make one hell of an easy target if you know what you're doing. What was Akihiko on about?

I decided to ask him.

We crossed the bridge to the concrete side of the Crucible,

the abandoned industrial remains where Akihiko liked to keep his van. The bridge began to shake ominously when we were almost across it, and I looked back over my shoulder. I didn't see anything, but I got a strong whiff of oni. The presence of the invisible ogre was almost reassuring.

Akihiko's main bodyguard, the harionago, didn't seem pleased to see us, but she stepped aside, her long braids swinging so that the small metal spiked balls in them clacked like a beaded curtain. She was dressed in a lot of protective leather tonight, and blades were sheathed all over her body. Akihiko greeted us with "I've been looking for you two. I thought you might have left the city."

"We pay our debts," I said.

He didn't miss the possible multiple meanings. "Good. I didn't realize that you and Britte were a couple. She didn't mention it in our talk."

"I'm afraid I misled you a little. He's my sidekick," Sig said.

I thought about objecting, but decided to make her pay for that later. Sig had been disregarded by the onmyouji. She could have her moment.

Akihiko looked at me with the first touch of amusement I'd seen from the man. It was scornful and cruel amusement, but it was genuine. "Indeed?"

"I'm also her front kick," I said. "And round kick. Back kick. Spinning kick. I'm good like that."

"What's going on with the fights?" Sig held up the scorecard. "These look easy."

"Your sidekick complained that the fights were too hard last night." Akihiko held up his hands. "So, I tried to be accommodating. Now you're complaining that they're too easy?"

"We're not going to draw out the rakshasa I'm hunting this way," I said, sticking to my original story.

His eyes were dark pits behind the tip of his lit cigar. "Perhaps."

Sig gestured at the creatures all around us. "I thought you were trying to give these beings something spectacular."

The onmyouji shrugged. "I give people what I give them. They can take it."

"Or leave it?" Sig asked softly.

He seemed to really look at her then. It wasn't an improvement. "They can take it."

I glanced around. The gashadokuro around us were motionless, but there were more of them than there had been when we started this conversation. A soft, chill breeze carried oni stink from somewhere behind us, and the way the temperature was dropping probably meant the snow woman was nearby.

"This seems like it would be a really good moment to giggle nervously," I observed. "But I'm not sure how to go about it."

Sig decided to leave and abruptly turned so that the hari-onago crowding her from behind had to step to the side or get shouldered. I bowed respectfully, and Akihiko bowed back, even though we didn't really respect anything but the danger that the other represented. That might be a guy thing.

"Well, that was productive," I said as I rejoined Sig.

She just grimaced, tension coming off of her shoulders.

We drifted to the edge of the dry riverbed, scouting out the crowd on that side of the Crucible, just moving and staying alert. We didn't know what else to do, or at least I didn't. If Sig had a definite purpose, she was keeping it to herself. Waiting for the first fight was maybe the longest hundred years of my life.

I mean twenty minutes.

When the kitsune addressed the crowd, her first words were "LADIES! GENTLEMEN! OTHERS! TONIGHT,

WE HAVE A SPECIAL EVENT FOR YOU! A DEATH MATCH THAT IS NOT ON THE SCORECARD!"

Of course they did. Sig and I kept drifting among the crowd. They were going to try to make Sig and me fight each other to the death. I'd been expecting this, was ready for it. I headed toward a gashadokuro who was standing motionless at the edge of the trench. If it started to move, I was willing to bet I could reach its swords before it could.

"WE ARE PROUD TO INTRODUCE A NEW FIGHTER!" the kitsune continued. "THE MAGNIFICENT JEANIE! AND HER OPPONENT, AN UNFORTUNATE SOUL WHO TRIED TO DISRUPT THE CRUCIBLE!"

Wait. What?

〜47〜

I DREAM OF GENIE

Jeanie" wasn't driven to the fight. She walked down the dry riverbed toward us, smokeless flames flickering around her outline. I couldn't see her well at first. She was tall, wearing a sleeveless black outfit that looked like a leotard made of leather. Her skin was dusky, her hair long and thick and black, falling down to the elbows at her side. I couldn't see her face at all. The fire licking around her head cast it in shadow.

The crowd was silent. Every predator in that throng sensed that some balance had just been tilted horribly out of whack. We were wolves and lions and snakes and tigers who had just discovered that we were standing near a *Tyrannosaurus rex*.

Jeanie? The siren had been called Big Bertie. Bertie, as in bird. Was Jeanie another one of the yuki-onna's little jokes?

Sig was thinking along the same lines. "Genie." She didn't say the word any differently, but I heard the G-E-N-I-E spelled out in her tone anyhow.

I uttered maybe the filthiest thing I've ever uttered. I won't repeat it.

"Stanislav always said that jinn are so rare they might as well be make-believe," Sig said uncertainly, not caring who overheard us anymore.

"It's not that they're rare." I was babbling a little. "I'm sure there's lots of them out there somewhere in jinn land. You know, fifth dimension to the right or whatever. It's not like jinn have any natural predators."

Sig eyed me suspiciously. "But they're not common here."

"It's rare for them to take physical form on our plane." My voice sounded a little strangled. "They prefer to act through dreams or emotions or visions and such."

"Stanislav said they could be good or bad." Sig really didn't like the way I sounded. "They're some kind of elementals, right?"

"Maybe." I tried to swallow. My throat was dry and tight. There are different types of jinn, and even though they were all born of some kind of smokeless fire, they each seem to work with different elements. Marids are associated with water. Ifrits with earth, and sometimes fire, maybe because of magma and lava and all that. Djinn are associated with air and also fire. You know. Oxygen. Fire. Those are the only three types the Quran specifically mentions, but some people think that djinn spelled with a D got confused with jinn spelled with a J, or jann, and that D djinn are primarily air and J jinn are primarily fire. And some people try to lump every kind of...oh fuck it. The point is, jinn are an ancient race of immortals and crazy powerful. I'm not sure if I said any of that out loud or not.

"Hey." Sig smacked me softly on my upper arm. "Pull it together. You're scaring me a little."

Jeanie had almost reached the kitsune. The jinn turned and looked in my direction. I felt the impact of that stare like heated air being pushed in front of an explosion, and I wasn't the only one. Several creatures around us took a step back. How good was a jinn's hearing? I had no idea.

I took a deep breath. "It's probably at least half human."

"They can mate with humans?" I couldn't tell if Sig thought that sounded horrible or was wondering what jinn/human sex must be like.

"Yeah," I said. It says so in the Quran, by the way, and a lot of people think Adam's first wife, Lilith, was a jinn, and that's why the Sanhedrin yanked her out of the Torah like a rotten tooth. She's still in the Talmud though.

"So, how powerful are the hybrids?" Sig still seemed a little unnerved by how hoarse my voice was.

I cleared my throat. "If we're talking the descendant of a descendant of a descendant of a descendant, who knows. If we're talking a human possessed by a jinn, their powers are mostly magic or mental. But the direct offspring of a human and a jinn? They're just insanely powerful instead of impossibly powerful."

"Fine." Sig wasn't getting it. "I'm more interested in the prisoner."

Oh. Yeah. Shit. Maybe I was the one who wasn't getting it. The headlights of a vehicle appeared in the opposite direction of the dry riverbed. The engine didn't belong to a golf cart, and it was pulling something heavy and metal behind it.

"The prisoner is a surprise." It was the yuki-onna. She had moved behind us as silently as ever. "And speaking of surprises, aren't you two a cute couple?"

"Fuck off, you frosty tart." Sig sounded bored but her heart was pumping fast. She's always more aggressive and impulsive when she's afraid, and the identity of the prisoner was eating at her like acid. What if it was Molly? Choo? Kevin? Even Sarah? And if it was just one of them...what had happened to the others? "This is a private conversation."

"I don't believe in those." The yuki-onna laughed, or at least, I don't know what else to call the sound she made.

"Do you believe in ass-kickings?" Sig wondered.

I was pretty sure that was a trick question. The yuki-onna must have thought so too, because she didn't answer it. The air turned warmer when she drifted away again.

Sig looked at me and I looked at her. What could we do? I could maybe pickpocket some creature's cell phone and walk outside the warded area until I got to a place where technology worked, maybe, and call the others. But the prisoner would be revealed by then, and it was entirely possible that the prisoner was a bluff...that Akihiko had just put some random person who pissed him off in chains and was keeping the identity a secret to mess with our heads. Maybe he wanted to see if we would try to contact someone. All of that passed between us wordlessly.

I can't remember what the kitsune yelled from the dry riverbed then. I was too fixated on the Jeep that pulled up dragging a heavy metal box shaped like a coffin behind it. Someone was pounding on the lid heavily. Sig gripped my arm so tightly that she cut off the circulation. I understood the impulse, but I gently disengaged. I wanted that arm.

The coffin was encased in chains, and the kitsune came up and began unlocking padlocks. That's when I found out what else had been taking up some of Akihiko's time and attention. A hand in a torn and smudged white Oxford collar shirt finally threw the lid open, and Ted Cahill climbed out.

∾48∾

DAMMMMMM!

Let's be clear here. I had no idea how Akihiko had tumbled on to Ted Cahill, and in that moment, I didn't care. Knowing what I know now, I suspect that Akihiko had connections in Interpol, and someone tipped him off that a sheriff from Tatum was red-flagging the fingerprints of one of Akihiko's men. But all that really mattered was that Cahill was the bait in a simple but elegant trap.

If Sig and I interceded, we would be violating Akihiko's hospitality and violating the truce that was the Crucible. The knights would have no grounds to avenge my death; in fact, doing so would harm their standing among the supernatural species who were witnessing the event, many of whom took contracts and rules deadly seriously.

Interceding would also connect us to Cahill, who Akihiko had obviously connected to Kevin Kichida. It would expose us once and for all and clarify the nature of whatever threat we represented.

And interceding would get us killed. All of the problems we

represented would be clarified, removed, and wrapped up with a neat little bow.

"Do you think he has a chance?" Sig whispered.

I didn't say anything.

"HERE WE HAVE…" the kitsune started, but Cahill wasn't playing by the rules.

Cahill screamed over the kitsune's spiel, I'M NOT MAX SELWYN! I'M NOT TELLING YOU PEOPLE SHIT!" Max Selwyn? The kid who had talked Kevin Kichida into donating sperm? What the hell did he have to do with anything? What was Cahill trying to tell us?

Then Cahill turned and took off toward the bridge at a run. Armor-piercing bullets blew large chunks out of the concrete around Cahill while the snipers on the bridge tried to adapt to his inhuman speed. I think Cahill just wanted to get under the bridge, where he could fight without the snipers being able to fire directly at him. I don't think he realized where the greatest danger was really coming from.

He found out. As fast as Cahill was moving toward the shadows cast between the bonfires and the bridge, "Jeanie" passed him in a blur and was waiting for him when he got there. He threw a running punch at her, actually hit her square on the jaw before shoulder-charging straight into her at a dead run. It was like watching someone run into a steel wall. Cahill slammed to a dead halt against her body and fell back with a crunch. He was still lying there on his back in front of her and trying to figure out what the hell had just happened when she pulled back her foot and kicked him. Cahill went skipping and tumbling over the surface of the concrete like a stone across water, if stones bled thick, dark blood and grunted painfully.

Something was wrong, though. Cahill's words indicated that Akihiko had been asking him about Kevin and that Cahill hadn't said anything. Akihiko wouldn't be asking questions if he'd already killed Kevin. But if Akihiko hadn't gotten his hands on Kevin yet...why would he be killing Cahill if he thought Cahill had answers? It didn't make any sense.

Maybe...dhampirs don't have much of a nervous system, and whatever else he was, Cahill was strong-willed. Maybe Akihiko had captured Cahill shortly before the Crucible and hadn't had time to both interrogate him properly *and* use him as a trap for Sig and me. If we didn't intercede, it would be easy for the jinn to beat Cahill into fragments and still not kill him. Was that...maybe...could this whole show be a bluff to draw Sig and me out?

I never got to pursue that line of thought.

As much baggage as I was carrying around, Sig had her own issues, and the most primal ones seemed to be wrapped around a complex swirl of obligation to authority figures that she didn't really love and feeling guilty for not loving them and desperately wanting to rebel against them and needing validation from them on some level at the same time. And she had introduced Cahill to the supernatural world. Sig had never stopped feeling responsible for that decision, and she was pigheaded, brave, and loyal to a fault.

And her father had been a cop.

Before I could stop her, Sig darted forward and grabbed a wooden torch holder out of the ground, shouldering the gashadokuro in front of us aside and running between several startled spectators, hurling the torch holder like a javelin toward the jinn. The missile wobbled and went completely off course as the torch dropped out of it, but that didn't matter. Sig had just declared war.

Fortunately, most of the crowd went quiet and still for a moment. I felt a light tremor in the concrete through the soles of my feet and heard the oni's club-like arm pushing air in front of it like a sharp breath. I even felt onrushing air on the back of my neck a fraction of a second before that massive fist would have broken it, but I don't think I would have been able to avoid the attack if I hadn't already been moving. As it was, I ducked the blow by throwing myself into a shoulder roll in front of it. The oni was moving a lot of weight and mass around, so it took a few seconds to regain its balance, and I came up behind the gashadokuro that Sig had shouldered aside.

The bone golem didn't weigh a whole hell of a lot and was just awkwardly regaining its own balance after some serious skip-stepping when I rose to my feet behind it. That skeletal fist began reaching over its shoulder for the hilt of its katana, but my hands got there first, and I removed the blade by stepping back and kicking the gashadokuro in the center of its spine. The skeleton went clattering and scraping over the concrete side of the riverbed.

No time, or at least none to spare. I darted left, not because I sensed an attack this time—the crowd around us was starting to make covering noise and vibrations as it parted—but because I knew an attack had to be coming. I was actually hip-checked into a spin as the oni rushed past me with an arm reached out in front of it. The ogre was invisible, but my infravision was beginning to kick in, and the oni looked like a large pink blur.

I went with the whirl, both hands on the sword's hilt now, one guiding, one powering. My feet weren't completely centered, but they were still directing my body and my hips were settling my weight when I slashed the side of the oni's throat. That stroke would have bisected a small tree, but not that Kevlar-skinned tree stump of iron muscle the oni called a neck. I did cut it, though. I don't know if I hit the carotid artery or not, but the oni's blood stopped being invisible when it flew from his throat.

The monster turned, and thank God it was so much taller than I was because I managed to duck under its backhand, and then I was inside the oni's reach and shoving the katana upward at an angle no sensei had ever taught me. All I had to orient on was the oni's misting breath, and the tip of the sword went through the roof of the ogre's open mouth and through its brain. The blade pierced the top of the oni's skull and got pinched and pulled out of my hands when the oni toppled backward, suddenly visible.

Still no time. A space had cleared around me, and a vampire was sighting on me with a sawed-off shotgun when a werewolf ten feet to his left fired a silenced Beretta into the side of the vampire's skull several times. I didn't pause to thank him but darted to scoop up the shotgun.

Akihiko wasn't the only one who had made preparations; I had a few more arrows in my own quiver, and I was looking around for Sig when surprise number one kicked in.

The sound of an alarm pierced the night, loud and deafening and disorienting. Most of the supernatural beings who had no direct stake in the proceedings had begun backing away to create their own personal space, but not all of them were running. Fangs and claws and mandibles and stingers were out, and a lot of the predators were considering joining the party. But the instinct to stay hidden and secret is primal among our kind, and the alarm tilted a balance. Even Akihiko's people were uncertain, pausing and looking for guidance among leaders they suddenly couldn't hear.

As it turned out, one of the members of Ben Lafontaine's local packs worked for the New York waterway system. An administrator, actually. High enough up the food chain to schedule a test of the alarm systems along the waterway. She was also connected enough to alert nearby police, firemen, news outlets, and emergency service personnel to ignore the sounds created. Choo had helped by installing two additional alarms in the woods about a half mile apart from each other, and they were actually keeping people away, not bringing them in, because they were loud enough to help cover distant screams and gunfire. But no one else knew that. All the monsters gathered there thought the noise was guaranteed to attract official human response in increasing numbers and authority, and the monsters scattered, providing both cover and confusion.

Surprise number two was just as dramatic: Beneath the bridge, a number of half-elves related or beholden to Holly Blake used the cover of that noise well. They were nestled among the trestles, coated in a layer of oil and grease and rust shavings that covered their scent and helped them blend in with the steel and concrete undermoorings of the bridge. Say whatever else you will about the Fae, they are masters of stealth and illusion. These half-elves had used their glamour-casting abilities to conceal themselves beneath the bridge earlier in the day, and their natural propensity for camouflage had helped them stay hidden during the night. Only the were-hyena guards might have sensed them moving in during the day, and they had said nothing. Now the half-elves crawled up from beneath the bottom and along the side of the bridge, coming up the side behind the human snipers who were all facing the Crucible.

The half-elves didn't have weapons because of Akihiko's ward, but the human servants facing the opposite direction had lots.

I won't count the were-hyenas as a surprise, because I doubt Akihiko ever relied on them completely—but the hyena pack didn't wait to see which way the tide was going, or consider their strategy carefully. They simply broke. Their nerves, their patience, their restraint, it all snapped. Half insane with fear and exhilaration, the were-hyenas *did* have weapons, and they mostly concentrated on Akihiko's human guards.

Some of the werewolves who were associated with the Round Table shifted to wolf form so that they could move among the rapidly scattering crowd low and unseen, and some used the firearms I had managed to plant inside the perimeter to good effect.

Still casting about for Sig, I caught a glimpse of the jinn down in the riverbed, cradling a flame the size and shape of a pineapple in her palm. She had apparently thought the gashadokuro I had sent rolling down the trench was a rude interruption, because the thing was a pile of smoldering bones, and Cahill was grabbing the short sword it had dropped.

I lost sight of them again as a gashadokuro charged me. I unloaded the shotgun into its exposed skull face and exploded its head into fragments. The skeleton staggered forward, at least momentarily disoriented, and I stepped inside the arc of its blade and reached into its hood. Stepping on the skeleton's foot, I ripped its spine out of the costume. The thing collapsed.

I barely got my hands on the sword when a great ball of fire came roaring in my direction. It wasn't anything like a Jerry Lee Lewis song; it was the bakechochin, Akihiko's personal fire spirit. He must have sent it out roaring like a sentient meteor to find me. There was only one way to escape that inferno, and I ran for the cold mist that had sprung up to my right, cutting the hand off the vampire who turned and tried to stick a gun in my face as I went. The ball of fire pursuing me consumed the vampire carelessly, and it must have turned him completely to ash because the screams didn't last more than a few seconds. Cold enveloped me and I disappeared into the thickening icy fog. The bakechochin lost me then, rising and looking for other prey when it came into contact with that supernatural cold.

But the yuki-onna? The snow woman found me.

I never smelled her, never heard her, never sensed her. I slipped on a patch of ice and a foot kicked the katana out of my hands while I was trying not to cut anything vital off of myself. My hand was numb and covered with frost. That fast. From that little contact.

I tried to move quickly and couldn't. My pants were sealed to the ground by dry ice. I desperately threw my torso backward, and it was a good thing I did. The pale hand that lashed out at me, over me, wasn't just clawed—it was so cold that my cheek got freezer burn just from being close to it. The ass of my pants came loose from the concrete with a tearing sound, and the legs of the fabric were stiff as I rolled to the side, barely escaping a kick. I tried to keep rolling, but it was awkward because ice was spreading on the ground beneath me faster than I could turn.

Then there was a small explosion, so loud that I could even hear it over the alarm, and the yuki-onna emerged from the dense mist screaming, burning, a staggering pyre, and then her head flew off her shoulders. Akihiko's other servant, the kitsune, appeared behind the snow woman, wielding the katana that had gone skimming across the concrete from my hand.

Surprise number three: The fox woman was free from Akihiko's control. Somewhere, at some point before or while all of this had been building up and going on, Kevin Kichida had opened his grandfather's safety deposit box.

I didn't have time to talk and couldn't have if I did have the time, not with the alarm still sounding. I tore my clothes free from the ground again and slid to my feet, half skating back out of the cold cloud that was already beginning to thin and disperse. A vampire was facing the opposite direction holding a TEC-9. A moment later she was facing me, but only because I'd broken her neck. I left her there, pausing just long enough to scoop up the firearm. The vampire wasn't destroyed, but she was out of the fight for a while, and I didn't have the half minute it would take to completely end that Kevlar-clad body.

Above me and to the left the great ball of fire was veering sharply away from something, and I headed in that direction. There was a good chance the bakechochin was veering away from Sig—she has a lot of tricks for dealing with ghosts, and even if it wasn't her, any place the fire spirit was scared of was a place worth checking out. I saw another vampire to my left, but as soon as I spotted him, his head exploded. The half-elves on the bridge were using their newly acquired sniper rifles to good effect on everything but the jinn. If any of them did fire on the jinn—and I sort of doubt it—the bullets didn't harm it.

Only one thing had any effect on the jinn, and that was surprise number four.

The administrator who worked for the waterway system—Ben's follower—had another bullet in her clip. The reason she could authorize a testing of the alarm systems was because she was also high-ranked enough or canny enough to schedule a dam release. Just to make sure all of the gate release mechanisms and hydro locks and spillways and other terms I didn't really understand were functioning.

Which is why a tidal wave came surging down the riverbed.

The jinn was single-minded. She had paused to see what was going on with the ruckus occurring above her, maybe even decided to do something about it in a moment, but she wasn't Akihiko's slave, and she wasn't worried. The jinn had started something that she was going to finish, and she intended to enjoy herself doing it.

Cahill's body was a smoking ruin. He lay there watching the jinn as she approached, taking her time, and he barely twitched. At least, not until she finally became aware of the approaching tsunami. The alarms had covered the sound of rushing water, but now the sheer volume of the oncoming flood shook the ground beneath the jinn's feet.

"Jeanie" turned then, turned and saw the solid column of water cascading down. She tried to run up the sloping side of the concrete trench, but Cahill's hand suddenly lashed out and grabbed her ankle while it was in midair. Incredibly powerful or not, that ankle had no leverage, nothing to push against, and the jinn fell sprawling to the ground while Cahill hung on like the doomed thing he was.

She kicked him loose, and the water washed them both away.

～49～

SURPRISE NUMBER FIVE

I didn't see Akihiko react to the chaos around him. He realized that some factors were in play that he had not anticipated and sent most of his emissaries out to either deal with those factors or cover his retreat or both. And then Akihiko made for the van he never strayed far away from while at the Crucible.

He probably believed that his forces would win, especially considering the presence of the jinn, but Akihiko was the most important thing in the universe—the next God, after all—and there was no point risking harm. And the van was the most important aspect of Akihiko's exit strategy. It all went exactly as planned. Akihiko slid the van door shut. He spoke a brief incantation. He slid the van door open so that he could step into his extradimensional escape route.

And a katana emerged from the van and pierced his heart. Akihiko's family's sword, as a matter-of-fact, held by a Kevin Kichida who looked exactly like Akihiko.

ᵔ50ᵔ

PAUSE, REWIND

I realize that this isn't how it was supposed to go. I was supposed to be the one to kill Akihiko. There was supposed to be a chase scene. Maybe some speeches. Sorry.

But not really, because Akihiko's death was the only thing that went exactly the way it was supposed to go. While Kevin was brazenly walking into Akihiko's bank and claiming his family sword, Sarah White was conjuring a mist and sending it through Akihiko's warehouse. It was a simple spell, so just to make it more interesting, Sarah had added some dye to her ritual preparations and made the fog green.

There were only two human guards on duty in the warehouse during the Crucible, and neither of them could call Akihiko with their cell phones while so much magic was in play around him. All they could do when a mysterious green cloud began filling the building was run outside, where Choo promptly shot them from a neighboring roof with his trank gun.

There were a few gashadokuro as well, but the skeleton guards stayed inside the warehouse, and when Kevin rejoined the others, Molly came with him. She went through the front door, and the bone golems charged...stopped...and recoiled, magnets propelled away from Molly by some reversed spiritual polarity.

Then Molly, Kevin, Sarah, and Choo went up to the paper doorway on the second floor. I don't know what Kevin's introduction to his family ghosts was like, but the sword in Kevin's hands really did channel the spirits of his ancestors. The same ancestors who had taught Akihiko, and those spirits really weren't happy with the onmyouji. The doorway opened into those endless paper hallways, and the sword led Kevin and Kevin led my team. They finally came to the doorway that was closest to Akihiko's location, the one that would open to the outside of Akihiko's van.

And there they waited. The sword didn't possess Kevin...it communicated with him, and he with it. Together, they waited for us to flush Akihiko out and drive him through the portal.

It's not very spiritually enlightened of me, but I like to imagine Akihiko's last conscious moments as he stared down the length of a bloody blade emerging from his chest, saw an exact duplicate of himself holding the hilt. I like to think that Akihiko didn't understand what was happening on any level as he swayed there in shock, struggling to focus. I imagine that for a brief moment, it seemed to Akihiko as if the universe had judged him—that his best self, his own soul, had finally rebelled and decided to take action against the obscenity he had become.

But I don't really know.

∽51∾

THE PLAN WITH THE VAN

As soon as Akihiko died, his human guards began to die with him. It was the bone golems.

When Akihiko shuffled off this mortal coil, his gashado-kuro did not instantly collapse. Instead, the spirits confined in those bone golems began lashing out blindly at everything in reaching distance, and that was mostly Akihiko's men. The flat terrain didn't offer much protection, and many of Akihiko's human guards had been using the bone golems as shields, standing close and firing around them from behind, relying on the skeletons' swinging blades to keep stronger, faster monsters away. Those same humans went down before they realized that their master was no longer controlling his creations.

Sarah, Choo, Molly, and Kevin took good advantage of the confusion. They had spent all day using Choo's van to practice emerging from a sliding door under battle conditions. And they hadn't practiced as if their lives depended on it, either... they had practiced *because* their lives depended on it. All four had a good working knowledge of what creatures were in Akihiko's retinue and what to expect from them, and each had worked out a strategy for covering the others without getting in the way. All of them except for Kevin were clad in Kevlar and riot helmets.

So when the ittan-momen—the rubbery creature pretending to be Akihiko's white coat—tried to flow up Kevin's blade, he was ready for it. Kevin used his higher elevation to kick Akihiko in the chest, propelling Akihiko's corpse off the sword so that the body carried the ittan-momen with it. This gave Kevin enough time to jump out of the van and to the left. If there were any henchmen or vampires sighting on that van, ready to fire, the sight of Akihiko standing over his own body confused them enough to buy Kevin some time.

Of course, the ittan-momen continued to ripple and surge over Akihiko's prone body, but Sarah White emerged from the van swinging a holly staff whose tip was burning like a torch. The flames trailing through the air behind that staff continued to arc forward, and the viscous flesh of the ittan-momen ignited. Maybe that shapeless monstrosity screamed, mouth or no mouth, but if it did, no one could hear it over the alarms. The ittan-momen recoiled away from Sarah and sent a last flaming tentacle lashing out at Kevin, but Kevin—or maybe a combat-savvy ancestor, if the family sword was guiding his movements—cut the pod off in midair. The pieces of the ittan-momen writhed on the ground like headless snakes, burning and blackening.

Sarah landed to the right side of the van, sending out licks of flame from her staff to keep back any creatures that might come running forward otherwise. A few enemies fired at her, but she was as prescient as Akihiko had been, and Sarah dodged incoming fire with minimal movements, using the flames from her staff to keep the dark thing hiding in Akihiko's shadow at bay, the otoroshi.

The otoroshi was moving by this time. Perhaps it had waited until the flames engulfing the ittan-momen were clear before it began to emerge, or perhaps it was not a highly intelligent being and events were proceeding too rapidly for it to process. In either case, it began to rise up from the ground, flowing over Akihiko's body before gathering mass, forming a dark tower of tusks and fists and teeth.

Choo shot it, center mass. He emerged from the van next, carrying an M2HB Browning machine gun whose belt feed was loaded with tracer bullets. Some of the hollow bases of the bullets were filled with phosphorous, some with magnesium, and Molly had carved crosses into the bullets' cases and blessed them. Something worked. Choo lit that creature up in every sense of the phrase. The otoroshi didn't die so much as dissipate.

Then Choo dropped the machine gun—the M2HB is heavy, and he couldn't use it for more than a few seconds—and pulled out a pump shotgun from a back sheath. He never got to use it. There were still vampires who were concentrating their fire on the van, and a bullet cracked Choo's helmet and slammed it against the side of his skull. Choo staggered and collapsed to his knees and elbows.

The vampires stopped shooting when Molly emerged. The undead couldn't even look at Molly, couldn't force their arms to point in her direction. Most of them struggled briefly and then began to retreat or, if insane with battle rage, looked for easier targets.

A number of bone golems began to converge on the van then, and they simply exploded. The skeletons came within thirty feet of Molly, paused, tilted their necks upward, and vomited bones through their hoods like obscene fountains. Other gashadokuro came streaming across the concrete to join them, and I don't know if Molly was somehow summoning the bone golems to their destruction or if they sensed that they had found a means to release themselves.

For a moment there was calm, and then the bakechochin came, a small comet hurtling through the air. Molly stepped forward to protect her friends. She pursed her cheeks as if to blow the fire spirit out like a candle, then paused, seeing or sensing something. Choo often joked about Molly's tendency to want to give ghosts a hug, but in this case, she physically opened her arms wide, inviting the spirit in rather than attempting to banish it.

And the bakechochin flew into Molly's arms, dwindling and shrinking as it did so. If her protective gear hadn't been fairly flame-retardant, Molly would have died instantly. As it was, her visor bubbled and browned while her Kevlar armor smoked and began to turn into burning goo. The bakechochin became a small flaming child in her arms, and then it became flame and simply disappeared.

Molly sank down onto her back screaming, her Kevlar armor burning her flesh through her clothes while Sarah frantically yanked it off.

They would have died then, but two strange things happened. The last remaining gashadokuro did not disintegrate. It stayed behind to help Kevin guard Molly and Sarah. The bone golem was joined by the kitsune, all four of the fox woman's tails waving behind her while she breathed fire and brandished the katana she had taken from me. The two beings brought my friends time to drag their wounded back into the van and close the door behind them.

~52~

LOOK, I DON'T CARE
HOW HOT YOU ARE…

The reason I didn't see Akihiko's demise was that I was next to the corpse of Akihiko's primary bodyguard. The long-haired harionago was lying on the ground with large chunks of her scalp missing. Her neck was broken. Someone very strong had ripped the harionago's expanding hair out by the roots. Somebody who smelled like Sig.

By that point, it was obvious that we would win the battle so long as the jinn didn't get involved, and I didn't like where that logic was going any more than I liked the direction Sig's scent trail was traveling. I liked it even less when I followed Sig's smell all the way to the edge of the no-longer-dry riverbed.

She had dived into the water after Cahill and the jinn.

I went running down the side of the riverbed as fast as I could, following the course of the water. The romantic thing to do would have been to jump in the newly formed river after Sig, but to hell with that. Sig can withstand low temperatures better than I can, and I wouldn't be much use to anyone if I washed up near any action half drowned and shut down by hypothermia.

I wasn't sure I would be of any use anyhow.

Ben's contact in the waterway system hadn't left the dam open. She'd scheduled a gate release just to make sure that the mechanisms were functioning, but the water gradually died out as the gates were closed again. The tidal wave went around two bends that broke its momentum, veering left and right up the concrete inclines and losing speed and mass. When the surge of released water finally petered out, there was about two and a half feet of standing water filling the bottom of the concrete trench for hundreds of yards.

The alarm had stopped ringing when the drill was over, and my hearing had healed enough that I heard Sig in the dark. Her teeth were chattering, but she was still managing to say, "Please! This is pointless! The Crucible is finished."

The voice that answered her was shockingly normal, or at least the pitch and tone and register of it were human. The cruelty and utter confidence of it were not. "Begging is good. Dying is even better."

I came flying around the last bend and saw the jinn with her back turned to me, one hand held up and burning brightly like a torch in that darkness. She had one foot on what I assumed was Ted Cahill's back, keeping him trapped against the bottom of the riverbed like a butterfly pinned against a poster board. His body was completely submerged, not moving. Sig was approaching the jinn slightly crouched, her fists held out before her in a boxing stance, though she wasn't able to do much footwork in water that came above her knees.

"Take your foot off that man and we'll talk." Sig's voice was low and urgent. A dhampir may be able to go a long time without breathing, but not forever, and Cahill had already been through a lot. "Tell me what you want!"

"Blood," the jinn said. "Fire. Screams."

I think the jinn was full of shit. I think she'd made some bargain with Akihiko, and she had no reason to betray the terms of that contract. I think it was a lot more fun for her to go off on a power trip than to reveal that a human had any kind of leverage over her, but I don't really know. The jinn had no reason to reveal her innermost motivations and weaknesses and complexities to an enemy, and she didn't.

I went splashing into the water some forty feet behind them, and the jinn briefly turned and flicked a flat palm at me. A column of fire ignited through the air with a sound like a sharp breath through a microphone, and I dived into the water beneath those flames, skimming over the bottom of the riverbed while light flared over me.

At least the water wasn't freezing anymore.

When I came up again, Sig had taken advantage of the jinn's momentary distraction and was hammering punches into the jinn's face. The jinn wasn't a trained fighter—whatever her life story was, she had probably never needed to work hard at anything, at least not physically—and Sig was playing it smart, using the jinn's unwillingness to move the foot pinning Cahill. Sig landed a solid punch, then moved back, just out of reach, tauntingly.

For her part, the jinn reacted like an adult being slapped by a two-year-old, annoyed but not really hurt. An adult with fire crawling over her shoulders. The jinn pushed both of her palms outward, but Sig stepped past the jinn's wrists and drove her knuckles into the side of the jinn's temple while flames rushed past. That did the trick. The jinn stepped off of Cahill and hit Sig with a backhand slap; Sig blocked that casual blow, most of it forearm and wrist, and it still sent her eight feet into the air. Sig back-flopped into the water with a huge splash, and that was good because the jinn sent another burst of flame after her. Sig managed to thrash sideways down into the water as the air around her ignited.

There was a lot of driftwood around us from the fire, and I picked up a six-foot log that was about half the thickness of a telephone pole. I never got to use it. The jinn turned around and kicked the bottom of the riverbed as if she was scuffing her foot. Several chunks of concrete shot out of the water, and one the size of a grapefruit hit me in the stomach. It wasn't going very fast—the water and the awkward angle of the kick and the limited motion and all that—but it still bent me over. The next thing I knew, the jinn was smacking the log out of my hands so hard that my body was yanked down into the water and splinters drove into the side of my face where the wood exploded. My hands were numb.

The jinn stepped on to my leg to keep me from going anywhere, and it was as if my foot was caught beneath a fallen tree.

Sig came running at her then, yelling, and the jinn almost casually turned and put a hand out to stop her. Sig blocked the hand at the wrist, and again it didn't matter. The jinn's hand just kept going, bending Sig's arm back as if it were boneless, and those inhumanly powerful fingers fastened on Sig's shoulder. The jinn forced Sig to her knees with one downward push and drew a fist back while Sig tried to tear her body free from those pincer-like fingers, her upper torso jerking and twitching. I was struggling just to get enough leverage to break my knee so that my hands could reach something useful.

That's when Cahill came up out of the water behind the jinn. The jinn's flesh was tough, but vampiric jaws are freakishly strong, even out of proportion to the rest of their bodies. Those fangs were sharp too, and bloodsuckers have an instinct for finding the softest places in the throat where skin doesn't cover muscle. Cahill sank his teeth into the jinn's neck. The jinn screamed and stiffened, releasing Sig and stepping off my leg, and something more than blood coursed through Cahill's body. One moment, he was just a shadow, his body heat almost nonexistent, the next he was lit up like a Christmas tree. He began to glow, and not just to my infrared-sensitive eyes; he actually glowed as orange and yellow hotspots began to appear under his skin.

"TED, STOP!" Sig screamed, but he didn't. Or couldn't.

The jinn didn't move, maybe from shock as much as the wound. Maybe it was the first time in her existence that she'd ever really felt pain. She stayed frozen, mesmerized by whatever sensations were coursing through her while Cahill's body continued to heat up. The jinn didn't move until Cahill was incinerated. He burst into heated fragments that floated there on the air with a lingering smell of roasted flesh.

Sig screamed and rose up, driving her fist into the jinn's diaphragm with all of her body weight and not-inconsiderable strength behind it. All of the jinn's power was irrelevant because her stomach muscles weren't tensed, and Sig's punch compressed the jinn's diaphragm and forced the air out of her in one explosive breath.

It wasn't weakness that doubled the jinn over. It was her half-human reflexes.

The jinn spun on Sig then, and I jumped on her back as if leaping onto a saddle. My weight tipped what was left of her balance—again, just physics—and the jinn went facedown into the water. She was still choking for air and inhaled water immediately, then instinctively spread her arms out and lifted them backward even while she was convulsing, trying to pluck my weight off. I managed to push my thighs under her arms in that sweet spot between the shoulders and bicep, caught her arms at an awkward angle, and kept them there while I brought my calves up so that they were behind the back of the jinn's head in a kind of inverted triangle choke. There was no plan, no finesse, I just rode her shoulders like she was a pony and locked my feet one over the other beneath her arms, over her neck, grabbing my ankles with my hands so that I could keep my head above water as the jinn stayed facedown in the riverbed.

I wouldn't have made it alone. The jinn's arms were beginning to slip loose and the muscles in my legs were literally starting to tear apart when Sig stepped on the back of the jinn's head and grabbed her wrists while those arms were hyper-flexed in the air behind the jinn's back. Sig pulled against those wrists with all of her might, all of her body weight, and even combined with my leg muscles and the jinn's lack of leverage, it was barely enough.

There was no way for the jinn's knees to get purchase lying flat on her belly. There was also no breath for the jinn to hold. A human would have already been dead, but she was only half human and thrashed while she choked. No rational thought, no strategy, just reflex and panic.

We lurched back and forth as the jinn flopped her body left and right. The water around us was suddenly warm. Sig screamed as her hands began to blister, but she still held on to the jinn's burning wrists until her fingers were too weak. The jinn managed to bend her elbows at an awkward angle then, hooked her arms and dug her fingers into my ribs. Those steely hands pierced my flesh as if she were poking them through cheese, and they were burning, just a half inch above the water, but it might as well have been half a mile. I could smell my own flesh cooking in my nostrils, but I still held on to my ankles and prayed. To God, to Allah, to whatever universal law the jinn had violated just by existing here.

Then, suddenly, the jinn's hands went still. Sig hooked her own useless hands inside the jinn's wrists and pulled the jinn's fingers out of me, then pushed the jinn's arms away.

As much pain as I was in, I stayed in the exact position I was in for a long time after that.

∽53∾

THE OFFICIAL STORY

Here's the official timeline of events:

Akihiko Watanabe had connections to the yakuza. His daughter ran away from home and married a serviceman and sniper, Jerry Kichida. She presumably told Jerry all kinds of stories about her father's abuse. Years after his wife was dead, Jerry Kichida told his son Kevin to make himself scarce for a while and got an old friend in Military Intelligence to investigate Akihiko Watanabe.

The friend from Military Intelligence was promptly killed.

Kevin went into hiding, but his best friend, Max Selwyn, disappeared shortly afterward.

Several Asian men wound up dead, shot by a sniper near the warehouse of an Asian importer whose identity turned out to be a complete fabrication.

Tatum's sheriff, Ted Cahill, turned in a fingerprint while investigating Max Selwyn's disappearance. The fingerprint was red-flagged by Interpol as belonging to an ex-yakuza member. Ted Cahill too disappeared shortly after this time.

The Asian importer who didn't really exist abandoned the warehouse and closed down his bank accounts.

Max Selwyn was found wandering aimlessly on the interstate. He had obviously been drugged, was dehydrated and disoriented, and didn't remember anything except for a vague impression of frightening Asian men.

Kevin Kichida reported that he hadn't heard from his father and was worried about him around the same time.

The official conclusion from all of these events seems to be that Ted Cahill and Max Selwyn were unfortunate casualties in a feud that erupted between Jerry Kichida and his father-in-law. Jerry burned Akihiko's cover and probably died in the process. Akihiko fled to start over again somewhere new.

Interpol is still looking for both or either of them.

∽54∽

ONE WELL OF AN ENDING

Choo drove the van back to Virginia even though he had a mild concussion. He's stubborn that way, and he was in a hurry to have an official doctor examine the right ear he can't hear out of anymore. Choo was also eager to salvage both his pest control business and the reconciliation with the ex-wife I still haven't met. He had gotten ninety thousand dollars as his share of Sig's and my combined winnings at the Crucible, but his business wasn't just a business to him. It was independence, and that independence was more important to him than ever. It wasn't entirely clear if he was leaving us or not.

Kevin was back in school, trying to scrape enough grades together to pass for the semester in case he decided that school was still something he wanted to do. He still had his family sword, but it wasn't as if he had to take the blade for walks or complete quests for it or anything. From what I understand, the sword was more like a CB radio to the other side. Most of the time, it was just a normal blade. Kevin was both relieved and felt like he had lost yet another part of his family.

Kevin has also gained a new family member. We found a

pregnant woman from Tatum in one of the rooms in Akihiko's paper corridors, being tended by faceless ghosts that
Sig promptly exorcised. It seems reasonable to assume that the
growing child is the pregnancy that resulted from one of Kevin's sperm donations. The woman, Leanne Collins, has been
traumatized by her experience, but she seems to be handling it
remarkably well. Or maybe she's still in shock. I'm not clear if
Leanne is going to assume a new identity rather than emerge
into a media shitstorm, or if she's going to claim some connection to Jerry Kichida and say she was abducted by Akihiko as
leverage, or just go back to her normal life and say that she took
a vacation because she was being stalked by an ex-boyfriend or
something. Sarah is insisting on handling Leanne, and I trust
her to do so. I do know that Leanne wants to keep the baby,
and Kevin is determined to maintain some contact with the
child after it's been born. I feel a little guilty for bringing so
many new responsibilities and complications into Sarah's life,
but I have to say, they seem like a good fit.

Kevin is coming to visit Sarah on weekends, and Sig and
I are still helping them continue to explore and clean out
those dimensional corridors. It was how we also found Aubrey
and Max Selwyn and a few other supernatural prisoners
who were dehydrated and abused and terrified but whole.
There are fortunes and secrets behind the sliding doors in that
dimensional labyrinth, but Sig and I have agreed without even
having to discuss it that anything there belongs to Kevin and
his kid. I'm not sure how he's ever going to explain his new
fortune if he ever decides to start spending it, but that's not
my problem.

Parth claimed that giant, possibly divine vision-granting clam
thing as his own reward for services rendered, and I didn't argue,
though the logistics involved in locating and transporting a chen

are a bitch. Don't get me wrong. Parth is extremely useful. He seems to honor contracts and has done more good than ill by me in our acquaintance. And I still have a hard time trusting him, but that may be because of my own issues.

Brother Takeshi is gone. It turns out that the gashadokuro who helped Kevin and Sarah defend the others wasn't an undead being at all. It was actually Brother Takeshi who had disguised himself and infiltrated the Crucible as a bone golem, hiding behind a ninja suit and a skull mask. God knows how many of Akihiko's servants had lost heads to Takeshi's swords without ever realizing that the gashadokuro who killed them was something else entirely.

I still don't know how many of the rumors about yamabushi and their near-mystical abilities are true, but I can now safely say this: Some of them really can lower their heartbeat and stay motionless for hours at a time.

I only had one conversation with Brother Takeshi after that last night in the Crucible.

"Why did you help us?" I asked. "Akihiko never did violate the Pax as far as I can tell. Not directly."

"I went there to observe," he replied. "But when those alarms began going off, I had to help end the confrontation as quickly as possible to maintain the Pakkusu."

"The police and emergency services had been told to disregard the alarms," I responded.

He digested this information with surprising equanimity. "An honest mistake." He didn't smile when he said that, but I'm pretty sure that's only because of his iron self-control.

The kitsune is also gone, though no one actually saw her leave. One moment, she was in the hallway of that paper labyrinth, showing Kevin where his friend Max was being held. The next, the kitsune had disappeared. When Kevin checked the pocket where he had been carrying the kitsune's hoshi no tama, the pocket was empty.

Chikako is a fox, after all.

Neither the knights nor the Round Table's standing in the supernatural community seems to be any worse than before. Rumors of a werewolf-and-knight pact are continuing to ripple outward at an increased rate, but according to Ben, the story is actually encouraging some of the more organized and altruistic werewolf packs to join his alliance. The general take on events is not that a bunch of lycanthropes went insane and attacked a mass gathering unprovoked. The consensus—to the extent that there is one—seems to be that some Japanese cunning man was insane enough to summon a jinn, and the knights sent their new werewolf agents in to shut down the situation. I wasn't at all sure that Akihiko had summoned the jinn, but rumor and logic and fact rarely go hand in hand. A lot of beings were still hostile, resentful, and paranoid at the idea of a werewolf/knight alliance, but the fact that this alliance had taken out a Japanese cunning man and a vampire gang *and* a jinn was at least encouraging predators to be hostile cautiously. The supernatural world respects competence.

The other factor causing some werewolf packs to think about joining Ben's Round Table was me. Werewolves are some of the weakest supernatural creatures individually, and I had done respectably well in the Crucible. A lot of werewolves are now under the impression that the Round Table will train them to fight as well as any knight, and maybe that will even become true over time. Sometimes ideas take on momentum and form their own reality.

What I find more worrisome is the fact that knowledge that a Charming is still alive has gotten out into the supernatural community at large. For five decades I managed to mostly stay off of everyone's radar, but now, when beings talk about a were-wolf and knight alliance, the name John Charming is starting to crop up. I'm not sure if I should huddle up in a fetal position and hide somewhere or have a tee shirt with a Knight's Templar logo on it made.

Molly is taking her time healing, even with the extra mojo that Sarah White has brought to the table. Or more accurately, brought to her guest bed. But at least, Molly isn't in too much pain. Molly is also another reason that Sig and I are hanging around New York for a time, and we were there above Sarah's bakery when Molly was coherent enough to talk.

"You're a fucking dumb-ass," I comforted her. I didn't care if I get struck down by lightning or something for saying it, either.

"It was just a child," Molly croaked, and Sig moved a glass of juice with a bendy straw closer to her lips.

"So are you sometimes." My voice was a little clogged. "You selfish, brainless..."

"Aw whassa mattuh?" Molly chided weakly. "Is the big bad woofums gonna cwy?"

Sig, who actually was crying a little, punched me in the shoulder. "You scared us. Ted is dead, Molly."

"That's too bad," Molly said. It was one of the things I loved about her. Molly never acted like she cared more than she did, and she never acted like she didn't care at all. "He still had a lot of stuff to work on."

"I think he figured some of it out," Sig said. "He saved our lives."

I remained silent. The revelation that Cahill had kept the abduction of Kevin's best friend a secret from us was still tossing and turning around restlessly in my cranium. I had sort of hated Ted Cahill despite my best efforts, and sort of liked him in spite of my worst efforts, and the fact that he had died before I sorted that out seemed a little unfair.

"We don't know who to leave Ted's share of the prize money to," Sig fretted. She had been obsessing about this a little. It was one of the things I was learning about her. Sig is an externalizer. She doesn't like yoga, she likes Zumba. When she's upset, she likes to hit things, and when she's tense, she likes to deal with abstract anxieties by hanging them on tangible deeds, even little ones. Honoring Cahill's legacy was proving a little difficult though. Cahill hadn't particularly liked his ex-wife by the time their marriage dissolved, and they'd never had any children. His parents were both dead. There was a sister somewhere in California, but they apparently hadn't been close.

"Maybe we can make a scholarship in his name," Molly suggested drowsily. "Give the interest off the capital to people who want to major in law enforcement. It ought to at least be enough for books and things, and we can add to it. I'll throw some of my money into the pot."

"I will too." Sig made a move like she wanted to squeeze Molly's hands than checked it. Sig's own hands were still burned, though her skin is tougher than normal skin. Sig's nose was broken too, but taping and setting broken noses is one area where I don't need any help from Sarah.

"I'll put some money toward that too." Sarah came into the room with some lentil soup and a salve that was a lot more effective than aloe. "I didn't know the man, but I could tell that he was in a lot of pain and trying his best not to be a bad thing in the world. He reminded me of someone else I met once."

She definitely didn't look at me while she set her tray down on the dresser. I just want to make that clear. I haven't had any more dreams that seemed to be more than just dreams either, or if I have, I don't remember them. If there's a part of me that's disappointed, I'm doing a pretty good job of hiding it from myself.

"That's three of us." Sig was looking at me pointedly.

I just looked back. "You know I'm going to do it. Let me grumble about it to myself for a while first."

She smiled.

Later, Sig and I were walking down one of Bonaparte's side streets. It was cold, but I was wearing the jacket she had gotten me for Christmas again. Against all odds, I had managed to keep it intact. We were almost at the top of a hill and the setting sun was shining right between the row of buildings ahead of us, just visible over the cresting pavement and glinting off surrounding store windows. I have survived a lot of things that should have killed me, but today, I wasn't traumatized or painfully shuffling through necessary tasks until I could find some hole to crawl into and heal. I was just glad to be alive. If being with people I cared about made me feel more vulnerable, it also made surviving more worthwhile.

Life is a series of trade-offs and contradictions. But it is life.

Sig was thinking about life too.

"You know, sometimes it feels like you're my soul mate, and sometimes it feels like I don't know you at all," she said. "I still have these moments where it feels like I'm waking up and I'm like *Akkh! Who's this stranger who's becoming such an important part of my life?!?!*"

"I know what you mean," I admitted. "Two years ago, I wouldn't have dreamed of being here with you. It still seems unreal sometimes."

She started laughing. It started out small and then it kept going, almost turning into something hysterical. I wasn't sure if I should join in or be concerned. "What?"

"We just got in a fight with a jinn," she gasped, leaning against a brick storefront. "And we're talking about what feels unreal."

Tension releases in odd ways, and it takes its own time doing it. I smiled and said, "It's all relative," and when she recovered, we walked a little more.

"Things are changing," she said.

Yeah, well, that's what things do. I stopped and pulled Sig to me and kissed her. She had to tilt her face a little awkwardly because of the broken nose, and our lips were cold, and she couldn't really hug me because of her hands, but we were both stubborn people. We stayed at it until our lips warmed up.

Some angry white male specimen drove past us in a red pickup truck, his window down in spite of the cold air. When he yelled at us, his voice was full of anger and derision and loneliness. "GET A ROOM!"

"GET AN INFLATABLE DOLL!" Sig called over my shoulder, and a few teenagers who were loitering nearby laughed. Sig smiled ruefully when we heard the truck's brakes squeal to a stop, but after the driver took a few moments to consider his options and their possible consequences, he hurled a few obscenities out the window and started the truck moving again. "You know, that's not bad advice," she murmured.

"Getting an inflatable doll?" I pulled her closer for body heat and kissed her below her left ear.

"Getting a room," she said. "The Waldorf Astoria seemed nice."

"Have I ever told you about me and New York City?" I asked.

I was with the wrong woman if I expected her to give up that easily. "I thought you Charmings were all about breaking curses."

I thought about that. "But the Waldorf? I'm more of a bed-and-breakfast type myself."

Sig made a raspberry sound against my neck. "You're more of a tent type. The Waldorf might be good for a special occa. on."

My blood started pounding faster. "Special occasion?"

She nodded solemnly, looking at me with eyes that were a little scared and happy and full of mischief and possibility. "Very special."

"Yes," I said simply.

What the hell. Maybe that place really does have magic sandwiches.

The story continues in...

Book 4 of the Pax Arcana

Keep reading for a sneak peek!

extras

orbit

meet the author

An army brat and gypsy scholar, ELLIOTT JAMES is currently living in the Blue Ridge mountains of southwest Virginia. An avid reader since the age of three (or that's what his family swears anyhow), he has an abiding interest in mythology, martial arts, live music, hiking, and used bookstores. Irrationally convinced that cell phone technology was inserted into human culture by aliens who want to turn us into easily tracked herd beasts, Elliott has one anyhow but keeps it in a locked tinfoil-covered box, which he will sometimes sit and stare at mistrustfully for hours. Okay, that was a lie. Elliott lies a lot; in fact, he decided to become a writer so that he could get paid for it.

Book 4 of the Pax Arcana

CHAPTER ONE

OOOH BABY

Once Upon a Time, I was too happy. I know that's not rational, but there's still a part of me that blames everything that happened afterward on that one simple fact. Something bad *had* to happen. I allowed myself to be too happy.

It had snowed while Sig Norresdotter and I were winter camping in the Cascades, and there's something about getting naked and keeping warm in an insulated tent while the world around you is frozen that adds a layer of intensity to the experience. Sig had kept up a running joke about how the weekend wasn't exactly the kind of date with Prince Charming that most women pictured—she would make proclamations about needing the Royal Roll of Toilet Paper before going off into the woods, or start yelling for footmen to come make us s'mores while we were entangled in our sleeping bag—but she was making cracks because she was in a good mood, not being passive aggressive.

I suppose I could have found the Prince Charming references a little annoying—my name may be John Charming, but I'm not royalty, and nobody in my family ever was—but Sig and I were in that physical intoxication phase of a new relationship where every word, gesture, and glance is saturated in a hormonal nimbus. She could have belched loudly and called my mother a whore, and I would have had to struggle not to view it as some kind of delightful postmodern irony. The truth was, I couldn't get enough of her smell or the way her skin felt against mine. I wanted to fill my hands and eyes and mouth and heart with her.

The hike back down the mountains had been like traveling through a series of paintings. The Freezing-Your-Ass-Off collection, maybe, but still beautiful. Then we'd decided to bypass the interstate and wound up getting lost in a little nowhere Appalachian town called Eccleston about twenty minutes outside Blacksburg, Virginia. We stopped at this brick building that looked like an old-fashioned general store and discovered that it was a restaurant called the Palisades. It was like finding a diamond in a plug of tobacco.

Warm air gusted through old-fashioned grates in the wooden floor while we drank hot cider and thawed out. I was trying not to release obscene-sounding sighs too loudly when the waitress brought out some of the best focaccia I'd ever had in my life. The outer crust of the bread was lightly dusted with spices, and when my teeth broke through that crispy surface, they sank into soft warmth lightly infused with cheese.

"Sweet mother of all that's good and crunchy," I said reverently. "Forget the pizza. I just want six more of these appetizers."

"I can't believe you ordered pizza anyway." Sig had refused to give up the menu even after she ordered, and she was still studying it intently as if trying to make sure that it wasn't some kind of trick. "You can get a pizza anywhere. How many places around here have food like this?"

Sig had ordered quail that was stuffed with chestnuts and Italian sausage and then covered with some kind of cranberry glaze, and I could see her point. "I ordered before I tasted this appetizer," I said. "This place doesn't look all that swanky, and it's hard for anybody to screw up a pizza so badly that I can't get behind it."

"It's not like we look all that fancy ourselves," Sig observed. "I haven't showered in two days."

"Don't worry." I reached over and got her to put her menu down by taking her hand and planting a lingering kiss on the back of her wrist. Then I made eye contact with her and promised: "I'm going to get you in a shower. And when I do, I'm going to clean you thoroughly."

Sig cleared her throat. Her voice was a little huskier than usual. "You do realize that *thoroughly* means focusing on more than two places, right?"

"Those areas behind the elbows and knees are very important," I said virtuously.

Sig laughed and released my hand. "Oh please. Whoever said *cleanliness is next to godliness* never showered with you."

That made me smile. "You know, you're joking around a lot more these days."

"I'm happier than I've been in a long time." She confessed this as if it were a character flaw. After a moment's reflection, she added: "You're joking around less. Or at least not in the same way."

"I'm happier than I've been in a long time too," I told her, meaning it.

That's when her cell phone rang.

We both froze. We'd had a no-cell-phone agreement for the weekend.

"Shit," Sig swore as the phone rang a second time, then confessed. "I checked my messages while you were in the restroom. I turned it off, but I forgot to power it off."

425

I nodded. "You'd better answer it." It might not be logical, but if some tragedy occurred while Sig and I had our cell phones turned off for the weekend, that's just the way it was. But if we ignored an active cell phone ringing and later found out that something bad had happened...

Sig answered the cell phone. My hearing is sharper than a normal human's, so I didn't have to wonder why her face went blank. The voice on the other end was Ben Lafontaine, and he sounded urgent and grim. "Hey Sig, this is Ben. Is John with you?"

Ben Lafontaine is technically my pack leader, a fact that we both skirt around because of my authority issues and the fact that neither of us is sure who would win in a fight. I'm pretty sure he would gladly let me lead the pack if I wanted the job and wouldn't be a complete disaster at it. In practice, Ben is somewhere between a mentor and a qualified ally and a friend, and I would pretty much do anything he asked me to do anyhow as long as he was asking. I owe Ben a lot. Sig handed the phone over to me wordlessly.

I didn't waste any time. "What is it?"

"It's Constance," he said. "Our goddaughter has been kidnapped."

CHAPTER TWO

THE TRUTH, THE HOLE IN THE TRUTH, AND NOTHING LIKE THE TRUTH

Sig and I got off the commuter plane and met Ben and an impossibly handsome blond man. The private airstrip was disguised as a straight patch of road between two vast stretches

426

of cornfields in the middle of nowhere, Michigan. It was dark and bitterly cold, but I already said it was Michigan, so at least one of those three facts is probably redundant. "This is Simon Travers," Ben said without preamble. "He's your Grandmaster's fixer."

The way Ben said *your* Grandmaster implied that he wasn't happy with the Knights Templar or me at the moment. Ben smelled bad too, and I don't mean he stank in any conventional sense. Ben was dumping rage pheromones into the air like a cheap perfume. Constance wasn't even a year old, and I don't think Ben had spent much more face-to-face time with her than I had, but our goddaughter's abduction was still hitting him on some primal level. Ben had lost a child at some point way back in his long life, maybe a century ago, maybe more, and that's all I knew about it. Maybe that's all I'll ever know about it, but I occasionally catch glimpses of how that loss has defined him.

"I won't say it's a pleasure, Mr. Charming, but I've heard a lot about you." The blond man offered me a brief handshake and a tight smile. He was so good looking that he was almost pretty, but if he was Emil Lamplighter's number one fixer, this Simon was a dangerous man. He turned his attention to Sig and his smile became less perfunctory. He took her hand and held it rather than shook it. "And I've heard about you as well, Miss Norresdotter. I've never met a valkyrie before."

This Simon was a charming fuck, dressed in some vaguely European-looking black outdoor jacket that was thin but well insulated in a series of ring-like layers that had been sewn together. His teeth were white and straight, but not too perfect. His eyes were green and bright and clever and cold. The four weapons that I could spot barely made bulges.

"Let go of my hand," Sig said pleasantly.

"Oh, right." Simon smiled a smile that somehow managed to be both sheepish and dazzling and released her hand as if suddenly realizing that he had become entranced. Which was bullshit. This guy didn't do anything by accident. "I'm sorry."

"That's not what your mom says," Sig said.

He looked at her puzzled. "Is that some kind of *yo mama* joke? I'm afraid I don't understand it."

"It's not a joke. Valkyrie talk to the dead," Sig reminded him. "Your mother says you're not sorry. In fact, she says you're a complete shit toward women. I don't think her spirit is going to find peace until you grow up, marry, and have children."

Simon paled. He somehow managed to physically recoil from Sig without taking a step backward.

"Let's fucking get on with this." Ben rarely cussed, and I checked off a mental box that said *uh oh.*

"Right, I'll get the car." Simon hightailed it for a nearby barn before we could offer to walk with him.

"Did you really see his mother's ghost?" I asked Sig conversationally.

"No." Her tone was matter-of-fact. "But I can tell that he doesn't have any living family. Some people carry that around with them. And men like him always have mommy issues."

Ben didn't give a shit. "The knights think Constance's abduction is an inside job, John. They think there's a werewolf traitor."

I doubled down on that *uh oh.*

introducing

If you enjoyed
FEARLESS
look out for

JINN AND JUICE

by Nicole Peeler

*Cursed to be a jinni for a thousand years, Lyla nears the end
of her servitude—only to be Bound once again against
her will. Will she risk all to be human?*

*Born in ancient Persia, Lyla turned to her house jinni, Kouros,
for help escaping an arranged marriage. Kouros did make
it impossible for her to marry—by cursing Lyla to live a
thousand years as a jinni herself.*

If she can remain unBound, Lyla's curse will soon be over.

*Unfortunately, becoming Bound may risk more than just her
chance to be human once more—it could risk her very soul . . .*

*Jinn and Juice is the first in a new series by fantasy writer
Nicole Peeler set in a world of immortal curses,
vengeful jinni, and belly dancing.*

The air whispered cool over my arms as I stood on stage, ready to be announced. The room was dark, the wisp-lights glowing on our small café tables the room's only illumination.

Suddenly Charlie's smoky voice oozed over the audience like KY at a porn shoot, getting all up in the audience's aural cavities.

"Ladies and gentlemen, I know you've been waiting for this. Straight from the sultan's bedchamber, a woman of fire too hot for the harem—put your hands together for our very own... Lyla La More!"

Applause, wolf whistles, and a few ululations echoed from the crowd, but the lights stayed off and I remained still. The crowd quieted, growing totally silent as it heard the first low strike of the bass drum. A deep, dark sound, it echoed through my bones as it thumped again, and again, speeding up by infinitesimal degrees. Stock-still, I moved only when the low sweet strain of a cello cut across the drum, and my left hip lifted and dropped. The cello sounded again as my right hip lifted and dropped. And then my hips erupted in a chaos of shimmies with the entrance of more drums and a violin. Beats Antique rocketed out of the speakers, taking the audience out of its seats and my limbs into hyperdrive.

The dance was a serpentine one, my costume signaling the theme with tight, sheer green fabric sheathing my legs from where it hung off the heavy, crazily Bedazzled belt slung low on my hips. The smooth, soft skin of my belly was bare, of course, and above my ribs metallic serpents cupped my breasts, holding more green fabric to protect my modesty.

It was the headdress that stole the show: a great papier-mâché serpent reared above me, its fangs glittering with rubies and its eyes with emeralds. Or the craft store versions of precious gems. It was heavy and awkward, but it looked marvelous in the low light, winking malevolently at the crowd as I danced for their entertainment.

My hips slowed as my chest took up the dance, lifting and shifting, my spine arching as I raised my hands in snake arms. I did a slow circle, alternating movements between hips and chest. As the music swelled into a crescendo I faced the audience again, letting my hands fall to frame my hips. My belly bowed and swooped, muscles pulling in and then relaxing. The beat increasing, I moved as much as my tight costume would allow, darting my hands at the audience like another pair of striking snakes doing the bidding of the great snake that loomed above. The audience went wild, thumping the tables and calling for more. But the music slowed, and I let my shifting carry me downward, my hands above my head. I knelt before them, my snake's head weaving and my arms undulating as the violin cut out, then the cello, leaving only that slow thrum of the bass drum once again. The lights lowered, and for a split second I could hear only the thudding of my heart and the rough pant of my breath through my toothy smile, until the first clap sounded in the room, sending everyone into another round of applause. The lights went up again and I stood, Charlie coming to take my hand.

Charlie was wearing all of his clothes, since it was relatively early in the evening. Soon enough he'd be stripped of his red velvet ringmaster's coat, underneath which he wore only lovely white skin and black suspenders holding up tight black jodhpurs. His mustache was twirled into two rakish whiskers flaring over thin lips, black guyliner smudged around his eerily colorless eyes.

He gave me his sexy ringmaster's leer as he approached, those pale eyes sweeping over my body. His interest was all part of the show, though—Charlie was both gay and taken.

The clapping slowed as Charlie grabbed my arm, jerking me around and toward him. For a split second we were nose-to-nose, me on my tiptoes and him bending over me. Then his arm wrapped around my waist, pulling my hips against his and arching my back. I melted against him, my hands slipping inside the lapels of his coat to lie against his chilly skin. We stayed in that classic pose for a second, Charlie's lean frame looming above me—the alpha male subduing his exotic female. I let my Fire flare just enough to swirl my hair, its sinuous weight mimicking the natural movements of the snake I still wore on my head.

On cue, Charlie whipped me around so I faced the audience. He stepped behind me, his hands moving to my headdress. He undid the strap beneath my chin, lifting the heavy snake's head off me. He set it by my feet, reaching for the belt at my waist.

The audience, having fallen silent when Charlie first grabbed me, began to clap with Trey, who'd initiated a slow beat from behind the bar.

The clapping sped up as Charlie's hand reached for the knot of the belt, undoing it with theatrical slowness. On cue, my next song began. "Hey, Miss Kiss, let us dance," echoed out of the speakers as Charlie whipped my skirt off, leaving me clad in a coin-covered G-string. The audience was on its feet, clapping as Purgatory's ringmaster grabbed my serpent head and, wielding my skirt like a bullfighter's cape, plunged offstage.

extras

They stayed on their feet for the second half of my act, a traditional burlesque number to which I gave only the slightest belly dance flair. I was already pretty nude, but that didn't mean I couldn't tease. And tease I did.

In fact, I got so deep into the dance I went ahead and let my Fire flare again, its dark shadow swooping around me like a doppelgänger, its preternatural heat caressing my skin like a familiar lover.

I would miss my Fire when my curse was lifted.

As the song ended I let the black flames fall around me like a cloak. My hands went behind my back, finding the knot that held on my bra. Then I let the dark swath of my Fire peel away, letting the coin bra fall with it and leaving me clad only in my coin G-string and a pair of pasties in the shape of genie lamps. The audience hooted as my Fire dissipated and my arms fell to my sides, leaving my mostly bare flesh sweating in the hot lights of the stage. Charlie came out again, leading me stage left, where I made a deep curtsy, peeping up at the audience provocatively through my lashes. I repeated the movement stage right, and then finally center.

Straightening from my final bow, I caught a glimpse of a man sitting toward the back, his silver eyes opened wide.

And glowing like fucking headlamps in the dark.

Magi, chimed my brain, unhelpfully.

I pulled sharply away, startling Charlie, who dropped my hand. A smart move on his part, because I was already running.

Panties a-jangling.

Trip hissed at me as I leaped over her and Trap. The twin spider wraiths were currently conjoined at the waist, their legs splaying around them as they prepared for their act.

I didn't respond, since I was in fully panicked fleeing mode.

Trip and Trap, after all, couldn't help me. Neither could Trey, or Big Bertha, or Charlie, or any of my other friends. Not unless they ripped that fucking Magi's tongue out before he could speak. For Magi he certainly was, his eyes Flaring to my Fire.

I heard crashing behind me as Trap cried out, "No humans backstage!"

The Magi ignored the spider wraiths, his footsteps closing in behind me. But he hadn't Called yet, and I used my Fire to propel me forward, pushing me toward Purgatory's stage entrance and the street. There I could hopefully put enough distance between me and the Magi for Pittsburgh's steel-stained environment to help me hide.

The cool spring air hit all my bare skin like a slap as I plunged into the night, cutting right down the alley. It was a wide, empty East Liberty alley, giving me plenty of room to run. But the guy chasing me was fast, and his hand managed to catch my elbow, twirling me around to face his glowing eyes. He stared at me in wonder for a split second and I thought I might just have time to kick him in the balls before he could speak.

But it was too late.

"Hatenach farat a si." I See you, he said, in a language older than humanity. Older than time. A language of smoke and fire; a language of magic. The language of the being that made me what I am today, which had the power to make me a slave.

Fuck if I was ever going to be a slave again.

With a harsh cry I launched myself at the man, skimming off the surface of the magical Node beneath the city to shift my nails into long, wicked talons. A look of surprise twisted his features, but he had good reflexes. He threw himself out of my way with a neat somersault that had him back on his feet, his fists raised as he balanced on the balls of his feet—the stance of an experienced boxer.

I lunged at him again, calling my Fire to flame around me. I hoped to intimidate him even if a jinni's black flames wouldn't burn a Magi. His eyes grew even wider at the sight, but he didn't budge. So I slashed at him again with my talons, but he got under my guard and I overextended badly, cursing my inability to use my strongest weapon even as I fell.

I landed hard on the ground, my breath knocked out of my lungs. He kicked away my hands and jumped on top of me. Concentrating on the words, he opened his mouth to speak. Before he could get out the rest of the spell, I struck upward with both my hands bent, the heels of my palms striking him in the chin.

His eyes, already glowing in reaction to my presence, Flared brighter in the darkness, causing my anger to blaze with them.

"Magi," I hissed, and I hit him again. This time he caught my wrists, his hands like vises. Now that he had me on the ground, his bigger size gave him the advantage.

At least for those few seconds.

It was his turn to hiss as suddenly, instead of being a tiny Jasmine-stripper look-alike, I blossomed into obesity. My fat hips knocked his thighs open, pushing him off balance. I heaved myself over, morphing into a taller, more muscular version of me as I did so. Unable to tap the Deep Magic unless Bound, I couldn't get that much bigger, but it made the fight a little more fair.

"Why don't you take on someone your own size?" I growled as I dove for him.

In retrospect, I should have taken the fight slower. I was just so pissed and so panicked. I hadn't heard anyone with those eyes speak that language in a century—not since I'd escaped

Europe for the New World, and found refuge in steel-soaked Pittsburgh, where only Immunda could survive. Recognizing a true, Initiated Magi, my crazy inner she-bear emerged, gibbering about never being taken alive. If I had any thought at all it was that my sense of self-preservation would give me an edge. I was fighting for my life, after all, while this guy was just a jerk trying to Bind a jinni.

Unfortunately he didn't fight like a jerk; he fought like a cornered wolverine. He fought as if he were the one who'd be enslaved if he lost this match. He fought like his life depended on it. Which, considering I was intent on killing him, I guess it did.

He fought better than me.

I was hitting him, hard, but I'd lost my talons shifting to a bigger size. Being unBound meant I was far less powerful, even with my unusual access to all of Pittsburgh's corrupted magic swirling at my feet. And now that I was unarmed, he wasn't hitting back, just using his big body to deflect the majority of my blows. Until I overextended a kick.

His own booted foot lashed out, knocking my leg out from under me. I was on the ground again and this time he didn't underestimate my abilities.

He pinned me down with all his weight, his knees pressing painfully into my thighs and his chest blanketing mine, his hands holding down my wrists. His face was inches from mine, but his features were entirely obscured by the bright glow of his Flaring eyes.

Not me, my brain howled. *Not when I'm so close to being free.* I started to shift again in a last, desperate attempt. But before I could change, he'd spoken.

It was the second part of the spell that was the real bitch. And I was too late to stop him.

"Te vash anuk a si," he chanted over and over. *I Call you.* His pronunciation grew more confident with every repetition. The harsh sibilance of the language of the jinn reached toward me, wrapping around my soul. I cried out, but the spell blanketed me, muting my powers. I stopped mid-shift, my power whoomping out, leaving me beneath him in my own small form.

My wide brown eyes stared up at him, begging him silently to stop, not to say the last bit. The bit that made me his; that made me do his bidding; that made me a slave until he either let me go or died.

He spoke the words.

"Hatenoi faroush a mi." *I Bind you.*

And just like that, I was caught. Bound to a human. Again.

There were no lights or sounds or other magical occurrences, but we both felt it. I was his. He stared at me with eyes gone wide with shock, his Flare fading as his magic accepted my acquiescence.

He was my Master.

"Göt," I muttered. Then I switched to English, so he'd understand.

"Asshole."